The Torment

of

Truth

By

Pamela Gaull

Published by: **Cauliay Publishing & Distribution**

PO Box 12076 Aberdeen AB16 9AL

First Edition

ISBN 978-0-9571330-8-2

Copyright © Pamela Gaull 2012

All rights reserved. No part of this publication may be reproduced, stored in a retrieval system, or transmitted, in any form or by any means electronic, mechanical, photocopying, recording or otherwise, without the prior written consent of the publisher. Any person who does any unauthorized act in relation to this publication may be liable to criminal prosecution and civil claims for damages.

A CIP catalogue record for this book is available from the British Library.

This book is sold subject to the condition that it shall not, by way of trade or otherwise, be lent, re-sold, hired out or otherwise circulated without the publisher's prior written consent in any form of binding or cover other than which it is published and without a similar condition including this condition being imposed on the subsequent purchaser.

For

My mother Janet
And my daughter Paula

In memory of

My father John whose advice was always to forge ahead and do your own thing.

My dear cousin Margaret who first suggested I should put my various stories and tales into a book.

My Aunt Ann who was the kindest hearted and most generous person I think I have ever known.

Charlie, the Jack Russell who was a delightful companion. The legacy of this young dog is that his DNA and lymphoma treatment plan is being used within research for finding a cure and improved treatment in lymphoma research for humans as well as animals.

Acknowledgements

I have to thank the following who have helped me in various ways to complete this book:

My newly found cousins in Pickering, Ontario, with whom I share great grandparents. They made me so welcome and shared with me that part of Canada where their families from Aberdeenshire had settled:-

Ian Hadden, his wife Ellen, his father Lewis Hadden and his wife Hanna who took me to visit Lake Ontario and showed me round Pickering as well as Guildwood where I had previously decided Catherine in the story would have lived, little knowing that a relative had previously lived in the same street.

June S Morrison who gave evenings and weekends to take me to local events in Toronto and to see the beautiful towns of Port Hope, St Jacobs and Cobourg as well as giving helpful comments on the Canadian part of the book.

The following who have patiently kept me motivated and given valuable and constructive criticism during the book's various stages:-

Christine Albert, Liz Campbell, Betty Clark, Francesca Clowes, Cathy Cowie, Pete Davies, Sue Fehlinger, Paul Hanratty, Laurain Keys, Peter Ruffell, Morag Russell, James Stott, Jim Stott.

Pamela and Bill Kelly who run Better Read Books in Ellon, Aberdeenshire.
www.better-read.co.uk
The Off the Cuff writing group that meet in Littlemoor Library, Weymouth.
http://www.offthecuffwriting.co.uk/
Paul Hazelle of Shmu Radio 99.8fm in Aberdeen.
www.shmu.org.uk

A special thank you must go to the rescue dog, sweet Amber, who came to me temporarily from a dog pound in Ireland. She was almost my sole companion during the winter months while I worked through a succession of edits. She now lives a most comfortable and happy life with her forever Mum, Chris, in Portesham where she romps freely in the beautiful Dorset countryside.

Chapter 1

(Toronto, Canada. Autumn, 1979)

Catherine gave a sigh as she laid her pencil on the glass-topped wicker table where she sat in the garden of her luxurious home on the shores of Lake Ontario. She'd been putting the finishing touches to her latest article for one of Toronto's most prestigious newspapers. However, although she knew it was a job well done, the usual sense of satisfaction was missing. What she wanted most of all from life continued to elude her and her eyes held more than a touch of bitterness as she looked out across the expanse of well maintained grass and trees that led down to the lake. But her expression softened as she admired the view. The various shades of green that had coloured the summer leaves were already fading and changing. Soon the landscape would appear to catch fire with the yellows and golds of the autumn leaves and burn with the spectacular red of the maple. No wonder it was the national emblem of Canada. It bedazzled her every year at this time and reinforced in her the feeling of wanting to belong to this marvellous new country. She loved Ontario with a lake so vast she couldn't believe it wasn't the sea. On the many occasions that she watched the waves dashing on the shore, a sense of familiarity would sweep over her, and her mind would be transported to the North Sea that fringed her home town of Aberdeen in far away Scotland.

Strangely, she had never felt the pangs of homesickness that had made many immigrants pack up and return to their native lands. Perhaps if she'd had family there she would have felt differently, but Uncle Eddie was happily married to Rosie in Essex and her stepfather Frank was ensconced with his brother and sister-in-law in picturesque Perthshire. So, even if she were still living in Aberdeen these dear people wouldn't be immediately available to her. It was her beloved parents, Maggie and Sam that she missed most of all, and it was to them in spirit that she often turned for advice and solace, knowing that they would be keeping watch over her. Memories of sweet little Lucy would bring an ache to her heart, that bright eyed toddler, who having died in early childhood never had a fair crack at life. She would have been almost twenty-four now. What Catherine wouldn't have given for the joyful companionship of a sister, especially now she sensed that many changes were about to disturb the easy flow of her life.

Of course, she was fully aware that her parents' and sister's presence at her wedding, and also at the birth of her son, Stephen, had been nothing more than the wistful pleasure of imagination due to the strong faith passed on to her from her mother that they would all be reunited one day in the afterlife. The reality was, that in this life at least, she would have to face the turbulent times ahead without them. She raised a crystal glass of iced gin and tonic to her lips and took comfort in the relaxation that it spread across her aching shoulders. So what, if giving in to the need for a few shots of alcohol to see her through each day was becoming a habit? What other tangible support was there for her to rely on?

An onlooker might have thought Catherine's life had reached perfection and to a degree it had. As she drifted into a reverie of the recent past she drank in the rich beauty of her home and garden. It made her catch her breath to think that she and Gregor owned all this. The past nine years shimmered like a mirage as if being acted out in front of her on the lawn. Time had flown so quickly by and was now only a dream, but the evidence was there for all to see that she and Gregor had done well for themselves.

She remembered their arrival from Scotland in 1970 with nothing but determination, hope and year old baby Stephen. Their lives had followed success after success and Gregor was on the verge of moving from purely medical work into the field of research. Catherine had become a top reporter, even going so far as to put her life in danger at times to scoop a newspaper-selling story. She had quickly mastered the skill of being able to recreate vividly on to the pages of a newspaper a range of happy, memorable or even tragic events so that the reader could experience these happenings as if they had actually been there. And now, just as it seemed there was no more room for improvement, the flaws began to manifest themselves in a way similar to that in which holes appear in a best winter coat where moths in wardrobes have been munching unnoticed until it is too late and the damage is done.

Baby Stephen had thrived and was now a healthy, boisterous young lad. And yet he had become a constant worry. Much to her irritation he had reached that frustrating cusp between the parent pleasing amiability of a child and the sullenness of a wannabe teenager. Most of the time she realised he was behaving like any normal son. Any offspring, desperate to shake off his mother's fussing would put up a fight for independence. But there was something else beyond that, beyond simply being challenged by a growing boy's hostility, and it caused the hairs on the back of her neck to rise and her heart to stand still in her chest.

Catherine's concerns came from the deepest and darkest chambers of her mind. She had struggled to keep under lock and key a certain ugly suspicion, but as Stephen approached maturity, there was increasing evidence that demanded its release and final recognition. Some of the disturbing characteristics Stephen was beginning to display grated on her nerves, threatening to damage their relationship, and her customary acts of fondness could change like quicksilver to the harsh rantings of a shrew when his behaviour and mannerisms stirred her fears. Afterwards, she would hate herself because Stephen had always been a loving son and didn't deserve these tongue lashings.

On this particular afternoon he had cleared off from under her feet to go swimming with his friend Leonard. Having her husband Gregor all to herself was a treat she had been looking forward to all week, but the only sign of companionship was the rattling in his nose and throat as he snored beside her on a sun lounger. If only she could confide in him. His commonsense approach to life would normally put her at her ease, but this was a matter so crucial to the stability of their lives that she knew she had to keep it to herself. Catherine twisted her wedding ring anxiously and sighed as she watched the brightness of the autumn sky fade as the day neared its end. The wonderful loving relationship that had kept them buoyant all these years was floundering and she felt her heart sink with the sun at the thought of the icy distance which was widening between them. Maybe that's what happened when things were going perfectly; they had to come asunder as if by some law of nature.

Catherine looked out towards the horizon frilled by the yellowing peaks of the tamarack larch trees that grew in stately procession along the banks of Lake Ontario. A twilight mixture of pale pinks and greys was already creeping over the bright blue of the afternoon sky. The days were shortening and autumn was drawing near. Although she loved this time of year it was also a warning of the winter to come when early darkness would creep over the countryside by mid afternoon and the trees would become eerie colourless shadows in the gloom. Only the proud conifers would retain their greenery, steadfastly lording it over the countryside regardless of the bitter cold which would cause the rest of nature to shrivel and shrink underground to hide until the spring.

She lifted the glass again to her lips and took a long slow sip, pursing her mouth not only because of the drink's tanginess, but also because so many unstoppable thoughts were charging through her mind. She twisted round to look at her snoring husband who was sound asleep under a scattering of Sunday newspapers. She'd been so looking forward to this opportunity to grab his attention and have the much needed discussion about their future which had reached a crossroads. Should they stay as they were or move back to Scotland as he kept suggesting? But due to his increasingly off-handed manner these days she could never quite pin him down and thrash it out once and for all. Much to her annoyance, on this Sunday when he was at home all day and might have had the time, he'd chosen to wear himself out mowing the immaculate lawn that stretched all the way down to the gently swaying trees.

A soft rustling through sun dried leaves played a hushing lullaby that might have been expected to soothe the most troubled of minds, but Catherine's was in too much of a turmoil to be quietened by the mere movement of cooling air. She reached down, stretching her body precariously over the edge of her chair and shook her husband's shoulder roughly to ensure he would wake up properly and not just mumble incoherently and doze off again. 'Gregor, listen to me, surely you don't think we made a mistake coming here in the first place?' He gave a jump, snorted and cleared his throat. He'd been listening to Catherine's constant whine for weeks now, and decided it was easier to close his eyes and resume his own steady drone than take part in one of her prolonged debates. Catherine's mouth tightened with exasperation. Gregor always shied away from disagreements and she knew he would pretend to be asleep as long as she was on the subject of his suggested move back to Scotland.

Once he'd made a decision he liked to stick by it and especially on this occasion he hadn't given careful consideration to its effect on anyone else. That's what had happened when they'd emigrated. He'd said that anywhere in the world would do as long as they were together, but that hadn't stopped him sending off for the emigration papers and telling his parents they couldn't wait to join them in Ontario. All this before he'd discussed it thoroughly with Catherine. 'Just do it' was the motto he always quoted and seemed to live by. Turn the page to the next chapter. Why waste time and energy analysing the life out of everything?

Catherine took a gulp of her drink and continued talking. 'I know we've done well. You just have to look at our home. It's absolutely palatial. But to return to Scotland! Will our time here not have been wasted?'

Gregor spluttered his way out from under the papers and eased himself on to one elbow on the wobbly lounger. 'Of course we haven't thrown away our best years. It's all part of life's rich tapestry and all that. Think of my parents. They had a wonderful twelve years here especially since Dad had a good private pension when he took early retirement, but their British pensions would never have increased while they were outside the UK so they couldn't afford to be here anymore; but so what? They've gone back with no regrets.' His jaw remained firm in an effort to maintain a sense of dignity since he'd had to roll himself on to the grass first before struggling to his feet by hauling himself up by grabbing the table leg and then the arm of Catherine's chair. He was annoyed that she had disturbed his much needed rest with what he called her neurotic compulsion to ferret around until she found problems in everything.

'Someone has to worry about our future,' she said sharply, holding out her hands as if pleading for some sanity. By now he was pacing backwards and forwards, whistling tunelessly, a sure indication of his anger. He paused, and as if to soothe himself, stood gazing transfixed at the magnificent view that was losing colour now as the sun dropped lower towards the horizon. The clean fragrance of pine wafted over them, carried on a soft, fresh breeze from the lake. It mingled strangely with the more heady smell of new mown grass.

A sudden shriek made them both jump. 'I'm home!' Stephen, who was incapable of speech when shouting would suffice, bounded towards them. 'I had a great time at Leonard's. We went swimming and then played baseball with some friends in the field near his house.' His face was flushed with exertion. He raced on past them and disappeared into a thicket of silver birches. In a couple of moments he emerged kicking a soccer ball, and, like a woodland creature, flashed in and out amongst the trees as he dribbled skilfully with no sign of his energy ever giving out.

Catherine called him over. He scowled and hunched his shoulders as he sloped reluctantly towards her, his lips forming a massive pout. 'What do you want me for?' he whinged. 'I was enjoying myself.'

Catherine pulled him towards her for a kiss. 'I haven't seen you since morning,' she explained with the motherly expectation of a full account of his activities that boys especially find so abhorrent. He hated having to report in after every short absence. 'Just look at your hair,' she said, 'it's all over the place.' Catherine shook her head and tutted. Stephen's hair did indeed stick up on end as if he'd suffered an electric shock. Using her thighs as a vice, she squeezed him close, and like a female cat with its kitten, licked her fingertips and used spittle to try unsuccessfully to flatten the hair that sprang back up in defiance.

Gregor, who was quietly allowing the early evening stillness to calm him, pulled a chair up to the table. He smiled as he ran his fingers through his own black mane that flopped down like a canopy over his eyes. 'You're fighting a losing battle there. Maybe you can nag your men into doing as you want but you'll never tame their hair.' In order to avoid any further confrontation, he eased himself out of the chair with a sigh and asked Stephen to pick up the rake he'd been using earlier. Egged on by his father's open rebellion and glad of an excuse to wriggle free of his mother's clutches he did as his father asked. Armed with the rake Gregor left them with the excuse of having to gather some loose grass cuttings he might have missed down at the far end of the garden.

Catherine grabbed her son, playfully this time, but Stephen detested being held and preened at. 'Leave me alone and give me space,' he snarled and when she put her hand to her mouth for more saliva, Stephen threw her a look that made her stiffen sharply with horror. His large eyes seemed to pierce into her very soul as if he knew everything about her, more than she wanted him to. She gasped and loosened her grip. Those eyes! That look! She'd seen them before but not on her child. Catherine thrust the boy away from her with such vehemence that he staggered backwards and nearly came a cropper on his father's lilo.

'Stop pushing me around!' he shouted. 'That was jolly sore.' The metal hinges had scraped his calf and he made a great display of pulling up the leg of his jeans and rubbing the white scurfy tram lines that had been raised across the tanned skin. Catherine snapped back that he should have watched where he was going. When he answered her with another fixed glare she jumped to her feet and rushed into the house as if the devil himself were on her tail.

'Why are you so grumpy all the time?' Stephen muttered after her as he straightened his denims. But he was young, and had enjoyed his afternoon so much it didn't take long for him to regain his natural exuberance. Only too glad to escape his mother's clinging arms, he was soon heading back to the foot of the garden where he began to practise roll over dribbling techniques. He lost control of the ball and this time it ran further away downhill towards the edge of the firs. His father was strolling nearby as he often did just as night began to fall as if he were saying his farewells to the passing day, and he would turn his eyes up to the heavens and observe the patterns of cloud in the sky as it slowly changed from light to dark. 'You know, it's never the same twice,' he would say every time without fail.

Stephen laughed and repeated the words parrot fashion before calling on his father to join him in a game of soccer tackles. Gregor turned and was about to step forward to play with his son when Catherine came tripping down the back steps of the house with some wine and two glasses. She resumed her seat at the table, looking forward to some conversation at last.

'Gregor, come and talk to me!' she called, not happy at being left alone. She held the bottle between her knees and plunged in the corkscrew. Tight-lipped she wrenched it round, pulling at it roughly. Her lips drew back from her teeth as she hauled the cork out. Part of it broke off, but she quickly stabbed it down into the wine and uttered a string of curses. Gregor strolled slowly towards her. 'Steady on;' he said having missed the earlier disagreement between her and Stephen. 'What's eating you?'

'You know damned fine. It's that son of ours; his whole demeanour. He's becoming so wilful and I don't need you encouraging him.' She poured out a glass and swilled it quickly down before offering Gregor any.

'No thanks; not when you're in this mood,' he said and turned away. Catherine gave herself another and made an angry start on that one too. She hated being seen to lose her temper. Gregor refused to sit down. He'd had enough and wanted to enjoy the peace and quiet. Still with his back to her and watching his son perfecting his ball control, he said, 'It's easily seen what's wrong between the two of you. Stephen is growing up. Name one ten year old who would want his mother flapping round him like a clucking hen.'

Catherine didn't answer. She was too busy trying to contain the wild idea that clamoured at the back of her skull to be let out, the horrible thought that haunted her like a ghost but one that she couldn't exorcise. Not only that, but its substance was strengthening daily and becoming increasingly harder to ignore.

Gregor abandoned his ritual meditation and made a clumsy attempt at figuring out the reason for his wife's recent ill humour and her frequently voiced desire to continue with their lives unchanged. 'If you want another baby, a little girl,' he mused, having totally misread this particular reason for his wife's ill humour, 'you have to give yourself a chance. Relax, and just let it happen. It's been less than two years. And how long had you been on the contraceptive pill? All those chemicals have to be cleared from your system, you know.' He was speaking in medical terms again and Catherine hated it.

'Yes, Dr Bruce,' she sneered sarcastically. 'Why can't you just agree with me about the unfairness of it all instead of talking at me as if you were my gynaecologist? We have everything to offer a child.'

'We've had Stephen,' he said, his eyes never leaving the lad who was practising toe top touches nearby. 'It stands to reason we'll have another.' Catherine opened her mouth as if to give voice to the stray idea that was threatening to break through again, but as her eyes darted from side to side as she considered the awful consequences of giving voice to her suspicions, she quickly changed her mind. She put the glass to her mouth to safely silence the thought and swallowed her drink quickly. As she had hoped, the remedy worked, and weakened by the alcohol, the dangerous concept shrank away to lurk in a shady corner until next time. Catherine sighed with relief although she knew in her heart it was only temporary. Gregor interpreted this as her having accepted his logic so he rubbed his hands together and changed the subject on to one he thought she would want to pursue and sat down opposite her.

'Have you thought any more about that offer from the British government to pursue my research into organophosphates and their effects on the environment? It does mean returning to Aberdeen, but it's the same line of work as I'm doing now and they have some of the best brains gathered to work on it over there.' Once started on his latest hobby horse, there was no interrupting him. 'It's a once in a lifetime opportunity for me. They want me to write a report that will carry weight worldwide when it's published, not to mention making the world a safer place for future generations.' As he delivered his well practised speech, he leaned over the table, his hands clasped in front of him in a combined gesture of enthusiasm and entreaty.

Catherine swiped away one of the swarms of tiny flies that had materialised out of nowhere since the fading of the sun. She closed her eyes and sighed. How many times recently had she listened to this diatribe while not getting much of a chance to air her own views? Gregor continued, 'Mum and Dad have gone back, albeit to the south of England, but they're living well, and being still in their sixties they have a long and happy life ahead. You know the score, once anyone leaves the UK there are no more annual increments on the pension, so the only way for them to be able to afford a few luxuries was to return.' Gregor paused as if to emphasise his point.

'But we're still earning. We don't have that problem,' replied Catherine, looking him straight in the eye. 'Why should we go back to square one?'

'That's not the case. We'd be furthering our careers. And my parents aren't retreating into the past. They're striking out to pastures new. They're adventurers and have no regrets. Even at their age they're seeking fresh experiences and have made their home in Weymouth. And anyway, after Uncle George died and their last family link over here apart from us had gone, the homesickness kicked in.' Gregor met her steady gaze with a persistence that he was sure would wear her down eventually. 'We've had a wonderful life here. Canada was so short of doctors, one per thousand in the nineteen-sixties that I was welcomed with open arms into this wonderful country and you got your work as a journalist just as you dreamed of. We've nothing to complain about even if we do up sticks and go home.'

'I keep telling you I don't care where I live. What I really want is a happy family life. A baby would be out of the question if we started moving around. We've more than enough money here after all these years of hard slog and I don't want to put off trying for a daughter any longer while traipsing the globe like gypsies.' Catherine frowned. 'You agreed that family must come before career. You're breaking your word.' Gregor leaned back in his chair and pressed his fingertips into his temples in anticipation of the next predictable stage in the quarrel which had become an almost daily occurrence.

Catherine stood up and put her hands on her hips to give added emphasis to the challenge which as always undermined his capabilities as a man. 'Come on, doctor, do something for me just this once. Give me another child.' Her face tightened viciously and she tipped the last of the wine into her glass before throwing it down her throat. 'Perhaps I haven't had umpteen years at medical school, but I do know you have to have sex first to become pregnant! I'm not the Virgin Mary waiting for a miracle to happen!'

Gregor's face blanched with humiliation at her cruel jibe and his fists clenched with rage. He was on his feet too and walked round the table towards her. He'd had enough of her belittling him. Taking a deep breath first, as if it were taking him all his might to restrain himself, he sneered back at her, 'You know the stink of stale booze turns my stomach and is a turn-off in bed.' This was a new excuse and Catherine flinched and stumbled backwards onto the expensive rattan chair as if she'd received a heavy blow. Her husband loomed over her leering menacingly. She'd never seen this side of him before. She'd always spat her venom at him during arguments without retaliation so she knew she must have struck a painful chord in order to raise the equable Gregor into such a passion of rage. More than that, she was horrified that her increasingly frequent indulgence in alcohol hadn't gone unnoticed.

Gregor blew his anger out into the coldness of the fast falling dusk, but not before he had grabbed the empty bottle by the neck and bounced it across the lawn. He stormed off leaving Catherine to seethe in her own vitriol. Pushing up his sleeves, he searched out Stephen who had run off to the far end of the garden to resume his solitary practice out of earshot of his parents' raised voices. He began to dribble the ball and his father rushed at him and tried to get it off him but Stephen was too fast. Pushing up his sleeves, Gregor prepared himself for success and began dodging from side to side in front of Stephen inviting him to try and pass him with the ball. Father and son roared with excitement.

'Your turn now,' said Stephen who was determined that although his father was so much heavier than him he would knock against him so hard he would give up the ball and he would have won that tackle as well. Father and son roared with excitement as Stephen bounded away with the ball nearly every time. They careered around the lawn with such a show of happy camaraderie that Catherine's face softened into a smile. They are so good together; she thought, such great pals. Casually she stretched out a hand to pick up her glass, but her lips thinned and curled down at the corners when she put it to her mouth and found it empty. She needed something to block her mind of so many things these days and especially the worry that Gregor's love for her was beginning to sour. They'd had their ups and downs before but had always pulled together. Problems had always been of an external nature; for example, where to buy a house, decisions on the layout of the garden, which social activities to pursue. But never before, had there been any personal differences between them. Catherine had never doubted the stability of their marriage, until now.

This was another issue to fog up her mind that was already clouded with an unspeakable dread. Nothing in particular that she knew of could be causing the rift. She suspected there must be more to it than merely her drinking. She'd been enjoying an occasional tipple for years so it must be something new, something or someone she didn't know about. Her head tightened into a dull headache as she wrestled with the puzzle.

She closed her eyes and began to nod drowsily. The alcohol

was finally having its desired effect and the tension was draining away from her body. In this state she could persuade herself that she and her husband were only going through one of those sticky patches she'd heard people speaking about when couples find they have little in common and just can't seem to get along. It would pass. Everything always did. That was the unshakeable law of life. The good times and the bad came and went. The happy times would return. Weren't she and Gregor always being held up as having the ideal marriage? She adored him and until the last few months he had seemed to worship her in return, but maybe all good things must come to an end. Finally, exhausted from thinking, she drifted into a light sleep. There wasn't an answer that made any kind of sense.

She was jolted awake by Stephen shouting in alarm. At first she thought he was only playacting, and irritated at having been disturbed from what had been a pleasant snooze, was ready to give her annoying son another ticking off. But this was no game. Gregor was lying flat out on his back on the grass and Stephen was hauling at his arms trying to lift him up.

'I'm coming!' she shouted. She struggled for a moment against the giddiness of inebriation and hurried unsteadily towards her husband. To her relief she found that he wasn't unconscious. She crouched beside him and told him to take his time to get his breath back. Hopefully he'd only been winded in a tussle for the ball. He raised himself on to his elbows and the colour slowly returned to his cheeks. Catherine put her hand under his upper arm expecting him to find his feet without too much of a struggle. However, he kept slithering back on to the grass and seemed to be having a problem digging in his heels to manoeuvre himself. 'I'll get my balance in a minute. Just give me time.' He was biting his lip anxiously and seemed close to tears.

'Daddy, get up; you're scaring me,' sobbed Stephen. 'I didn't mean to fight you for the ball so hard that I would knock you over.' He was distraught with fear and guilt. He had never before seen any sign of weakness in his father and it scared him.

'It's all right son, I lost my footing that's all. It's nobody's fault.

We were playing a game.' He rolled over until he was on his hands and knees, and even from that position he was unable to push himself to an upright position without Catherine's help, although she too was staggering slightly. 'I don't know what happened. My legs buckled under me as if I my body had cut out.'

'Old age,' said Catherine, trying to make a joke of it. She didn't want to worry Stephen who was grinning and jumping up and down now that his Dad was all right again.

'Probably mowing the lawn after a heavy meal and then all that running,' murmured Gregor. 'Nothing that a good strong cup of coffee won't put right.' He brushed the loose bits of grass off his clothes and arm-in-arm the couple strolled towards the house with Stephen leaping and whooping ahead of them into the house. 'Just look at how happy he is,' said Gregor planting a kiss on the top of Catherine's head. 'Don't you agree we're fine as we are? We don't need any more children.'

That was definitely not what she wanted to hear. She broke free and ran quickly up the steps of the house. 'You utter bastard!' she shouted back into the cold, raw air. 'You haven't a clue how I feel.' She stopped and took a few deep breaths. For Stephen's sake she must make an effort. He'd had enough upset for one afternoon.

Gregor walked slowly, eyes on the ground, concentrating. Stephen was shouting from the doorway. 'Come on, Dad! Hurry up! Mum's dishing out ice cream.' Gregor gritted his teeth and persevered. On reaching the house he hauled himself up the stairs by the handrail. However, at the last few steps he had to physically take his free hand and clutch hold of his trousers at the thigh in order to lift his legs one at a time. Catherine's shrill voice yelled from the kitchen, 'Make sure you take off your shoes before you come in. Stephen's already got earth all over the kitchen floor!' Gregor sighed but did as he was told. He couldn't face her flying off the handle again. Having wiped the muck from his feet, and in stocking soles, he began to fool around. 'Make way for an old man,' he called in an attempt to lighten the atmosphere. He hobbled to the table with an exaggerated bending of his back in order to camouflage the genuine limp. Stephen laughed. 'Dad is such good fun.'

In bed, Gregor lay back against the soft white pillows with his hands behind his head, staring up at the ceiling. Catherine sat up beside him trying to read a newspaper. She was punching at it and shaking it in an effort to fold it properly. 'What's wrong with you that you can't straighten up the Sunday papers once you're finished with them?' she snapped.

'I'm really sorry,' said Gregor, clearing his throat and heaving a great sigh. 'Give it here and I'll sort it. A little patience is all it takes.' Catherine tugged the by now tattered mess from out of his fumbling fingers and flung it down the side of the bed on to the floor. 'That temper of yours is getting out of hand,' he said sharply, 'and I'm thoroughly sick of it.'

'I'm sorry Gregor, but I don't know how to approach you anymore,' Catherine replied with a whine in her voice, 'you're never interested in how I feel. I want you to try to understand how important having a baby is to me. Sometimes I awaken from dreams of having her. I hear her gurgling cries and tinkling laughter and when I hold her close I smell her powdery baby fragrance and feel her skin soft against my face. While my eyes are still closed I can almost see her pink cherub's face framed with silken curls. I can't bear it when I waken properly and find it's not for real.' She rolled on to her tummy and pressed herself close to him. She stroked his hair, pushing it back from his eyes that were red-rimmed as if he too had been crying. 'If you're not well, just say so,' she said. 'Is there something wrong you're not telling me about? You look upset.'

'I always get hay fever when I've been cutting the grass,' he explained. 'Why can't you leave me alone when I'm tired? I'm beginning to realise how Stephen must feel when you haul around at him incessantly and won't let him be himself.'

'My God,' she said, 'anyone would think I had leprosy the way you two treat me.' She switched off the bedside light with a flourish and threw herself over to her own side of the bed where she curled up with her knees and elbows sticking out over the edge of the mattress as far away from Gregor as possible without actually falling off.

'Goodnight, dear,' he said quietly. He hated fights and always made a point of not letting the sun go down on his wrath.

Catherine hoped this might be a signal that they were back on friendly terms. She turned over and lay with her arm across him. He was breathing evenly as if not far from sinking into sleep. Perhaps now that he was relaxed he would be willing to make love. She began kissing him ever so softly, brushing him with her lips, on his face, his ear, his neck, his chest. She began to move her head lower and shoved the quilt aside. She was kissing the hair that ran downwards from his navel and moaned softly. Gregor laid his hand on her shoulders and held her gently at first, but when she struggled to keep on going he pushed her aside and turned his back leaving her empty-armed in the middle of the bed. 'It's no use,' he said gruffly, but when he heard her gasp of shock, he mumbled hastily, 'Maybe tomorrow.' Catherine let out a howl and, slinking back to her own side, pulled the quilt right over her head and sobbed into the pillows as if her heart were breaking into tiny pieces.

Chapter 2

Catherine was still reeling from the overwhelming danger of her latest undertaking as she drove home from Mississauga which lay thirty-five miles south of where she lived in Guildwood, a prosperous suburb of Toronto. She'd just completed the most demanding assignment of her whole career. On November 10th, a 106-car freight train had derailed on the Canadian Pacific rail line. It had been carrying explosives and poisonous chemicals. Gregor had been furious when she'd made hurried preparations to go there. 'What about us?' he'd shouted after her.

'What about us …?' she'd shouted back with a sneer as she raced for the car. She had to be there among the first of the reporters. If it was career opportunities that mattered to Gregor, then she'd show him she was high up in her field too. When she arrived on the scene in Mississauga the train was going up in flames but being allowed to burn itself out. However, a ruptured chlorine tank was the main cause for concern. With the possibility of a deadly cloud of chlorine gas spreading through suburban Mississauga, nearly a quarter of a million people had to be evacuated. The danger had thrilled her. Dicing with death made her feel more alive. She knew it was selfish but the risk taking had exhilarated her.

The lure of one of the most important reporting missions of her life had been too much of a temptation for Catherine. She had been feeling strangely at odds with her family and this perilous mission had satisfied her need to feel wanted, to have a sense of purpose. Mississauga had been turned into a virtual ghost town. Within a few days it was practically deserted until the contamination had been got rid of. It had been a massive evacuation, probably the largest during peacetime in North American history. Later, when the mess had been cleared and the danger neutralised, residents were allowed to return to their homes. Catherine had been completely caught up in the drama of the emergency and wrote frantically for her readers congratulating the authorities on the efficiency with which the whole operation was conducted without any loss of life? She was on a high. She had been involved in one of the greatest events in Canada in recent times. The city was finally reopened on the evening of November 16th and the chlorine tank was emptied on November 19th.

For nearly two weeks she had been totally immersed in the major rail disaster and had managed to wash personal worries from her mind. As she made her way home on Wednesday 21st her body still surged with adrenalin. Catherine knew it would be a struggle to come back down to earth. Her mind was racing; she had seen so much devastation. A national disaster had been successfully averted and she'd been there to see it first hand and by writing about it fed the intoxication that disasters strangely create amongst the public. She'd successfully transferred the event on to the pages of her newspaper and into the homes of her readers.

Now that she was on her way home again, Gregor and Stephen became uppermost in her thoughts. Gregor hadn't wanted her to go. She had a child to think of. Catherine's head was pounding. Maybe Gregor was right about returning home to Scotland. Perhaps Canada wasn't the healthiest of places after all to raise a child. Gregor had always been 'wittering on', as she put it, about the proximity of the nuclear power plant in Pickering where they'd settled after emigrating from Scotland when Stephen was only one. It was the largest in the world. In fact, when they'd lived in Pickering they had been issued with iodine pills to keep handy in case of a nuclear meltdown at the plant. Her friends in the press who personally knew people involved in the building and planning of it had assured her of its safety. The finest engineers in the country had been involved in its design.

In any case they had learned to live with it and, as their careers had taken off, had moved to the more upmarket area of Guildwood. Catherine had been immediately drawn to the drama of a reporter's life especially after having spent years staying at home to look after Stephen. These had been a great joy and she'd loved every moment of watching him growing from a baby to a toddler and then into a smart young schoolboy. Once back at work though, she had entered a new phase in her life, one of travelling, staying in the best of hotels and sparkling at the centre of scintillating company, or so it seemed, after a skinful of gin in some busy lounge bar. For so long previously her social life had been chatting to other young mothers about the best detergents and what snacks to prepare for growing children that it had been a welcome novelty to be immersed in totally adult company as she discussed the latest news with reporters from the provincial and national press and even radio and television.

All these thoughts ran through her mind as she drove. Could she bear to abandon this life? For a daughter she would, but Gregor couldn't, or wouldn't understand. She was only a handful of miles now from Guildwood on the Kingston Road, but felt too hyped up to go straight home. Perhaps some relaxation would help. She would pop in past the golf club. It wasn't part of her usual routine to join Gregor there on a Wednesday evening. That was his circle and they had agreed that it was necessary for each to have a separate part of life to call their own, but just this once could hardly be called an intrusion. After all, she was his wife.

A quiet social interlude would help her to unwind and soothe her jangling nerves. Surely he wouldn't mind. Neither would Mrs Thomas, their widowed neighbour, who was a godsend and looked after Stephen any time she and Gregor were both out. Stephen loved her and had called her Granny Thomas from the word go and the name had stuck. Would it be fair to move the child from all that was familiar? Gregor's opinion was that it was now or never, especially before Stephen started his secondary school education.

The back of Catherine's neck began to tighten as familiar problems began to rear their ugly heads. Was opposing the move really worth all this friction? Mightn't it be best in the long run to simply let fate run its course? Gregor saw it as simply moving on to the next phase instead of stagnating. Although Gregor enjoyed challenge and change, it wasn't in his nature to take completely unreasonable risks. Probably, all things considered, the time was right. Once they had made the move he would be less stressed and be willing and able to give her another child.

She parked the car at the club and rotated her shoulders forwards and then backwards. Feeling a little less tense, she looked around for her husband's car but there was no sign of it. Perhaps he'd got a lift from someone. She had to be calm when she sat down for a drink with him. No more unpleasant outbursts. She signed herself in at reception and headed straight for the bar. The loosening-up exercises hadn't been enough. She was desperate for some alcohol to steady the tremor that ran through her right down to her fingertips. Mike the barman smiled and dispensed a large gin on the rocks. Catherine's hand shook as she lifted the glass, but she felt her muscles ease as the iced liquid hit the back of her throat. Mike scrutinised his territory while he polished clean glasses and placed them carefully on the shelf above his head. 'Gregor's over there,' he said, nodding in the direction of a secluded alcove tucked away from the main bustle of customers. Catherine thanked him, emptied her glass, gave a little cough and ordered a double of the same before strolling casually over in the direction of her husband.

He was deep in conversation with Marion, one of his golfing companions. Their heads almost touched as Gregor leaned in towards her. Neither was aware of Catherine drawing near. Catherine said Gregor's name, expecting him to turn immediately and make her welcome. However, much to her annoyance, she had to repeat it quite loudly before he noticed her. He was visibly flustered to see his wife standing there watching with an accusing look in her eyes. Marion moved quickly back from Gregor and gave Catherine a broad, but embarrassed smile. 'How lovely to see you,' she said, her face colouring. 'We were just talking about that terrible derailment. It must have been terrifying for you being on the scene first hand.' She jumped up and almost stumbled in her hurry to leave the table.

Catherine's face was rigid with suppressed rage and she made no effort to mask her annoyance. 'All in a day's work,' she replied brusquely, but her eyes were on Gregor who looked back at her all red in the face and stammering. 'I'll go and get you a drink,' he said struggling to his feet desperate to compensate.

'Don't bother,' said Catherine. 'I only popped in for a quick one on my way home.' She drank the double gin in one gulp, gasped and closed her eyes for a moment as the heavily pine scented spirit hit her stomach. It looked as if she might spit at him but she merely glared and rushed off. Gregor was too slow to stop her and was still struggling to his feet as she disappeared out through the door. Instead of the anticipated calm after a pleasant chat, Catherine's temper was fuelled to boiling point by having seen him paying more attention to another woman than he ever did to her. She slammed her way out of the building ignoring Mike's cheerful goodnight. Blind with rage and not too steady on her feet she headed for her car where she threw herself into the driving seat, revved the engine to a roar and crashing through the gears, careered perilously through the icy streets to their house.

The gin bottle stood open in the middle of the kitchen table where Catherine sat staring straight ahead. Her cheeks ran black with mascara and her hand trembled nervously as she drank from a large tumbler. She had ushered Mrs Thomas home to her own house although she had been watching a favourite television programme. She needed to be alone with her thoughts while she waited for her husband to come home. A car drew up at the door and she heard Gregor calling his goodbyes. Steadying herself on the furniture she scrambled to the window and peered out from behind the nets like a prying, jealous wife. She was in time to see Marion's distinctive green Toyota disappearing along the road. Marion was a 'good' woman who didn't drink when she was driving and was always in training for some sports event or other. So that's why Gregor's car was still in the garage; Marion must have come round and collected him from their house, the brazen hussy! How much Catherine had come to hate that woman in little more than an hour. Marion was there in her mind's eye as clearly as if she were standing beside her in the flesh, a great mouth of even white teeth smiling from that pink cheeked, healthy face and a body as trim and taut as an Olympic gymnast's.

Catherine could scarcely control her fury and made it back to the comfort of her drink. She listened to Gregor fumbling with his door key as he struggled to get it into the lock. If he couldn't manage then he could spend the night outside for all she cared. After what seemed like an eternity she heard the door creak open. There were a few moments of quietness when she imagined he was incapable of walking and when he did finally make it into the house he stumbled over the rug in the lobby and knocked the vase of artificial lilies off the hallstand. He moved slowly and deliberately through to the kitchen and stood sheepishly in front of her. Catherine glared at him. He said not a word, but his eyes were fixed on her glass. 'Don't start with all your parsimonious lecturing. You're as drunk as me,' she said, slurring her words.

'Look here, Catherine, I wish I could make you understand,' he said. 'We were only talking.' He held out his hands, but seeing that Catherine was only interested in getting back to her drink, he clapped them together again. 'I see there's no point in trying to reason with you in that state,' he said with a shake of his head, 'but you're barking up the wrong tree.' He opened his mouth to continue but realised he was wasting his breath. He bade a wrathless goodnight before climbing laboriously upstairs to bed with an occasional stagger and holding tightly to the banister.

Knowing he wouldn't take part in a row at this late hour she screamed after him all the same, 'You haven't even asked me how I got on. You don't care that I might have been blown to smithereens or poisoned with chemicals. You don't give a damn what happens to me. We're not like a real family ...' She slumped forward with her head on her arms and cried herself into a fitful sleep. At some point during the cold, dark night she carried the last of the gin over to the sofa where she lay with the bottle pressed to her lips until she passed out too drunk to cry any more.

Chapter 3

(Spring 1980)

After many long discussions and tantrums and tears over the winter months, it had finally been decided that Catherine would travel to Aberdeen with Stephen to prepare the way for the whole family settling there once Gregor's work in Canada was completed. It was the day before Catherine was due to fly out and sentimental memories helped to still the emotions that had been running high and causing heated rows over recent months. Catherine and Gregor walked hand in hand in the early morning mist along the beach on the shores of Lake Ontario. They had driven to Rouge Hill, their favourite walk. The lake was calm, shiny as glass that has been polished with a soft cloth. Along the horizon a red band of light announced the imminent arrival of the sun. Above it, pink puffs of cloud wiped clean the dark blue of the night and fresh sunlight brought brightness to the daytime sky.

Stephen skipped on ahead of them, stopping every now and then to skim stones across the smooth water of the great lake that lapped in soft frothy waves on the shore. Their warm breaths looked like white smoke puffing out of their mouths and nostrils to meet the cold morning air. Stephen loved this effect and ran towards them roaring ferociously. This caused great white billows to burst from his lips to swirl and disperse in front of him. 'Look out, here comes the dragon,' he shouted and pretended to be a monster threatening to claw them. Catherine laughed and cowered back in mock terror. Gregor laughed but didn't give chase as he usually did. Stephen pulled a sulky face. 'You never play with me now like you used to. You're no fun anymore. I'll be glad to get to Scotland. Uncle Eddie will play with me. He likes me. He told me so.' The boy sped away and soft white sand sprayed up behind him.

Catherine felt Gregor stiffen and she squeezed his hand tightly. 'He doesn't mean it. Children don't know how to express their feelings.' She looked at the greyness around them. Winter was reluctant to give way to spring. The bare twigs of the trees reached out their bony fingers to the pale pink of the morning sky. They looked as dead as she felt inside. Would she ever feel the surge of living happiness again? Winters were harsh in Canada, even more so than in Aberdeen, but she had never minded that. The summers were much warmer in comparison and she remembered with nostalgia their trips to the pretty towns such as Port Hope where they would bask in warm sunshine and even swim in the lake. She'd never swum in the North Sea off Aberdeen. She thought longingly of their drives past the vineyards, even stopping for samples of the local wines and purchasing a few bottles of their favourites. They wouldn't be doing that in Scotland, that's for sure. Whatever life had to offer in Aberdeen, her fondness for Canada would never ebb like the waves of the North Sea at the turn of the tide.

She admired the fir trees that had stood like proud, dark sentinels all winter refusing to lose their greenery. She loved these conifers. They were to her a sign of strength and hope that spring would eventually win through, and even as she looked, some of the deciduous trees did in fact seem to be taking on the yellow tinge that would soon burst into the bright foliage of the willow. Then would follow the beautiful silver maple with its distinctively shaped leaves that gave Canada its emblem, in the same way as the thistle represented Scotland. The ground would change from brown to green as new grass shoots peeped through and the world would explode into glorious Technicolor again instead of wintry grey and white. Would she too begin to blossom once they were settled as a family again? Gregor's decision to pack them off and stay behind on his own had riddled her with doubt and her body felt weak with depression.

The silence was broken by Gregor who let out a loud groan. He too had been mulling over the changes that were taking place in their lives. 'Stephen doesn't like me the same as he used to. He seems dissatisfied with me as a father because I'm no good at sports and can't make runs at baseball.' Catherine was taken aback by this outburst. She hadn't given any thought to how Stephen and

Gregor were or weren't getting along. She had put Gregor's reluctance to romp around as he had previously done with his son down to the same exhaustion as that which had brought their sex life to a standstill. In fact, his lack of energy helped to overcome her fear of his having any involvement with Marion. She daren't think it might actually be the cause.

'Of course Stephen loves and admires you. He's anxious about leaving his friends and of course Granny Thomas.' The panic that had caused Gregor to choke on his words forced a note of compassion to enter her voice. He had been so busy recently that even his Wednesday nights at the golf club had gotten the occasional go by and he had used exhaustion as the regular excuse for not having sex. She had no choice but to believe him. Apart from not being able to withstand the emotional strain of constant rowing, she couldn't bear it if she forced him to confess to something she didn't want to hear. Life without Gregor was unimaginable. Her heart fluttered like a frightened bird at the merest thought of their splitting up. 'Stephen is going to miss you just as much as I will.' This was the last day before she and Stephen left. Everyone had to be on amicable terms.

'I've been ignoring you both and I'm sorry,' he replied stopping for a moment as if to catch his breath. 'I've been putting in long hours trying to finish off this side of the research before I go to Aberdeen. Measuring the effects of organophosphates on plant and animal life, not to mention humans, has consequences worldwide. I can't accept the offer to carry out the programme and then say my wife wants me to sit with her in the evenings and my son wants me to play pitch and catch in the back garden.' He was off on one of his long speeches about work again that he had increasingly been using to avoid any direct discussion about family relationships.

'I do understand,' said Catherine. She had stopped listening to these tedious explanations but it did make her feel happier that there may be a legitimate reason for cutting himself off from them. This present discord was a flash in the pan. When he joined them in Aberdeen the initial findings would be finalised and the long hours would no longer be necessary. She smiled and imagined those happy days to come. 'Just look at that sunrise,' she said brightly, changing the subject. The red streak that had spread itself along the line of the horizon had mellowed into a beam of orange light that resembled an open fan with the emerging sun at its centre. 'Those colours are amazing.' They looked at the golds, yellows and oranges that streamed quickly now like the spokes of a sunshade round the red ball of the sun and whose reflection was spreading like a silken garment over the lake transforming its drabness into splendour.

'It's a pity about that nuclear power plant,' replied Gregor with more than a hint of surliness in his voice, 'which has been producing more electricity than any nuclear power station in the world.'

Catherine found her patience sorely tested. 'Can you not forget the science for five minutes?' she snapped and strode on ahead to catch up with the other sullen male in her life. She stopped and looked out across the lake, waiting for Gregor to catch up. 'Scotland's not going to be any better in that respect,' she said. 'Between the Dounreay power plant and the submarines in the Holy Loch, the air will be thick with radioactivity, not to mention that we'll be in the direct line of fire if we ever have a war with the Soviet Union.' She was needling him deliberately. She didn't even know if there was the slightest shred of truth in what she was saying.

'You can start on all your marches again; team up with Uncle Eddie in Trafalgar Square,' was Gregor's trite reply.

She looked ahead at Stephen. Even from a distance of twenty yards or more she could see he was scowling and the stones were being thrown angrily rather than skimmed skilfully. She had wanted so much for them to be happy on their last complete day together. Stephen hunched his shoulders still in a sulk because his father wouldn't chase him. He had been feeling the edge of Gregor's indifference as well. Maybe things would be better in Aberdeen. They'd all miss this wonderful lifestyle but at least Gregor might be happier. He'd changed since his parents had returned to the UK. Maybe that was it. He missed his family. She dropped Gregor's arm and hurried towards her son. Perhaps she could find a way of cheering him up.

'You give in to that boy far too much,' said Gregor. 'We can't be at his beck and call every minute of the day and night.' He raised his voice and called on him. 'Come here beside us and stop worrying your mother. And stop pulling that face.'

Stephen sidled up to his mother and began muttering under his breath back at his father. 'You never do anything with us nowadays. The sooner we're away from you the better.'

Catherine started to cry. 'Let's not all fall out.' She turned on Stephen. 'Surely for one day you can act your age. Can't you see how tired your father is? I'm past caring about you and your tantrums. I for one am going to miss him.' She sniffed into her handkerchief until Gregor drew alongside her and pulled her to him. Stephen stood well away with his back to them and scuffed up the stones on the path until he had left a pattern of holes in the earth. His face was drawn into itself like a squeezed glove puppet. Gregor looked from one to the other of his family. He blamed himself for making them both so miserable and wiped his wife's eyes with his clean handkerchief. How to put things right with Stephen was beyond him and he decided that ignoring him might be for the best. He spoke gently to his wife. 'Things will work out; you'll see. You have a cakewalk of a job to look forward to, writing a weekly column from home for that women's magazine. Think of all that spare time to visit Rosie and Eddie with days out in London, and Frank's only along the road from you in Perth.'

Catherine raised her head from where she had been snuggling against his chest. 'Why had she ever applied for that job which meant having to go on ahead of Gregor? And why had he seemed almost pleased to be left behind for a while? Her face was pale and her cheeks had lost their firmness. Anxiety filled her eyes. 'Why did you want to marry me?' she asked in a subdued voice.

Gregor looked at her, his brows suddenly scrunched down over his eyes in surprise. 'That's a strange question, Catherine,' he said in a voice that sounded almost schoolmasterly. 'I fancied you;

simple as that. And I admired your determination. I knew that life with you would always be interesting.' Catherine longed to ask if he still did, but she was scared, too frightened to face up to what his true answer might be. Instead she leaned against him, rubbing the side of her head against the roughness of his lumber jacket and allowed her secret tears to be absorbed into its cloth.

Chapter 4

At Toronto International Airport, Catherine lost her composure completely and wept openly when Gregor kissed them goodbye. 'Look after your mother, son,' said Gregor. His eyes too were brimming over. 'Phone me often. Write and tell me about your school and all your new friends.'

'I will. And I'm going to write to Granny Thomas too.'

'You'll have your real Grandma and Granddad Bruce to visit soon,' he said referring to his parents. 'They live in a great little town by the seaside. You'll love Weymouth in the summer holidays. It's got a beautiful beach with miles of sand where you can build sand castles and swim all day in a warm blue-green sea; and they have donkey rides and candy floss and a fairground.' Stephen's eyes lit up and he shook his knees restlessly back and forth as if impatient to get to Weymouth there and then.

'Let me know as soon as you arrive,' said Gregor, giving Catherine's hands a final squeeze. 'Fiona and Robert will be there to meet you and it's all arranged you'll get a flat near them. You'll be well looked after in a cosy little community of my future colleagues.'

Catherine blew her nose and squared her shoulders. 'Goodbye, dear Canada,' she whispered, 'you've been so kind to me. Maybe one day I'll come back to you. Wish me luck, I'll think of you often.' As the aeroplane soared into the heavens a rush of memories flooded Catherine's mind: the wonderful scenery, the visits to First Nation reservations and her admiration for their customs, the modern buildings in Toronto, the cosy friendliness of her community, the close friendships she had made at the newspaper and the thrill of the chase when battling competitively with other journalists for a scoop.

Stephen had been only a year old when they'd first arrived and lived in a tiny detached house in Pickering. It had also overlooked the lake. She had been so excited to discover that a number of its inhabitants had been descended from Scots who had travelled there at the turn of the century seeking new lives, some of them also from Aberdeenshire. She had felt entirely at home. She knew she would miss them all to the point of heartbreak, but, as Gregor always said: 'Step bravely on to the next chapter.'

For the long haul flight Catherine had brought her notebook to make a start on the first of her columns for the UK magazine. Stephen had his comics and an adventure book. 'Let's play I-spy,' he suggested cheerily. Catherine looked around at the other travellers wondering why they were flying to Britain. Glancing out of the window she watched the bird's eye view of Toronto and the roads and countryside around it slowly receding, and through an early morning mist she took a last lingering look at the land which had taken her to its heart. The land was browned by the heavy snows of winter and scattered patches of white still clung on despite the warming air of springtime. Soon, as they gathered height there was nothing to see but billowing cotton wool clouds beneath them. Not wishing to let go of the life she had just left she allowed herself to reminisce. They had certainly lived the good life and built up a satisfying level of financial security that gave them the freedom to branch out in their careers without too much worry about money. Gregor had become obsessed with the potential danger to animals that grazed on land treated with organophosphates and had managed to secure for himself a post at a research unit near Aberdeen. Catherine had the good fortune to have landed herself a cushy number with a magazine, writing about a career woman's observations of the changes brought about by the Sex Discrimination Act of 1975.

But she didn't feel the expected buzz from starting a new career. Her heart wasn't in it any more. What she really wanted, although it now seemed beyond her grasp, was a little girl to make her family complete. She had toyed with the idea of having a second child straight after Stephen, but had decided that would mean abandoning her career for so long she might never be considered experienced enough to resume it by any of the worthwhile newspapers. Why had she allowed her head to rule her heart? Imagine how happy she would have been with another baby; how wonderful to have had that second child to love and cherish. Her desire for success had destroyed what she had really wanted. And now there were these nagging doubts that Gregor had stopped loving her, not to mention that other outlandishly weird idea that kept her awake at nights and filled her with dread.

Stephen had always been such a delight, there was no denying it. And now he was just a normal boy growing up. There wasn't a child living who didn't cheek their parents from time to time and he was simply making a strike for his own eventual independence. Surely it was only right and proper that he should stand up for himself.

She smiled as she remembered how she had revelled in those infant and toddler years when she had stayed at home writing only a short story here and there to keep her hand in. These had been her blissful years while Gregor had been a GP in Pickering. Their small house, 'Catherine Bruce's domestic domain' as Gregor had called it, was attached to the surgery. Their subsequent move to suburbia had provided evidence of their prosperity and they had made friends at the tennis club, swimming club and the golf course. However, the baby girl she had planned once they were well and truly on their feet had never materialised. Work had begun to take over for both of them almost to the point of it being their god. The perfect dream life had faded into memory and her resentment had forced her to seek solace in gin while Gregor had turned further away from her into his all consuming studies.

And now it seemed as if he were packing Stephen and her back to Scotland in an effort to free himself. It was with great difficulty that she fought off the idea that he had no intention of joining them. Perhaps he had other ideas for himself. For all she knew it might even be with somebody else. She must stop this. She was becoming maudlin. She wished she could fall asleep for the journey as so many around her seemed able to do. The stewardess approached with the trolley. 'Large gin and tonic,' she heard herself say. She turned to her son. 'Would you like an orange juice, Stephen?'

Stephen grizzled. 'Okay then. But I wish you'd pay attention. I said, "Something beginning with s" ages ago and you've not been looking round for the answer.'

'Sandwich!' she said quickly and Stephen's face brightened. 'Now it's your turn,' he called excitedly and sucked his drink furiously through the straw as he scrutinised the cabin for something beginning with t as his mother had suggested. In spite of Stephen cringing and making a face, Catherine, her eyes sparkling with tears, put an arm round his shoulders and cuddled him close for a good minute before releasing him. Each gave a sigh and mother and son settled contentedly into the long journey ahead.

Due to the time change, it was late afternoon by the time the plane circled Heathrow and the sky was feathered with red. 'Red sky at night shepherds' delight.' Catherine automatically chanted these words in her head. Looking down from the plane, the greenery of the surrounding countryside fascinated her. Spring was so much further ahead in England than in Ontario. Maybe not so much in Aberdeen, but regardless, Catherine felt happier now that sunny days were on their way. A spark of excitement made her stomach tingle and she began to look forward to her new life, or at least not dread it so much. She decided to ignore the darkening clouds of evening's approach that hung ominously overhead.

They had a short space of time to wait for their connecting flight to Aberdeen and a piece of pizza and cola made it bearable. Stephen's scowl lifted as he chomped his way through the cheese and pepperoni and slurped his drink. Catherine had a gin and bitter lemon with hers. Nerves were playing havoc with her stomach and most of her food was left on the side of the plate. Soon they would be on the final part of the journey to Aberdeen.

It was dark when they approached the town but the sparkling city lights gave them a bright and cheerful welcome. After circling ever lower, the wheels of the plane hit the tarmac with a thud and then rolled along the runway reducing speed until eventually they ground to a halt. For better or worse they had arrived.

Catherine gazed wide-eyed round Dyce Airport. How it had

changed. She could hardly believe it; all those new shops, restaurants and bars. Since their leaving in 1970, Aberdeen had been transformed beyond all recognition by the oil boom. Catherine was in for quite a shock. She'd been back to the UK for a couple of holidays, but that had been to visit Rosie and Eddie in Basildon and then the train up to Perth to see Frank. This was the first time she had caught the connecting flight on to Aberdeen. Her heart quickened and her eyes stung with hot tears. The reality of it all began to sink in. She was home again but she felt like a stranger in a strange land. At least there was Rosie, dearest darling Rosie, and she would be seeing her and Eddie again very soon. They'd promised to be up at the beginning of summer whether Gregor had come over by then or not and she couldn't wait to visit her step-father, Frank, who had been a constant support since her university years. She could imagine him now as clearly as if he were actually standing in front of her.

Catherine's stomach leapt uncomfortably as another face loomed into her mind's eye and she gasped in spite of its not being real. This one filled her with dread and she would be glad never to see him again as long as she lived: Jimmy Simpson, her bête noir. Although he was Rosie's only son, and she had loved Rosie all her life, Jimmy had given her nothing but aggravation and worse. Suddenly her heart gave a lurch as she realised that Stephen was no longer beside her. She turned quickly and to her relief saw him trailing behind gaping open mouthed around him. 'Hurry up!' she snapped through clenched teeth, and grabbing his hand, dragged him after her as if escaping the very spot where Jimmy had entered her thoughts in case he might actually materialise like a spectre that was determined to hunt her down. 'We'll never get to baggage reclaim if you keep loitering.' She was shrieking now and Stephen's face grew angry at the apparent injustice of it all.

Chapter 5

The weary travellers sat round Fiona's and Robert's table that was laid as if for a feast. They had been close friends before the emigration and were delighted to put Catherine and Stephen up in their spare bedroom until all the arrangements for finding their own place were finalised. There were a number of medical and university people new to town in these flats that had been difficult for the Council to let out and they were being allocated for rent to incoming key workers. They were spacious, reasonably priced and not too far from the centre of town. 'The best part is that you won't be lonely,' said Fiona, passing Catherine a dish of Brussels sprouts as she spoke. 'It'll give you time to decide where you want to settle and maybe even look for a house to buy.'

'That's true,' agreed Catherine, although deep in her heart she didn't know what her plans were. She speculated on what Gregor might be doing. It was Wednesday. She wondered if he'd be playing golf today and if he'd round it off with an evening's socialising. Fiona had kindly allowed her to phone him but there had been no reply, only the answering machine.

'Are you all right?' asked Fiona. Catherine was holding the bowl of vegetables but making no move to take any as she visualised Gregor chatting and laughing with Marion. 'Oh, er, yes;' she stammered, 'jet lag, I guess.' She managed to joke at her own absentmindedness as she scooped a tiny helping on to her plate. She couldn't face food as her stomach churned at the vivid memory of the last time she'd dropped in past the club.

Catherine and Stephen spent a comfortable night in Fiona's spare room. In spite of the time difference of five hours they slept well and were able to spend an interesting day being shown round the city. Catherine was amazed at the changes. Union Street with its magnificent Edwardian architecture built of granite, grey in the rain and silver in the sun, sparkled in a glorious spring day as if it had been showered with diamantes. But it was so busy now compared to when she'd last seen it. The heavy traffic was squeezed into the narrow streets and there were hold ups, engines revving and horns blasting from a congestion of cars, lorries and buses that needed more space.

The streets in Toronto were wide and the traffic flowed along with ease. The highways were vast and built to accommodate modern life, whereas Aberdeen, like so many other cities in the UK, had originally been built for horses and carts and stagecoaches. However, Catherine thought there was something reassuring about the compactness of Aberdeen. It felt cosy and safe.

Fiona couldn't wait to show Stephen the beach. They strolled along the prom and looked out along the endless stretch of golden sand running up along the coast and disappearing into the horizon. Stephen ushered them down to the shore and took great delight in running barefoot towards the waves and escaping them just before they splashed over his trousers. 'Of course you can go for a swim, but I'd wait until the warmer weather,' laughed Fiona. She and Catherine sauntered arm-in-arm talking over old times as well as telling each other all they'd been up to in the years in between their last meeting.

The nippy sea air that smarted on her cheeks, the salt taste when she licked her lips and the smell from the fishmeal factory carried on the moist breeze all made her feel in a strange way that she had never left town. The last ten years might never have happened. Perhaps they were only a dream. She knew that was only a fanciful thought and Stephen's shrill screams of joy and the sight of him leaping amongst the white foam convinced her that her other life had definitely taken place. But where was it now? Apart from Stephen, blurring shadows of memory were all she had to show for it. As she watched her son playing in the familiar landscape a ghostly hand gripped her heart. He wasn't dissimilar in build to another boy she'd known and played with many years before. Was her worst nightmare in actual fact a reality?

'Let's go for coffee and maybe even a plate of chips to heat us up,' Fiona suggested on seeing Catherine's face suddenly blanch. 'There are a couple of wonderful cafes up on the promenade.' She hesitated before adding, 'I've something to tell you and I think it's best if you're sitting down to hear it.' Stephen howled his displeasure at having to stop his game of competing with the North Sea but the lure of French fries as he was accustomed to calling them, and maybe ice cream to follow, soon saw him scuttling up the steps from the beach. He hauled on his socks over the wet gritty sand that stuck to his feet and shoved them into his shoes without taking time to undo the laces. Catherine was about to tell him to do things properly when Fiona laughed gleefully, saying, 'Isn't he just something! You're so lucky to have a son.'

They entered the warm cafe and the smell of freshly frying chips 'warmed the cockles of their hearts' as Fiona said and they smacked their lips in unison while Stephen also rubbed his tummy and said, 'Yummy.' As they tucked into their tasty treat, liberally sprinkled with salt, vinegar and ketchup, Fiona dropped the bombshell. 'Robert and I are going on a field trip to South America, all expenses paid,' she explained. 'It's for six months to begin with; the rest is in the lap of the gods.' Fiona and Robert were geologists and both worked for the same company. It was the chance of a lifetime. 'It'll help you to get properly settled in,' she said in an effort to soften the blow. 'If you stay in our flat, it will give you time to decide if you want to rent a similar one or go for something private. There's plenty room as you've already seen.'

Catherine's regained appetite changed to a wave of nausea. Having these friends to support her had been the main reason she had agreed to leave Canada without her husband. She thought of her lovely home in Toronto that was piled high with crates ready to be shipped as soon as Gregor gave the word. Fiona's street of council flats where she and Stephen would be living by themselves was dismal and several of the windows were boarded up. Catherine had to wash down a mouthful of food with a great swig of hot coffee otherwise she would have surely choked.

Making a supreme effort to be cheerful for her friend's sake, she replied with a congratulatory smile, 'I'll miss you both, but what an opportunity. You certainly can't turn that down.' She forced another forkful of chips into her mouth and chewed vigorously. Fiona mustn't see her anguish at being left alone in a strange part of town. She continued brightly, 'I can't thank you enough for trusting us with your home. It'll give me a chance to find something more suitable before Gregor comes.' Catherine wondered how Stephen would settle in with only herself for company, but for the moment he was enjoying himself and his eyes lit up when a dish containing three flavours of ice cream lined up on top of a banana and smothered in swirls of caramel was placed in front of him.

'You don't mind if I spoil him,' said Fiona smiling indulgently at the happy child whose mouth was smeared with all the colours of the rainbow. 'Once Robert and I have done this stint of work we'll start a family,' she said.

'Don't leave it off for too long,' said Catherine seriously, thinking of her own predicament.

'Don't worry; one more year and then it's all go on the baby front,' Fiona replied confidently. 'Having that flat cheap has enabled us to save a deposit on a house but we don't know where yet. We haven't even decided on a country. Our line of business could have us moving anywhere on the globe, but one day we're hoping to strike gold or even more oil.' Fiona was wired with excitement. In her mind she had already left.

Catherine shoved her plate away. She'd had enough. A cold lump of loneliness had hit the pit of her stomach and fear for the future spread a chill through the rest of her trembling body.

Chapter 6

Catherine told Stephen to hurry up and eat his breakfast. Fiona and Robert had been gone almost a fortnight and Mondays were grim now that Stephen had started school and complete weeks of being on her own stretched endlessly ahead. The letterbox rattled and she ran to the door hopefully. She was desperate for news from Gregor. Anxiously she tore open his letter. Surely there would be word of him coming over in this one. His telephone calls were brief and he refused to be drawn into setting a date. This short note was no different. He was missing them but had taken up playing golf again on Wednesdays and swimming on Fridays. Mrs Thomas was feeding him well and the garden was coming back to life in the warm spring sunshine.

Disappointment had become the order of the day and Catherine casually shoved this latest piece of uninspiring correspondence into the kitchen drawer with the others, in amongst the circulars, the pieces of string, a half used roll of cellotape, old biro pens and other detritus. These letters could hardly be called billets-doux to be lovingly tied together with ribbons of pink silk and stored in a pretty box to be read at intervals to set her heart aflutter. They were drab and repetitious with no mention of love or longing. She hurried Stephen on to finish his food. He had stopped asking when his dad was coming, his main preoccupation being with his new school and the friends he had made, or rather was struggling to make. 'I wish everyone would stop saying I'm American,' he wailed. 'My accent is nothing like that, and I don't understand half of what any of them are saying.'

Catherine tutted and gathered in the dishes from the table. 'You're the new kid on the block, that's all. Give it another few weeks and you'll be one of the boys, and then somebody else will be new.' She dredged up yet another reason why he should stick with it. 'Do you remember Jack Nelson who came from Quebec and spoke with a French accent? He was older than you and lived across the street from us. His mother used to cry every day over coffee in our house because Jack thought no one wanted to speak to him, but in no time at all he was one of the High School's best ice hockey players and everyone wanted to be his friend.' Stephen wasn't convinced. He heaved a great sigh and reluctantly dragged his feet across the kitchen to pick up his satchel that dangled by its strap from the door handle. His eyes were cast downwards and there was the suggestion of a tremor in his lower lip.

Catherine's heart went out to him. She knew how it was to feel like an outcast and she thought back to her first days at the senior secondary after passing her eleven plus. She had spoken in the Doric of Aberdeen whereas many of the better off children had spoken 'proper English'. Stephen had an even worse problem. Although some of the children communicated in English, many did revert to their local 'mither tongue' in the playground. The poor lad had quite a problem on his hands. The Doric was an alien language all together for a Canadian speaker plus he had a misrecognised accent. Being taken for an American was an added insult to this child whose ambition had been to swim for Canada one day and maybe even be chosen for the 1988 Olympics team. He had photos of his local hero, young Victor Davis from Guelph, Ontario, stuck up all over the walls of his room. Although at 16 Victor was too young to win the 1980 Olympics, Stephen was sure that Victor would win in 1984 and then he himself would be champion four years later.

She drew the lost boy to her and gave him a long hug. 'You'll get there, Stephen. Anyway, you're my champion. Just look at you. You're nearly as tall as me already,' she laughed, hoping to cheer him up. 'You're my man about the house.'

Stephen didn't relish his mother's kisses and pushed her away from him. 'You don't know what it's like. I hate it here. And I hate you for bringing me.' He stormed out swinging his school bag behind him. It struck Catherine hard on the side of the thigh.

'God give me strength,' she muttered between her teeth as they made their way down the path to the car. Stephen sat in the passenger seat beside her, pulling his face into various horrific contortions and muttering under his breath about hating school, hating Aberdeen and hating her.

'There are lots of children in your class who've come from different countries because their fathers work in the oil business; you'll just have to make more effort,' she growled as the car stalled for the second time. Stephen's smart comment about kangaroo petrol cheered him up no end and he began to laugh which grated on her nerves and only made her feel more despondent and even more of a failure. What a bloody mess, she thought furiously. Gregor sends us half way across the globe while he stays put with nothing to worry about except what he scores on that blasted golf course, and who he scores with afterwards in the club house. She wished she could clear her mind of that image which was distorting with time into a lurid love scene.

Catherine drew up at the gates of Stephen's school. The parents were a mixed bunch. Some were local but many came from out with the city, drawn from other parts of the UK as well as from around the world, especially the United States, by the lure of the oil boom. So much work, so much money. Men were making fantastically high earnings in the oil industry that were previously unheard of for the ordinary worker. Houses were being snapped up despite their prices soaring, expensive cars were speeding through the town, and pubs, restaurants and hotels were doing a roaring trade. The streets were alive until all the hours of the night and early morning with throngs of revellers and party goers.

Men who endured the tedium on the rigs far out on the grim North Sea for two weeks at a time more than made up for the bleak isolation by playing extra hard when they came ashore. They partied, some of them, morning, afternoon and night for the two weeks they were on leave. For many, the only link with their wives and families was a snatched telephone call. Some were lucky and had settled with their loved ones in Aberdeen or roundabout and could have a share of home life. Others only had to journey to various parts of the UK, but even the lucky ones were only part-time fathers or boyfriends. Most of them lived with the worry of what their wives or girlfriends might be up to during the lonely times in between.

Catherine dropped off Stephen and managed to force a smile out of him by promising to take him swimming after school. She watched forlornly as he walked away albeit unwillingly to take up his studies and meet other boys. At least he had the marvellous Bon-Accord swimming pool in Aberdeen where more than one world famous swimmer had trained. It was the correct length for Olympic practice and Stephen had made it his second home.

Catherine decided to leave the car where it was and walk into town. There was so much running through her mind as she strolled along busy Union Street that seemed to have more estate agents than any other kind of business. A steady drizzle moistened her skin but not so much that she had to run for shelter. It gave her a readymade excuse for holding on to, and even enjoying her bad temper. Their plans seemed to be going awry. Gregor wasn't playing his promised part. She couldn't bear it if she and Stephen had been tricked into coming back home in order to give him a free hand. Her life was in tatters.

She stopped at one of the windows that displayed the many houses and flats for sale. They seemed shockingly expensive for what they had to offer. She thought of her beautiful home in one of the most exclusive part of Toronto and balked at what little the money for it would buy in Aberdeen. Even if Gregor did decide to join her, perhaps it would be more sensible to let out her home in Canada and rent for a while in Aberdeen. And what if he didn't come at all? She broke into a sweat every time she thought of it, but she had to. She must prepare herself for the worst if she and Stephen were to survive on their own. This had become her regular line of thought. At least she had the reassurance of knowing she could afford to support them with her income from writing, but she could never afford to pay the sort of mortgage these houses would entail if she were to become the sole breadwinner. She had to live in hope of one day soon resuming family life with her husband, but there was no guarantee.

She decided there and then to go personally to the Housing Department and put her name on the waiting list. It may be in a less popular part of town which was why they were being offered so readily to key workers, but she met that criterion, while she was married to Gregor at least. He was a doctor carrying out important research. In the meantime, she had the use of Fiona's home and that gave her independence and didn't run away with too much money. She thought of the council house her mother had been allocated: the dream home with the lovely garden and the cherry tree where the birds would gather merrily as if to entertain the frail Maggie with their cheerful chatter and joyful singing. There wasn't a hope in hell of her getting somewhere like that nowadays. What would her parents think if they could see her now, especially in comparison to how she had been living only weeks before? She had never felt so cast out and lonely.

The memory of her mother forced her to buck up. She had been told often enough of her mother's determination to survive the wiping out of her entire family in a fire when she was only twenty-two. Catherine could still remember how hard she had worked when she was widowed to ensure that Catherine would have a university education. A tear ran down Catherine's cheek when she thought of her father too. Life on the trawlers had been harsh in those days and yet he had done it to put food on their table, work that had led to his untimely death from a heart attack. Catherine felt ashamed of being so self-pitying. Her life was so easy in comparison. 'Nihil desperandum.' She could hear her Uncle Eddie's voice urging her on to succeed. 'Never give up.'

She wiped away her tears with the back of her gloved hand and scrutinised the notices in the estate agent's window. Fiona's flat was certainly roomy and once she had found her feet she might consider buying somewhere smaller but affordable. After all, didn't house prices rise and fall continuously. She had to remain positive. I can't believe what Gregor has done abandoning us like this, she thought, and despite the vision of him and Marion that was beginning to cloud her every waking hour, she set off boldly towards the Townhouse.

In her desire to establish herself, Catherine had taken to writing an occasional short story for the magazine as well as the column commenting on the News and how the latest events would affect women. However, these tales of clean living and happiness with only minor hiccups in the characters' lives left her bored. In Canada she'd had a job she could get her teeth into, meeting with other writers and reporting on life threatening events.

   She hadn't minded the short story writing during Stephen's early years. It hadn't been tedious then. She had loved being with her baby son, witnessing every new development and being there to comfort him through the teething and the knocks and bumps when he was taking his first unsteady steps. Also, she had been a young wife and mother who adored her husband and was worshipped in return. No money worries, a secure life with kindly in-laws in a wonderful new country. She had been one of those safely married ladies that she wrote about now, women who passed their time flicking through the pages of glossy magazines, searching for ideas on knitting, cooking flans, growing pretty little flowers in the garden and wearing fashionable, figure enhancing dresses to wear for their husbands when they came home from work.

   Somewhere along the line life had gone pear shaped and she knew exactly how and why. As Stephen became more independent home life hadn't satisfied her. She'd wanted more challenge, the harbinger of doom to many a happy situation. Contentment hadn't been enough. And then to crown it all, two years ago, Gregor's parents announced their return to the UK in order to be assured of financial security by receiving the annual increments to their pension which had dwindled dramatically since living abroad. They had decided to set up home in Dorset, by the sea in Weymouth, where winters were mild and property prices hadn't rocketed as they had in the oil capital of Europe. Missing their frequent and happy visits from nearby Pickering, Catherine had grown lonely and there was no doubt that this had played its part in turning Catherine into the workaholic who had lost sight of family life and made journalism her baby instead. These were the thoughts that crowded Catherine's mind as she struggled to acquaint herself with her new situation and those multiple regrets began to feed and intensify her depression.

In order to stave off the isolation while Stephen was at school, Catherine had taken to roaming the streets, occasionally stopping in some tearoom for coffee and a rowie, the famous Aberdeen morning roll made of flour, salt, lard and butter, sometimes called a buttery. These tasty rolls that she often had with jam were both satisfying and addictive, but not as lethal as her need for alcohol when she was feeling low. The pubs started selling drink at eleven o'clock and the hotels at twelve. There she would sit, a lonely figure huddled in a dark corner, sipping gin and looking expectantly from time to time at the door pretending that someone would be coming to join her.

As the day wore on, the streets of Aberdeen would come alive with an intriguing mix of nationalities, especially the Americans in their Stetsons and cowboy boots. Now and again she would take a stroll round the harbour and think of her father. She could almost feel her hand warm and safe in his as she recalled how she would listen enthralled as he told her adventure stories about life on the high seas. She recalled the Soviet ships unloading timber and the coal company boats delivering from Berwick and Newcastle. He had known each and every boat and ship that was berthed there. However, she kept well away from the street that led to the Bosun's Locker. She'd shied away from there ever since her 'unfortunate encounter' as she called it in the alleyway nearby. She flicked back the thick chestnut ringlets that were being blown like a veil over her face and ran the tips of her fingers along her jaw line where the scar from that horrific attack had faded and blended with the natural lines of her face.

How quickly this area round the docks in particular had been transformed. The hooting of the ships that now trafficked the harbour in a steady stream made her heart leap with excitement. It was bustling with cargo vessels from the far flung corners of the earth. She stopped alongside one ship that was from Louisiana, all the way from the distant southern states of America. The sailors were slapping around the deck in their sea boots, bandanas round their long dreadlocks. There was so much work to be done and despite the coolness of the sea air, some were stripped to the waist, the sweat shining on their black skins like polished ebony, while on others the perspiration broke through their brightly coloured cotton shirts in wet patches as they hauled at the ropes and the mysterious workings of the ship. Some carried supplies aboard, muscles rippling like those of boxers prepared for the ring. She heard the mingling of their voices in the patois of the Cajun, rising and falling, shouting and laughing, competing with the voices from the crews of the other ships and the general hubbub of the harbour. And above the human badinage rose the steady thud of ships' engines that were throwing out a thick waft of oil fumes that filled her nostrils. A huge Norwegian vessel was berthed opposite. It had arrived carrying spare parts for the rigs. Her inquisitive reporter's mind wondered why they had to come from Norway.

Bypassing the trawlers whose numbers were now in decline was a steady flow of supply boats slinking out across the waves to the oil platforms. She wondered at their funny shape. Were these flat backs for carrying cargo or for helicopters landing? There was so much now she must learn about this industry that had taken over from all else. Above her sounded the heavy drone of two choppers heading out with workers ready to begin their stint. They would return loaded with men desperate to reach shore. In no time it would be their turn to swagger in and out of the public houses, hotels and nightclubs, seeking the good life and desperate to make up for lost time.

Suddenly, right at her back she was aware of a bunch of men jostling past. 'You lost, Pet?' said one. It wasn't a harsh voice and possibly he genuinely wanted to help. Most likely he only said it because he felt the need to pass some kind of remark to any unaccompanied woman; no more than an irritating habit, but to Catherine in her present state of anxiety, and being so near to where she'd been set upon by that horrible man who'd torn her face with his ring, it made her heart lurch with fear and she froze. Her stomach jumped up to her throat and she felt the sharp taste of bile flowing into her mouth and burning her lips. The men slowed their pace and stopped right behind her. 'You sure you're okay, Pet?' came the same voice in an unmistakable Geordie accent.

Although there was no cruelty or mocking in his tone, Catherine turned. 'Clear off and leave me alone, you wasters!' she ranted. 'Must you accost every woman in sight?' Then she turned and ran, her heels clacking against the cobbles as they had on that tragic Saturday night when she'd been attacked and her father had died. She remembered too how Gregor had come to her aid, but had been too late to prevent her being injured.

Catherine continued to run, gasping for breath as she made her way up through the side streets in a part of town that was lined with dockside pubs and turf accountants, the modern name for bookies these days. As she ran she had to dodge on to the street to avoid a couple of brawling drunks as they crashed out through the door of a dingy bar. Her foot stuck in a grating and there was a snap. One of the heels of her shoes had got caught and broken off. She grabbed it out of the litter strewn gutter and hobbled her way past chattering office workers that dawdled on the pavements looking for somewhere to take their early lunch break. Windswept and dripping with perspiration, she stopped to catch her breath at the entrance of a hotel. This place would have to do. She had a quick tidy up in the Ladies and, thanks to having bits and pieces belonging to Stephen in her handbag, super glued the heel of her shoe back on.

Presentable again, she made a beeline for the lounge bar and her usual fix. Thankful of a sit down, she gazed resolutely into her glass to avoid the glances from men she knew had come rolling in looking for easy pickups in that notable part of town. There were a couple of women in the window seats who welcomed the attention of a group of loud oilmen and happily had their bill paid for them before they all left together laughing loudly with their arms round each other. It didn't seem to matter that there were four men to only two women, or that the lot of them were wearing wedding rings.

Sheer terror had brought her in here. If she'd carried on for only a short walk into the town centre and up towards the West End she might have been seated in her favourite restaurant, served by charming waitresses in neat black skirts, starched white aprons and little lace caps. She would be making a selection from the tasselled leather-bound menu: usually smoked salmon with fingers of brown bread and butter accompanied by a light salad and washed down with a pot of finest Assam. In her hurry to escape the streets, and desperate for a drink, she had ended up in hotel bar on the fringes of the red light district. Catherine picked at the chicken Maryland in front of her. What on earth had possessed her to come into a dive like this? She would have preferred a bought sandwich to eat at home while she tidied the house or worked on her stories until it was time to collect Stephen rather than skulk in this dubious establishment.

She scrutinised the empty glass in front of her. She was calmer now and decided to order a refill regardless of her surroundings, anything to pass the time. Now, with a second drink inside her, the thought of going home to make the beds and clear the breakfast dishes until it was time to collect Stephen made her close her eyes and shake her head in protest at the wearisome routine of her lonely life. Another drink would fill another half-an-hour. She remembered her promise to Stephen to take him swimming. Was that only this morning? She felt as if she'd moved into a different time zone, a parallel universe. She knew she should really go home and sleep off what she'd already consumed, but the craving for more alcohol was too overpowering.

She looked at her watch, two o'clock - nine in Toronto. Gregor would be finishing his breakfast, carefully prepared no doubt by the loving hands of Mrs Thomas or even ... but no, she mustn't think of her. Men always had to be looked after, she thought with a burst of bitterness that made her head tighten with anger. She and poor Stephen were expected to fend for themselves. Any suggestion of her hiring help would be frowned upon as lazy and incompetent. She had considered paying for a cleaner but that would be in name only. In reality she would be paying to have someone to talk to, a person who would understand her struggle, and not make the usual comment that she had it easy earning a living from home. There was bound to be another human being somewhere who would be glad of a few hours' wages in return for companionship to break the monotony of her isolation.

She fingered the cool glass of her fresh drink but before she could raise it to her longing lips she was surprised to hear her name being called. She glanced round, thinking at first it must be for someone else called Catherine. Who could possibly know her, especially in here? Her wandering gaze fell on a familiar face belonging to a glamorous young woman who was waving and calling on her to join her and a couple of men. Although Catherine recognised this rather ostentatiously dressed fashion piece, she struggled to place her. Nobody in her narrow circle of Gregor's academic friends would be making merry in the early afternoon and especially not in here. The penny suddenly dropped as she carried her glass over to the sociable group. It was Heather, one of the parents she sometimes chatted to at the school gate. Instead of her workaday pink and purple shell suit, she was sporting a tailored suede skirt and open necked blouse that revealed a lacy bra and generously sized breasts as she leaned forward over her two male companions to greet Catherine. 'Don't sit there all by yourself,' she said, dragging Catherine into the seat beside her. 'Let me introduce Ray and Earl. They work with my husband for an American oil company.'

'My friend hasn't turned up,' explained Catherine, embarrassed at having been spotted in what she knew Gregor and her in-laws would describe as place frequented by lowlife. 'I was on my way home to get ready to collect Stephen. I'm taking him to the Uptown Baths,' she explained. Briefly she wondered why the Bon-accord Baths had this second name.

'I'll be collecting Michael from school soon,' said Heather. Her voice rose with excitement as she continued. 'I'm throwing a party at my house. Why don't you come? Michael would love to have Stephen to play with.' As Catherine shook her head and was on the verge of forming the word no, Heather became more persuasive. 'There are plenty other days to go swimming. Go on, come with us and enjoy yourself.' Catherine remembered telling Heather that her husband was still in Canada and inwardly cursed for making herself an easy target. Heather kept up the pressure. She knew how to win over a lonely woman. Catherine swallowed and her pursed lips moved from side to side as she deliberated on the offer. The thought of being amongst adults for an evening was certainly tempting.

Without waiting to be asked, Earl signalled to the waitress and a tray of drinks was soon on its way. 'Do I detect the trace of a transatlantic accent?' asked Earl, his eyes lighting up at the thought of meeting someone who might have come from near to his home town which he said was in New Jersey.

'It's Canadian,' Catherine replied, startled to think that here was someone from near to where she'd lived. 'I've recently returned from Toronto where I lived for almost ten years.'

'Maybe a different country, but only a few hundred miles along,' said Earl and his smile broadened. 'I'm from Paterson to be exact, only eight hours' drive from Toronto. I should know, I've done it on a business trip, but unfortunately didn't know you'd be there at the time.' Catherine felt herself blush and quickly took some of her drink to cover her embarrassment. Surely, from spending so much time on her own she wasn't becoming nervous in the company of strangers. Earl didn't seem to notice and continued with his story. 'I moved to Houston, Texas, a few years ago to work in the oil. It's my home now when I'm not in Aberdeen.'

Catherine found her heart quickening. She was having an actual conversation. A real exchange of personal information with a living, breathing adult and her voice became animated for the first time in weeks as she recalled and told her companions about that beautiful part of the world. 'I've been to New York State a number of times but never unfortunately travelled south to New Jersey.' All three sets of eyes were upon her. She was the centre of attention. The conversation continued and Earl spoke nostalgically about his hometown of Paterson while she described life in

Toronto, the main city in Ontario. She felt her confidence returning. People were actually focusing on her and listening as she reminisced with excitement on the fishing, the golf, the swimming and every last detail of her suburban life and how it had been only a short journey from the bustle of the vibrant city. They seemed to understand too that she had lived in Ontario for such a long time that she had grown unfamiliar with Aberdeen. She bubbled over with energy and the desire to go with them back to Heather's once they'd collected the children proved too much. Stephen would understand. Hadn't he been complaining all weekend that he hadn't any friends? He would be delighted to spend an evening with Michael, and probably some other boys as well.

Chapter 7

Stephen's face had set firmly in a sulk from the moment he was collected in the taxi. He knew she'd had a few drinks and had picked up from his father that this should be treated with an element of scorn. And who on earth was this funny looking American with the big hat and his jeans tucked into leather boots that were patterned with deep swirls and scrolls? 'Are you a cowboy?' he asked petulantly before lapsing back into silence. Catherine gave him a nudge. Earl laughed. 'I sure wouldn't mind being one, but you know, I ain't never been on a horse in my life.'

'My father says it's wrong to say "ain't". He says there's no such word in the English language.' Stephen was determined to be obtuse. Hadn't he participated enthusiastically in an afternoon of elementary algebra and conversational French purely because he'd been promised an evening's swimming? Otherwise, he was certain he would have died of boredom and had to be carried out of school in a stretcher.

Earl had picked up immediately on the reason for Stephen's surliness and treated him with the sympathy of someone who knew full well what it was like to be a thwarted schoolboy. The lad had been hijacked. 'Well, I'm sure your father is a real smart guy, and he's quite correct,' he said, humouring Stephen along. 'But, you see, I ain't English; I'm American and I say "ain't" all the time.'

'Humph ...,' said Stephen and he turned away to look out the window as they left the city and entered the suburban countryside. 'Michael lives a terribly long way from school,' he said in a voice that was trying to be plaintive but was beginning to sound intrigued. They turned off the main road and along a freshly tarred street leading to a crop of houses that appeared to have been planted in a settlement of new-builds with no foundations like the green plastic properties of a Monopoly board. They drew up at a smart detached house in a cul-de-sac that looked not dissimilar to some of those he'd seen near his home in Guildwood. 'I like it here,' he said much to the surprise of Catherine who had been preparing herself for a nightmare few hours of endless whingeing. 'This is so much nicer than our flat. I wish we lived here instead of in that dingy street.'

'Stephen's never short of something to say,' said Catherine, following her son quickly out of the taxi in case he burst out with something wildly embarrassing once he reached the house. Earl laughed. 'I like a kid with some spirit. We're going to get along like a house on fire, him and me.'

Catherine stumbled at the doorstep and Earl steadied her. The fresh air had hit her and she found herself having to concentrate in order to speak clearly. 'It's all right,' she said gripping his arm tightly, 'these high heels aren't made for walking on gravel.' Stephen was already inside looking for his pal Michael who had arrived with Heather and Ray.

This was clearly going to be more than the quiet cup of coffee and biscuits that the parents at Stephen's last school enjoyed in each other's homes on Fridays. The party was already in full swing. It had kicked off earlier that day and Heather had left some friends and neighbours in charge. Through a haze of smoke Catherine could make out a table laid with plates of nibbles and an assortment of bottles that any bar would have been proud to stock. The latest music blared from a quadraphonic sound system. 'Michael, show Stephen your room,' Heather shouted above the melee. 'Vicky and Kirsty are up there already.'

'What?' Michael shrieked as he raced upstairs to defend his territory, 'You've let other people into my room without me? And two girls! I've told you before, it's private.'

Heather merely laughed. Her arms were already round Ray's neck laying claim to him. Her friends might be allowed the run of her house, but this man was clearly marked out as her property. 'Make yourselves at home everyone,' she shouted, 'but remember, upstairs is out of bounds. There's a bedroom through the hallway for anyone in need of a bit of privacy.' She dragged Ray towards the table of drink, grabbed a bottle and a couple of glasses and disappeared out through a side door with him.

Catherine looked round the large through lounge as these living rooms that stretched from front to back had commonly come to be called. The thick shag pile fitted carpet and the spotlights dotted around the artex ceiling completed the typically fashionable suburban dwelling. What the hell induced me to agree to come here? Catherine thought as she watched the couples that were draped rather than seated on the soft calfskin sofas and swivel chairs. They were fondling and groping each other in a variety of clinches, the forerunner of more to come. Of course she had heard plenty about swingers' parties but she and Gregor had thankfully avoided any participation in such activities and mingled only with sedate professionals whose pinnacle of excitement was a good hand at bridge.

But this could hardly be described as swapping; it was more like freelance sex romps while absentee husbands and partners were tucked away on oil rigs braving the harsh North Sea, and the men's wives and girlfriends waited patiently at home for letters or phone calls. At least the children were safely upstairs away from it all. She noticed one of Heather's friends was on her way up with a supply of cola, sandwiches and cakes. The ceiling above their heads gave a bump every so often followed by the thumping of running feet and she was reassured that the children were well catered for and having a good time.

Catherine clung to Earl as they sank into a most uncomfortable suedette bean bag with Earl squashed beside her. It was impossible to keep her feet on the floor and she could feel her skirt riding up her thighs. At least she had an excuse other than being tipsy for grabbing him round the waist in order to stop herself from rolling on to the carpet among the overturned ashtrays and spilt glasses. Eventually they managed to wriggle around enough to make secure hollows for themselves among the polystyrene beads.

A plump blonde called Gladys with large, fleshy thighs strode amongst the sprawling couples with a tray of drinks and shoved a large gin and bitter lemon into Catherine's hand and a rum and coke into Earl's. Catherine thanked Gladys and took a grateful sip. Earl placed his free hand on her knee and smiled into her eyes. Suddenly she felt more at ease. She couldn't remember the last time anyone had seemed glad to be in her company. This was the first party she had been to for absolutely ages. Thankfully at this one there would be no need for the customary small talk that frequently made her feel awkward and out of place among Gregor's colleagues. Her own journalist acquaintances were more relaxed though not quite as much as this totally uninhibited crowd.

She couldn't help noticing the abundance of leather: boots, jackets and trousers as well as the couches that lined the walls. These men were so big; their legs spread out to fill the floor space and their booming voices made the room echo with laughter and jokes. They were desperate for women's company being so far from home and lonely. The wives were the same, their husbands away for two weeks at a time, some for much longer. Why not make the most of all the money that came rolling in and enjoy themselves? Didn't they keep saying the oil would run out pretty soon? Plenty time then to be miserable.

Earl suggested a dance and how they giggled and laughed as they struggled out of the bean bag that had moulded itself round their bodies until they'd sunk deeper and deeper into it almost to the floor. Earl held Catherine's hand tightly in his as they stepped over feet and shins to a clear space over by the far window. They relaxed into each other in a slow smooch, Catherine with her head resting on his broad chest and Earl with his arms around her with his hands pressed firmly on the small of her back so he could enjoy every small movement of her swaying body.

She felt the heat of him through his shirt, and when she looked up at him when the music paused, he gently rubbed the roughness of his face against her own smooth skin. A shiver ran up her spine and she felt giddy. Her heart was beating in a heavy pulse that throbbed through her whole being. She was embarrassed to be so noticeably aroused and swallowed nervously. She tried to pull away but Earl drew her firmly towards him and turned his head just enough so that his lips were brushing her face. He allowed them to run along the dewy skin of her cheek until they met her mouth in a warm, moist kiss. His moustache tickled but he pressed his mouth firmly against hers and she gave a little shudder. She could no longer resist him and returned the kiss with ardour. It was such a long time since she'd had the opportunity to respond to someone's lips on hers and the sheer thrill of being wanted proved to be a powerful aphrodisiac. As he swung her round in time to a slightly faster tune she closed her eyes and sank breathlessly into the delightful dreaminess of desire. She laid her head upon his shoulder and allowed his arms to support her while the heady scent of his aftershave made her moan helplessly. Her body melted into his and they moved as one to the steady rhythm of the mellow, chocolaty voices of the singers.

It was nearly ten before they left. Stephen was crushed into the back seat of the taxi between his mother and Earl. Catherine found it hard not to be turned on by Earl's manly smell that wafted and filled the cab. With Stephen there as chaperone it would be all right to invite him in for coffee and a little chat. She wanted this day never to end, but knew in her heart of hearts that this couldn't become a regular way of life.

Heather's party had been surreally alien to her accustomed coffee mornings and tennis club meetings where conversation was polite and everyone was so scrupulously careful to say what was right and correct. The sessions with her colleagues had been different. The topics there were more full-bodied and controversial. But that was work. There had been no suggestion ever of any sexual tension between her and the men. She had always been just another person, one of the boys.

Once inside the flat, Stephen started up what Catherine called 'his nonsense' again. He was hanging about and strutted around the middle of the floor refusing to go to bed. 'But I'm not tired. Michael says he only goes to bed when he feels like it. I'm nearly eleven. I'm not going to be treated like a baby anymore.' Catherine wasn't too drunk to notice Earl laughing and giving him the 'thumbs up'. She banged the tray of coffees and Stephen's hot milk on to the long john and sat down on the chair by herself although Earl had indicated the cosy place beside him on the sofa.

Stephen put his hands on his hips. His face bore that annoying, arrogant expression that burrowed under her skin. He was obviously racking his brains for something really outrageous to say to make her rise to anger. She fought against it and moved over to sit beside Earl. She needed the comfort of someone beside her. Earl drew her close. He knew he had annoyed her. 'Sorry,' he said, 'I was only fooling around. I didn't mean to encourage him.'

Stephen glared at the two adults. He was beginning to feel shut out and he turned on his mother with the look that tore into her soul. 'Why does my dad never come?' It was frightening to think he knew exactly how to hurt her. He continued in the same vein, 'The other boys' fathers come home on helicopters and take them out somewhere different every day after school. Dad hardly even talks to me.' Catherine didn't feel sober enough to answer with the sympathy and understanding the child deserved. The accusations made her wince and she felt the insistent banging at the back of her head. Was she going insane or what? Perhaps every parent undergoing the stress of coping with a child approaching puberty had these crazy thoughts. Maybe it was a mechanism provided by Mother Nature to soften the blow of losing the child and to make parents almost glad to see them grown up and moving out.

She glared at Stephen, bulging her eyes out at him as far as she could but he retaliated by opening his naturally large eyes monstrously wide and stared hard at her in defiance, looming over her until she was forced to blink and turn away. She turned to Earl who was tapping a cigarette on the packet in preparation to light it. 'Ahem ..., Earl ..., we don't smoke in front of Stephen.'

Stephen sat in the easy chair opposite, swinging his legs and sneering. 'For goodness sake, Mum, I'm not a baby. Anyway I've tried it myself. Richard Parker brought one to school and we all had a puff of it in the outside toilets at lunchtime.'

'I hope it made you sick,' said Catherine making a mental note to go and see the headmaster. 'Okay, Earl, go ahead, light your cigarette,' she said in as pleasant a voice as she could muster, but continued in a snarl, 'It's obvious Stephen will survive. He seems to know all about everything.'

'It's no problem,' said Earl wisely, sliding the offensive white stick back into its packet. He sensed the tension in the air between them and didn't want to take responsibility for a full-blown fight. 'I'll go make more coffee,' he said throwing a glance at Stephen who had thrown himself sideways across the chair with his legs dangling over the side of the wide arm and was kicking his heels against the fabric. Catherine wanted to scream. Where was the little boy she had loved so much? Stephen was no longer her little soldier who did everything his mummy wanted without question. Would she ever win him back, if only for the rest of this evening? 'Come on, let's phone Dad,' she offered with a joyful note in her voice. 'He'll be home from work now.' She knew Gregor wouldn't be pleased at Stephen being up at eleven o'clock but she was past caring, and after all, wouldn't he be going out himself later to have fun? Surely she was entitled to have a friend in occasionally.

Stephen's eyes lit up. 'Let me ring him. I know the number.' His finger was already in the holes of the dial, twisting it round furiously. He waited for it to be answered, refusing to allow Catherine to grab it from him. She glanced quickly at Earl. What on earth would Stephen say to his father? 'Hello Granny, it's me, Stephen ... Yes, I'm working hard at school ... No, I didn't go swimming after school today ... Mum took me to a party and we met a cowboy ... No, not that kind of cowboy ... He works on an oil rig away far out in the middle of the North Sea ... Yes, Mum's here ... Bye ...' He turned to Catherine and handed her the phone at last. 'I don't think Dad's there.'

'Hello ... Yes ... I'm fine ... It's only a friend, he drove us home from a get together with some of the parents at Stephen's school ... Is Gregor not home from work yet? It's after six ....' Her hand tightened on the receiver as she sat on the floor leaning against the back of the settee. Her expression darkened as she listened to Granny Thomas telling her that Gregor had gone to the clubhouse to eat. In fact he had been there the night before as well. So that's why no one had been there to take her call. Mrs Thomas had only called in past to do the washing. Gregor it seemed was hardly at home these days and was playing more golf to pass the time without her. After a few more pleasantries and reassuring Granny Thomas that Stephen was usually in bed well before nine she rang off. If Gregor had taken up with that Marion she would never forgive him. They would be finished. She daren't ask too much. If anything was going on, did she really want to know? That would mean the end and the very thing she dreaded.

'Even when Dad does answer he doesn't say very much,' said Stephen, breaking into her thoughts. She clambered to her feet and resurfaced from behind the sofa. Her hands were cupped over her face and she smoothed the tension from her forehead with her fingertips. When she looked up after taking a few deep breaths to calm herself she noticed with surprised dismay that Stephen didn't really seem to be caring that much. His attention had been diverted to the novelty newcomer in their midst. He was curled up cosily beside Earl examining his hat and asking all sorts of questions. She drew him back to the subject of his father, anxious that the bond between them should be maintained. 'You know he loves you. He never was one to chat on the phone. Just wait until he joins us; he'll want to know everything you're up to then.' Stephen pushed his lips out, those lips of his that seemed to be growing more rubbery every day. 'He doesn't laugh like he used to either,' he moaned. 'Is Dad getting old?' He twirled the fringes that ran along the edges of Earl's leather jacket sleeves as he spoke.

'Don't be silly and stop annoying Earl,' she snapped. 'It's about time you got yourself ready for bed, there's school tomorrow.' She was horrified that her son had begun to share the same impression of Gregor as herself, the only difference being that he didn't seem to mind as much, but then he didn't lie awake night after night visualising his father enjoying the company of Marion McIver.

She forced a smile and tried to make light of their apparent dissatisfaction with Gregor. 'My husband is a very busy doctor,' she said by way of explanation, grabbing Stephen by the arm and hauling him off Earl and leading him towards the door. Stephen seemed to be all knees and legs these days. By this time next year he'd be bigger than her. She waited for Stephen to finish his milk which he was drinking ever so slowly in tiny sips. He knew every trick in the book when it came to prevaricating.

'Gregor works the oddest of hours. He's involved in research, you see.' Catherine was speaking, but to no one in particular, as if by giving voice to her thoughts she might actually manage to convince herself. Earl had been showing Stephen his identity card for work, and as he slipped it back into his wallet, he nodded but said nothing, probably wondering, as she was, why, if Gregor loved his wife and son so much, he couldn't find a few minutes to ask how they were.

'I wish I could fly in a helicopter,' enthused Stephen, his upper lip covered with a white froth. He wiped his mouth and stood at the door beside his waiting mother, their shoulders almost level. Suddenly the small child that was still in there somewhere surfaced and he put his arms round her, his head tilted back slightly so he could look her in the eye as he spoke, repeating excitedly the fascinating information he'd gleaned from his new friend. 'Mum, Earl flies all the way out to sea in a chopper. It's not tiny like you would think. It's as big inside as a bus or like the plane we flew in up here from London. It's not as big as the jumbo jet from Canada though; that was ginormous.' He barely paused for breath as his imagination began to take over. Catherine was enjoying this unexpected show of warmth towards her and held him close, glad to draw on the youthful energy that bubbled up inside him. With an almighty roar he broke free from her embrace and began to run around the room with his hands above his head twisting them like rotor blades. 'I wish I could fly to and from school in a helicopter,' he shouted before starting to make loud whirring noises in the back of his throat to imitate the noise of the engines.

Catherine smiled but she was staring straight ahead, glassy eyed and only half listening. How could Gregor be so callous, abandoning them to a soulless life while he started afresh with another woman? She wondered what Marion's plans were. Would she leave her husband and move in with Gregor? She put her hands up to her head and massaged her scalp with her fingertips. What a nightmare her life had become. She felt sick to her stomach and, ignoring the fact that Stephen was making the whole building shake at nearly midnight, thumped in her stocking feet over to the cupboard in the kitchen where she knew there was a bottle of gin. Marion was definitely the reason Gregor didn't chat and laugh like he'd once done. He was so unwilling to share anything of himself nowadays. He had become a stranger. Why, even Earl, whom she'd known for only a few hours communicated with her more easily.

She unscrewed the top and the juniper berry smell drifted comfortingly out through the neck of the bottle and into her nostrils. She was out of sight of the living room and raised it straight to her lips and took such a gulp of the spirit it made her gasp. Oblivion would be a blessed relief. She replaced the cap and put it back on the shelf. She didn't want Stephen to see, or Earl, for that matter. Drink had obviously been part of the reason Gregor had turned against her. She didn't want to lose everyone. She rushed the tap and returned with a glass of water. 'I have a tickle in my throat,' she said. She could feel the flush triggered by the sudden intake of alcohol rising up from her neck and over her face. 'I hope I'm not starting a cold,' she said, 'I'm suddenly very hot.'

Earl stretched himself. He must be at least six foot three, she thought, and so slim, solid muscle; no spare fat on him; no flabby paunch creeping over the top of his trousers. It was unfair to compare him to Gregor who worked so hard. But where was Gregor? She just had to stretch out her hand and she'd be able to touch this man, but she remembered that even when Gregor had been physically near, he had distanced himself from her and denied her any contact. All the while she had been musing about her husband's indifference Stephen had finally tired himself out and gone to bed. 'I think I'll hit the sack too,' said Earl, rising to his feet. 'It's getting late. Do you mind if I phone for a taxi back to the hotel, all expenses paid thanks to American Oil.'

Chapter 8

Catherine sat at the table beside Stephen helping him with his maths homework. The tiny figures of the fractions on the text book blurred in front of her bloodshot eyes and the mess of Stephen's jotter made her squirm with horror. Not only was the page a tangled network of scorings out but there were black rimmed holes in the paper where he had gone mad with a dirty rubber. He kept yawning and saying that maths was rubbish and the teacher didn't explain properly. Despite having to squint in order to see clearly, the calculations themselves came easily to Catherine. She turned to a clean page and worked each one out afresh, trying her best to explain exactly why she had made every change. All she received in return were tortured groans as Stephen covered his face with his hands refusing to look, far less listen. 'It will all make sense tomorrow after a good sleep,' she said patiently. She really wanted to take him by the shoulders and shake the lethargy out of him, but kept her rising frustration under control. She would have gladly used his fatigue as an excuse to give up the unequal struggle if it weren't for the fact that she always insisted he did his schoolwork. But she knew she was reaching boiling point and dreaded having yet another blazing row.

Up until then Catherine had been in a good mood in spite of a hangover. Her day had gone well. The music and dancing of the night before had invigorated her and immediately after walking Stephen to school to collect the car from where she had left it the day before, she had hurried home and rattled off an article before slipping under the covers for a few hours' sleep. Taking an interest in what she looked like for the first time in months, she'd put her hair up in a new style, winding the coils carefully into place and securing them with a pretty jewelled clasp that hadn't seen daylight since happier days when she'd shared an active social life with her husband.

'Divide the top line by the bottom to convert it to whole numbers and the leftovers are fractions of the whole,' she instructed, but Stephen chewed his pencil and muttered on and on about helicopters. He'd even drawn one on the cover of his exercise book. 'One day I'll fly in one; just see if I don't.' He pushed the books away from him. 'Mr Wilson Skinnypants says we don't have to hand this in until Thursday. There's no maths lesson tomorrow.' Catherine sighed and only just managed to bite her tongue. Suddenly a mischievous twinkle sparkled Stephen's eyes and he drew his face into a mock frown. 'A nurse is coming to talk to us about nocturnal admissions tomorrow,' he said wonderingly. 'What's that mean Mum? I know that nocturnal means like badgers and foxes and admissions are when people go to the pictures. So why do we need the nurse?' Catherine's face cracked into a reluctant smile. He could be such a comic at times and she was sure this was another of his windups. He'd no doubt found out all there was to know on the subject at the smokers' union in the boys' toilets and was deliberately saying the wrong word to feign innocence. 'Ask your father the next time we ring him,' she suggested. Stephen had been trying to be funny but the mention of his absent father killed the humour and neither of them laughed.

Mercifully, a knock at the door rescued them from reconstructing seventy-nine twenty-fourths. Stephen had rushed to open it before his mother had even lifted her eyes from the book. 'It's Earl!' he shouted and ushered him in, hanging off his arm. Earl strode over to Catherine who flushed bright red as she jumped to her feet and patted at her hair which had begun to fall loose from pulling at it during the fraught maths session. He gave her a quick kiss on the cheek and she mustered a welcoming smile. 'Have you two eaten?' the handsome caller asked with a knowing grin. His own hair was hanging in ringlets down his back. 'You look like Wild Bill Hickok,' screamed Stephen. His face glowed with pleasure, his tiredness flown out the window along with Mr Skinnypants' infernal calculations.

'I prefer Willie Nelson myself,' Earl shot back at him before asking, 'Do you like Chinese food? There's a fabulous restaurant just a few blocks away.'

'Do I ever?' shouted Stephen. 'Chicken chow mein is my favourite.' The boy was already pulling on his jacket that lay over the settee where he'd flung it an hour earlier. Catherine hesitated. She'd enjoyed this attractive man's company but hadn't planned on making a habit of it.

'Penny for them,' said Earl, as he and Stephen gave each other a high five. 'You're away in another world. I asked if you'd fancy a Chinese.' Catherine had to admit she was hungry. All she'd eaten was a cheese sandwich from the corner shop for lunch and was planning burger and chips for tea. 'I think that would be rather nice,' she replied politely. 'I'd forgotten what it's like to be asked out by a gentleman.' There would be no harm in having a companion. In fact, this new friendship was already doing Stephen, and her, a power of good.

On the landing on the way downstairs they squeezed past three youngsters who loitered there, sniffing from large plastic bags filled with glue. They nudged each other and quickly shoved them behind their backs. Round their mouths were the telltale red spots and their eyes were glazed. Catherine didn't even know if they lived in the building. They seemed to take shelter in whatever block of flats had a front door left open. After several mouthfuls of cheek from them when she'd asked if they lived there, she decided she didn't really care and ignored their antics. 'Glue sniffing is the latest craze,' said Catherine as she nonchalantly made sure her coat buttons were fastened straight. 'They'll grow out of it.'

'Or move on to something worse,' replied Earl, his nose twitching. 'Somebody's enjoying a joint somewhere not too far away.' He looked at Stephen and then at her. 'I hope you're keeping a close eye on that boy.'

'Stephen doesn't mix with anyone from round here and he knows what happens if you take drugs,' she said, putting an arm round her son's shoulders to guide him past the lads on the landing.

'You get sick and your brain turns to water and you get taken away. You might even start to see monsters,' replied Stephen shrugging her off. Catherine was desperate to hurry him down the stairs before any trouble broke out.

'Where's your horse?' one of the youngsters shouted at Earl.

Quick as a flash, Stephen shouted back, 'My friend's got a gun. He's going to shoot you.'

'Shove off, mummy's boy. Anyway your mother's fancy man looks like a girl with that long hair. Give's a kiss, Geraldine.' Earl pretended not to hear but in his mind's eye he would have enjoyed grabbing them by the scruff of the neck and throwing them out into the street. He had to clench his fists to make sure his dream did not become reality. Stephen, meanwhile, was hurling insult for insult. Nobody was going to call him a cissy.

'I'm going to get a gun one day,' he shouted back at them, 'and I'm gonna shoot the lot of you. Just you mark my words.' The boys stuck up their middle fingers before opening the bags and burying their faces in the foul smelling fumes. Catherine grabbed Stephen by the top of his arm and dragged him downstairs warning him not to cause trouble.

In the restaurant, the lights were low and piped music tinkled in the background. An assortment of the delicious smells that are unique to Chinese eating places spiralled around them and made them lick their lips. Stephen eyed the décor with obvious admiration. 'I love how they've done it all up in red,' he said as a young waiter with a welcoming smile and a friendly good evening showed them to a table in a corner where a huge lantern with long tassels hung directly over their heads. 'I've seen a Chinese parade in Toronto,' he continued as they took their seats. 'There were dragons with huge heads and sharp teeth, much bigger than the skinny headed creatures of mythology that Mr McKay, the Greek freak, keeps going on about.' He looked around him again and asked, 'Is it a special occasion?'

'The Chinese had their New Year in February,' said Earl, taking up the conversation. 'They celebrate all round the world and seem to like having decorations up the whole year.'

'Mmmm ... ,' said Stephen thoughtfully, 'I'm a Rooster according to the Chinese calendar. We've been studying it at school. Mum's a Boar and Dad's a Horse. When were you born?'

Earl was proud to be able to answer immediately. 'I know about these things, and I'm a Monkey.' Stephen was suitably impressed and spoke about processions and costumes until the food was brought in. Did these oilmen never stop spending money? Catherine thought to herself while Stephen laughed at Earl's photo in his identity card that he'd taken out again to show the boy what he'd looked like years ago when he'd had short hair and worn spectacles. She was aware of Stephen's increasing attachment to Earl and didn't know whether to be worried or pleased. He needed a man in his life even more than she did, but she didn't want the child to switch affection away from his father on to someone who was little more than a passing acquaintance.

'Stephen's dad loves celebrations,' she said quickly with a surge of loyalty to her husband. She took a sip of white wine. 'Why don't we look at the photographs later? There's a lovely one of Gregor with Stephen hoisted high on his shoulders so he could see over the crowd.' Now that she had established Gregor as head of the family once more, she relaxed. The pleasure that Earl and Stephen took in each other's company no longer bothered her and she was able to fully enjoy the meal.

Earl was in Stephen's bedroom fixing up the VCR which didn't seem to be working properly and was lying unused on a shelf. Since their evening at Heather's, Stephen had been whingeing incessantly that his bedroom was boring. Michael had a television, a VCR and a computer for playing games. All the while that Earl was fiddling with wires, plugs and scart leads Stephen was pestering him with questions about helicopters. What made the noise? How many men did they carry? How did they stay up in the air? Earl knew all the answers, or at least Stephen believed that he did.

Catherine watched the proceedings while perched on the edge of a basket chair that was piled high with clothes waiting for Stephen to put past. She screwed up her face. Stephen had long since stopped showing the same excitement about his real father and said he was boring and never did anything. She thought it was wrong for him to be choosing a stranger over his own dad and she felt resentment taking root again. It was as if she and Gregor weren't what he really wanted as parents and once more she wondered if other mothers felt this way. Perhaps it was normal behaviour for teenagers to be self-obsessed and turn to whoever happened to be there at the moment, and in their selfishness be oblivious to how they might be offending or hurting their parents. 'Time for bed, Stephen,' she said more sharply than she had intended. Stephen made a face and then turned his attention back to Earl. 'Do as your mother tells you, Steve,' he drawled.

'All right, sir!' Stephen nodded and jumped to his feet giving a quick salute before marching to the bathroom to clean his teeth. 'Mum, will Earl be back tomorrow?' he asked, standing in the doorway with white foam dripping from his chin on to his pyjamas and a toothbrush dangling from his hand. Catherine wanted to slap them both. How dare this visitor call her son Steve! How dare this wayward son of hers ignore her and obey a stranger! She was losing control of her life. Earl seemed to sense her discomfort and leaned over to kiss her forehead before inserting another video, this time about a boy and his dog. Stephen cuddled down under the covers to watch it but was asleep in minutes.

Back in the living room, Earl flicked through the sparse collection of records and chose a jazz trumpeter to play for them. They sat back and listened, only now and again passing a comment about the music or to mention other artistes whose music they enjoyed. Earl was wearing the same aftershave that smelt tantalisingly of musk, although there was no sign that a razor had been anywhere near his face. Catherine sensed the pressure of his body leaning against her and a tingle ran like electricity through her from head to toe. She was aware of her breathing coming faster, and a woozy feeling spread up the back of her neck and into her head. This wasn't right. Why didn't he just go? She was exhausted.

'I think I'll phone Stephen's father,' she said, thinking that would make him leave. She pulled the phone cord tight so it would stretch into the privacy of the kitchen. What was there to lose by asking Gregor straight out who he had been sitting chatting to in the club? She counted twenty rings. No reply and the line automatically went dead. She wanted to scream but steadied herself. If he was having an affair it was best she didn't find out. Straying husbands always returned to their wives didn't they? – Well, according to what was written in the problem pages...

She put the phone back on the shelf and was about to storm her way to the cupboard for a quick shot of alcohol when Earl jumped up and caught her by the wrist. The glisten in her eyes grew into giant salty teardrops that spilled down her cheeks and fell splashing on to both their hands. The floodgates opened and she fell against him, leaning into his warmth and the manly smell of fresh perspiration mingled with the aftershave. He rubbed the stubble of his chin softly against her face and sensing no resistance kissed her full on the mouth. His moustache tickled as it had done during their first kiss and she laughed and pulled away. Earl pulled her back firmly and pressed his lips hard against hers making it difficult for her to breathe. He kept up the pressure and used his tongue to excite her further. She felt his hand on her tingling breast and a tickle low down in the pit of her stomach made her arch her back and push her body against his. Her heart was pounding and her breath came quick and heavy. Soon they lay panting on the sofa. Earl's hands had found their way under her clothing and were massaging every part of her.

Trembling with desire, she excused herself and hurried to her bedroom where she rummaged desperately in her underwear drawer. Yes, there it was in its smart plastic box, her diaphragm. By some twist of fate she had kept it from the time the doctor had suggested her coming off the pill for a short spell. That was in the days before she'd begun to try for another baby. She put her head round the living room door to reassure Earl that she would only be a minute. She no longer wanted him to leave. She needed him. She'd been on her own for too long. Fortunately she had contraception. It was one thing making love to another man but having their child was out of the question.

In bed, Catherine curled into her lover. She had enjoyed sex with a stranger. She had broken her vows and betrayed Gregor. But her husband had denied her; wasn't that every bit as bad? She knew she was only rationalising the situation to save herself from guilt but surely she deserved some happiness.

The early morning sun was shining through the flimsy curtains when she put her hand out to feel for Earl beside her. There was no one there, only an expanse of cold sheet. It shocked her that she missed him already, but she was glad too that no explanation was required for Stephen. How could a child understand her needs? She got up and showered and prepared breakfast as usual. When she woke her son who was usually in more of a coma than a sleep, it took only seconds for him to shake off drowsiness and ask excitedly if Earl was still there. 'Of course not;' she laughed, 'he went back to his own place soon after you went to bed.'

'He told me he lived in a hotel. He doesn't have his own place,' Stephen replied fully alert. 'Why can't we live in a hotel? Some of the boys in my class do.' Catherine thought back to the encounter with the glue sniffers. 'I think I'll start looking for another flat,' she reassured him as she went about preparing breakfast. 'There's no point in us living here when we never see those so-called friends of ours that live nearby. Everything would be different if your father were here.' So far there had been no reply from the Council apart from a routine acknowledgement and although this flat had suited Fiona and Robert, it wasn't the best place to be raising a child.

'Do people have to keep the same father forever?' asked Stephen through a mouthful of toast. 'We could go and live with Earl. Michael told me in school yesterday that Ray was going to be his new dad and his first dad was moving in with another family.'

Didn't anyone live a normal life these days? Catherine thought to herself. She put down her cup of coffee and looked across the table with her eyes level with Stephen's and spoke gently but with a firmness that precluded any further argument. 'I really don't want to hear anything else about what Michael does and what

Michael gets. Your dad will be your dad forever, Stephen. He and I will never stop loving you.'

'Can we phone him again tonight then? I want to tell him I'm in the school team for the gala.'

'Of course you can. Why don't you write as well? He's going to be so proud of you.'

That night, as she snuggled into Earl's warm body, he took a long slow drag on a cigar, filling the room with its fragrance. 'I have something to say to you, Catherine. You're married and I'm sort of involved with someone back home. I don't want you expecting anything to come of this little ... er, encounter. You do realise that this is just a bit of comfort to help us both survive our loneliness?'

'I know that,' she retaliated. She was horrified to think that Earl thought she might be 'after' him. 'I've been trying to pluck up the courage to say much the same to you.'

Earl squeezed her hand. 'You're a good mother and in spite of what we've been to each other, you are still a faithful wife at heart. However, the next thing I have to tell you is that I'm leaving Aberdeen in a couple of weeks. I'm going back to Houston with the same oil company. We'll end it then, but in the meantime, let's have a ball. I don't have to go back offshore, just report into the office every morning.'

'That suits me just fine!' said Catherine fighting against a tremor in her voice. She had dreaded breaking up with him and now it would happen as a matter of course. But she hadn't expected to feel such a pang of sorrow at the mere suggestion of Earl's leaving.

The happy pair went to every party going and had a whale of a time. Catherine was quite shocked by the amount of daytime debauchery that went on in the well-heeled suburbs. Horse riding and badminton weren't the only sports that took place in these private clubs in the afternoons while children were safely tucked away in school studying grammar and basic arithmetic. Catherine's only interest was making the most of her time with Earl and wallowed in his company, drawing on his love of life to compensate for her own lack of it. With his arms around her she could come to no harm and the world was a better place.

It was the slow, smoochy dancing that Catherine enjoyed most, tucked cosily against his chest and moving rhythmically to the Country and Western or American Motown that was their favourite styles of music. The words reflected the sweet sorrow in her heart and gave meaning to the sensual feelings that coursed her body whenever she felt Earl's slightest touch. Of course there were 'goings on' at these daytime parties but Catherine had eyes only for Earl. What other people did was up to them; and of course there were drugs in abundance. Oil people could well afford whatever kind of experience they desired, but Earl was adamant that he would never touch them. He had seen too many of his friends coming adrift. Catherine was glad. Sex, drink and dancing were enough for her, although her alcohol consumption was more than Earl realised. He was unaware of the quarter bottle that was always carried in the smart leather handbag and swigged from during nearly every visit to the bathroom. However, Catherine did make sure it was Stephen who took priority in her life and didn't neglect his needs. In the evenings they took him to the cinema to see films of his own choosing and at weekends they went swimming, to the park, to the beach and to practically every Chinese and burger bar in town. To onlookers they seemed a normal, happy family.

The last night together came much too soon. Earl held Catherine's tearstained face in his large but tender hands. 'I won't write but I will leave you a phone number. It's a mate's who lives in Aberdeen. If ever you need me in the future, call him. He'll put you in touch.' He gazed at her lovingly and kissed her forehead before taking her in his arms and squeezing her tight. His eyes were moist and his voice nearly breaking as he whispered: 'Promise me you'll look after yourself. You do matter to me and I've really taken that scamp Steve to my heart. I can see him making a fine upstanding man one day.'

Catherine's gave several short, sharp quivering breaths before gathering herself to say her farewells. 'You mean a lot to me too, Earl. You've been like an oasis in the desert, but from now on I'm going to concentrate on Stephen and nothing and no one else until Gregor comes.'

Chapter 9

In the playground, after seeing Stephen through the school gates, Catherine successfully avoided speaking to Heather. She would put her hand to her mouth to cough, saying she'd a bad cold or turn quickly to talk to someone else. The hedonistic lifestyle wasn't for her anymore, so any time Heather approached she'd make an excuse and rush off.

A quiet life was all she wanted from now on, and if Gregor didn't want her, well, she could earn enough to live on and there was also the house in Canada to sell. No bit on the side like Marion McIvor was going to fall heir to what she'd slogged her guts out for. No sir! She would force a sale and get half the proceeds. She had worked it all out during her time with Earl when her confidence had been high and she was able to form solutions in her mind.

Most of her days were spent at the dining table typing and editing. She worked off her devastation at Earl's departure by completing a series of short stories in record time. One morning, as she was sharpening a pencil to make a few changes here and there, she heard the rattle of the letterbox and the flop of mail hitting the mat. She rushed to the door hoping it was a letter from Gregor. He had sent a couple of postcards in the beginning but they had tailed off too. There was a handwritten envelope amongst the bills and circulars but it hadn't come from abroad. She recognised the clear script written with a fountain pen: Uncle Eddie! Eagerly she tore open the envelope and hurried into the living room to read it.

Eddie said he'd phoned a few times after six and never got a reply, but knew she was probably at the swimming baths with Stephen. Catherine's phone was a simple model and she hadn't bothered yet with an answering machine. Catherine smiled to herself. Trust Eddie; he would never phone before six when long distance calls were expensive. The main reason for the letter made her heart leap with joy. Rosie and Uncle Eddie would be arriving by sleeper next Thursday morning. They'd be staying with Rosie's son Jimmy and his wife Patsy in their luxurious house. This was the only drawback of her dear uncle having married her mother's best friend: Jimmy, being Rosie's son would be part of Catherine's extended family forever and she had to listen to Rosie's interminable ramblings about every little move that he made and every little success that came his way. He had apparently done 'ever so well' and had two 'wonderful' daughters. However, she would still enjoy seeing Rosie and Eddie over the next few weeks when they'd be in Aberdeen. Life was picking up again.

Catherine and Stephen could hardly contain themselves when Saturday, the day of the visit arrived. Catherine gave herself one last look in the mirror and put on yet another layer of lipstick. Turning to Stephen she licked her fingers and tried to stroke his hair flat. 'I know you don't like it but we have to look our best for Auntie Rosie and Uncle Eddie.' She was hopping about like a cat on hot bricks. Time for one more visit to the loo. Catherine paced the floor, sat down, looked at her watch and got up again to scan the street from the window. She was on tenterhooks. Her visitors were already more than quarter of an hour later than they said they'd be. Stephen's face was red and moist from having had his nose pressed to the glass for what seemed like the whole day. Now he was fed up and lay on the sofa moaning that he was bored.

    Catherine went over to sit beside him and stroked his forehead. 'Patience is a virtue,' she said without conviction. She was about to tell him one last time to be on his best behaviour when she heard a sound and put her hand to her ear. 'Sh! Listen. I think I hear them on the stairs.' She made for the door. It must be them. Rosie's unmistakeable voice was rising loud and clear above the thump, thump of many feet on the stone steps. Who else was coming? Catherine nearly choked at the thought of who it might be. Surely Uncle Eddie would have intervened if Rosie had suggested bringing *him*.

    'I hear children too. Maybe they've brought Sophie and Sylvie,' cried Stephen and rushed out past her excitedly to meet them. Catherine heaved a sigh of relief. It wasn't Jimmy after all, only his two girls. Stephen had never met them, only heard plenty about them from their Granny Rosie. However, when they entered the house immaculately groomed and so polite, he curled his lip and looked appealingly at his mother. 'Why couldn't they have been boys?' he muttered. Catherine put her finger to her lips to silence him and offered up a prayer for a straightforward afternoon. She hugged Sophie and Sylvie, all the while glaring at Stephen to remind him to watch himself. She told them that he would let them see videos in his bedroom and she would bring them all juice and biscuits. The girls edged their way over towards him and he welcomed them with a forced smile that was more like a frowning grimace.

However, before he could disappear with his uninvited guests, Rosie clasped him to her bosom and nearly squeezed the life out of him. Once he had suffered a sloppy Rosie special kiss he was only too glad to wriggle free and rush to the bedroom with the girls if only to escape his auntie's clutches.

Eddie held his arms out to Catherine. 'Let's have a closer look at you,' he said. Tears spangled his eyes that had grown red rimmed and bleary from years of reading far into the night. 'A sight for sore eyes,' he said and held her close as if frightened she would disappear if he let her go. Rosie was meanwhile rummaging in the foot of her bag for the sweets she'd brought for the children. Eddie continued to gaze lovingly at his great niece. 'As gorgeous as ever; still got the Clark hair. I'm sure I see glints of red amongst the hazel.' With Catherine tightly in his grasp, he allowed his free hand to run over his own head that nowadays had only an occasional whisper of auburn amongst the grey. 'Thin on top now I'm afraid. Losing my crowning glory. Soon be polishing it with a silk hankie.'

Now that Rosie had found the bag of mixed penny treats for the children and put it on to the table, she was all set to greet Catherine properly. She pushed Eddie aside and threw her arms round her neck. 'Oh, Catherine, my darling girl!' As soon as she felt the warm and familiar embrace Catherine let fall her guard. She clung to Rosie almost desperately. The accumulated strain of the past weeks burst out from her in a shudder of sobs against the warm, ample body that had held and comforted her ever since she was a tiny baby when Rosie would take her to give her mother a break. 'Oh, Rosie, how I've missed you! You've no idea. I thought this day would never come.'

'What's Gregor thinking of sending you over here on your own?' Eddie said, his voice full of concern, when he saw the sorry state his niece was in. He looked round the room, a typical let, sparsely kitted out with the cheapest of furniture. 'Does he not know what you're living amongst? We'd to fight our way in past a crowd of ne'er do wells hanging around the entrance. Nothing but the height of cheek from them, and the phrases they've chalked all over the stairwell are sheer filth.'

'They've nothing better to do, that's all,' said Catherine, surprised at herself for leaping to the defence of the youngsters she was always chasing from the front door as if they were the plague. She knew fine what went on, but she didn't like her home being criticised.

'They should be helping out their mothers at home. Your bit of stairs is the only bit that's ever been swept and scrubbed, it seems to me,' said Rosie sharply. 'What would your mother say, you living like this? We weren't so well off in those days but you could have eaten your dinner off our landings.' Catherine's mind flashed back to the time they caught Rosie cleaning in the middle of the night – during her amphetamine period. Memories of hard but happy times stirred her emotions and she didn't know whether to laugh or start crying again. Eddie noticed her discomfiture and put an arm round her, stroking her hair and kissing her cheek.

'I'm sure Catherine can look after herself without you nitpicking,' he said pointedly to Rosie who had taken off her coat and thrown it over the settee before sitting down to release her hot, swollen feet from her white patent leather high heels.

'It was supposed to be so I'd be near to Gregor's colleagues, but we never see them. I've been to the Council and the estate agents to see about renting somewhere better. I hate it here and so does Stephen.' She helped Eddie off with his coat and was about to admire Rosie's beautifully hand knitted jumper in order to change the subject when Stephen came running in followed by the two girls, who in their shyness were stuck to each other like glue. The three of them stood in a row, Stephen demanding the promised juice and biscuits.

He was shoulder to shoulder with Sophie who was only two months older. A cold shiver as if someone had just walked over her grave stopped Catherine in her tracks and she felt her jaw drop. The likeness between them was striking although Sophie had the same blonde colouring as her mother. Was it something about the eyes or was it the mouth? By contrast, Sylvie had the same dark hair as her father but her features were undoubtedly inherited from her mother. There was no mistaking the likeness between Sophie and Stephen. The banging at the back of Catherine's mind marched like a procession of kettle drums to the front of her head. She turned to look at Rosie hoping she hadn't noticed. But she had. Rosie was staring in shocked silence, her mouth wide open too and it took her a full minute before she finally turned to look at Catherine right into her eyes all the way through to her soul. 'What's wrong?' said Eddie innocently. 'They're not getting up to anything. It's only their sweeties they're after.'

Catherine hurried into the kitchen and threw cupboard doors open noisily in a frantic search for cups and teabags and mugs and biscuits. Rosie cleared her throat with a great cough and started distributing the stack of goodies which she almost threw at the amazed children who were sent away with enough drinks and goodies to see them through the whole afternoon. Catherine set down the tea tray on the coffee table and motioned Rosie and Eddie to make themselves at home on the sofa. Eddie was still asking if he'd missed something and Rosie was tutting and slapping him to make him shush. Although nothing had been openly said about the reason for Rosie's horrified reaction, Catherine had seen it only too clearly. In order to cover up the frightening revelation, she threw wide her arms and shrugged, but the speed at which she spoke and the way her voice rose by at least an octave exposed her nervousness. 'They're just kids. They all look the same these days with their jeans and sweatshirts,' she said in a high pitched frightened squeal. 'Just listen to them laughing. They're having a great time.'

She was relieved that Eddie was there to prevent Rosie from interrogating her further and she gladly encouraged Rosie in her non-stop bragging about how well Jimmy had done. Apparently he was a great father, rightly strict for this day and age and a hard working provider. Patsy, or rather Patricia as she liked to be called since becoming a mother, was a very lucky woman to be married to her son. 'He didn't have to take her on, you know, just because she got herself pregnant. He could have left her like someone less responsible might have done.' Catherine shook her head, inwardly amused at Rosie. She was about to say it took two to tango but thought this might draw her attention further on to a subject she was desperate to avoid.

Catherine encouraged Rosie to stick to her favourite topic of proudly singing Jimmy's endless praises. His house was newly built and in a lovely area with a Neighbourhood Watch. It had two bathrooms plus a separate toilet and he was thinking of putting in a sauna. One bathroom already had a Jacuzzi. 'I have to be honest; Patricia really has been the making of our Jimmy,' Rosie said with the emphasis on the name Patricia. Was she making a dig at Catherine as if he was better off with the wife he had than he would have been with her. Catherine decided to let it pass and Rosie continued to boast about her beloved son. 'He is such a caring family man now. That's all our Jimmy ever wanted from life; all he ever spoke about even when he was still at school - a wife and children to take care of. He's so happy with Patricia and she's such a good influence on him. He stays home every night, takes her out regularly to lovely restaurants and he is so watchful over these girls of his. I don't know who's going to be good enough for them. They'll have to fight their way through their father first to get to these two. He has done marvellously well for himself, especially since the oil boom. Welders make a fortune offshore.'

Catherine mustered a weary smile. There was no stopping

Rosie once she started on the subject of Jimmy. 'I'm so pleased for him, honestly I am,' she said. Catherine's head was spinning. She resisted every temptation to boast about her own successes in Toronto. Anything Rosie had to say, as long as she was sidetracked from speaking about Stephen and Sophie, she would gladly endure. How much longer could she ignore the persistent clamour inside her head that felt as if the massed pipes and drums of all Scotland had gathered to play in competition with each other all at the same time? She had to have a drink. Rosie joined her in a gin and tonic and Eddie was happy with one of the cans of lager Catherine had bought in especially for him. He was happily immersed in the latest edition of the local newspaper and, switched off to his wife's bragging, only looked up to mutter an obligatory yes or no at the appropriate times.

As the visit drew to an end and Rosie was stacking the glasses and dishes on the draining board, she drew Catherine to her side and said in a whisper, her mouth almost touching Catherine's ear, 'I don't want Eddie suspecting anything. You know fine what I mean ... some things are best kept under wraps ... but you and I will have a little chat on our own before I go back to Basildon.'

Catherine pulled quickly away and crashed the dishes into the sink, breaking the stem off one of the glasses as she did so. 'I don't know what you're driving at, Rosie. I am looking for a better place to live.'

'Don't give me that, Catherine. You know very well there's something far more important than flats and houses to consider.' She fixed Catherine with such a gaze, that for the first time ever, Catherine saw a likeness between Jimmy and his mother, and, if truth be told, her Stephen as well. 'If I have a grandson, then no one is going to keep him from me, even you,' Rosie said, and with a tightening of her lips flounced out of the kitchen and grabbed her coat and Eddie's, throwing the bewildered man's gabardine at him. 'Hurry up; Jimmy will be waiting for us.' She put her nose round the door of Stephen's bedroom. 'Come on girls, jackets on. You know Daddy doesn't like to be kept waiting.' She turned to Catherine. 'Jimmy's taking us for a meal at the Tree House. It's really upmarket there. Just round the corner from where he lives. I'll give you a phone to arrange that little talk. We can't have a proper woman-to-woman with Eddie around.'

Eddie raised his eyebrows. 'She's always blaming me for something and all I ever do is sit quietly reading.' Rosie ignored him and called Stephen to her and caressed his face with both hands. 'I've enjoyed meeting you again so much. Has anyone ever told you that you're a very handsome young man? You must come and visit Eddie and me in Basildon.' With that, she ushered out her charges and closed the door hard behind her. Catherine knew that Rosie was a force to be reckoned with and meant every word of what she'd said. She picked up the pieces of the broken glass and threw them in the bin. It was all too much. With tears running down her cheeks she reached up to the cupboard. Thank goodness, just as she'd hoped, there was another bottle untouched behind the nearly empty one.

Chapter 10

Catherine was working at the table in the living room. Ideas were thankfully flowing well. She'd be finished this article with plenty time to spare before collecting Stephen. So far, there had been no word from Rosie about Stephen. Hopefully, she'd come to her senses, or better still, forgotten all about it in the excitement of visiting Jimmy. Catherine's spirits began to rise and a sense of optimism made her sigh with relief that the whole mind boggling episode would pass and eventually fade from her own thoughts too.

Suddenly, there was loud insistent knocking at the door. Some of those kids making a nuisance of themselves, she thought at first, but when she looked through the spy hole her blood ran cold. The tall figure at the other side of the door was none other than Jimmy Simpson. There was no mistaking him. He hadn't changed much, only heavier and better dressed in an expensive leather jacket. His hair was the same, sticking up but shorn, like an ugly, worn down lavatory brush. Catherine's heart sank. Rosie must have given him the tip off after all. She put the chain across before opening it.

'What do you want here? I don't think we could possibly have anything to say to each other.' She managed to keep her voice steady. It certainly didn't reflect the agitation that fluttered her stomach to the point of nausea.

'You can say what you like, but I think we do,' Jimmy replied with equal assertiveness and with not a flicker of expression on his face. He paused and said in a voice that let her know he wasn't going to leave until they'd had it out, 'In fact we have a great deal of talking to do. Some things are just too important to ignore.' Catherine's face paled and she held on to the door jamb to steady herself. She thought her heart was going to burst out through her chest. Jimmy saw her distress and tried to reassure her. 'I'm not going to hurt you, I promise,' he said as she opened the door just a fraction more. When he saw the stark terror in her eyes, his tone softened and he seemed to take on board how earth shattering the reason for his visit must be for her.

'Where have I heard that before?' she retaliated. The memory of what he'd done the last time he'd paid an unexpected call flashed back as clearly as if it had happened only yesterday and filled her with utter revulsion.

Accurately reading her reaction, Jimmy jumped to his own defence and took a step forward. 'Good God, do me a favour. That was nearly twelve years ago,' he said as if that entitled him to immediate exoneration. 'I'm a family man now with a wife and two daughters to consider. And anyway I've changed. I've grown up.' Jimmy spouted one reason after another why she could safely let him in. Catherine dreaded hearing what she knew he had to say and kept the door almost shut. She hadn't laid eyes on him since his mother's marriage to her Uncle Eddie when she had been heavily pregnant and Patricia had already given birth to Sophie. Both she and Jimmy had lived separate, happily married lives since then. It was only in the last couple of years since Stephen's baby face had matured into Jimmy's likeness and he had taken to giving smart comments that verged on the impudent, which she recognised as a trait of Jimmy's and nothing like Gregor's, that earlier suspicions had begun to re-emerge.

Catherine undid the chain and the man she detested most of all in the whole wide world stepped back into her life. Without being asked, Jimmy carried on along the hall and into the living room. He drew up a chair at the table and sat straight backed and wooden. His jaw was set determinedly. Catherine resumed her seat opposite, her stomach cramping with fear as if facing an interrogator who was capable of meting out torture if the answers she gave weren't pleasing to him. She shuffled together the pages she'd just typed before turning them face down. She didn't want him spying on anything she was doing.

'I believe you've done pretty well for yourself in Canada,' he said lightly in an effort to break the ice.

'No better than you with your happy little brood, complete with fitted wardrobes and deep freeze.'

'My mother has been keeping you informed I see.'

'She always did have a lot to say when it came to you.'

'Look, Catherine, I didn't come here to argue.' He leaned over to touch her hand but she withdrew it quickly and twisted it into the other on her lap until her palms ran with sweat and her fingers felt as if they might break off. Jimmy knew it was going to be difficult, impossible even, to hold a productive discussion unless he managed to put her at her ease. 'If only I could make you understand how sorry I am. You don't know the number of times I've wished I could turn back the clock and undo what I did!'

'If I'd gone to the police, you could have landed in jail. What you did wasn't only wrong, it was a crime,' she said accusingly. She had to get him running scared. She feared the outcome of this meeting more than anything else in her life. It could ruin her marriage, as if that weren't already on dangerous ground.

'You think I don't realise that now, especially with changing moral attitudes. However, I don't think the law would have given you any cuttings in those days.' Jimmy was determined that Catherine wasn't going to worm her way out of this conversation regardless of the criminality of what he'd done.

'Don't start making excuses for your actions. You came at me like a maniac and completely against my will,' she said, determined to hold her own. As soon as he had her on the defensive she would break down and all her suspicions would come flooding to the surface and he would have won the day. A man as cruel as Jimmy was capable of taking her son from her, especially if she and Gregor split up and he had the wonderful Patricia by his side.

Jimmy persisted in playing down his own guilt and overestimating the part she had played. 'Looking back on what really happened, do you think the police would have been all that interested?' he said with sarcasm, as if she were crazy to argue otherwise. Jimmy was determined to clear his name. He had to hold fast to his line of defence or else Catherine would have the ammunition she needed to wreck his marriage and therefore his life. His voice lowered and became almost gentle in his endeavours to be on an equal footing with her. Little did he realise that she thought he had the upper hand and had come seeking custody of the boy, when in fact all he wanted was to be acknowledged as the father without Patricia ever finding out.

He had to win her over just enough to allow him to have his say, but even that was proving difficult. 'I was different then. I would never do anything like that now. You see, I felt we belonged together. I always did. I thought you cared about me because you helped me when my mother was going through a hard time getting off prescription drugs. We were brought up in the same tenement. I always thought you would be my girlfriend and we'd get married. When Patricia fell pregnant I didn't want her. It was always you I had my eye on. The night I came round and saw you wearing only a thin dressing gown, I lost my mind. I was deranged. Nothing else mattered to me but you.' Jimmy looked across at Catherine who sat grim faced staring down at the table top as she contemplated every line of the grain of the wood. Surely this must be a bad dream and she'd waken soon. He decided to continue; for all he knew she might flare up at any moment and throw him out. If that happened he'd have to come back another time and start the process all over again. Of one thing he was sure, if she didn't relent this afternoon and give him a proper hearing, he would return as often as was necessary until she did. 'I didn't realise then how much Patricia was going to mean to me. I made a mistake thinking you were the one. But regardless of never wanting to lose Patricia I am still entitled to know if Stephen's mine or not.'

What Jimmy said next sent such a shudder up Catherine's spine that her whole body shook as if electrodes had been deliberately and cruelly applied to it. He threw her the words of confirmation that she'd hoped she'd never live to hear: 'It didn't even last ten seconds.' She knew exactly what the 'it' stood for. His voice flowed over her and she felt as if she were drowning in it. She gagged as it brought horrific memories flooding back as he continued with the words that confirmed their consummation: 'But it was long enough to know you'd been with someone else before me.'

Catherine gasped. At the time, because she'd been barely

conscious, she hadn't been sure that intercourse had actually taken place, but it seemed that it had, and now that Jimmy had started talking he wouldn't stop. He'd obviously been rehearsing for days, stockpiling his arsenal before going in for the kill. He knew he had her full attention and stared straight into her bemused eyes as he continued. 'And then Boy Wonder came crashing in just at the critical moment. Sorry, I shouldn't call him that. After all, he did me a favour. When I lay on the pathway with my face in the mud, I literally came down to earth with a bang. I knew then that there was more going on between you and him than I had ever suspected and there was no future for you and me. I wanted a woman who was untarnished and Patricia had been pure when she came to me. I realised that I did love her after all. When I married her I didn't want to be like my father. I had to do things right. I admit I felt tied down to begin with but when baby Sophie was born it was love at first sight and my wife and family have been my whole life ever since. You see, that's what I had wanted for us - you and me - a home and children, and I suppose because I had dreamed of it so desperately I lost all control. Going by today's standards I did deserve to be charged, but those were, as I've already said, different times. Do you seriously think back there in the nineteen sixties that there would have been any sympathy for a woman who invited a man she knew well into her house wearing little more than a nightdress?'

Catherine was aghast. He seemed to have the whole episode stored so clearly in his mind and the account of it so well practised, whereas she had spent years trying to block it out. She didn't know fact from fiction any more. 'I don't care what "happily ever after" you had fantasies of, and it doesn't matter what I was wearing, there was no justification for your attacking me.'

'Catherine, you answered the door and let me in wearing only a skimpy nylon dressing gown and see through nightie. You know perfectly well that when you pulled it tight round yourself you may as well have been naked. I could see everything. Your nipples stood out like ripe berries and you wiggled yourself in front of me, taunting me. You even stood aside to make sure I could watch that couple snogging on the TV film behind you. You wanted to turn me on. You always were a tease and then revelled in saying no. You got a kick out of thinking that I wanted you.'

'How dare you! I want you out of here right now, you bastard.' Catherine stood up. Her face was bright red and her eyes flashed with anger.

'Just sit down will you, and listen for once in your life.' Jimmy's voice remained steady and commanding, but still with its note of patient politeness. 'We were both young and didn't realise the dangers of playing games. But you went too far that night. I know I have no excuse, but I was somewhat tipsy and I'd been brought up to think that one day we would be together.'

'Your mother!' shouted Catherine indignantly. Rosie had always infuriated her with suggestions that she and Jimmy would make a lovely couple. 'I always made it perfectly clear to her and you, that there wasn't a hope in hell of that.'

'But give my mother her due; nothing much goes past her, and that's why I've called round. I want to know if it was me that made you pregnant. I'm maybe only a welder and not brainy like you, but I can count, and anyway, nine is all that's necessary in this case. Tenth October to twelfth July - only a few days out.'

'You've kept the date in your head all these years? But we never ... and I didn't feel anything ... your hand ...' Catherine knew from what he'd said earlier that it must have happened after all.

'Thanks a million. Not very flattering for a bloke I must say. I admit it wasn't the best experience I've ever had, but do me a favour, that was more than my fingers. How else do you think I knew you weren't a virgin? It wasn't one of my better times, I'll give you that, but if your boyfriend at the time hadn't come bungling in, I might have held on longer.'

'That was more than a boyfriend. It was Gregor. We were engaged to be married.'

'Okay, that husband of yours interrupted me and it was all over, you know what I mean. But forget about it not being the most earth moving experience I've ever had; it certainly was one of the most productive, and I believe I have a son.'

Catherine tried to remember as she had done every time the thought that Stephen was Jimmy's had hammered at the back of her head. She remembered the walls closing in around her during the attack and everything going blank. 'But I didn't feel it ... I didn't think that anything ... surely not ...'

'You never were one for compliments. But I was drunk remember. And how else do you think I knew it wasn't your first time?'

Catherine heard again his parting shot as Gregor threw him out: 'At least Patsy was a virgin when I first had her.' So it was true; the pounding suspicions; those penetrating looks from Stephen - Jimmy was his father, not Gregor.

'I'm sorry, Catherine. I didn't mean for any of this to happen, but if I have a son, then I want to know. It's nothing to do with the past. It's the here and now that matters and I would like to see him. Beyond that is anybody's guess. And don't go blaming my mother; she had a right to tell me the kids resemble each other. She wanted to get to the bottom of it and clear up any doubt.'

'I could do with a drink,' said Catherine. Nervous exhaustion had subdued her. 'Do you want one? There's lager in the fridge, supposed to be for Eddie.'

'You go ahead; I'm not much of a drinker these days, but I could murder a cup of tea.' He was drumming his fingers on the edge of the table as if giving great consideration to the next step.

They sat in stony silence, drinking and thinking, but strangely the animosity was gone. It was too much to take in for both of them. They shared a child. There was no greater link between two people. Jimmy reached across the table and put his hand over hers and gave it a gentle squeeze. This time Catherine didn't pull away immediately. She needed so much to feel comforted and now that the moment she had dreaded for so long was upon her, she was glad of human touch no matter who was the source. After all, she thought briefly, he is the father of my son. Catherine looked up at him. 'I don't know what to do,' she said in a cracked whisper. Then, as if coming to her senses she shuddered and quickly withdrew her hand. With deliberate intensity she began rubbing at it with the other as if to cleanse all trace of him from her skin. She made no secret of what she was doing and worked her hands in front of her face just under the chin, the place where it was usual to lock one's hands in prayer.

Jimmy tensed, aware of her sudden show of revulsion and quickly removed his hand from the table and hid it by folding his arms. He leaned forward towards her and gave her what seemed to be a list of instructions for what he had planned next. 'You're obviously tired and suffering from shock, so let's leave it for today. I'm ashore for another week while Mum and Eddie are here. I'll meet you in town tomorrow afternoon and we'll collect Stephen from school together. I'll take you somewhere for your tea. It'll be a chance for us to get better acquainted; but no word of my being his father mind. My wife must never get to hear of this. Only us ... for now ... understand? I don't want anything to spoil things for my Patricia. I couldn't live without her.' He paused for breath and looked her straight in the eye. Catherine felt like a rabbit caught in the headlights of a speeding car. Was there any way she could get out of this situation? But no matter how hard she thought, it seemed she had little choice.

Jimmy took her silence to mean acceptance of his suggested meeting and also the fact that he was Stephen's father. 'So, what are you going to tell Gregor? Do you think he knows?'

'Well, if I didn't know until now, how could he?' Catherine replied.

'Don't give me that, you've more or less admitted that this hasn't come as a complete shock. Gregor's a doctor. If I can do the sums ... he's probably guessed all along. But then, he is a good man, going by what I've heard through the grapevine.'

Catherine clutched at her throat in alarm. Her heart was doing cartwheels in her chest. It made her wonder if maybe that was why Gregor had gone off her. Maybe he'd noticed Stephen's resemblance to Jimmy. She was about to say that his mother shouldn't have brought Gregor into the equation but thought better of it. She knew that everything she said would be immediately relayed to Rosie, and she didn't want to give Jimmy any opportunity to stir up bad feeling between them.

'What about your mother?' she asked knowing full well that Rosie would give the game away. 'If she ever found out she'd never keep it to herself. Patricia would know in a twinkling.'

'I told her she was imagining things; that you and I had never been together. She didn't seem too happy hearing that but she has no choice, especially if you stick to the same story. Anyway, they've gone to Ullapool so she won't be bothering you for a few days. Give you time to concoct your side of things.'

Catherine sat quietly staring ahead with unseeing eyes. She was living through her worst nightmare. She would never wake up and be normal again. It was like the gruesome plot of some midnight horror movie. The intermittent banging at the base of her skull had become a persistent throb in her temples. She pushed her chair back and made for the kitchen. Jimmy followed her through. Catherine made no secret of what she had come for. She filled her glass and took great gulps from it. Jimmy put his hand on her arm, his eyes following closely the quantity of liquor that she was pouring down her throat. 'And to think how you used to look down your nose at me,' he sneered, 'when I failed the eleven plus and you passed with flying colours.' Catherine said nothing but carried the bottle and glass back to the table. Was there to be no end to Jimmy's diatribe? 'From then on we were in different worlds, but look how we've ended up. I'm a success and you can't face any problem without "poor me, poor me, pour me a drink". I wasn't stupid just because I went to a junior secondary; and time has shown that my feet were planted more firmly on the ground than yours. I'm my own person with nothing to prove. I must have been crazy. Patricia is worth a million of you.'

Catherine's confidence crumbled and she bowed her head in submission over her glass before downing another mouthful. She envied him, though not his house or his family, but the fact that he could take whatever life threw at him without resorting to drink. What was wrong with her that she needed this crutch? She disgusted herself but still she continued to do it. How could she give it up with this latest crisis on her hands?

'You always thought that you were superior to me,' said Jimmy and she detected the contempt in his voice as he continued to spew out years of resentment and ill will. 'I agree that I was a brat to you, but I was a boy, and I liked you. How could I put that into words? You always did look down on me as just another failure while you swanned off in your posh uniform to the senior secondary. I agree I was nasty to you, but I didn't understand my own feelings, while you were a ...'

Suddenly Catherine spoke. Jimmy's heartfelt sense of injustice caused her to view their childhood spats from his perspective and she completed his sentence for him. 'Yes, I was a ... smartass. I see that now and I really am sorry. I got carried away in some fantasy. You were right. My world came from the pages of books. My ideas of life were fiction. I had no concept of reality and I thought that being "better at school" somehow made me a better person, but I realise how false and shallow that was.' Tears were rolling down her cheeks as the effects of the gin dented her self confidence, dragged her down and made her see herself through his jealous eyes.

'Please don't be upset,' Jimmy said. 'You have to trust me. I've changed, Catherine, honestly I have.' His voice had grown more tender now that he had the satisfaction of seeing her reduced to a snivelling, drunken wreck. 'I haven't come here to cause trouble. Can you blame me for wanting to know if I have a son? Do you think I would want to damage my own child?' He was speaking now as if he considered himself to be a decent, hardworking family man who had never done anyone a bad turn in his life.

However, his smug satisfaction was to be short lived as Catherine, begging for mercy, also gave him a few home truths: 'You're successful with a loving family and beautiful home,' she said. 'Why couldn't you have been happy with that and left me alone? For as long as I live I shall never forgive you for what you did to me that night, and for what you're doing to me now. There is never a day passes when I don't regret ever having set eyes on you.' Jimmy rose to his feet and pulled up the zip of his jacket.

He'd had enough. There was no way she was ever going to find him acceptable. The clock on the tiled mantelpiece chimed the half hour. Catherine pushed past him to the bathroom to fix her swollen eyes and blotchy face. 'Stephen will be coming out of school soon. I have to go and fetch him.'

'I'll give you a lift. You can't drive in that state.'

Catherine knew he meant because of the gin. 'I was going to walk. I need to clear my head.'

'I understand,' he said, nodding condescendingly. Catherine bit her tongue as she watched a smirk cross his face. It annoyed her to see him take the moral high ground. 'I'll drop you off in the street next the school and disappear sharpish,' he added, 'but tomorrow I'll be there smack on four o'clock and we'll all go out together. Just tell Stephen that his Auntie Rosie wanted us to meet; that's all ... for the time being at least.'

That evening Catherine tried her best to be cheerful and extra kind to Stephen. That poor little lad; what did the future hold for him? They were tucking into their fish and chips, still in the paper as a special treat, when the phone rang. 'It's Daddy!' Stephen only said Daddy when he was feeling at his most affectionate and happy. His face was a picture of joy as he turned to his mother and shouted, 'He says he's coming soon ... He's been missing us ...' Catherine's heart went out to her son as she watched him babbling with glee as he tried to tell his father all that he'd been doing. 'Love you so much ... Can't wait to see you,' he squealed before handing the receiver to his mother and he bounded round the room like an overexcited puppy, jumping on the sofa and hurling himself into the air.

Stephen was right. In no time Gregor would be on his way. He said that his research had reached its conclusion in Toronto and the rest would have to be carried out in Aberdeen between the university and the institute. 'I won't be over immediately of course, but it could be in a month or very soon after,' he said. 'I can't wait to hear all your news. Got to go now and sort out my packing. The men are coming tomorrow to collect the tea chests. I've arranged for them to go by sea and have them put in storage when they arrive in Scotland. I love you, Catherine ... Bye.'

'I love you too, Gregor.' Catherine wished that all she had to worry about was a few boxes. She dreaded Gregor coming now and having to explain why Jimmy had reappeared in her life. Anxiety raged through her and she felt a pool of acid gathering in her stomach.

'You don't seem very happy, Mum. What's wrong?' asked Stephen. He came over and gave her a hug, laying his head on her shoulder as he had used to do so often when he was a child.

'Of course I'm happy. I'm just, as they say, struck dumb. Let's heat up these chips. They're stone cold and you can have any ice cream you want later when the van comes round.' Robotically, Catherine dealt with the food. Her mind had seized like a car engine that's been running without oil. With great effort she pulled her face into the happy smiling expression that she knew her son expected and listed all the fun things they would do together when Dad came, and all the places they would take him on days out.

How she wished she'd taken some action over finding somewhere else, a place on a par with their beautiful residence in Canada. How could she make Gregor glad to have left his swimming and golfing friends behind when all he would find was a wife as grumpy as hell, struggling to survive in this hovel? How long would she be able to keep up the pretence that Stephen was his? At the thought of the clubhouse, doubt flooded in. Was he coming over for good or only on a flying visit? Why hadn't he sounded more excited and why had he enunciated 'I love you Catherine' so deliberately, making a meal of every syllable? She wondered if he really was spending the evening sorting through his stuff. She would phone Mrs Thomas.

From the bumps and bangs in Stephen's room she guessed he was already tidying up in preparation for his dad's arrival. His chattering was incessant as he foraged in drawers and searched amongst his belongings on the shelves. In no time his swimming certificates were firmly cellotaped to the door of the fridge and an array of cups stood proudly on the unit in the living room.

Catherine's mind wandered to what his 'real' father might be doing; no doubt stretched out on his white leather sofa sleeping off a cordon bleu meal prepared by that paragon of virtue 'Perfect Patricia', while his virginal daughters completed beautifully set out homework in sumptuous bedrooms that were decorated in soft shades of pink. Her hand shook with a mixture of rage and fear, making the neck of the green bottle of best London gin clunk against the heavy glass of the tumbler.

Chapter 11

The hangover next morning had been particularly bad. Catherine told Stephen she had a headache and he had to prepare his own cereal and walk to school alone. He didn't seem to mind. In fact he gloried in his new found independence and proudly brought her a cup of tea in bed to prove he was indeed the man of the house. She mumbled a thank you but let it stand on the bedside table. Anything, even a plain hot drink, would have started her vomiting again.

She had finished almost a whole bottle of gin in twenty-four hours thanks to Jimmy's visit. The sheets had been soaked with sweat when Stephen shook her out of the comatose state into which she'd fallen sometime in the early hours. She'd lain awake supping alcohol in an effort to blank out the vision of Stephen being lured from her to go and live with Jimmy and Patricia in preference to herself. Her mind had become devoid of all reason while scary paranoid thoughts took over and ran riot. What if she became a single parent and Social Services intervened at Jimmy's behest? They'd never allow a child to remain with her in an environment of drug addicts and glue sniffers in preference to a perfect family in a beautiful home. Jimmy was sure to mention her drinking in order to persuade the courts to award him Stephen. Gregor wouldn't be there to stand up for her. He'd be too busy looking after Marion. She'd barely made it to the toilet to throw up the sour residue of liquid from her stomach that contracted in agony to rid itself of the poison. Most of it had already escaped into her bloodstream and circulated her body eating at her brain and shattering her nerves.

Once Stephen had left, whistling his way down the stairs that were thankfully clear of catcalling youngsters at this early hour, she dozed off and on all morning. How on earth was she going to survive the evening? The substance of her worst nightmare was about to become reality. She rose and took a long soak in the bath, but however hard she scrubbed at her weakened body no amount of tearing at her skin with the back brush would ever wash away the truth. Life had become a torment.

Her mind was befuddled and filled with paranoia. She was certain Gregor wouldn't want her but she couldn't let Jimmy know that she was on the verge of splitting up from her husband. As long as Jimmy thought her marriage was stable it would provide a sure protection from him as he probably still held Gregor in awe after the thrashing he'd got from him on the night of the attack. She had to appear confident and calm.

She chose a knee length royal blue suit with a white and yellow patterned silk scarf loosely knotted at the neck. Her hair was wound into a neat chignon on the crown of her head with a full fringe falling over her furrowed brow to break the severity of the style. The shoes she chose were a dark navy with a low heel. She couldn't risk overbalancing in this fragile state. She checked her reflection thoroughly in the mirror. Smart and respectable; power dressing they called this latest look for women who wanted to appear successful in their lives. Jimmy wouldn't be able to criticise her for slovenliness that's for sure. However, it took a straight slug from the new bottle of gin she'd fetched from the off licence before she could brace herself to face Jimmy again. She would explain the dark glasses by saying the blinding migraine had worsened.

Catherine recognised the dark maroon BMW parked opposite the school. She had walked in order to clear her head, but despite that and the numerous coffees and glasses of pure water she had consumed all day, her system still bore the ravages of alcohol, headache, raging thirst and worst of all a nervous tremor that set her on edge. On sight of her, Jimmy climbed out of the car and pressed the remote that locked it with a bleep. Trust him to have all the latest gadgets, she thought. He ran over to her side and put his arm protectively around her making sure that he was walking on the outside of the pavement. He'd done that for as long as she could remember. In order, he always said jokingly, to make sure that any passing horseman with a sword would stab him and not her. He was well groomed in what might be called 'smart casual' trousers and a suede bomber style jacket. As he moved close to her she caught the spicy scent of a tasteful aftershave which was quite unlike the overpowering stuff smelling like air freshener that he'd doused himself with in his younger days.

'I've had a headache all day,' she said tapping the side of the dark glasses in order to explain the need of them on a dull day. She knew she must be looking rough despite having coated her haggard face with layers of makeup. Jimmy caught the rancid smell of alcohol from her breath. 'I hope all this isn't making you ill,' he said before turning away to gulp some fresh air. She wished she had cleaned her teeth a second time. Sometimes these mint sweets weren't powerful enough to mask stale drink when she'd been soused in it. It oozed from her pores and even the expensive perfume she wore couldn't camouflage the traces of sweated gin. He passed no complimentary comment on her appearance but at least there was no criticism.

'I told Stephen that we would be meeting you,' she said, before continuing with a warning note in her voice, 'Gregor will be here in a couple of weeks.' She added an inaudible aside to herself, 'As if I hadn't enough to deal with already.' Jimmy was about to say something too but she held up her hand to silence him. 'Sh, here he comes.' Catherine arranged her face into a welcoming smile as Stephen ran towards them, stopping a couple of yards away to give himself a chance to weigh up the stranger. Jimmy held out his hand and spoke before Catherine had a chance to put together some words of introduction. 'Hi there, Stephen, I'm Jimmy,' he said. His face had taken on a glow that may well have been interpreted as instant love. 'I'm so glad to be able to meet you at last. Your Auntie Rosie has told me so much about you.'

Stephen was obviously delighted to be greeted in such a formal, grown-up manner, and immediately thrust his hand out to shake Jimmy's. Catherine felt the sting of hot tears as she watched father and son greet each other for the first time, their eyes meeting, holding steady as if each sensed automatically the link between them. From the broad smiles that crossed their almost identical mouths, they liked what they saw. 'Jimmy is Sophie's and Sylvie's dad,' explained Catherine. 'He couldn't make it with them last week so he's come to meet you today instead.'

'That's right, Stephen; and Rosie is my mother. Your mum and I were friends years ago and want to get to know each other again.' Stephen wrinkled his brow in an effort to piece together all these relationships and was quietly mulling things over as they strolled along. For the first time ever he walked in the middle of his real parents, down the steps, through the Union Terrace Gardens and up and on to Union Street.

'Are you going to take Sophie and Sylvie out with us another day?' Stephen asked innocently. Jimmy stopped walking as a look of horror swept across his face. He looked over at Catherine and although his words were supposed to be for Stephen their meaning was directed straight at Catherine. 'They are much too busy with school work. It's most unlikely they'll be able to visit ...,' he said, and over the top of Stephen's head he mouthed silently to Catherine with his eyes wide as organ stops, '... ever, and I mean ever!'

Catherine put her hand to her forehead. It was moist with perspiration. 'I never thought of that,' she whispered, her lips barely moving.

A train whistling as it went past on the railway running alongside the gardens caught their attention and helped to change the subject. 'It's going to Inverness,' declared Stephen. 'I know that because Uncle Eddie told me. He said that he and Auntie Rosie would be on it on their way to the West Coast and to wave to it going past. And I did, at half-past eight on the way to school yesterday.'

'You never told me that. I thought you were just waving to be friendly to some traveller who had waved out at you,' said Catherine. It made her nervous to think her son was developing his own life beyond her.

'You don't have to know everything about me, Mum,' he said, glad of an opportunity to show Jimmy to whom he already felt a close alliance that he was an independent character and not a mummy's boy.

Jimmy laughed. 'You're quite a lad, young Stephen. I can't wait to know you better.' Stephen pulled his hand out of his mother's tight grasp and drew himself up to his full height to walk proudly in step with the man on his right.

They went to a Chinese restaurant at Stephen's request. 'This is a bit like the one we were in with Mother's other friend, Earl.' Catherine noticed that he'd started calling her Mother from time to time as part of his growing up campaign.

'We met Earl when we were visiting Michael, one of Stephen's school friends,' she explained. She couldn't risk Jimmy knowing any more than that. 'He gave us a lift home.' She didn't admit to it having been what might have been termed a 'date'.

'Earl flies out to the rigs on a chopper hundreds of miles out in the middle of the North Sea,' announced Stephen so loudly that several diners turned their heads.

Jimmy laughed. 'So do I; right out to one of the furthest rigs there is.'

Stephen's eyes nearly popped out of his head. 'Do you hear that, Mu ... Mother? Jimmy knows about helicopters too.'

'I believe your dad is coming over quite soon,' said Jimmy, obviously interested in finding out more about how they got along.

'He drives to work, my dad, and sometimes he cycles, on an old fashioned bike. It doesn't even have a horn. He rings a bell if someone's in front of him on the Lakeside Path.' Stephen stopped and his eyes moved upwards as if trying to remember clearly. Then he added thoughtfully, 'But he's been tired lately and usually drives.' Stephen frowned as if wondering whether this was something he should have mentioned or not.

'Your dad's a doctor. And that's one of the most important jobs around. He probably cycles because it's healthy.' Jimmy was being noticeably respectful of Gregor and Catherine's worst fears began to fade. Jimmy was as terrified as she was of a marriage breakup.

'Mother keeps telling him to buy a more modern bicycle,' Stephen replied, and added with genuine pride, 'I have a mountain bike with loads of gears.'

'It sounds to me as if your father loves his old boneshaker and

I think you should let him enjoy it.' Jimmy picked up the menus and handed one each to Catherine and Stephen.

'I hope he doesn't bring it over here. What an embarrassment if he met me from school on that!' Stephen had already commented on Jimmy's highly polished BMW, his eyes bulging with admiration when he'd seen his mother and Jimmy standing beside it. He knew this would bring complimentary comments from his classmates the following day, and for once he was looking forward to going to school.

'You should be proud of your dad, Stephen, regardless of what he rides on to get about.' Jimmy spoke in a fatherly tone. Already he wanted to make sure his son would grow up with decent attitudes. 'He's always worked hard for you and your mum. Never forget that.'

'That's right, Stephen,' said Catherine. She threw Jimmy a faint smile to show that she was pleased with his handling of the situation. He could so easily have hijacked Gregor's position. 'Your dad is a kind man who has helped countless people. Does it matter that he doesn't scoot around Ontario in a helicopter?'

'I suppose not. But that's what I'm going to fly one day when I'm a man,' replied Stephen. The insecurities of being in what was for him a foreign land had led him to welcome the masculine influence of both Earl and Jimmy and they had become his new role models. The meal continued pleasantly and proved to be less stressful than Catherine had anticipated, but was it to be yet another step towards ruining her family?

Jimmy insisted on giving them a lift home. As they approached his car, he took out a hand held control and with a bleep the doors were unlocked. It was all show with him. When he opened the door for her, the back door of course, because Stephen the male would be sitting in the passenger seat, the whiff of new leather mixed with air freshener was overpowering. Stephen was agog and asked about every dial on the dashboard. Jimmy beamed with pride and with a press of a button made the windows slide open and shut. 'A far cry from the old bikes we went out on for runs in the country,' he laughed. 'Remember when that cattle truck flashed past us and drenched us with urine? Those were good times.'

'Yes,' replied Catherine drily. 'It was the same day as the picnic by the river.'

Jimmy became subdued. That had been the day he had asked her to marry him and she had laughed outright in his face. This embarrassing part of the memory had quelled his exuberance and a heavy silence filled the car. Even Stephen stopped talking. He knew all was not as well between them as it had at first seemed.

Chapter 12

Catherine hadn't had a minute's peace of mind since Jimmy had come to the flat despite his sworn promise that the secret would remain firmly between the two of them. She knew he wasn't likely to blow the whole mess up in her face. But what if Gregor had suspected the truth right from the beginning? Would he abandon them or continue to tolerate the situation especially now that Stephen was old enough to suffer if he ever found out his true parentage.

Another overwhelming worry was the hold that alcohol had on her, the new bottle having been emptied within a day of Jimmy meeting Stephen. She'd even downed the lagers from the fridge that were meant for Eddie. There was no doubt it would count in court if ever Jimmy wanted to lay claim to Stephen. He might do it regardless of Patricia simply because he didn't want his son brought up by a drunk. She had to give it up. What had begun as a social pleasure had turned into a monster controlling her life.

In her determination she had tried by stopping buying any but had only managed to endure the withdrawals from her massive binge for a couple of days. As the toxic substance cleared from her system she began to suffer horrific nightmares and even hallucinations. She could bear it no longer. Lack of sleep, hot and cold sweats, apparitions and waking dreams brought her to the end of her resolution to stop suddenly. She would have to cut down gradually.

Catherine was first in the queue waiting outside the off-licence to open at nine o'clock for a drink to steady her nerves. She had endured a night of terror as visions of blood stained hands reached for her from the ceiling and clouds of buzzing insects had swarmed noisily round her ears. She wasn't the only one desperate for more of the same to quell the tremors of her body and the fear in her heart. Heavy lidded and blood shot eyes peered at her questioningly out of scruffy unshaven faces. 'Hair of the dog, missus?' asked the little man nearest to her with the wizened face of a hardened drinker. He laughed as he looked her up and down.

'Been out on the game have you? There's not many round here can afford that cut of clothes unless it's from the wallet of one of them Yanks on the rigs. Was last night a bit too hard for you, eh?' He gave a throaty laugh at his own joke.

His friend joined in the banter. It wasn't often that a high-class dame like her joined their desperate queue. 'There's plenty room in my bed if you're looking for somewhere to spend the night,' he said and gave her a wink that made his whole face crumple like a dried out chamois leather. He had taken a spindly thin roll-up out of his toothless, gurning mouth just long enough to pass comment. She turned away in disgust but more at herself than at them. Another hunched up creature, who had recently slunk in about, laughed out loud at the remarks. The sudden harsh intake of breath caused his tar stickied lungs to throw up some filthy green and brown phlegm which he spat in thick, glutinous blobs only inches in front of the pointed toes of her designer shoes.

She had no alternative but to wait. Sweat was seeping through the front of her blouse and she had to lean back against the metal grid that covered the shop window. When another five minutes of listening to coarse comments had passed, the shopkeeper finally strolled lazily along the pavement with the keys at the ready and a pleasant 'good morning'. It seemed to take forever for him to unlock and raise the metal grid and open the door. Catherine was hard on his heels into the shop and first at the counter to hand over the cash for two half bottles of gin, any brand would do. She swore this situation would never happen again. She remembered how Rosie had won her battle with prescription drugs – gradually - cutting down a bit at a time. Would it work the same with drink?

This was the third night she'd tossed and turned while her tortured mind created the bleakest of futures. She had decided to allow herself two half bottles of spirits and three of wine in a week. However, in only two days she'd drunk the lot. There was no one she could offload her problems to. She'd even considered counselling but her worries were real, not figments. Alcoholics Anonymous with their twelve step programme had a good reputation for success but who could she trust to look after Stephen? They would find out about her drinking and perhaps alert the authorities. Facing reality was a nightmare and the loneliness of handling it on her own was eating into her like a cancer.

Rosie and Eddie had been in touch and thankfully arranged a day out away from the flat at the beach and then the carnival. There had been lots of frivolous fun at the fairground but with no opportunity for real conversation. Catherine longed for time alone with her uncle but certainly not to spill the beans about Stephen. Eddie was the type to want to have everything out in the open and she couldn't risk the hurtful fallout that honesty can bring. Rosie was desperate to have her suspicions verified and kept a gimlet eye on them, straining her ears to catch every single word that was said, but Catherine was only interested in someone to talk to on topics that would lift her mind from the pain of her emotional drama. Eddie didn't waste much breath on personal matters and spoke refreshingly on a wide variety of subjects, his latest hobby horse being the struggle against pit closures up and down the country.

He would be the last person she'd tell about Stephen. He would insist on telling everyone the truth immediately and throw everyone's lives into chaos. It distressed her too that it was her long time confidante Rosie who played the most central but opposing character in this whole sorry mess. She would have been a tower of strength and immediately on her side in any other situation but this one where she would naturally side with Jimmy. As far as Rosie was concerned there were no holds barred when it came to supporting her son and logic and fairness went out the window. The one aspect of their relationship that had caused sparks to fly in the past, namely Catherine's potentially romantic involvement with Jimmy, would become an all out conflagration. She couldn't help noticing that Rosie's eyes, when they weren't watching Eddie and her, would fix on Stephen, searching for the clues that would prove he was her grandchild. Never had

Catherine felt so isolated with the link to her most trusted ally severed by her involvement.

Stephen had been on every ride and had eaten ice cream, candyfloss and chips but still remained buoyant and excited. Catherine had ventured on to the wild mouse and regretted it. Eddie stuck to bumping cars on the dodgems. Rosie screamed in delight on the waltzers. 'I always had a good head,' she scoffed at Catherine who was still green about the gills from the mini roller coaster. 'Takes Eddie all his time not to stagger on the dance floor after a couple of foxtrots,' she laughed. Together Rosie and Stephen climbed on to the waltzers for a second turn. Catherine and Eddie turned their backs. They couldn't even bear to look.

Rosie smiled smugly when she and Stephen tapped them on the shoulders and laughed once the exhilarating turn was over. 'That man kept spinning us extra,' squealed Stephen and he and Rosie doubled up with laughter at the horrified expression on Catherine's face. 'Stephen's just like me when it comes to enjoying himself, and Jimmy's the same,' she said. 'We could go on every ride here twice and never feel the slightest twinge of nausea.' She had her arm possessively round Stephen's shoulders. 'Let's go and get some bags of chips and a few pickled onions,' she said pointedly, knowing full well that the Clarks would be knocked sick at the very thought.

'Auntie Rosie's good fun,' said Stephen, and to make matters worse added that his father often threw up when flying in an aeroplane. 'He'll have to take loads of his special travel medicine when he comes from Toronto,' he said stuffing a handful of greasy chips into his large grinning mouth.

When the time came for Rosie and Eddie to return to Basildon, Catherine couldn't bear to let them go and cried openly as she held them tight, begging them to return soon. They'd popped round to the flat for a last minute visit. 'Go easy on the hard stuff,' said Eddie who had noticed her problem and had been somewhat put out when he discovered his cans of lager had also been consumed. Surprisingly, Rosie had said nothing on that front but no doubt it had been discussed thoroughly by everyone in the Simpson household. Had Jimmy warned his mother off? Had he told her about their meal out together? The uncertain mystery made Catherine even more reluctant to tell Rosie anything about her private life. 'Try not to worry;' Rosie said to her gently, 'life has a way of sorting itself out in the end.' But that was exactly what Catherine feared most.

Chapter 13

Catherine's sense of isolation intensified. Alone in the evenings, she found it almost impossible not to turn increasingly to alcohol once Stephen was in bed. She refused every offer to go to parties with Heather who turned out to be one of those people who can become quite nasty if you stop doing exactly as they want. 'Please yourself. Be on your own night after night,' Heather had snapped. 'And what of poor Stephen? Playing with Michael was doing him the world of good, that poor, lonely little boy.' Catherine wasn't caring what she thought. She had a personal fight on her hands and she would never beat the demon drink if she continued to mix with Heather's crowd. It had been all right while Earl was around. He was comparatively moderate in his drinking and certainly, as far as he was concerned, drugs were off limits. Even so, Catherine had relied on secret snifters to carry her through the partying and had never left home without a quarter-bottle in her bag.

Now that these hectic times were over, Catherine tried her theory of cutting out the drinking by going without every second day in order to reduce it steadily until she was dry. This was easier said than done when life was handing her one bad card after another in such rapid succession. One evening as she paced the floor of the living room when her supplies for the day had run out, the craving for more became too much for her. When she was sober she would clench her fists and swear she was capable of keeping her promise to beat the curse. The difficulty was that as soon as her alcohol levels began to rise, so her strength of will began to fail and her mind began to trick her into believing that she was entitled to seek oblivion any way she saw fit.

She was amazed at the ready availability of any quantity of alcohol, literally on the doorstep with no questions asked, which made any attempt at resistance virtually impossible. A couple of extra bottles thrown in with the shopping or a quick run round to the licensed grocer soon increased the quantity far beyond her intended limit. In Canada, apart from the private clubs, there were only the Beer Stores that could sell beer and the provincially-owned Liquor Control Board of Ontario (LCBO) that was allowed to sell hard liquor or wine as well as beer and a small number of privately owned speciality wine stores. She'd had to drive a good half hour to get her gin supplies, whereas in the UK it was possible to stock up with a vast range of alcohol from any one of an abundance of 'offies' liberally scattered round each city and town.

It was a Saturday night and she had convinced herself she should be allowed a drink. Stephen would be safe enough. She'd left him for a few minutes before. So, after peeping in to make sure he was fast asleep, she threw on her jacket and nipped out, locking the door. No sooner was she at the entrance of the dingy corner shop than the shopkeeper reached up for her 'usual', two half-bottles of gin. She found it easier to stop after a half than if she'd had the lot all in one. He put them in brown paper bags on the counter for her. One fitted snugly into her pocket. The other was easy to hide in her handbag. Head down, she scurried back to the flat wondering why he had bothered with the bags which just as readily identified the contents as any well known label would.

She had to run the gauntlet of the children hanging round the front door. 'Here she comes, fur coat and no drawers Boozy Betty,' they shouted. Their sneers and rude gestures followed her up the stairs. She had never been smart enough to smile occasionally and befriend them. Her attempts at retaliation in an accent that sounded posh to them alienated her and made her appear to be looking down on them. They had their own brand of pride and gave her hell for despising them, especially when in their eyes she was no better, and in fact a lot worse, than many of their mothers who struggled through poverty to live decent and sober lives.

In desperation to shake them off she hurried up the steps trying to take them two at a time, but she misjudged how intoxicated she was. On reaching the safe haven of the landing, she missed her footing and a bottle fell from her pocket, smashed on the concrete floor and spilled the clear liquid through the sodden paper bag into a pool mixed with broken glass. She fell headlong on to all fours amongst the mess and crashed against the door of her immediate neighbours. Suddenly there was blood everywhere. Her hand had been torn open as it scraped along on a shard of glass. She was losing it quickly on account of its having been thinned by the alcohol. She pressed the heel of her other hand against it in an effort to stem the flow.

'What the hell?' said Gerald, her young neighbour, throwing open his door. His voice rose in tone and volume and from shocked to threatening as he looked quickly beyond her expecting to see an attacker fleeing down the stairs. 'Help me,' Catherine said weakly, I fell and cut myself. Satisfied there was no one else involved, Gerald squatted down beside her and, before adding the pressure from his own hands to that of her own, he rushed back in to the house and came out wearing a pair of rubber gloves such as those a dentist or a doctor might use and a large towel which he held tightly against her wound to stop the blood spurting everywhere. With a steadying arm round her waist, he helped her to her feet, which was no simple task as Catherine continued to stagger due to a mixture of distress and being the worse for drink.

He shouted to his wife Mandy to hurry up with the mop and dustpan and brush to sweep up the debris. A blonde, skinny girl peeped out, ran back in and then re-emerged with the necessary equipment and squeezed past them to clean up. She too was prepared as if for performing surgery. Even then Gerald wasn't finished dishing out orders. 'There's been a lot of blood spillage so you'd better get some bleach as well.' Now that Catherine was on her feet he wouldn't allow her one step further on to his precious off-white carpet until he was satisfied no blood was oozing out past the towel. Then he led her into the sparkling white bathroom where he meticulously bathed the cut at the sink before applying a thick pad of cotton wool bound round with half a roll of sticking plaster. This seemed to successfully staunch the flow so Gerald was finally happy to lead Catherine through to the white plush sofa in the pristine living room.

He went into the kitchen and put on the kettle. Catherine looked round the room which sparkled with fresh paint, polish and chrome. Several African style wooden figures stood on the gleaming surfaces and a couple of wall hangings that looked as if they might well have been authentic Persian rugs added the only colour to the room which wouldn't have been out of place in a quality magazine. She jumped when Gerald suddenly stood in front of her. 'Sweet black coffee and plenty of it,' he said, offering her a large mug. Catherine was up to speed now on the expected etiquette of the house and, after gulping half of it under Gerald's watchful eye, placed it dead centre on a silver coaster well in from the edge of the glass topped coffee table.

'You've got a kid haven't you?' he asked accusingly. 'You shouldn't let yourself get into that state.' Catherine brought the steaming liquid to her lips and took a few more small sips. It wasn't what she wanted. She didn't want to sober up. She was frightened of the withdrawals she would have to endure, but out of politeness she nodded. 'You're right,' she said. 'I'm trying to cut down but I fell by the wayside tonight.'

'Literally,' Gerald said and they both laughed. Mandy had returned the bucket and mop to their rightful place in a cupboard in the hallway after emptying the contents down a drain outside. She'd scrubbed her hands and was busying herself in the kitchen. After much rushing of water and rattling of tins she emerged with a plate of little biscuits. This was the last thing on the face of the earth that Catherine wanted but she bit into a lemon puff so as not to appear ungrateful. This couple were so correct, so tidy. As soon as the crumbs hit the floor, Gerald was off to the cupboard for the carpet sweeper. 'I think I'll go now,' said Catherine, stressed out by their obsessive behaviour.

'No, stay, at least until you're steady enough on your feet to go home without falling. You have to think about your little boy.' They were insistent, probably rightly so. Catherine settled back against the fluffy cushions. She looked around. There wasn't one speck of dust and everything shone. Gerald nodded to Mandy and they disappeared into the kitchen, no doubt washing dishes or cleaning under the sink from the sound of things. She moved her position on the sofa so that she could peer through the door that joined the kitchen to the living room. 'O my God,' she gasped aloud. A little tray with syringes, cigarette lighter, spoon and rubber tubing was neatly set out on the work surface and a pan of what she took to be plain water was simmering on the gas flames of the cooker. The girl suddenly rushed out and just made it to the bathroom where the sound of retching loudly proclaimed that Catherine's hunch was right about what she suspected had been going on round the corner out of sight. Gerald had now disappeared into the concealed part of the kitchen.

Mandy meandered back into the room and slumped into one of the easy chairs and closed her eyes. A satisfied smile spread across her face prior to her head falling forward. Catherine noticed the brightly coloured chiffon scarf on her arm, loose now but obviously having just recently been tied tight just above the elbow. The tell tale red runs down the inner part of the girl's forearm confirmed that she'd been mainlining. Feigning naïveté, Catherine asked Gerald if she was all right as he too staggered over to the other chair, leaned to the side, and seemed on the point of zonking out. He had chosen rubber tubing as a tourniquet and he pulled it from his arm and flung it across his knees. 'Mandy's good for a couple of hours,' he said in a voice that sounded like a 45 record being played at 33 rpm. 'I've only had a wee hit, take the edge off, you know what I mean?' His eyes were large and red rimmed as he looked over at her. Catherine wondered if he could even see clearly and he obviously mistook her inquisitive look for one of interest.

'You want some? Better for you than all that booze.' The drug addict obviously considered himself better than the alcoholic and would be doing her a favour by enticing her to change from her awful addiction to theirs. 'We're very careful,' he said, beginning the sales talk, 'very clean. We use antiseptic and you'll get your own never-used-before needle. I pick them up from the hospital where I work. Nobody notices. There are stacks of them in the store cupboard.'

Catherine didn't know what to say. She certainly didn't want to risk annoying him. 'I'll leave it for now if you don't mind,' she said, getting to her feet. The shock of what she'd stumbled into had sobered her up. She looked over at the slumbering Mandy and couldn't help noticing the beginnings of a bulge on the girl's tummy. Surely not! But then hadn't she been drinking all the time she'd been trying to get pregnant in Canada?

Gerald gave a wry smile. 'Sorry, shouldn't have offered. We only do this at weekends. A lot more civilised than those drinkers brawling through the streets. We've good jobs and we like a quiet life.'

'You may well be right,' she agreed, remembering the last time she'd been in town on a Saturday night.

'The only trouble with this game now,' he said, and a deep frown drew his lean young face into the worried lines of a much older man, 'is that there's this new disease called AIDS. It's deadly and it's spread by blood. A lot of folk in Edinburgh have it already. That's why we're so thorough about hygiene. Drug users are catching it from dirty needles. We boil everything even if it's new. Got to look out for the baby now.'

The room swam round her when she stood up but she persevered. She had to get home and only just managed to teeter across the landing to her flat before letting herself in. She leaned back with overwhelming relief against her firmly locked door for a good minute to catch her breath before heading straight to the kitchen sink where she opened her handbag, took out the half-bottle, twisted off the top and turned it upside down. She listened thoughtfully to the glugging sound as it emptied and then she rushed both taps to clear it away to the furthermost drains and out to sea to be dispersed throughout the oceans until diluted into nothing. She rinsed out the bottle not wanting its smell anywhere in her house and took it outside to throw in the communal bin. She tossed her head in the air as she passed the glue sniffers and, ignoring all their comments, said cheerfully on the way back in, 'Hi, how's it going, lads?' They were stunned into silence for the first time ever.

This was it! After that experience, which felt as if she had taken part in some mad March tea party, she had no desire to ever drink again. Once she'd survived the physical withdrawals she knew she could kick the lousy habit for good. For goodness sake, what had she been thinking of? She couldn't believe she'd let it take hold of her like that. She thought of Rosie and the awful struggle she'd had to come off a concoction of amphetamines and tranquillisers, and she'd been going through a divorce at the time. If Rosie could come off pills, she could come off alcohol. She remembered too how smoking had affected her mother's tubercular lungs and how her father's gambling had almost destroyed her parents' marriage. They'd managed to overcome both. She had to brace herself and prove she shared their mettle.

Chapter 14

For a whole week she never left the house. She phoned the school and told them she had a debilitating virus and that Stephen would be arriving and leaving on foot. There was a stock of food in the house and it was possible to send out for pizzas and fried chicken. Stephen was delighted to be allowed to buy in the basic groceries from the local shops while his mother lay day after day sweating it out. She woke one night and hid under the bedclothes from the mice that scurried over the floor and up on to her bed. Her drinking days were over. Surely she had hit lower than rock bottom when a junkie looked down his nose at her and the glue sniffers despised her.

She had to be careful. If word ever got out about her drunkenness she could lose Stephen. He'd be taken into care and that would be the end of her life. What had started as a social pleasure had ended as a nightmare addiction. She knew that vitamins would help to rebuild her nervous system as her body fought the withdrawals. She gave Stephen a note to take to the local chemist for them. She drank pints of water and ate dishes of fresh fruit and plates of vegetables to flush out her system. Soon she would be clean.

However, it wasn't long before Catherine began to realise that her fight wasn't only against alcohol but she also had to learn to cope with reality. As her mind regained its ability to function, it presented her with the hard facts of life that she had been using alcohol to avoid. It wasn't just some frame of mind or imaginary guilt. The gin had been a cover-up and if she could confront this nightmare in a state of sobriety then she need never drink again. She had rid herself of demons in the past, but this present problem she would have to learn to live with for the rest of her life. Her darling son had been a baby born of rape. The man who had impregnated her was someone she had always despised and whom she found revolting, but she was entwined with this beast through her connections with his mother, Rosie, who had married her dear Uncle Eddie. She would never be free of him. She would have to live with that.

And now he knew that he was Stephen's father, he would be a permanent feature in her life whether she liked it or not. As Catherine mulled this over in her mind, panic would sweep over her and palpitations would shake her body. Once or twice it brought her to the point of being violently sick, but she saw it through. She allowed the truth that had bedevilled her for years to penetrate and she knew that if she stuck it out and came to terms with life mentally then her physical reactions would gradually lessen. She would never be happy with the situation but if a problem exists it exists. She would learn to accept that which she couldn't change. What was the point of drinking when returning to sobriety meant going through this torture again?

The only cure was to endure the suffering. It was the same as the grief she'd felt after her father and then her mother had died. Even many years later, the pain had never quite gone away but it had gradually lessened. Learning to live with these hard facts would be the same. She would face up to the torment of truth and endure it. Poor Stephen; she had treated him abysmally at times when he had reminded her of Jimmy. The child wasn't to blame for what his father had done. He was a person in his own right. How many people went into making one human being anyway? There were her parents, grandparents, Rosie, Jim, their parents and grandparents, thousands of ancestors in fact, all overlapping and intertwining through hundreds of generations of all sorts of people, some good, some bad, some no doubt cruel, some even crazy. It was all chance. She had never known her own grandparents but they must be in her somewhere. She had heard plenty about the kindly Daisy and the fatherly Joe Clark who had died in the fire. They would be in Stephen too. So would her mum and dad. She had overlooked all these beautiful components to her little boy's wonderfully unique soul.

She felt ashamed for ever allowing herself to treat him badly just because his hair stuck up like Jimmy's. Her behaviour had been unjustified and even insane. Stephen was an individual in his own right. She had no right to punish or reject him. He wasn't a clone. And there had been so many other influences that would affect him and make him into the worthwhile man he would grow up to be. He'd had a comfortable life. Gregor had set him a wonderful example over the years. His grandparents too had shown him great love and affection. Why all the fuss? She was proud of him and she would start to show it more.

And so what if Jimmy wanted to visit? However much she abhorred the idea he did have that right. She found it impossible to rid herself of a lingering anger at his having escaped any form of punishment however. Instead, he was regarded as a wonderful family man who could do no wrong. She would just have to accept she had these feelings. She would have to tolerate Jimmy in her life. But although she was learning to cope with the truth, there were too many others who might not. It would have to remain a secret.

After a full three weeks of the horrors of cold turkey and almost sinking into madness as she underwent vomiting, dry heaves, terrifying hallucinations and dreams, she felt no urge to drink, no craving. She was through with suffering and there was no returning to that hell. She knew she was one of the lucky ones. It had been a matter of facing full-on the problem that had bothered her most and been poisoning her thinking.

If Gregor had tired of her, then she would cope. There was nothing else for it. Other people managed; so would she. Nihil desperandum - never give up. She thought of her mother turning out day after day to the freezing fish house to make ends meet while here she sat able to make a comfortable living by tapping out a couple of wishy-washy short stories at her own table. She flushed with shame but she wasn't going to cry sentimental tears. After a quick shower she dressed smartly and went into town to buy food. She returned soon after to clean the house. If her time as a wife was over, then she had to be the best mother she could be.

Taking the bull by the horns, she phoned Gregor. One o'clock in the afternoon, eight in the morning over there. The couple of weeks that he'd promised had already lengthened into four. She told him straight. He'd better mean it. If he wasn't over to join her within a fortnight then they were finished. Better bring things to a head than live in this perpetual limbo. Gregor sounded surprised, shocked even at her outburst but quietly agreed to make it to Aberdeen as soon as was humanly possible. Stephen was overjoyed. 'You look like a real mum,' he said proudly when she stood at the school gate that afternoon. When she told him his dad would be home by the end of the following week his eyes lit up and his face shone like a newly polished rosy apple.

Chapter 15

At the airport, Stephen was bobbing up and down like a jack-in-the-box, scanning the face of every male passenger making their way from the London plane as if by staring he could turn any one of them into his long awaited father. Catherine's stomach was doing wild somersaults. She didn't know which was worse - the feverish longing to be in her husband's arms or the dread of being told by him once and for all that their marriage was over. And of course there was the choice she would have to make between coming clean with the truth about Stephen or living a lie. She knew that whichever she chose her life could never flow smoothly again. The happiness she had known over the past twelve years had been wrenched from her in one cruel swipe the day Rosie had brought Jimmy's offspring into her home.

Suddenly Stephen was tugging at Catherine's arm. 'Mum, it's Dad, but I think he's had an accident.' The words that had begun so excitedly tailed off in fear. She turned with no immediate sign of recognition. Of all the suspicions that had engraved themselves in a list on Catherine's mind this was one she'd never dreamt of. She stared at Gregor in amazement and allowed herself to be dragged in a haze of disbelief towards a frail looking man who resembled an older version of her husband leaning heavily on a stick. He was calling her name with Gregor's voice and there was no mistaking the look of love in his eyes. She stood open mouthed as he repeated her name and it was only after a few long moments' hesitation that she hurled herself weeping into his tight embrace.

Stephen's confidence returned when he saw that his mother was crying tears of joy and laughing and kissing his dad all at the same time. 'Did you fall off that old ramshackle bike and hurt yourself?' he asked, knowing that a bit of cheek would bring their attention back to him.

'I see somebody hasn't changed,' said Gregor, releasing Catherine and pulling Stephen to him for a hug. 'What have you been feeding him, Catherine? He's shot up like a hothouse plant.'

'I'm nearly the same size as Mum,' Stephen said and stood with his back ramrod straight next to his mother.

'There's maybe more feeding in fish and chips than I thought,' Catherine said to keep the conversation light, trying to keep from Gregor how upset she was at the state he was in. 'And what's happened to you?' she asked. 'You look as if you've been in an accident.' There was no hiding the horror in her pallid face. She waited for his reply.

'I'm truly sorry,' he said shaking his head so that he didn't have to look her squarely in eye. 'It sounds weak and cowardly but I couldn't bring myself to tell you.'

She had been looking forward to rushing into his arms and feeling his strength enfold her once more but all she could do now was gaze at this near cripple. It came as no great surprise to Gregor to see how worried she was. He took her arm. 'Why are we hanging around here? Let's get on home.' As they walked, he offered her a potted version; the full story would have to wait. 'This is why I stayed behind for so long,' he said, giving his cane a little wave in the air in front of them. 'I didn't fall off anything or have a crash. It's a sort of illness and I had to have some tests carried out, but now that's done and I have the confirmation, there's no point in any more pretence.' At baggage reclaim Catherine kept an arm firmly round Gregor as if he might suddenly disappear. It was such a relief to see him again and thankfully he hadn't had some kind of injury. Now these tests were completed it was simply a matter of recovery. Stephen was beginning to annoy her however. His mood seemed to have changed and he dawdled behind as if he weren't with them. Catherine grew angry and dragged him along beside her. 'Stay by us or you'll get lost!' she commanded.

Stephen's reply hurt her to the quick and intensified her fear of losing her child to go and live with Jimmy. 'I don't want him,' he wailed, pointing at his father, and he forced his hand out of hers and ran away.

'Leave him. He'll be fine,' said Gregor. 'What do you expect? The boy's had a shock seeing me transformed into a weakling.' Stephen hung around at the entrance watching all the strong, muscular men leading their families home. He stuck out his bottom lip and his brows knitted into a thick black caterpillar over eyes that filled with embarrassment when he saw his own father being helped along by his mother, not even able to carry his case. Stephen was so nasty that Catherine almost wished that Gregor had been having an affair instead of this.

Catherine and Gregor leaned back on the sofa almost too exhausted to speak. Stephen had gone to bed early in a sulk. 'Don't feel bad,' said Catherine, 'He's been living for this day ever since we arrived. He'll be fine in the morning.' Neither responded to the slamming of cupboard doors and yelled curses that emanated from Stephen's bedroom. 'I should go to him;' said Catherine 'but things haven't been plain sailing between us lately and I don't want to antagonise him further. I think it might be best to leave him for a while.'

'If you say so, perhaps that would be wisest,' said Gregor nervously. He was at a loss as to how to handle the bewildered boy. He lifted Catherine's hand from her lap and squeezed it to his cheek and closed his eyes as if trying to hide from the nasty scene in the child's room. Soon there was quietness and Catherine went through. Stephen was under the blankets still fully clothed and crying. Gently she took the child in her arms and rocked him. 'Let's get you undressed. Things will seem better in the morning when we've all had some sleep.' Stephen allowed himself to be led to the bathroom. When he re-appeared in his pyjamas he went over to his father and snuggled in beside him on the sofa. 'Sorry, Dad,' he whispered.

Gregor drew him close and kissed him on the cheek. 'Tomorrow we'll have a special day,' he said and this time he was the one that was hiding his tears.

Once Stephen was settled and asleep, Gregor sat staring ahead with a helpless expression on his weary face. 'To be honest, I feel I've let you both down so much he must hate me. I don't deserve either of you.' He turned to Catherine who was sitting quietly by his side and took her hand. He drew her fingers round to his lips and kissed them hard in almost the same way that a child would shove its fist in its mouth to stop itself from crying. He released her and spoke in a voice strangled with guilt. 'Most wives would have taken off with somebody new instead of waiting so patiently.'

Catherine made no immediate reply. In that regard she knew she was nothing special. After a moment's thoughtful silence she asked the obvious question, 'Why have you never mentioned these tests before? We were totally unprepared for seeing you like this.' She withdrew her hand from his grasp as she remembered the long nights of painful anxiety she had endured while he had kept her in the dark. Surely she'd had a right to know. Her joy at Gregor's return was rapidly changing to resentment and she felt it wouldn't be long before she had a Stephen-style fit of pique.

Gregor, sensing her mood, lightly stroked her arm but didn't attempt to take hold of her again. As he prepared to answer he closed his eyes and worked his lips together, chewing at them as if wishing his mouth could be sewn up to save him the coming ordeal. This wasn't going to be easy. At last he took a deep breath and spoke. 'There were two reasons for having these tests and there are things I have to tell you, Catherine;' he said in a husky whisper, 'things that I know you won't like and that may take some getting used to.'

Catherine took a deep breath. 'Well, Gregor, better get it off your chest and then we can maybe get some rest. I don't know about you, but I'm shattered.'

'I agree; I think it's better left for another day,' he said, relieved to have an excuse to postpone the telling. 'I'm jet lagged. Let's have our rest and be fit and ready for a nice day out, the three of us, tomorrow. Plenty time to talk over problems later.'

Catherine was desperate to know what had been happening in Guildwood but realised that if there was any more bad news it was best left until morning. 'We can go to the park, the swimming baths, the pictures,' she said brightly. 'Take your pick.'

'Well, if it's all right with you, and Stephen agrees,' replied Gregor with a distinct note of enthusiasm in his voice, 'swimming would be fine. I can move better in water. I may even beat that young upstart in a race.'

Despite Catherine's fears that Stephen would upset his father, the day out was a great success. At first, when Stephen saw the effort he had to make just to walk downstairs to the car he lowered his head in anticipation of more jeering from the louts in the lobby. But when Gregor chased the teenagers with their bottles of cider along the entrance and out the front door with his stick, Stephen adopted an attitude towards his father akin to hero worshipping. This was greatly enhanced by the fact that his father had given a great roar that he had learned during a Native American Powwow in which he'd participated the year before. It was a war cry that may actually have been heard during the Great Indian War, but in the stairwell of some flats in 1980's Aberdeen it did the trick just the same and scared the hell out of the cowardly brats.

As for the swimming, true to his word, Gregor held his own with Stephen in the water, but that was a man against a child. 'Just wait until next year, Dad,' Stephen shouted and flexed his already developing biceps, 'I'll beat you hollow.' However, the fact that his father was still a good swimmer pleased him no end. He wanted a dad he could be proud of. Afterwards, when they went for a burger and chips, it was Stephen who made sure the walking stick was propped up within easy reach.

Catherine too was developing an admiration for Gregor's patient handling of the disability. She wanted to know more about it and how long it would be before he was back to normal. That would have to wait until Stephen was in bed and they could talk privately. Dear Stephen, she was so proud of him. He was such a decent human being.

There could be no more putting it off. Catherine snuggled up beside Gregor on the sofa. 'Thanks for a lovely day. We managed to wear Stephen out. He was asleep before his head hit the pillow.'

'We have to talk,' was Gregor's serious reply.

'Here it comes;' thought Catherine, bracing herself, 'the affair!' She sat up straight preparing herself for the worst but sure she would handle anything he might throw at her.

Gregor cleared his throat. He'd built himself up for this during the long flight and it was now or never. All he knew was that any peace of mind they had now was about to be shattered for all time. He was glad Catherine was side on to him and he didn't have to immediately see the look in her eyes. 'Do you want me to pour you a drink before I start?' Gregor asked. 'I could do with one myself.'

'I don't drink anymore,' she replied, her voice steady, 'but if you want one I can go to the licensed grocer for you. I don't keep any in the house.' She was absolutely confident of passing the acid test of refusing alcohol while someone else was drinking. All desire for the stuff had gone, regardless of what trouble she had to face. Those dark days of blind intoxication were over.

Gregor placed his hand gently on Catherine's forearm. He passed no comment on her abstinence. He was oblivious to the fact that his silence had caused her such heartache and had been the cause of so much of her drinking. He did sense, however, that he might be in for some cold shoulder treatment and was careful in case one wrong word from him that sounded in any way patronising or critical might send her into a frenzy and racing round to the shop. How could he be expected to know that his wife had undergone an agonising metamorphosis in his absence and was much tougher now as a result? What he had to tell her would take broad shoulders and he was worried sick it might topple her, that other, emotionally weaker Catherine, over the edge. But this was a new and stronger Catherine.

He took a chance anyway and laid it on the line. 'Stephen isn't my son,' he blurted out without any preliminary lead up. He fired the words out one by one like bullets, but they seemed to hover in the air in front of them before finding their mark. At last Catherine gasped as if she really had been shot. 'How do you know? Who's been talking?' Her immediate thought was that Rosie or even Jimmy himself had been in touch with him. Matters were reaching a head. They were about to lose Stephen.

Gregor was astounded. 'It sounds as if you know already.' His voice became loud and accusing, 'Or have you known it all along?' Without pausing for breath or giving Catherine a chance to explain, he continued to offload in one go what had been on his mind for years. 'You know, I suspected right from the start but kept quiet. I knew you hadn't been unfaithful. The only possibility was the night Jimmy attacked you. I couldn't make a police case out of it in those days. You allowed a man you knew into the house in your flimsy nightwear. An accusation of rape wouldn't have held water. We'd have been laughed out of court. That came into my mind immediately I saw what you were wearing, and that's why I gave him such a doing over. The law would have let him off scot-free. In those days the police could have made things a lot worse for you, the scantily dressed woman, and not him, the man who had been strung along. Attitudes have thankfully changed but women must still carry some responsibility both for their behaviour and their clothing. No amount of legislation will put an end to the amount of crazy people there are out there.'

Catherine was confused. What had brought all this on? But his words struck a familiar chord. 'That's what my father said the night I went out wearing the short skirt. And he was right. No matter how much society changes, there will always be the predatory men who are tempted and interpret a provocative style of dress as an invitation.'

Gregor held her tight. He knew she was reliving that awful night from the way she was running her fingers along the line of her jaw. 'You were a young girl. You were unlucky that's all.'

Catherine wasn't interested in that any more. The paternity issue had taken precedence. 'You never said anything before ... all these years ...' Catherine was angry. 'Why didn't you voice your suspicions twelve years ago? And how did you find out?' She sidled away from him to the opposite corner of the couch. Why was he so suddenly and so cruelly raking up the past?

'I didn't want to lose you; that's all. When you came into the Shiny Teapot that day and you'd been crying, I thought it was because you knew the baby wasn't mine. You always said you took precautions. But you wouldn't have of course when Jimmy ... and then I deliberately pushed it from my mind. I wanted our wedding to go ahead as planned.'

'And I didn't want an abortion. I was hoping that maybe the contraception hadn't worked; nothing works a hundred per cent. I was hoping ... I convinced myself the baby ... Stephen ... was yours.'

'Did you think I wouldn't want you? That I'd make you get rid of it?'

'I don't know. I couldn't face it being Jimmy's. I loathed him.'

'But for God's sake, Catherine, I'm a doctor. I try to help people. I brought up the child as my own regardless of my suspicions. I knew you hadn't willingly slept with Jimmy. Do you take me for a monster? Any child of yours is mine to bring up. You were going to be my wife and I was determined to look after you.'

'But that was then. Now you're saying you know for certain. How did you find out?'

'How can I tell you this ...?' Gregor covered his face with his hands and took several slow breaths. Then he clasped his hands in front of his mouth and knocked them against his lips several times as if preparing himself to say what was coming next. He dropped his hands and let them hang loosely by his sides. All was about to be revealed. 'You see, Catherine, the truth is that I can't have children. I could never have been any child's father. That's what clinched it.' Catherine winced when she heard these awful words coming from Gregor's own lips.

'I had tests done to find out. I'm sterile, Catherine.' He waited a moment or two for this unexpected information to sink in before continuing. 'I could never have given you a daughter.'

Catherine began to interrupt, 'But ...'

'Please let me finish,' he said, patting her on the thigh to show he respected her right to speak but that he must have the chance to have his say. 'When there was no sign of another baby in spite of our trying desperately month after month I began to wonder seriously about my fertility. You were obviously capable of having a baby but what about me? I had the tests done shortly after you left Guildwood. My sperm count is exceedingly low and what few I have are what are known as "lazy sperms". They're not any better at running than I am myself.' His attempt at bringing some humour into the situation was wasted on Catherine as she left his side and began pacing round the room as if not knowing what to do with herself.

'You mean to say you had tests!' Catherine's stilettos beat a tattoo on the linoleum as she marched rapidly from one side of the room to the other. She threw her arms in the air. Her voice was shrill and every syllable was uttered with angry precision through tight lips. 'You went skulking behind my back with something as important as that!' Catherine was on her high horse now. Was there no end to this man's deceit? She felt she had a stranger in her house and one she didn't like at that. She stood with her back to him at the window seething with rage and biting her lips. She was beyond words now.

Gregor buried his face in his hands. He couldn't bear her icy silence. He pushed himself up and limped slowly over and put a hand gingerly on her shoulder. She turned on him venomously. 'Why didn't you tell me? I am supposed to be your wife after all.' She bit her lower lip hard, sucking it back into her mouth and her whole body started to shake. Gregor put his arm round her.

'So what, I had tests done, eventually. It had always been a niggling doubt in my mind but it didn't seem to matter that much. I loved the boy and still do. As far as I am concerned, Stephen is my son.'

Catherine rolled her eyes up to the ceiling deep in thought. 'So that's what's been annoying you. But why wait until now?'

'I wanted to know for sure whether or not I could make you pregnant. And don't act all innocent with me. You knew already, didn't you? In fact, you've probably always known.'

'What do you mean? I only found out myself a few weeks ago. Rosie saw Stephen and Jimmy's daughter, Sophie, together and spotted a likeness. And then Jimmy came round and said …' Catherine began to cry and Gregor drew her to him. 'I think we're talking at cross purposes,' he said. 'Something's been going on around here you haven't told me about.' Catherine was so upset she had to sit down again. Gregor brought her a glass of water.

Between sobs she blurted out the whole story. 'Jimmy's been round. A few weeks ago Rosie tipped him off that Sophie and Stephen looked "like two peas in a pod".'

'What!' Gregor's knuckles were white as he clenched his fists with rage. 'That bastard Jimmy knows. Things are worse than I thought.'

'It's all right. He doesn't want to come between Stephen and you. He did at first. He quite liked the idea of having a son, but he doesn't want to cause any distress to Stephen and he certainly doesn't want his wife Patricia to find out.'

'What about Rosie?' There was panic in his voice.

'We both told her categorically that it was impossible.'

'And Frank?'

'He's never seen the two of them together and it's only someone with needle sharp eyes like Rosie's and her computer mind that would spot the likeness. I've racked my brains and I still think it's best to keep all this under wraps. I can't face the fallout.'

'Let's get something clear. When and how did you find out?'

'Jimmy came round. He did … he did have sex with me. I thought that he only …'

'I should have said more at the time. I had my suspicions, of course, and don't tell me you didn't either. I used to watch you sometimes pushing Stephen away from you every time he showed a trait you recognised as Jimmy's.'

'I hated myself every time I did that,' sobbed Catherine. 'He seemed to change overnight. He didn't look like anyone in our families. My father was strong but stocky with black curls and my mother's side are slim and have reddish or blonde hair. And his build is nothing like yours and there's no resemblance facially either.'

Gregor moved over and put his arm round her. 'I never blamed you. How could I when Jimmy had attacked you? It's not as if you'd been a willing participant.'

'So it really is true. Even after what Jimmy told me and their looking alike I still held out some hope.' Catherine sniffed and said thoughtfully, 'Strangely, it doesn't seem to be too much of a shock for either of us. We've lived with the idea of it for so long, but what might it do to Stephen finding out at this late stage?' She stopped crying. Something else seemed to be bothering her. 'I thought you said there were two reasons. This second one had better be good.'

'It's the same reason as I'm walking with a stick, may even be crutches before long.' His voice was shaky now. Catherine assumed it was because of his nervousness at her being so annoyed at his deviousness.'

'Now can you understand why I couldn't tell you over the phone? How could I put it into words in a letter? I had to wait until I saw you face-to-face.'

'That's not excuse enough. I've been to Hell and back.' Catherine stormed off to the kitchen and rushed water into the kettle for a strong cup of tea and it splashed all down her front and wet the brand new blouse she had bought for Gregor coming home. 'Damn, damn, damn!' she shouted. 'So much for the happy reunion.' She leaned against the sink in tears.

Gregor slowly made it over to her side and took the kettle from her and filled it. 'A cup of tea is probably a good idea,' he said. He placed the kettle on the work surface and made to insert the plug in the socket but however much he struggled he couldn't quite get the pins to fit into the holes. His face grew white with strain and beads of perspiration stood out on his brow. His hand shook and he broke out in a sweat that soaked through his shirt. Catherine watched him speechlessly as he gave up trying and began wiping his wet face with a tea towel. 'Go and sit down, Gregor,' said Catherine. Her tears had dried in smears on her cheeks and her voice had taken on a note of puzzled concern.

Gregor sank into the sofa. His face was as white as a sheet and he was shaking. 'I want to be able to do these little things for you still. You've had a hard time and I know I've been callous leaving you to handle so much on your own.'

Catherine sat beside him and put the cups of strong, sweet tea in front of them. She was determined to keep her temper and not burst into tears again.

'The real reason for the DNA test was that I wanted to make sure that Stephen can't inherit this awful disease. There is a chance that I may have some genetic disorder, especially now that this disease is full blown, so not being his father came as a great relief. At least we don't have to worry about him becoming a cripple like me.' Catherine had curled herself into a ball at his side. She didn't want to hear any more but Gregor went on to explain. 'It's called Lou Gehrig's disease in North America after the famous New York Yankees baseball player who had it. In the UK it's called motor neuron disease. Its medical name is ALS – amyotrophic lateral sclerosis. They don't know if it's in you when you're born just waiting to come out, or if it is caused by environmental factors.

Even then, no one knows for sure if once you have it you can pass it on. There may be a slim chance that any children I did have now would carry it and pass it on in turn to their children. Nobody knows the answers yet. Research is going on all the time. It's maybe better this way. At least we know that Stephen will never end up like this.' He looked at the walking stick that had fallen on the floor beside him. 'I can't even pick that up myself without your help. Catherine dared to ask the next question. 'Is that why you wouldn't make love to me? Did you know what was wrong then and not tell me?'

'I admit it, I behaved like a brute. But I couldn't risk having sex with you while I waited for confirmation. I was terrified of making you pregnant. I've treated you so cruelly, Catherine. All I can say is that when I began showing symptoms of what I knew to be some kind of motor neuron disease I lost all sense of reason. I couldn't face it. But I couldn't ignore it either. And instead of including you, the person who mattered most, I shut you out completely. I've been the worst sort of coward. Knowing how much you wanted a baby, a little girl, I thought you would abandon me. For all I know you may do that yet.'

Catherine threw her arms round his neck. 'I'll never leave you,

Gregor.' She pulled back from him and gave a funny little laugh. 'I thought you were planning to leave me.'

'Whatever made you think that? You're my whole life.'

'It was because of Marion,' whispered Catherine. 'When you were excluding me, you and she became so close. And Mrs Thomas said you were spending all your time at the clubhouse. I thought you didn't want me anymore. I thought you had stopped loving me and wanted me out of the way to be with her.'

'Oh, Catherine, I never dreamt you'd taken it so hard. Take your time now and think carefully - what does Marion do for a living?'

Catherine didn't have to rack her brains long before she was nodding her head and it all began to make sense.

'I'm asking you again. What job?'

'A nurse or something like that; a physical therapist ...'

'That's it exactly, Catherine,' said Gregor. 'Marion's a physical therapist. She treats all kinds of sports injuries and helps to rehabilitate people who've had strokes. Marion has a reputation for being one of the best. She even has celebrities among her clientele. I was interested to find out what she knew about Lou Gehrig's disease. I wanted to know if anything could be done. I went round everyone in the medical profession looking for an answer that might mean I had a chance. I was in a daze. I was out of my mind. I told her to keep it a secret from you, even though she thought that was a bad idea.'

Of course, thought Catherine with a sigh of relief, Gregor had been picking her specialist brains for advice. That was the reason behind the secrecy. He hadn't wanted her to reveal the real reason for their apparent intimacy. She felt her face flushing as she realised without being told any more that Gregor's reasons for speaking head-to-head with Marion had been perfectly innocent. 'I'm so ashamed,' she said, 'Marion was only giving you advice. She must think I'm a dragon. However, you can't really blame me when you think about it. I should have been told and then I wouldn't have thought you were planning a new life without me. I was jealous. I felt left out.'

'Marion was a great help and I wasn't playing golf all the time. I asked Mrs Thomas to make any excuse while I was in hospital for tests and that must have been her chosen one. I did go to see Marion a few times, but always as a professional. She knew which medical papers to look up.' Gregor spoke with respect rather than affection. 'She could interpret the findings more accurately than I could myself, and she's given me strengthening exercises to do that might help.'

'So what's the prognosis?' Catherine had heard of debilitating viral illnesses such as ME lasting for years.

'I've looked into it. It's definitely five years or thereabouts.'

'But five years is such a long time to be on crutches. Can't they do anything sooner?'

Gregor turned and sat sideways on to her. He knew that whether he liked it or not, he had to be brave enough to look into her eyes. The news he had to give her was the worst any man could give his wife. Tears ran down his face and dripped from his chin as he uttered the awful words. 'The five years, Catherine ... It's not that I'll take five years to recover,' he said before clearing his throat and swallowing. 'That five years, Catherine, isn't when I'll be better ... It's when I'll be dead.'

Catherine let out a cry. Gregor took her in his arms. 'My dearest, beautiful wife, the love of my life, I really am so sorry. I've investigated every possible avenue. This illness usually takes three to five years and there is no treatment, let alone a cure.' He paused before adding, 'The exercises, the walking and the swimming give some relief, but no more hiding from the truth; there is no cure and the deterioration is fast.'

Catherine closed her eyes. Although seated, she felt as if she were about to pass out. Noticing the colour had drained from her face, Gregor gathered her into his arms. 'There's nothing we can do about it. Believe me, I have read every paper written on the subject. I have spoken to every nurse and doctor on the face of the planet. We have to make the most of every single minute we have together.' He stroked her hair to keep her calm. 'I haven't even told my parents yet.'

Catherine began to whimper as if she'd been whipped. 'It can't be. I need you so much. I've never loved anyone else. What will we do without you?'

'I'm sorry,' he whispered gruffly. 'I really am.'

A cry of utter pain broke from Catherine's dry lips and she threw her arms round his already weakened body with her head crushed hard against his chest. 'No, Gregor, no ... You can't ever leave me. It's only you I've ever loved. Only you I've ever wanted. I'm sorry, sorry, sorry ... I didn't know, I didn't understand ....' Catherine sniffed into his jumper like a small child clinging on to an adult as if expecting them to perform a miracle that would make it all better.

Gregor held her tight, the tears flowing down his face and dripping on to her bowed head. He rocked her backwards and forwards like a mother nursing a hurt and frightened child while she sobbed her heart out, beseeching him to stay with her, to stay alive for her. Gently, like a mother teaching a baby to walk, he led his heartbroken wife through to the bedroom. Neither spoke as they undressed. Catherine threw herself under the blankets and flung them up over her shoulders. Her body shivered and she began sobbing into the pillow. Gregor eased himself in beside her and held her close, her bottom tucked warmly against his thighs so that they were like spoons in a drawer. They lay in silence for quite a long time except for the occasional stifled cry of deep sorrow that came sometimes from one, sometimes from both.

Gregor kissed the side of Catherine's neck and his hot breath made her ear tingle. 'I love you so much,' he whispered. 'I always have and I always will.' He kissed her shoulders and down her back. Slowly she turned over to face him and their lips met, softly, lovingly. She edged herself over his weakened body until she lay on top of him. Slowly, scarcely moving, they made love with such tenderness that they seemed to flow together like two streams joining and mingling into one. Catherine smiled, closed her eyes and fell into an easy sleep for the first time in over a year.

Catherine and Gregor stood together at the window looking out at the back area. This early evening view was a far cry from the tree lined garden in Toronto. 'Why do people have to live like this?' asked Catherine, fixating on a pile of debris against the back wall – the springs of an old bed, some broken chairs and a rusty old pram thrown on the top for good measure.

'I wonder about that myself,' said Gregor, 'but maybe life has worn them down and they just can't cope any more. Phoning the Council to take away rubbish isn't the easiest thing in the world you know. You need a degree in English to fight your way through all their bureaucracy, apart from requiring a phone in the first place.' Catherine recognised in Gregor a humanitarian understanding of people that she didn't always share. She thought of the drug dealers next door and the glue sniffers in the outside lobby.

'Let's make a fresh start,' she said, turning away from the unwholesome view of their back yard and rushing over to a drawer and bringing out some brochures she had acquired from an estate agent in town. She slapped them down on to the table and insisted that Gregor come and have a look. After a few minutes of browsing Catherine was beside herself with joy when Gregor selected the one that was her favourite too.

'I like this house that's on the way to the hospital, up a lovely tree-lined quiet street not far from the Westburn Park,' he said, waving the leaflet in the air triumphantly. 'I remember I wanted to live there when I was studying. It's near to the tennis courts and handy for a game of cricket or football at the weekends.' A wistful expression crossed his face but his eyes were simultaneously full of acceptance. 'I realise I can't take part in them now but it's ideal for Stephen. And there's a swing park too.'

'I love the beautiful Victoria Park across from it with those colourful flower beds and a fountain. I can sit there and dream up my stories,' Catherine added with bittersweet joy.

'We'll be made. A perfect home for a perfect little family.' He kissed her fondly on the cheek before taking out his briefcase of papers and settling himself at the table. 'Now I've got work to do. Got to pay that mortgage somehow! The house in Canada won't be enough to pay for this one outright. The institute are happy to have me in a more or less advisory capacity carrying out the research, and rather than lose my expertise all together, they'll make allowances for my illness.'

Stephen crept in from his bedroom where he'd been since his arrival home from school. He looked at his father commandeering the table and Catherine urged him to bring in his homework and work alongside him. 'I'll nip out for chicken and chips and leave you two together,' she said blithely. Stephen perked up at the thought of working beside his dad and having fetched the maths books, opened them, albeit with a grimace, and placed them alongside his father's papers. Determined to master his homework by himself, he pulled the zip on his pencil case to open it and sucking on the end of a pencil began writing on the page of his jotter. Catherine put on a pretend act of horror at the sight of the maths books. 'Better you than me, Gregor. The dreaded Mr Wilson Skinnypants and his evil fractions are about to take over your life,' she said, pulling on her coat and skipping downstairs. She threw a glance at the youngsters gathered on the doorstep sharing a can of lager. 'Hello, lads,' she said in a friendly tone. What chance in life did they have? Her recent predicament had brought out a latent compassion in her. Soon these no hopers would be but a distant memory.

What a difference from her early days in the tenement when no matter how little everyone had, the men went out to work and the youngsters aspired to do the same and by fifteen the young lads were serving apprenticeships and the girls working in shops or offices. What had gone wrong in these years in between that the youngsters had lost the motivation to demand the right to work and little effort was made by the adults to keep their immediate surroundings clean and respectable?

The contrast between this block of flats and the tenements she had lived in was startling. She remembered the strong smell of polish that met you on entering the front door, the gardens kept tidy where everything from rose bushes to potatoes were grown with pride and bicycles and prams could be left in lobbies with no fear of them being stolen. Soon she would be away from all this but it didn't stop her from caring that somewhere along the line a dangerous apathy had crept into people's lives despite the installation of bathrooms and heating. One would have expected more happiness and appreciation as a result, but instead, the old sense of community and purpose was diminishing and she couldn't understand why.

Meanwhile, the two men in her life worked companionably until she returned with their supper which brought a smile of anticipation to their faces as the seductive smell of chip shop food wound itself round their hearts. 'Mum, you'll never guess,' shouted Stephen as he cleared away his books and helped to set the table, 'I like maths now. Dad explained them to me and all the problems fell into place. I think it's going to be my favourite subject from now on.'

'Well, wonders will never cease;' laughed Catherine, 'old Mr Skinnypants is going to die of shock!'

'Later, as they cleared the last morsels of crunchy chips from their plates and emptied every drop of cola from their cans, Catherine thought dreamily that this was a treasured moment in their lives. They were as happy now as they would ever be. Hard times stretched ahead. She knew that for sure and she was equally sure they would pull together, although the last remaining piece in the jigsaw, a baby girl, would always be missing. The plump rosy cheeks of the child who would never be born swam in front of Catherine's inner eye. She breathed in the baby perfume of her despite the air being filled with the overpowering smell of vinegar. Her eyes filled with salty tears. She and Gregor were still in love but there would be no little girl for them to cherish and choose pretty dresses for. Catherine blinked and the vision floated by like gossamer chased on a passing breeze.

Catherine and Gregor had had little choice in the matter of allowing Jimmy to visit in order to see his son. It didn't seem unreasonable to Patricia or any of their friends and relatives that Jimmy, whose mother was married to Catherine's uncle, should want to lend his support while she looked after her husband as his condition deteriorated. Frank had reservations. He knew about the time Jimmy had turned up at Maggie's home and had a drunken outburst of violence against Catherine. Rosie had witnessed this firsthand but decided to excuse her son on account of his being worried over Patricia's pregnancy. No one but Jimmy himself, Catherine and Gregor knew about the rape, so, to all intents and purposes Stephen wasn't the reason for his popping by for a couple of hours every time he came ashore.

Jimmy was subdued at all times in the presence of Gregor. His respect for the sick man was obvious and he never hesitated to help in any way he could whether it was to collect shopping from the supermarket or drive him to appointments. Stephen wasn't always at home when he called but to insist on his presence every time he came round would have created suspicion. The one thing that Jimmy insisted on, and he repeated this often, was that Stephen and either of his daughters should never meet.

Chapter 16

(Weymouth 1984)

Catherine and Gregor inhaled the fresh sea air on Weymouth beach while basking in the warm sunshine that beat down on their browning bodies. Catherine got up and shook the cushions on Gregor's wheelchair to make him more comfortable before sinking back down into her deckchair to watch his parents, Thelma and Donald, make the most of a family day at the beach. It was the highlight of their year when Gregor and his family came to stay with them. Thelma paddled in the sea almost up to her knees with her floral skirt gathered in a tight bundle round her thighs. She waved excitedly to Stephen and her husband who shrieked with laughter as they steered themselves round the bay in a pedallo. 'Just look at the fun they're having,' said Gregor. 'Bringing Stephen for the summer has knocked years off them.' Gregor's speech by this time was indistinct, and because he found it hard to carry out the necessary swallowing and breathing that speaking requires, it was only the patient and practised ears of Catherine and Stephen who could follow what he struggled to say.

Catherine replied with a muffled 'Mmmm...' She'd allowed herself to drift into a snooze and lay with the magazine she'd been reading open across her face.

'Stephen adores them,' said Gregor. 'He loves writing to them. Dad calls them his "Letters from Abroad", not that Scotland is abroad of course, but they were started off in Canada when the poor lad was missing having his granny and granddad living nearby.'

'It's maybe a pity Weymouth doesn't have the same research facilities as Aberdeen so we could have all stayed together,' replied Catherine. She sometimes felt lonely in Aberdeen not having been able to develop a social life while caring for her husband and son as well as keeping her hand in at writing.

'Mum and Dad might have gone to Aberdeen in the first place if our move back to the UK had been definite. Anyway, Stephen can come here whenever he wants when he's older,' Gregor replied optimistically. Catherine agreed but couldn't prevent the thought passing through her mind as she looked over at his wasted body that he probably wouldn't live to see those times.

'You must promise me something, Catherine,' he said as the pedallo was recalled and they watched as Stephen clambered out and ran to his granny splashing her with the incoming waves to make her scream. 'If at all possible, they must never know the truth. It would break their hearts to find out Stephen isn't really their grandson.'

Catherine eased herself out of the low slung canvas of her chair and stood up to wave her arms so Stephen and Donald would find them in the densely crowded beach. 'There's no reason for that. Even if, as you see in the movies, Stephen needed a blood transfusion, he's "O positive", the most common type there is and the same as both of us. If in the unlikely event he needed a kidney, and I wasn't a suitable donor, then we'd have to use the donor bank or as a last resort involve one of the Simpsons. But honestly, what are the chances of that?' She knew she was being flippant but sometimes that was the best way for her to handle these hypothetical scenarios.

Stephen came running up from the sea and flung himself at his mother making her fall sideways on to the sand with him on top. How they laughed as they scrambled to their feet and she squeezed her son to her. At fifteen he had overtaken her in height and was almost as tall as Gregor. Since the revelation about Jimmy, Catherine had relaxed more in her attitude towards him, not growing nervous when he showed any traits inherited from him and their easy relationship was a joy to watch. Her only concern was the difficulty he had in gathering friends. When he wasn't helping to look after his father he would retreat to his room with videos and music. For them there wasn't the problem of a teenager running up phone bills while chatting to mates; quite the reverse, in fact. They would have loved it if someone had rung and asked for Stephen.

Catherine smiled at her dripping wet son and brushed the

damp sand from her bathing costume and legs. 'Fancy an ice cream cone? Race you to the kiosk.' Catherine and Stephen ran as fast as they could in spite of their feet sinking into the soft dry sand. 'We'll have to eat them all,' she joked on the way back, licking some melted ice cream from the side of her hand.

As they tore along the beach with the cones dripping all over their fingers they heard a blood curdling cry which they recognised immediately as coming from Gregor. All the excitement had caused him to take an emotional outburst. Thelma's face had changed from a happy smile to a look of sheer horror. She'd been sat at his feet contentedly drawing patterns in the sand with her fingers and as soon as the fit came over him had jumped up as if being stung, and moved away from him in alarm.

This was the first time she had ever witnessed one of his attacks. Making a brave effort to comfort him since she was after all his mother, she had put an arm round his shoulder but was too shocked to utter words of comfort. Instead she called out to her husband, 'Donald, do something! Hold him in case he falls.' Donald stood by in a state of confused paralysis. His hands twitched as if wanting to help but his body refused to move forward. 'I don't know what to do,' he said. 'You're his mother.' Catherine and Stephen appeared through the sunbathers, sticky ice cream trickling up their arms. Gregor started to laugh uncontrollably. By this time Thelma was hysterical and Donald remained frozen, statue-like. Gregor stopped laughing and he hunched forward, slavering and crying.

'Here, take these,' ordered Catherine hoping that this small act might steady her mother-in-law. Donald stood helplessly by, his arms dangling by his sides and his mouth opening and closing like a stranded fish. Thelma refused to let go of her son and continued her wrestling match with him to make sure he didn't fall out of his wheelchair. Catherine shouted at Donald to take the ice creams and he jumped back to life and took them obediently and started licking what he considered must be his own one. Catherine crouched beside Gregor and gently stroked his head, starting with her hand firmly on his forehead and then bringing it over the top in much the same way as patting a friendly dog. Then she kissed him tenderly on the cheek telling him that he was all right.

Thelma had moved over to Donald and was hanging off his arm sobbing. Stephen munched nonchalantly at his soggy wafer. 'Dad does that sometimes. It's part of his illness. He'll be all right in a minute.' He looked at his grandparents' ashen faces. 'Don't worry, you'll get used to it.' Stephen's admiration of Gregor's bravery had built over the years until he was the one behaving in a fatherly way. He thrived on responsibility, and his new found maturity, coupled with his childlike matter-of-factness, made him an excellent carer, though too old beyond his years for his own good.

His granny reached out to him and drew him to her. 'You're a brave lad, Stephen, and we're so proud of you.'

'One of the best,' continued his granddad. He knew it wouldn't be long before the child would need every last ounce of his courage as Gregor's condition worsened. But what selfishly worried him more was how he and Thelma were going to cope.

Catherine did her best to regain the happy family atmosphere. Gregor had recovered and was once again his usual self. 'The ALS causes these outbursts of inappropriate laughter or tears,' she explained. Fortunately Gregor's colleagues understood. Catherine spoke with pride about her husband's achievements, but made sure he was included and not spoken about. 'I think your parents would like to know how well your research is coming along,' she said before turning to address them. They were standing at the side of her looking awkward.

'Without his work the use of organophosphates might have continued without any understanding of the consequences,' Catherine said and turned again to smile proudly over to Gregor who looked at her with adoring eyes. 'Your son's certainly going to leave his mark on research into farming methods.' Too late she realised the grave implications of her words. She'd been so careful not to treat Gregor as an object that she had carelessly reminded his parents that he wouldn't be around for much longer, something Gregor had long since come to terms with. Thelma had her face buried in her handkerchief. Donald watched her. There were too many tears in his own eyes for him to be able to help.

'I know!' It was Stephen who came to the rescue. 'Let's climb Portland Bill Lighthouse tomorrow.'

'Sounds like a good idea,' said Gregor quickly in the slurring voice Catherine had grown used to and could understand without too much difficulty. 'Granny and I can wait in the tearoom nearby while you three go up to the top.'

'You'll love the fresh crab sandwiches,' said Catherine to Thelma. Gregor would only manage some milkshake through a straw. The paralysis that had reached his throat muscles would prevent him sharing in the seafood delicacies on sale there. But she would make a point of telling Thelma later so that Gregor would be protected from hearing yet again the never ending instructions that anyone who was to be alone in his company had to know.

Catherine and Stephen carefully manoeuvred Gregor up the stone ramp from the sands and on to the seafront. 'I've already climbed Girdleness Lighthouse in Aberdeen. There are a hundred and eighty-two steps,' said Stephen as he straightened again the cushions that were needed to prop up his father. 'I counted them all.' The adults laughed and praised him, glad of his youthful energy to see them through what was going to be the hardest time of their lives.

And it was Stephen who proudly commandeered the wheelchair as he strode ahead pushing his father in front of him. Donald hurried to catch up and took hold of one of the handles. Thelma and Catherine walked behind. Thelma seemed anxious to talk. She slowed her step and turned to Catherine. 'I must ask you something, dear,' she said quietly and she looked down at her sandalled feet with embarrassment. 'I saw how lovingly you handled that awkward situation. I'm his mother and I didn't know what to do.' Donald and Stephen were away ahead of them and had stopped to wait. 'Hurry up you slowcoaches,' shouted Stephen.

Thelma and Catherine began walking again. Catherine

explained that every moment with her husband was precious. 'Gregor still has the capacity to be a wonderful companion,' she assured his mother. She remembered the torture of worry when she thought he might be leaving her for another woman, but said nothing on that score. She felt the pain of dread that one day she wouldn't have him and had to clench her teeth to squash down the tears that this realisation would provoke. She put her arm through Thelma's almost in fear of falling over as her heart skipped a beat and almost choked her. 'I admit that our life now is no bed of roses but we carry on and the reason I never give up is simple;' Catherine said, but her voice was shaking as she struggled to force out the rest of the words, 'Gregor isn't only the love of my life. He is my life. I'm preparing myself for the toughest battle I shall ever have to face. When Gregor dies it will be a long time until I can fully live again. It will be for Stephen's sake that I carry on. You see, living has become so hard for Gregor that he would willingly give up the ghost right now. But it is for us and not himself that he draws breath every day, and if that's not a labour of love then what is?'

'And as for Stephen, I couldn't be more proud of him. When the news came through yesterday that his hero Victor Davis had won a gold medal for Canada in the 200m breaststroke in Los Angeles, my heart went out to him although he was leaping and shouting for joy. It was always his ambition to swim in the 1988 games. And who knows he might have been well on the way to achieving that dream if he hadn't devoted so much of his time to caring for his dad. Stephen has sacrificed so much that my heart nearly bursts with love for him.

Chapter 17

(Aberdeen, Autumn 1986)

Catherine clicked the end of her pen as she thought through the plan for the next scene in her short story. Gregor was beside her propped up in the recliner in front of an afternoon murder mystery on television, his head lolling forward onto his chest. He was having a short but welcome break from his time on the breathing apparatus and snoozed off and on. Over the past six years Catherine had tended to his every need. The sexual side of their love for one another had given way to an intimacy bordering on the spiritual that few couples could dream of even after a lifetime of married bliss. It was as if they could read each other's minds and sense one another's moods and needs with a telepathy that often made speech unnecessary. Catherine was amazed at how much could be 'spoken' with the eyes and they shared laughter and sadness and opinions every bit as easily as those who could speak without effort. Gregor's speech was more or less incoherent except to Catherine who was tuned in to it because she had listened and responded every day while it had gradually deteriorated. Stephen too was so devoted to his father that he was able to communicate with him quite easily.

Gregor was no fool and knew what the outcome of his disease would be and already he had cheated death by a year more than he'd expected. Maintaining a healthy exercise programme, one especially created for him by Marion whose expertise had served him well, and his lust for life had no doubt contributed to his winning that extra time. Right from the outset, while still in control of his faculties, he had made it perfectly clear to Catherine that once he had become helpless he had no desire to linger on this earth. He knew the lengths that some doctors would go to in their efforts to prolong life but in his view this was defying the natural course of events when a person was ready to take leave of his physical body.

Gregor had signed a declaration that he did not want to be

resuscitated and should be allowed to die naturally. Beyond that, all he could hope for was a quick, painless and peaceful end. Catherine had been horrified at first when he spoke so freely about his view of death being one of blessed relief but was persuaded to share his opinions as she witnessed his steady deterioration. She wouldn't have wished this loss of dignity on herself. That's always what Gregor used as the mainstay of his arguments. When you watch a person struggle to breathe with no movement in their body would you want to be them? But he was determined to postpone that day for as long as he was able to maintain a standard of life where pleasure was still possible.

It would have been an entirely different story if he had been struck down all of a sudden with a coronary. A person with a heart attack or lesser illness who suffered a cardiac arrest deserved every life saving technique in the book. But Gregor's situation was different. There would be no quality of life worth fighting for if his heart stopped or his breath stuck in his throat. Neither he nor Catherine told his parents that he wanted a speedy end when the time came. They might not have understood. They who had brought him into this world wouldn't want to see him depart for the next.

A few weeks before, Gregor had been rushed to hospital during a choking fit with aspiration of the lungs. The paralysis of the throat that curtailed his speech also prevented him from swallowing properly and although he hadn't eaten or drunk for a few hours he had begun to choke on his own spittle which was going down his airways instead of into the stomach. A team of doctors prevented his choking to death and fortunately, by laying him on his side the physiotherapist was able to gently pat his back and sides to bring the liquid back up. Massive doses of antibiotics prevented the pneumonia that results from foreign matter entering the lungs.

The ALS had reached such a stage that the part of the throat controlling swallowing had succumbed to the paralysis and there was now the constant danger of choking on any food or liquid which would pass down into the lungs instead of the stomach. In his condition, starvation and dehydration were also on the cards.

Because it was impossible for Gregor to swallow, the insertion of a naso-gastric tube through which nourishing liquids could be passed into his stomach was impossible. For such a tube to be inserted, the patient has to be able to swallow it down. Gregor refused to be anaesthetised for the procedure. He knew his time was nearly up and couldn't see the sense of unnecessary suffering. Neither did he want a tracheotomy whereby his windpipe would be cut and a tube inserted. 'These procedures work for temporary illnesses,' he insisted, 'or for people who wish to cling to life regardless, but as the old saying goes, "Doctors make the worst patients" and I want to leave here and go home even if it means signing myself out.'

This decision wasn't wholeheartedly welcomed by all of the staff, some of whom cruelly considered his return home would provide Catherine with a quick and easy way out of her responsibilities. But these matters had long ago been thrashed out and Stephen was in on the decision too. His father had decided against intervention and his desires must be respected.

Whether it was because Catherine was watching him intently as she pondered these things or whether it was the sudden loud noise of the adverts, but Gregor suddenly woke up with a start and began to choke. Catherine was at his side in an instant wiping his mouth with a cloth and holding him steady until he caught his breath again. It felt as if she were cocooning a frail little bird fluttering in panic against her. His limbs were wasted almost to the bone and his clothes fluttered loosely around him. The taut fleshless skin of his face was stretched like transparent silk over the contours of his cheeks and his eyes that bulged too large for their sockets were glazed and pleading.

'Take me out round the park,' he gasped. Although his voice was barely more than a whisper, it carried a note of command that Catherine found impossible to argue against. 'There's a fine rain so I'll fetch our coats,' was all she said. Anything he wanted she would make sure he had. As she wrapped a warm woollen scarf round his scraggy neck she wasn't at all surprised that it couldn't properly support the weight of his head. The breathing tube was placed carefully close to his mouth in case he should suddenly need it. They had to carry at all times an oxygen cylinder in the rack under the seat of the chair. She also made sure his head was well covered against the cold and damp and off they set.

It took such little effort to push the wheelchair in contrast with the first time when his body still had some bulk and she'd had to strain when going up the slightest incline. Now, because there was barely any flesh to act as padding on his fragile bones, he needed a foam disc to sit on to cushion him from any bumps along the way and he was as light as a feather. Catherine was thankful for the wet weather. At least the shower would mask her tears if they should meet anyone on the way and she was forced to speak. She found these trips so emotionally moving due to Gregor's absolute delight in them. They were his only pleasure in life. Today, despite the drizzle, he insisted on a complete tour of both parks. The dewy rain on the grass sprayed behind the wheels as they crossed the Westburn.

No games to watch today, but from the wan smile on Gregor's face and faraway look in his eyes he was seeing plenty from memory. On Saturday mornings he rejoiced in cheering on the schoolboys in their five-a-side matches. Their enthusiasm, as they played from the heart, seemed to pump energy into him. Sundays too brought a wide assortment of activities to watch and even participate in, especially the family picnics which Gregor and Stephen both loved. While Stephen took charge of his father, Catherine would bring over from the house an assortment of sandwiches, chicken legs, juice and a flask. They would stay out in the sunshine for hours.

People taking a constitutional walk past the flowerbeds on their way back from the local newsagent with their Sunday scandal sheets would nod and say their hellos. They would also get cheery waves from groups of men, old and young, heading pub wards for a laugh and a joke while their roast dinners were being prepared for them at home. Gregor loved them all and he had become a known character in the area. These people were his contact with the world at large. Some even stopped for a quick chat. He had a place in their lives. He belonged.

Catherine never grudged him one moment of her time. She enjoyed watching his face light up at the tiniest event, and even in his weakness he was able to transfer his pleasure to her and anyone else fortunate enough to be sharing his company at the time. Old Mr Grant with his frisky Labrador dog appeared in the distance. It would take more than a few spots of rain to keep them from their twice daily walks. Gregor couldn't even manage to raise his fingers but gargled a welcome. His friends had seen him and that was enough. Mr Grant's arms signalled as if he were on semaphore patrol and Laddie came bounding over panting with excitement, his long red tongue hanging out like a piece of well boiled ham. He knew Catherine carried treats in her pocket. Gregor loved his four-legged pal and giggled when Laddie nuzzled his hand and then sat in front of Catherine to give a paw in return for a dog biscuit. Then with a wag of his tail and a yelp of excitement he galloped back to his owner to lead him over to Gregor so he too could pass a few precious moments with him.

After that amusing adventure they crossed at the traffic lights to the Victoria Park, a gorgeous haven of trees and colourful flowerbeds. Catherine sighed with relief. The fountain was playing, its waters shooting high into the air. On the days it wasn't working, Gregor would look at Catherine with tears in his eyes and even cry. Today, however, he bubbled over with excitement like a child and would have clapped his hands had he been able. The fact that he made sounds of pleasure every time he saw it, and raged with his eyes and would emit a rattle from his throat like a grumpy old man if it had been turned off, amused Catherine. He had always been a man with strong opinions. Catherine pushed him over to a nearby bench and after wiping the rain off with a few tissues took a seat. Together they watched as the water sprang and fell, cascading over the pink granite bowls and spilling into the rippling pool at the bottom.

On the path beside them little sparrows were flapping their wings merrily in puddles where water had gathered in the little hollows carved out by their tiny bodies when previously taking dust baths. Catherine and Gregor were the only human beings around and, because they made a point of remaining silent and scarcely moving, the birds took no heed of them and entertained the couple with their amusing antics. Catherine handed Gregor the paper bag of crumbs to hold steady for her in his lap. He had in the past enjoyed scattering them for his feathered friends, but for many months now it was Catherine who had to throw them while he could only watch.

The blackbirds flocked from trees and bushes to snatch up the tasty titbits and fly with them back among the branches to eat at their leisure. The air was so full of their merry chirping it made the couple glad it was raining. They breathed in the warm earthy smell that always rises from the ground when showers fall after a long spell of dry weather. When Catherine felt Gregor had had long enough time watching the birds she continued on to the Garden for the Blind where every flower and plant had such a powerful fragrance it could be easily recognised without having to be seen. They stopped in order to savour the assorted perfumes.

Catherine closed her eyes and allowed herself to remember the walks with Gregor along the shores of Lake Ontario to the wonderful park near to their home. She thought too of the large open garden where she and Gregor had played so happily with Stephen when he was a toddler finding his feet on the smooth lawn that Gregor had tended so carefully. The memory was so vivid she thought she could hear Stephen's tinkling laughter and Gregor's voice encouraging him in his first few steps.

She could almost smell the pine of the evergreens and hear the distant splashing of the waters on the shore. If only she could stay in this dream state for ever with Gregor permanently by her side ... but she was brought back to the present and reality by a couple of school children running past. Gregor gave her a happy smile as if he had been reading her mind and participating in her nostalgic visit to their past life. No doubt he enjoyed these same wonderful pictures from time to time and felt the same mix of emotions that their memory evoked. Catherine pulled another few hankies from her pocket and wiped the dribbles from his mouth. Inevitably, as the outing had been a mammoth exertion for him, his breathing became a violent fit of retching as the air seemed to stick in his almost paralysed throat and lungs. Immediately but calmly Catherine attached the little clips to his nostrils and the oxygen began to flow. It was time to go home.

Back in the house Catherine stripped Gregor of his wet raincoat and helped him into bed. He'd had enough for one day. Although it was virtually impossible for most people to understand what he was saying, Catherine, through a mixture of familiarity, patience and the telepathy that people in love share, could understand his every word. 'Thank you,' he said. 'Today couldn't have been better.' She brought him hot chocolate in his beaker and held it while he drank it a little at a time through a straw. The whole lot nearly went flying when Gregor burst out with one of his laughing and crying fits. However, it didn't last for long. Exhausted, he slumped forward in a deep sleep. Catherine gently eased him back so that his head sank into the soft goose down pillows. She covered him with a warm blanket and stroked his damp forehead where his wispy hair hung down in a soft fringe that refused to be combed back. How much longer could she keep up his treatment at home? He had always said from the outset that to be put into a home regardless of nurses being able to give him better care would be intolerable. Life was hard enough but would be intolerable without his beloved Catherine there beside him to make living worth the struggle.

Catherine never slept soundly during her night-time vigils. She chose fatigue over convenience. How could she allow him to be taken to a hospital or nursing home when she was as capable for the time being as any carer of keeping him fed and clean? However, the nurse did pay a call every morning and evening to check his 'readings' as she called them and to change his drainage bag and help Catherine to dress and undress him. Catherine listened to her husband's shallow breathing in the bed next to hers. Her back ached from all the lifting but she valued every breath that he took. There was still some joy to be had from life as that afternoon had proved. He was still capable of giving companionship and she lived in dread of the day he would be taken from her either to a care home or by dying.

She had mixed feelings about his death. She would be devastated on her own behalf, but decidedly relieved to see his suffering at an end. Her anger at the unfairness of it all often rose during the night when her mind raced. Someone like Gregor deserved more time. He of all people shouldn't be taken away so young. He was only forty-four.

She stopped and listened through the darkness and threw back her duvet. Had his breathing grown fainter or was it only her imagination? Sitting on the edge of her bed, holding her own breath to listen for Gregor's had become a nightly occurrence. A warm drink might help to soothe her and maybe a quick read of the evening paper; anything to occupy her mind.

She was in the kitchen on the point of pouring the hot frothing milk into a mug when she heard the only too familiar choking and retching coming from the ground floor bedroom where she had left him only minutes before. Stephen who always slept with half an ear open, just in case, was already hurrying down the stairs. They rushed through the open door together. Gregor was rigid, his head thrown back and his body writhing. His face had turned a pale shade of purple as the air stuck in his throat. 'I'll dial 999 for an ambulance!' Stephen shouted and ran towards the phone in the hallway.

'Stop! Just stop!' his mother shouted. Her voice was almost a scream. 'No, you mustn't. We've spoken about it so often. The hospital knows your father's wishes and so does our G.P. But the paramedics don't. It's as if they are programmed to carry out C.P.R. regardless of anybody's condition when they receive an emergency call. Anyway, we have the signed document to show them that states that your dad refuses resuscitation and wants to slip away with us by his side. I've rehearsed this moment so often in my mind. No one is going to start laying into that poor dear man, pummelling at his body, breaking ribs and inflicting electric shocks on his heaving chest. He must have peace.' Stephen hesitated. He had been involved in his father's decision making discussions. He knew his mother was right. The look of stark terror in his father's eyes confirmed that he wanted to be allowed to die peacefully. 'Come and sit by us,' she said quietly to Stephen. 'Just be with him. That's all he's ever asked for.' The look of tranquillity that replaced the fear in Gregor's eyes spoke volumes.

Catherine cradled his head in the crook of her arm and his body gradually relaxed. Stephen wiped the saliva from his dad's mouth and put on the oxygen mask which was used to make it easier for him than the prongs in his nose when his struggle for breath was at its worst. His breathing, though shallow and laboured, grew easier but he was barely conscious. Catherine gently lifted the mask to clean with a soft tissue the foam from his lips that dribbled continuously. He opened his eyes and Catherine could read the desperate pleas. 'Hold me tight, Catherine. Don't leave me,' was written clearly in them.

He grew agitated and tried to speak in his crackling voice but he had already whispered the words to Catherine earlier when she'd tucked him in for the night. 'I couldn't bear it if they took me away. I want to die in your arms. I know my time is coming. When I was sitting there in the park with you I heard the voices of angels singing in my head and I saw the brightness of Heaven.' She had seen him looking around with an expression of wonder in his eyes. 'I never believed in such things before but I'm ready to go there now,' he'd said.

Catherine knew he was trying to say these words again and gently shushed him. 'I know my darling,' she whispered. 'No one is going to take you from me; only the angels will have that right.' Gregor seemed to want to speak and the gagging started; the desperate fight for breath. She tried to put the oxygen mask back on but it was obvious he was trying to move his head away. His voice, as weak as the moist air coming out of a slowly deflating balloon, managed to convey the words, 'Please don't let them take me away.' Catherine, who had her ear pressed close to his mouth to catch what he was saying, knew exactly what he meant. 'It's all right, darling. You're safe with us.' He remembered Stephen saying he would phone an ambulance and needed reassurance again. After putting the mask over his mouth to ease his final breaths she rose to allow Stephen to take care of him. He moved his father who had shrunk to the weight of a child to a more comfortable position among the pillows.

Gregor's eyes rolled in the direction of the door. Regardless of their many attempts to convince him that he would never be taken away, his obvious fear of hospitalisation kept on returning.

His breath was little more than a continuous rasp with no words forming but both Catherine and Stephen understood exactly what he meant. In hospital they might be able to prolong his grip on life, but he had always said many years ago, even before the onset of his illness, that he would hate that sort of existence. 'I want to go fast; maybe drop down out of the blue in the middle of a game of golf.' He'd make statements like these especially after a stint in the long term wards of the chronically sick when he'd been doing the rounds as a hospital doctor. Catherine could sense the panic rising in him now and she held him against her to stop the trembling. She would make sure that wasn't going to happen. 'Don't worry, Dad. I understand.' Stephen knelt down at his bedside and leaned forward to kiss him on the forehead.

Then Stephen went to the kitchen to finish making the drink for his mother and put a steaming mug on the bedside cabinet next to her. He was maturing into such a thoughtful young man. There was no doubt he had acquired Gregor's caring ways. He was a homely lad. Sometimes they worried that he didn't have many friends and seemed happy in his room studying or playing his music or watching videos. But the one sure thing in his life was his love for his father. If he were to find out the truth now it would surely break him. On the occasions when Gregor was hanging on by only a thread to his flimsy life Stephen would lapse into long silences. And now at the moment of his father's death his lips trembled and he sat on the edge of the bed weeping. 'How can we go on without him?' he whispered. 'I've never known anyone else like him.' He gave a shudder in an effort to compose himself. He turned and stroked his dad's bony hand that was almost purple now as the circulation slowed. 'I love you, Dad. You'll always have a place in my heart.'

Gregor's eyes were rolled back in their sockets but they were sure he had heard. Wasn't hearing the last of the senses to go? The dying man leaned into Catherine. He was trembling and the beat of his heart grew steadily fainter through his pyjama jacket until it couldn't be felt at all. His breathing was non-existent, replaced only by frantic dry heaving as his body stopped being able to draw in air. There was little chance of any reaching his lungs now. Catherine looked beseechingly at Stephen and uttered a prayer to God to take him painlessly before turning back to hold her terrified husband as if he were a baby in a shawl. 'You've been a wonderful husband to me, my dearest darling Gregor,' she said and she kissed his dry lips while the tears flooded down her face. 'It's all right my darling,' Catherine said, nursing her treasured husband in her arms and stroking his cold, clammy brow one last time. 'Don't worry, we'll never leave you,' she whispered. Stephen gave his beloved father one last lingering hug as the life shuddered out of him and he moved on to a place of no more anguish, the 'happy golf course in the sky' as he used to joke.

Catherine brought a bowl of warm soapy water and a flannel. 'Fetch a clean pair of pyjamas for him, the wine ones with the white stripe,' she said robotically to her son. After all she had rehearsed this scene so many times. With loving tenderness she washed her husband and together they put on his freshly ironed pyjamas. She took the soft baby brush that was all he could stand next to his skin and tidied his hair. It had retained much of its black colour but had tinges of grey at the side and was streaked with white in places. It continued to fall over his brow no matter what she did.

Images flashed in front of her eyes of Gregor as a youthful student in his medical school scarf taking her to casualty to have the wound on her face attended to. She saw him as an enthusiastic young doctor hurrying through the corridors of the hospital where her mother had lain dying of consumption and she smiled when she remembered how he would wait for her in the Shiny Teapot where they would often share a plateful of bacon softies. A tear spilled down her cheek at the memory of them walking hand in hand along the shores of Lake Ontario and how they would turn to watch the colours of the sky changing as the sun went down.

'You can phone the doctor now for the death certificate,' she said huskily to Stephen. 'Leave it to him to call the ambulance. It's better that he's here when the paramedics arrive.'

Chapter 18

Mourners crowded into the crematorium as the organist played Handel's Dead March from Saul. Every seat was taken and people had to stand at the back. Despite Catherine wishing daily that Jimmy would do them all a favour and disappear from the face of the earth, there was no way she could exclude him from the funeral. For years he had paid occasional visits to her home on the pretext of keeping a concerned eye on her while she struggled to cope with Gregor's illness. Rosie and Eddie were glad that he did so and had encouraged him to make sure that Catherine and Stephen were managing. Jimmy's true motive was a closely guarded secret. The pretence that he was merely going along with the age old custom of keeping his mother, Rosie, happy was accepted without question by Patricia who was a kind and thoughtful woman. Anyway, what threat could Catherine pose when she was so entirely devoted to a husband of her own?

A steady bond of avuncular friendship had grown between Stephen and Jimmy but there was thankfully the constant reassurance that Jimmy placed too much value on his marriage to endanger it by ever confirming Rosie's suspicions that he was Stephen's real father. Despite wishing he was absent from the funeral, Catherine had to accept that under the constant influence of his mother, there was no way that he would have been allowed to miss this family occasion. After all, wasn't his the perfect example of happy family life? If only the world knew the truth!

Catherine sat with Stephen on her left and her stepfather Frank on her right. The poor man had struggled all the way on his own by train from Perth. He knew about the violent attack on her before the rape and detested Jimmy. However, beyond that he knew nothing and now only Catherine and Jimmy shared that knowledge. Frank, who had married Catherine's widowed mother, Maggie, and enabled them to get their lives back on track after Sam's death abhorred the thought of anyone harming Catherine whom he treated as the daughter he'd never had. He had moved to Perth after Maggie's death to help in his brother's jam making business and was living out his retirement there. Although he hadn't visited Catherine and Stephen very often due to failing health, today he was their main support.

Gregor's grieving parents sat on the other side of Stephen. Thelma's eyes were puffy and red from days of crying. Clinging to her was Donald, broken hearted, his shoulders bowed as if life had defeated him as he stared fixedly at the coffin where his son lay. Rosie and Eddie sat next to Frank. Catherine could hear Rosie sniffing as Eddie tried to comfort her. 'Come on, girl, you have to be brave.' It seemed as though Catherine and Stephen were the only two who kept their composure, each one bearing up for the sake of the other. They had been shedding tears for six long years and the well had almost run dry.

Profound relief superseded their grief. As first hand witnesses to Gregor's decline, they knew what lay behind his clean and well groomed appearance. Neither had shirked from the intimate nursing care they'd had to provide for that beloved man of theirs. However much they had benefited from their all too short time with him, and regardless of how distraught they had been on the few days following his departure from this life, Catherine living on hot milky coffee for sustenance because her stomach rejected solid food, they were nonetheless glad that Gregor had finally been granted his well deserved reward - the heavenly bliss of death.

It was Reverend Forbes who took the service, the same kindly minister as had married Maggie and Frank in hospital. Catherine had kept in regular touch with him since the day she had talked her heart out to him during a particularly lost and lonely spell soon after she discovered that Gregor only had a few years to live. She had seen his name on the notice board outside a church by chance one day and gone in. There he was just inside the door as if waiting for her and he listened without judgement to how there were days when she found caring for Gregor so demanding that she even felt like running away. He relieved her of her guilt, saying this was a perfectly normal and understandable reaction and gave her the confidence to stay strong. In the years that followed, any time the going was getting tough, she would go to his church and take the words of his sermons as sustenance. This kindly minister had found time amongst all his other duties to visit Gregor. What they spoke about was private and even Catherine had to leave the room while Gregor poured out his worries and fears about facing death to this kindly, spiritual man.

Reverend Forbes, through a mist of tears, spoke admiringly of how much good Gregor had packed into his short life. He read out messages of condolence wired from friends and colleagues in Canada as well as from Aberdeen. Gregor had been a man of substance and his work would be recorded for ever. Doctors and professors in turn spoke of the valued research he had carried out in spite of the awful paralysis that had crept through and finally overtaken his young body.

Catherine walked shakily to the front and read a short poem she had written especially for the occasion with Stephen at her side holding her by the elbow in case her body would give way as she read her final tribute:

To My Husband Gregor

Your strength carried us through the difficult years,
And will help us continue and face without fear
The future....
For always I know your love will be there....
So we leave you now in God's tender care;
Goodbye my dearest darling.

Stephen helped his mother back to her seat. By this time she was crying uncontrollably and few in the congregation were able to hold back their tears. Frank was weeping too. Gregor had been a great favourite of his. He had seen him as a knight in shining armour who had come to Catherine's rescue when her mother was ill. Catherine whispered to him to remember Gregor as he was as young man free of pain, but that made Frank worse. 'I would rather it had happened to an old codger like me instead,' he sobbed. 'Gregor deserved better.'

When it was Stephen's turn to pay tribute to his father, Catherine deliberately glanced over at Jimmy. He was dabbing at his eyes with a folded white handkerchief. What a hypocritical swine, she thought. Why didn't he stay away and allow us these precious farewells without his horrible presence. However, she knew he must be suffering too. He would never hear on his own behalf the beautiful words Stephen was going to say about Gregor. By the time Catherine turned back to give her full attention to Stephen's eulogy, Jimmy's shoulders were heaving up and down as his body revealed for all to see the full extent of his grief. Unaware of the real reason for her husband's distress, Patricia half turned towards him and leaned over to put a comforting hand on his arm. Their daughters, in the middle, sat ramrod straight with heads demurely bowed.

Stephen spoke of how close he and his father had become during his struggle against Lou Gehrig's disease, ALS. Both had loved swimming and Stephen had been able to carry his father to the edge of the pool and lower him in, and with his son's support had been able to enjoy time in the water. Catherine bit her lip. She knew the massive sacrifice Stephen had made. He could have been competing in world class championships if he'd spent the same amount of time developing his own prowess. Now the poor lad had lost heart as swimming brought back so many sad memories. Maybe one day ... she dared to hope.

Catherine had requested that 'Ae Fond Kiss' by Rabbie Burns be played at the end. It had been sung too at her mother's funeral and its haunting melody and heart rending words on the agony of separation matched her own sorrow that twisted like a knife deep into the pit of her stomach.

At the end of the ceremony, the multitude of mourners filed past to offer Catherine and Stephen their heartfelt sympathy. Stephen had to grab her in both arms to stop her from sinking to the ground when Rosie and Eddie drew near. She leaned into Rosie's comforting arms and stayed there for almost a complete minute, the two of them sobbing. So much joy and pain they'd shared over time that it seemed that they clung so tightly for fear that the other might be snatched suddenly from life without warning.

The people Catherine had dreaded most meeting stood in front of her - Jimmy and his family. Stephen held out his hand to this man whose eyes were red rimmed and sunken in total ignorance of their true relationship. Jimmy seized it in both of his and squeezed it, holding on as if he'd never let go. His eyes seemed to bore into Stephen's. 'Look after your mother, son, you're the man of the house now.' Catherine looked on in a trance. She had expected that she would automatically dredge up some remnant of revulsion but too many other emotions were causing her slight frame to ache that day for there to be any room for hate. When Jimmy turned to her with tears in his eyes, she allowed him to hug her close, but there was no comfort in his touch and thankfully the outright disgust had lessened. Patricia's eyes were full of genuine sympathy and the kiss on the cheek she gave Catherine tingled as if charged with electric energy. There was nothing false about this woman. Jimmy had indeed struck lucky. Catherine wondered how she would react if she ever found out the awful secrets that lay hidden behind his respectable exterior.

Chapter 19

At the buffet gathering afterwards, Rosie came over and sat beside Catherine. They chatted about Gregor and what a sad loss he was, not only to them, but also to the wider world. It didn't take long, however, before Rosie veered the conversation on to her favourite subject: Jimmy and his successes. Catherine couldn't really be bothered listening to it anymore and glanced across the hall to where Jimmy and his beloved family had discreetly settled themselves. He was impressively attentive to his wife and talked to Sophie and the younger girl, Sylvie, in a grown up fatherly manner that she would have found admirable had he been a stranger. 'Sophie's quite the young lady now,' said Catherine and she added, looking directly at Rosie, 'so like her mother.' Rosie glanced at Stephen and back at Sophie. 'That's only due to the blonde hair and fair colouring. If she were dark like her father it would be more noticeable that she takes after him.'

'I think she favours Patricia,' Catherine persisted, 'and definitely not her father.' She kept up the flow of opposition to Rosie's determined insistence. 'It's like my Stephen. He looks more like his father's side than mine.' She had meant of course Gregor's parents, but Rosie, as smart as new paint, shot in with, 'I'll grant you that, he looks more and more like that side of the family every time I see him.' She pressed her lips together in a satisfied smirk. It was clear she meant Jimmy's and her own. Catherine's growing irritation was replaced by a wave of relief when Stephen approached with a plate of sandwiches and cakes.

'Give your old, ahem, auntie a hug,' Rosie said, eyeing him closely up and down and then glancing at Catherine. The two women held each other's gaze for several moments before Catherine, tight lipped, looked down at her food and picked up a sandwich with a shaky hand. Stephen's brow creased with surprise. 'Is something wrong?'

'Don't be silly,' said Rosie. 'I thought the two of you looked tired that's all.' She drew the young lad to her and held him close before kissing him soundly on the cheek. 'Come and sit down between us. Look, there's a spare chair at the next table. Eddie's gone off with Frank and will be boring the life out of some poor folks as they sort out all the ills of the world.' There was an exasperated edge to her voice as she scanned the faces down near the bar. She turned to Stephen who had remained protectively by his mother's side and scrutinised him from head to foot. 'Just his father's double,' she said, running her tongue thoughtfully along her lower lip and nodding her head, 'especially around the mouth and eyes. Similar build too.'

'Yes, just like Gregor,' Catherine retaliated sharply. Would Rosie never let up?

Both Jimmy and Catherine had agreed that Rosie should never know the truth. She wouldn't be able to keep it from Eddie and with his strong principles he would insist that everyone be in the know. Two families and three children would be destroyed with one blow. The truth could be a very dangerous instrument.

Eddie and Frank emerged from a cluster of men of their own age group and returned to offer to buy drinks. They were obviously eager to return to their new found friends after the necessary check-in to keep Rosie sweet. 'Would you be kind enough to buy me a ginger beer?' asked Catherine. Beads of perspiration had broken out on her forehead and she chewed on her lips to suppress the angry words she longed to let loose on Rosie. However much she loved her uncle's wife, she was overwhelmed with the urge to throw at her the fact that her beloved son was nothing more than a rapist.

Frank noticed the strain on Catherine's face but put it down to grief. 'Why, sure,' he said, mimicking her accent which, although it seemed strongly Scottish in Canada, was tinged with a Canadian drawl in Scotland. They all knew she never touched alcohol and thankfully respected her wishes. Stephen asked for orange juice and Rosie ordered a brandy and coke for herself. She was also feeling the strain of the argument and felt rightly indignant that she was being deprived of a grandson. 'And don't say the coke will spoil it,' she snapped at Eddie before he could get a word in. 'That's how I like it and that's how I'll have it.' Eddie gave a wry smile, shook his head and ambled over to the bar with his ally Frank at his side.

Catherine noticed that they no longer strode, and that they both seemed shorter somehow. As if reading her thoughts, Rosie spoke quietly, 'Eddie's getting old, but he won't accept it; refuses to retire completely and drives everyone at the community centre mad with his ideas for what more they could do for the area.' She turned to Stephen whom she had forced to sit in beside her. He was scrubbing at his mouth where Rosie had caught him with a special kiss. 'When are you coming to see us? Be a nice break for you.' It was noticeable that Catherine wasn't included in the invitation.

The idea of travelling alone appealed to him enormously. 'Mum, Mum, can I?' he asked. Youthful exuberance had overtaken his funereal depression at the thought of a new experience.

Catherine shot Rosie a withering look. Rosie's smug smile indicated that although there was an unspoken truce on the subject between them, she was determined to get her clutches into the young man whom she considered to be Jimmy's son. She wouldn't give the game away, but it was as if she were warning Catherine that allowing free access was the best way of silencing her. 'Next school holidays I'll see you on to a train and Uncle Eddie and Auntie Rosie will meet you,' Catherine replied reluctantly.

'I am seventeen after all and can easily go on my own,' said Stephen, the teenage whine disappearing as he got his own way. He moved closer to Rosie who had a way of winning him over that seemed to separate him from his mother. Catherine saw they were engrossed with each other as they discussed a list of possible day trips around Essex and up to London and was glad to withdraw into her own world for some respite from the day. Thelma and Donald had returned to their hotel room immediately after the ceremony unable to face anyone. There was a steady troupe of people to the table and Catherine was glad of the reprieve from Rosie's interminable hinting as she accepted the many condolences and politely asked in return how her well wishers were doing.

However, her optimism was short-lived. Patricia was on her way over with her daughters in tow. She could see Jimmy over at the buffet talking intently to one of her neighbours. She knew from many brief chats with him in the park that he was an offshore driller. It was such a small world. Perhaps they worked together on the same platform. They were deep in conversation, waving their arms and even seemed to be counting on their fingers from time to time, no doubt analysing world oil prices and how they might affect their future chances of employment.

'Catherine and Stephen,' said Patricia, breaking into her thoughts, 'you've never met Jimmy's daughters before, have you? This is Sophie and this is Sylvie.' She held them out in front of her as if putting them on display. All three youngsters smiled at each other but were naturally embarrassed at having everyone's attention drawn to them. Rosie took over, saying, 'Come and sit beside Stephen, girls. There's plenty room; Eddie and Frank could be long enough.' Patricia pulled in another chair and joined the group, wanting to keep an eye on her daughters. Catherine gritted her teeth and forced a polite welcome. 'My goodness, just look how you've all grown since last time; must be more than six years ago.' She explained to their mother whose face had taken on a confused look that Rosie and Eddie had taken her daughters to visit once. What she omitted to add was that Jimmy had banned any more such contact and had even told his daughters to keep quiet about that first one, using the flat's dubious location as a perfectly feasible reason for not letting on to their mother. Catherine directed a smile at the three youngsters as if there were no reason to hide anything. 'Isn't it lovely to see the children together again?' she said.

Stephen squirmed and glared at her. 'We're not children anymore. Why must everyone discuss our growth as if we were forced cabbages being got ready for the Turriff Show?'

Sophie and Sylvie laughed. 'I keep telling Mum the same,' said Sophie quietly, and Sylvie added loudly, 'So do I.'

'I'm waiting for the day Mother sticks a rosette on me,' quipped Stephen, delighted that his comment had brought a response.

'That's right, lad, stick up for yourself,' said Rosie, egging him on.

'I keep telling Mum to let us speak for ourselves,' said Sylvie, the younger but more confident one, and Sophie nodded in agreement.

'What will Catherine think of you, talking to me like that?' said Patricia.

Catherine shook her head to indicate she wasn't in the least bit shocked. 'Stephen's even worse as you can see; never short of a smart comment.'

'Yes, they're all the same,' said Rosie with a smirk. 'Jimmy was full of cheek at that age; and talk of the devil, here he comes.'

Jimmy came storming over to investigate the reason for the impromptu get together. He didn't entirely trust his mother. She was too cunning by far. 'I thought Stephen and our girls would like to meet one another,' said Patricia innocently. She spoke rather shrilly and her face flushed as she excused herself and yanked her offspring by their hands to stand quietly by her side. Despite what she had said, she obviously didn't want her daughters picking up bad habits from any teenage boy.

Jimmy had noticed his mother's smug look and tried to stay calm; no point in raising her suspicions further. 'I was talking to Bert Brannigan there. It's not good news; some of the oil companies have already stopped drilling. I've never known him so troubled.' He blew hard through his lips and shook his head to emphasise his concern, glad to have a credible reason for his agitation. With a brief but disapproving look over at Catherine who knew why he was so flustered, he ushered his clan back to their own table to eat the food he'd gathered for them. 'Look after your mother, Stephen,' he said for the second time in less than an hour and his eyes suddenly softened as he looked at his son and as he turned away, he closed them and screwed up his face as if a sudden stab of agony had caught him off guard.

Stephen was full of the impending journey to Basildon. 'You must come too,' said Eddie as quick as a flash to Catherine. He had just reappeared with Frank and their faces glowed with a combination of having enjoyed both good company and fine drink. 'We can do our own thing while these two do theirs.'

'A very good idea ...,' said Catherine. She waited, and sure enough, it was quickly followed by Eddie's '... son.' They doubled up with laughter as they repeated the popular catchphrase. The grief-filled tension eased. Life would continue after all.

Catherine decided to leave them to their plans and strolled over to Jimmy's family. She didn't want any unpleasant confrontations adding to the stress of the day and wanted to prevent his returning to pay his respects properly with Frank there. Catherine was pleased Frank hadn't encountered Jimmy face-to-face. He detested the thought of anyone harming her or Stephen and had never forgiven Jimmy for the first attack on her and would be after him with murder in mind if he ever got wind of the rape.

As soon as Catherine approached, Patricia was on her feet. 'Give Catherine a seat, Jimmy, we can't have her standing?' It was obvious from her tone that she couldn't understand this unusual lack of manners in her husband.

'Sorry, Catherine,' said Jimmy jumping up quickly at his wife's command. 'I was miles away. Let me fetch you a drink.'

'A cappuccino with sugar would certainly help me through,' replied Catherine, maintaining the air of politeness that surrounded Patricia and her brood.

'Jimmy has a lot on his mind,' explained his wife. 'Things are taking a tumble in the oil industry it seems. He's worried about his job, although I've told him that we'll manage somehow even if it means my taking on a little part-time work somewhere.'

'Over my dead body,' he declared, his eyes flashing angrily at his wife's unimaginable suggestion. He turned quickly to Catherine. 'Oh my God, what am I saying? I didn't mean it.'

'No offence taken.' Catherine had grown a thick skin over the years and disregarded these accidental though potentially offensive comments. Jimmy hurried away for her drink, his face red with embarrassment. Patricia smiled. 'Jimmy can't contemplate ever being unemployed,' she said. 'He's going around with his mind in a whirl.' The girls remained silent but listened eagerly. The current topic under discussion in their house since their father had come ashore from his last trip was their possible move far away from home to where their father could find work.

The cup rattled in the saucer as Jimmy returned with Catherine's coffee. His hand shook as he placed it on the table. 'We'll move if we have to,' he said, knowing full well that the uncertainty of his keeping a job had come under discussion. 'If the oil falls through then Aberdeen will have no work for me. They've shut down most of the traditional industries. All my school days and throughout my apprenticeship I planned working in the shipyards for life, but there's none of that now.'

His wife shushed him gently. 'Catherine doesn't want to listen to our problems. She has enough of her own.'

'Don't mind me. I only came over to thank you for coming. I didn't mean to intrude,' Catherine said.

'Stephen seems a good lad; very grown up. You must be proud of him,' said Patricia in an effort to include her. 'We would have liked a boy, wouldn't we?' she said. 'But we thought two was a nice size for a family.' She had turned to address these last few words to Jimmy who now flushed a deep crimson and stammered, 'Eh, er, I suppose so. Sophie and Sylvie more than make us happy.'

Patricia noticed how uncomfortable he had become. 'I'm sorry dear; I shouldn't have started on about work.'

'Jimmy's bound to be troubled if there's a recession looming. It scares all of us.' Catherine was desperate to ensure that any awkwardness would appear to be on account of the precariousness of the country's economy.

'Thanks, Catherine,' said Jimmy loosening his tie and opening the top button of his shirt.

'I'm training to be a nurse.' It was Sophie who spoke in a quiet but clear voice. 'It's a career you can follow anywhere, so travelling doesn't bother me.' It was obvious she wanted to help out. She had a sweet little face, high cheek bones like her grandmother, Rosie, but slight of build like her mother. But there was no mistaking those eyes, and that mouth!

Jimmy smiled adoringly at his daughter before turning back to

Catherine. 'We'll be in touch. Don't you worry about a thing.' As she walked back to join Rosie and company, she felt a firm hand on her arm, and as she was swung round to face Jimmy whose hand it was, she winced at the steely glare of his eyes. Why had he come after her? 'People will think I'm only adding my words of support so listen closely to what I have to say, and take careful note.' Catherine couldn't think what had brought on this covert aggression. As he continued, his lips drew back from his teeth making him like a predatory wolf. 'Never, ever let me catch Stephen anywhere near my girls. Do you hear me?' Catherine winced. 'Get my meaning? Just think about it.' He looked her straight in the eye as he said this and slowly the penny dropped.

Catherine gasped and her lip curled as if a horrible taste had entered her mouth. 'Trust you and your dirty mind,' she retaliated but this wasn't the first time this particular topic had come under discussion over the years and she had taken on board the implications of what he was saying and she knew he was right. But the venom in his tone of voice shook her to the quick. Of course, there would never be any need for Stephen and his darling daughters to meet. At the same time, however, she inwardly breathed a deep sigh of relief. Another reason for Jimmy to want to move away and he was obviously dead set on the truth never coming out. In fact they were the only two people in the world now who knew. Rosie could do all the guessing she wanted but it would always be denied. A glimmer of hope was finally shining its way into her life. The black cloud of the recession seemed suddenly adorned with a silver lining. Jimmy could depart at any time with the whole shebang of his family and out of her life and Stephen's for good.

Chapter 20

(Autumn 1987)

Catherine looked at the brandy glass on the shelf with the Happy 40th Birthday engraved on it. It had been there for months and it was about time it came down. Stephen too had celebrated an important milestone that year, his eighteenth. He had been accepted at Robert Gordon's Institute where he was studying to become an engineer. She on the other hand had reached stagnation. Life was supposed to begin at forty she mused as she browsed through old family snaps.

The nights were drawing in already and it was barely after seven o'clock when Catherine got up from the sofa to close the heavy curtains and put on the main light. She had become so engrossed in memories that she hadn't realised she was sitting in the half dark until the unmistakeable sound of a taxi's radio outside had startled her. Then she'd heard a man's voice and a car door slamming. She certainly wasn't expecting anyone. As she reached out to draw the warm winter curtains in preparation for switching on the light, she noticed a stranger hanging around outside. He stood under the hazy yellow light of a street lamp peering at a scrap of paper in his hand as if he were trying to trace an address. As she watched, he approached her house and put his hand on the gate but seemed hesitant to push it open. She certainly didn't recognise him. He turned his head and catching her eye at the window, waved and proceeded up the path. 'Another insurance salesman,' Catherine muttered. She'd been plagued with these people in the year since Gregor's death. What a way to earn a living, she thought to herself; scouring lists of the recently deceased and then tracking down gullible widows as a possible market for their latest products.

She flung open the door ready to chase yet another cold seller away with a flea in his ear, but this one didn't start immediately with a spiel about giving thought to the economic survival of any dependents as was the norm. Instead, he stood waiting for her to say something, looking her up and down and making her feel decidedly uncomfortable. It was a chilly night with a grey haar rolling in from the sea. Catherine wanted to return to the warmth of the fire. His silence unnerved her and she was on the point of slamming the door on this unwelcome canvasser when he eventually found his tongue. Her knees nearly buckled under her when he did. 'Don't you recognise me, Catherine? It's me - Earl.' Catherine stared at him through the dim light until his features and overall appearance began to take on a familiar look. Earl stammered nervously, 'I didn't mean to impose. Perhaps I should go.'

'No, please, come in,' she whispered hoarsely and then cleared her throat in order to speak clearly. 'It's just that you've changed so much.' Catherine was glad when he stepped inside and she was able to close the door against the wintriness of the night, drawing her long cosy cardigan round her shivering body. What a fright she must look. No make-up, old jeans and her hair scraped back into an elastic band, not to mention the heavy rimmed spectacles perched on the tip of her nose from when she'd been straining through the gloom to see the details in the photographs. As she showed her surprise visitor into the living room, she whipped them off and shoved them in her pocket, hauled her hair loose and fluffed it up, all the while chewing desperately on her lips to give them some colour. She couldn't let him see she'd turned into a frump.

Earl stood with his back to the gas flame fire and Catherine switched on the main light so she could observe the transformation in her former lover. 'You haven't changed a bit,' said Earl as a wide smile spread across his handsome, rugged face. 'Still the same shining curls and the soft peachy skin.'

Catherine stammered her apology. 'I'm sorry I didn't recognise you at first; you do look the same, but your hair ... it's short and you've shaved your moustache; and your clothes ...'

Earl opened his arms to her. 'Come here and give me a big hug. I've grown up. I couldn't stay a cowboy forever. Times have changed and we've all morphed from carefree flower children into staid, middle-aged adults.'

'Don't be so pessimistic,' Catherine scolded, 'I've a lot of living to do yet.'

Earl smiled. 'Of course you have. But I think you'll agree the lives we were living then would kill us now in less than a fortnight.' He'd meant it as a joke but stopped in horror when he realised what he'd just said. 'Sorry, Catherine. I read about Gregor in the newspapers. I know it's been a year but I should have been watching what I was saying.'

'Don't worry,' said Catherine, settling herself into his comfortable embrace, 'you'd be amazed at how many similar sayings there are in the English language. I'm growing a tough skin in my old age; and that last bit is unfortunately no metaphor.'

Earl stroked her face and gently kissed her forehead as if to disprove her words. 'I don't want to worry you and please be assured that I'm not stalking you.' His eyes were full of genuine concern and sadness for a few moments. And then he smiled. He wanted to cheer her up not pull her further into the doldrums. 'You really are a great girl, Catherine,' he said with a broad smile. Catherine felt at home as she leaned her head against his manly chest. She'd often wondered what had happened to 'Wild Bill Hickok'. 'I thought you'd left Aberdeen. And how did you know where to find me?'

He took her by the hand to sit beside him on the sofa. He was grinning from ear to ear while Catherine's face was pale from the shock of seeing this ghost from her past. 'I come and go between here and Houston quite regularly now. When I read about Gregor the address was in the obituary and I wrote it down ... and kept it. The papers were full of your husband's story. He must have been a great man. I was paying a quick visit to a colleague who's in the hospital round the corner with stomach pains and when his family arrived I decided to leave them all to it and come and see you instead. I'm so glad I plucked up the courage. I was so nervous I almost let the taxi driver sail past your door.'

'I'm glad you kept my address. Gregor did get quite a write-up in the local press. He spent his life working for the benefit of mankind and I'm so proud of him. All the secrecy I told you I was worried about turned out to be his hiding from me the fact that he was being tested for that horrible illness.' Catherine bent her head forward and put her hand over her face as if to hide her shame.

Earl pursed his lips. 'What that poor guy must have been going through! I've heard about ALS, Lou Gehrig's disease. There have been fund raising events right across the States but they seem no further on in finding a cure.'

'One day they will,' Catherine said optimistically and I try not to feel angry that he had to be one of its victims. There will never be anyone quite like him again. I'd known him since I was seventeen.'

'That's why I didn't come round straight away,' said Earl. 'You needed time.' An anxious frown had chased the laughter from his eyes. 'Please don't get the wrong idea; this is only a courtesy call.'

Catherine squeezed his hand. 'Don't worry; I'm delighted to see you. I'll make some coffee and we'll talk over old times.' She hesitated before adding, 'I've given up alcohol; seven years now. It began as a habit when I was on reporting assignments but I ended up using it as a prop to block out stuff I should have been dealing with.' It was almost as if she were delivering a speech. Earl nodded as he listened to how she had struggled against the addiction and Catherine wondered if he had guessed she'd had that problem. He said nothing that would have confirmed that suspicion but he drew her into his arms and hugged her close. 'I understand, Catherine,' he said gently as he stroked her back. 'I'll always be your friend and I'm proud of you. That was a massive achievement and not everyone is strong enough to do it. You are one brave lady and I can't believe I'm seeing you again after all this time.' He let her go and held her out in front of him to look at as if proving to himself he wasn't dreaming. Catherine sighed as if a great weight had been taken from her shoulders. True friends had been hard to come by and here within touching distance stood one of the most valuable she would ever make.

'Thank you, Earl,' she said softly. 'It's kind of you to be so understanding.'

'Right, let's have that coffee,' he said firmly. He took off his heavy padded jacket and folded it over the back of a chair before seating himself on the sofa where Catherine had been sitting in lonely reflection only minutes before.

She brought through the tray and set it in front of them on the light mahogany coffee table. She felt comforted by his presence, and the strong smell of the percolated Columbian, which she hadn't forgotten was his favourite, brought back memories of the heady days when she'd first arrived in Aberdeen. 'Those were crazy times,' Earl said and took a sip of the strong, sweet black liquid. 'It's exactly as I like it; you remembered! I must have made more of an impression than I thought.'

'How could I forget you,' she smiled, 'and the wonderful times we spent together? Everyone went a bit mad during the oil boom. The town seemed to explode with people out to enjoy themselves.'

'Only a bit?' he said with a chuckle. 'We were completely insane. And all that money flying around; people buying houses, cars, going out every night to expensive restaurants; I never ate so much steak; and wild parties morning, noon and night. The pubs were open from eight in the morning if you wanted them.' They laughed as they reminisced, but a sad flicker of nostalgia passed over both their faces for those long ago days they knew would never return. 'We're all getting older and now the oil industry's in trouble. I'm over here to organise the folding up of the Aberdeen side of things.'

'You don't mean?'

'That's exactly what I mean. Another few weeks and that's me away for good. My wife, Theresa, will be pleased. We've not long had a baby girl, Hannah. Theresa's the woman I told you I was going out with back home. We were married five years ago.'

'Why, that's lovely,' declared Catherine with exaggerated enthusiasm and she started to stack the cups in order to hide ... dare it be said ... jealousy. Life with Gregor had fulfilled her as a wife and of course she had loved being a mother to Stephen, but there still lingered the dream of a daughter which she had long since made up her mind would never come true. She was forty. The hands of the body clock as they called it were ticking their way too quickly round, and had almost moved beyond the years that were still possible for child bearing. With forced effusiveness she continued, 'It'll be so much better for you to be with your family; children need a father.'

Earl took the tray from her. 'Let me take you out for a meal sometime. I know a hotel that serves the most fabulous T-bones.'

'That would be lovely,' she replied; the intimate joking had gone and been replaced with polite phrases.

As they were saying their goodbyes on the doorstep, a red car shot along the street towards them and turned into the driveway, screeching to a halt with the minimum use of gears.

Stephen stepped out. He frowned, weighing up the stranger who was standing too close for his liking to his mother. 'My, you've turned out well,' said Earl, holding out his hand to the handsome young man who came marching up the path towards them with a quizzical frown that pulled his brows heavily over his peering eyes. 'Bet all the girls for miles around are chasing after you,' grinned Earl not to be put off. He knew how possessive Stephen could be of his mother.

Stephen scowled. 'There are no girls.'

As quick as a flash Catherine intervened. 'Look who it is, Stephen; it's Earl, from when you were still in primary school.' She was hoping against hope they would still get along.

Earl kept his palm open in welcome towards Stephen and added for him the description that was obviously being weighed up in Stephen's quickly computing mind, 'Think cowboy boots,' he said, 'a Stetson and a long yellow pony tail.'

Stephen's eyes rolled up to the left and to the right and then as a smile broke over his face he nodded. 'Helicopters!' he shouted joyfully. 'It's all coming back to me now. I would never have recognised you in a million years.'

'Well, it's only taken a couple of seconds with a few clues here and there,' laughed Catherine. The two men shook hands. 'Glad to renew your acquaintance,' said Earl. 'I'd be honoured if you'd join your mother and me for a meal tomorrow. I'm in town for a couple of weeks.'

'You're on;' said Stephen, 'I wouldn't miss it for the world.'

Catherine and Earl smiled into each other's eyes across a corner table in the Steak Emporium and the happiness they'd known before broke through the surface of the ice of their initial reserve and the years melted away. Stephen wiped the grease from his chin with the linen napkin and let out a loud belch. 'Excuse me!' he said and did it again. Earl suppressed a smile while Catherine glared. Being his mother, she felt obliged to correct him, but how could she be annoyed with a son who had done so well in his Highers? 'Four As and a B,' Stephen informed Earl proudly. 'Mum promised me a run-around for my eighteenth birthday if I studied hard and I expected an old banger, but the car she's bought me is fantastic.'

'It's his pride and joy,' laughed Catherine. 'He's out driving around the countryside non-stop and if it's not that then he's cleaning it. He'll soon have it polished down to the bare metal.' She turned to Earl, 'And he's so grateful that he's learned how to operate a vacuum cleaner at long last!' Stephen tutted. Why did his mother always have to talk about him as if he were still a child or not even there to speak for himself?

There were many more such enjoyable meals and Stephen and Earl got on famously. 'He sure is a credit to you, Catherine. I'm going to miss both of you like mad when I leave.' Earl's reminder that his stay was only temporary brought a heavy pall of sadness over the table. In only a short time he had regained the status of dear family friend.

Stephen added to the finality of the occasion by making an announcement that made his voice shake with emotion. 'This could be our last meal together because I have to go to Glasgow tomorrow for a weekend's introductory course on hydraulic valves in combustion engines and won't be back until Monday afternoon.' He looked over at Earl and his eyes misted over. 'Thanks for everything,' he said huskily, 'especially for looking after Mum. It's been great to see her happy again. She's been through a rough time.'

Catherine took a sharp, shuddering intake of breath so loud there was no hiding the fact she was close to tears. Earl put his hand on her arm. 'Don't take on so. We'll keep in touch; Christmas cards and all that.' He forced a smile. The sorrow of an almost imminent farewell was hitting him hard too and he sank his teeth into his lower lip as if to prevent himself from saying anything over sentimental and unsuitable for a married man.

'We'll never forget you, will we, Stephen?' Catherine said as she dried her eyes. 'We've had such a wonderful time. Now, why don't we cheer up and end this lovely meal with some strawberry cheesecake?' The replies were unanimous. 'A very good idea ...,' said Stephen, and Earl who had cottoned on to the old family joke added, '... son.'

Catherine put yet another chocolate in her mouth. It was a mint cracknel and she followed it immediately with a marzipan delight and a nut cluster. Maybe if she filled herself with sugar it would ease the emptiness that she knew would make her feel like caving in when Earl left. Once he reached Heathrow, he'd board a jumbo jet for Houston and fly through the clouds out of her life forever. It was small recompense that Earl had given her a huge box of her favourite candies as he called them, as well as a gigantic bunch of roses that had filled three vases, causing her to joke that the living room looked more like the dressing room of some famous actress or singer. 'You're more than a celebrity to me. You're ultra special,' he'd replied and planted a kiss on her forehead. 'There won't be a day goes by when I won't think of you.'

Earl was flicking through her record collection. Like Catherine, he was a jazz fan. He chose a moody saxophone number and instead of sitting down to listen he swept her into his arms and they clung together, swaying rather than dancing as the haunting melancholy of the music drenched them in sadness like a depressing cloud of damp, grey fog. Catherine gulped down the residue of the sweet chocolate, and choking on sobs that made her heave against Earl's chest, she tightened her arms round his neck as if compelling him to stay and never leave.

'I have to go, Honey,' he whispered in her ear. 'It's going to be just as hard for me. These last few days your name has been echoing round and round in my head as if you were the only one that mattered to me.' Earl pushed her gently from him and taking her hands in his he tried to explain. 'I never meant for this to happen; I'm a happily married man. I can't hurt my wife. She's a good woman. There are children to think of too. We must be brave. What other choice have we?'

Catherine took the handkerchief that he offered and blew her nose. She laughed nervously. 'I must look a dreadful mess. I bet my face is all red and blotchy. I know you're right. I knew this wasn't going anywhere; we're good friends, nothing more.' The music had stopped and reality began to set in. 'It's loneliness that's making me like this. Since Gregor died I've allowed myself to shrink away from the world. You've brought me out of my shell again. I'll be fine; I know it. You belong in Houston with your wife while I belong here and I have to start living again.' She sat on the sofa wiping away tears and taking deep breaths.

Earl disappeared into the kitchen. If she'd seen him splashing cold water on his face she would have realised that he was taking it equally hard. He returned with a broad smile and laid a large mug of milky coffee in front of her before sitting down beside her to drink his black. Catherine had calmed down. Thoughts were obviously racing through her head. 'Why don't you stay with me,' she said quietly. She looked up into his eyes holding his gaze as if to make sure he understood her meaning. 'Just for these last three nights, please. Stephen will be back on Monday. I'll be able to cope once he's home.'

Earl shook his head. 'It's not that I don't want you,' he said, his voice lower than a whisper. 'It's because I would never want to hurt you. I thought you would be all right as long as we didn't sleep together.' Earl's hand trembled as he stroked her damp cheek before kissing it.

'It's what I want – to spend these last few nights together. I'm not making any demands on you or trying to spoil your marriage. I just want to feel like a woman again. I want to know that someone might find me attractive again one day.' She leaned her face into his hand that still lingered on the side of her tear stained face and he gently turned her head and pressed his open lips on to hers. In moments they were clinging passionately to each other on the sofa and it didn't matter that the hot drinks were growing cold in the cups. 'Not here,' said Catherine, 'I want it to be special. I'll go upstairs and you can join me in a few minutes.'

She looked in her underwear drawer. She had sensibly renewed her diaphragm even though there was no man in her life. It was from the time she'd joined a dating agency a few months previously, just in case. It was what any responsible single woman would do. But that little foray into the dating circuit had soon died a death after a few calamitous meetings with men she felt uncomfortable with. Gregor couldn't be replaced and she'd cancelled her membership.

She was contemplating the contraceptive device when a flash of something akin to genius but of dubious intent struck her and she replaced the cap in its box and shoved it back in the drawer. Why not? She didn't want another husband, ever. But she did want a baby girl. She'd always dreamed of having a daughter and surely this was her last chance. Earl was good looking, well educated, kindly – what more could she want in a potential father? She didn't want him as a husband. She knew it was only fear of being alone again that had made her hang on to him and long to possess him. Although she'd always care for him deeply as a friend, she'd be over him in a week as a lover. But she did want his child. And even if it were a boy, it wouldn't matter. It would give her someone to love now that Stephen was growing up.

As she looked at herself in the mirror, there was no denying she hadn't lost her sex appeal. Even after seven years she was still every bit as seductive in the black silk negligee that clung to every curve of her body, showing it off as clearly as if she'd been naked. She jumped. Earl had crept upstairs and was standing behind her. His lean, muscular presence enticed her to turn and hold her body next to his. She smelt the muskiness of his fresh sweat and the velvety softness of the blond hairs of his chest as they brushed tantalisingly against her nipples. Her breathing quickened and the thudding of his heart beating fast in time with her own let her know that he was equally aroused and would soon be inside her with the goods that she so desperately wanted him to deliver.

Earl's stay lasted over three nights and two complete days. He made a mad dash to his hotel early on the Monday morning after one last hurried consummation. Catherine wept openly and uncontrollably, but she was sure that the excessive amount of sex they'd enjoyed over that memorable weekend, smack in the middle of her monthly cycle, would bring a farewell souvenir to be enjoyed for the rest of her life.

Six weeks later, Catherine stood naked in front of the long mirror on the door of the wardrobe. She passed a hand lovingly over her belly that was swollen with the bud of life inside. Her breasts bulged heavily and were lined with a network of rich blue veins. The nipples, like ripe berries, stood proud in the centre of bright purple haloes. The symptoms that confirmed her pregnancy filled her with delight. It would be a summer baby, and already she was dreaming of walks in the park and the wondrous sensation of holding the warm, plump newborn to her bosom. She had loved this child since the moment of its conception, watching and waiting daily for each early sign of its existence.

Even the morning sickness was bearable and nothing like as bad as the daily dry heaving sessions she had endured when expecting Stephen. She hoped this was a sign of its being a girl this time. They did say that the nausea was worse with a boy than a girl. An old wife's tale or some hormonal reason perhaps? Some dizziness and occasionally feeling faint and having to sit down quickly before keeling over were easily handled. Working from home meant being able to time her writing to take place during spells of well-being. She was building a reservoir of stories and articles for the months immediately after the birth when every waking moment would be devoted to the new arrival.

Her situation was perfect for having a baby on her own

without a husband. Memories of Gregor gave a satisfying comfort and the gnawing loneliness had been replaced with a wonderful burst of joyous fulfilment. A quick glance at the clock on the dressing table made her hurry to the bathroom for a shower. She trembled with excitement; today was her first appointment at the ante-natal department. She couldn't wait for the day when a scan would confirm that this was a little girl. There was no doubt of that in her mind already. However, she wouldn't mind if it were another boy. Stephen had been a delight to bring up. Deep in her heart, she knew that the only thing that really mattered was for the little one to be healthy.

Chapter 21

Rosie and Eddie were paying their regular New Year visit to Scotland. Catherine waited until the fourth of January to drop the bombshell. The bulk of the festivities were over and Aberdonians with sore heads from a surfeit of parties were thinking downheartedly of a return to work. Catherine wondered if the fact that Rosie and Eddie were tipsy and worn out from nights on the tiles would somehow weaken the impact of her earth shattering news. She waited until they popped in past her house for a nightcap after a reunion with some of Rosie's old neighbours which had made them both merry and mellow.

However, at the news, both their mouths fell open and they sat on her settee like hungry baby birds, only silent. That didn't last long and it took only a few moments before the squawking began. The pair of gadabouts were unfortunately far from being tired out and they insisted on analysing the pregnancy situation as if they had the power to change anything they didn't like.

'Why couldn't you have chosen a man who was unattached?' asked Eddie. 'Why have you gone for a man that you knew could never give you a future?'

'I did make efforts. I joined a dating agency. But I couldn't forget Gregor. It was too soon for anyone to take his place,' she explained, although she considered they really didn't have any right to be prying into her private affairs. 'Perhaps I'll never feel what I felt for him again.' Rosie's expression had changed from a disapproving frown to wide eyed interest. She put down her whisky and soda that she'd needed to steady her nerves on first mention of the baby and leaned forward, hands on her lap, pushing her skirt down between her thighs. Rosie had an insatiable appetite for juicy gossip. 'You've been dating strangers? These people are usually just a lot of misfits. You do hear some awfully strange stories.'

Catherine wasn't in the mood to discuss it, but at least it would create a diversion. 'There was one I thought at first was a lovely gentleman - Jeremy - so kind, so polite. He was a widower and had gone back to live with his mother. They both saw me as the answer to his prayers although we'd never even kissed.'

'That's what they always say – nothing happened,' quipped Rosie, winking over at Eddie.

He closed his eyes and shook his head. 'I can't stand all this women's talk,' he said. He looked up at Catherine and said with a sigh, 'This is all too much for me.' Without another word he took his pipe out of his pocket and left the room for the fresh air at the back door.

'Never mind him,' said Rosie, leaning forward even further so that she nearly overbalanced. 'Get on with the rest of the story.' She had to steady herself by gripping on to the seat. Catherine could hardly keep a straight face. 'Hilda, as his mother was called, knitted me out of the goodness of her heart a bright pink cardigan. It would have let in two of me. In fact I've still got it upstairs.'

'Mmmm ...,' Rosie said thoughtfully, 'that colour really suits me; it compliments my fair complexion.' Catherine sighed. Rosie was incorrigible. In the midst of being told the life changing news of a baby, all she could think about was something new to wear, something possibly glamorous and all for nothing at that.

'You can have it, if that's what you want,' said Catherine. 'I'll fetch if for you right now.' She knew that all their lives would grind to a halt until Rosie got her hands on it. Catherine hurried upstairs and Rosie listened to the banging open and shut of a couple of drawers and when she saw Catherine return with the sweetie pink garment she was up on her feet in a flash and grabbed at it excitedly.

'It's gorgeous!' she exclaimed, rubbing her face against the soft angora wool. 'Let me try it on.' Catherine's hopes were raised. She was off the hook. Her condition had been forgotten in the mad rush to hold a fashion parade. Rosie wanted to know more about Jeremy and his mother as she twirled round the living room in a flurry of pink fluff. Catherine sat down to keep out of the way of the fluorescent dervish and explained under duress that Jeremy had started discussing their future together. With no conferring having taken place between herself and him but obviously plenty with Hilda, he began talking about how things would be living in his mother's house and selling hers. No mention was made of what would happen to Stephen. Rosie actually stood still for a moment to say she would have had none of that. Her eyes were all the while moving sideways to admire herself in the mirror. Catherine's face was flushed as the telling of this brief encounter had brought back the annoyance with Jeremy that she'd felt at the time. 'It would have been like going to prison,' she said angrily. 'I'd rather have spent the rest of my life in Holloway than with that mother and son. And so, that was the end of that little experiment.'

'You get mothers like that,' Rosie agreed with a shake of her head. 'Can't keep their noses out.' Catherine was tempted to say something but stuck her tongue firmly in her cheek instead. 'How did you get out of it?' Rosie asked, genuinely intrigued. 'They sound a ghastly pair.' She was sitting on the sofa running her hands up and down her front, stroking the cardigan as if it were a pet cat.

'Jeremy kept phoning and coming to the door saying his mother was ill over the heads of me, so I pretended that a previous suitor had been in touch and we were trying to make a go of it. He became quite nasty when I pointed out that we were only friends and he called me a two faced besom and stormed off saying I had ruined his life.' Catherine clapped her hands together as if dusting off some unsavoury dirt and added with a happy flourish, 'He hasn't been heard of since, and luckily for you, Rosie, neither has there been any demand for the return of the cardigan.'

Rosie smiled broadly. With her eyes on her reflection she gave another twirl and when she saw Eddie coming back in through the door, she straightened her shoulders and puffed out her well endowed chest to give him the maximum benefit of her latest acquisition, expecting a flattering compliment. However, when Eddie caught sight of his wife, his eyes nearly popped out of his head. 'Good Lord, what's this?' he exclaimed. 'I didn't know there was a fancy dress party in the offing. Are you going as a stick of candy floss?' To make matters worse he started to laugh, bending up and down and clutching at his stomach. Catherine couldn't contain herself any longer and the two of them were soon in hysterics holding their sides with tears rolling down their cheeks while Rosie watched them with increasing anger.

She glared at her husband and tore open the buttons of the fuzzy wuzzy and shoved it angrily back at Catherine. 'Why didn't you tell me I looked a fright?' she shouted accusingly as she hauled back on her favourite black fitted 'cardie' with the tiny white pearl beads stitched on tastefully round the neck and cuffs. Catherine struggled to keep a straight face. This pair were rapidly turning into a music hall turn. Eddie only stopped chortling so he could swill a can of lager down his throat.

'You're a fine one to speak!' snapped Rosie, reaching inside her blouse to haul at a bra strap so that her bosoms at least would be under some kind of control. She wasn't to be beaten by her husband's tomfoolery. 'You would pass as Wurzel Gummidge in that moth eaten jacket of yours,' she sniped, and making a dive for the can, snatched it clean out of his hand. 'No more drink for you tonight, smart Alec, you're drunk as a skunk.' With a toss of her head, she marched out to the kitchen and poured the remains down the sink.

Eddie held out his empty hands with a sad, hard done by look and lovingly caressed the sleeves of his sports jacket. 'Best Harris Tweed, this; had it since my university days,' he said as if to console the insulted piece of attire.

Catherine managed to bite her tongue. She longed to say, 'And it looks like it too.' Chewing the insides of her cheeks to stop herself from laughing at her uncle, she stuffed the shocking pink bundle into a corner of the sofa. 'I'll put this ugly thing in the pile for the charity shop,' was all she said. A sweep of tiredness has gripped her suddenly and all she wanted now was a bit of peace.

Rosie returned and glared at Eddie who was sucking at his unlit pipe. 'It helps me to think clearly,' he explained. A Christmas box of chocolates lying on the coffee table caught Rosie's attention and she was happy again, taking a handful and passing round the rest. 'Catherine's been telling me all about the dating agency,' she said through a mouthful of caramel.

'So what;' snapped Catherine, giving her a look that should have turned her to stone, 'it's hardly worth putting on News at Ten.' She respected her uncle and didn't wanting him thinking she was turning into a man eater.

'What's all this about lads, Catherine?' asked Eddie, prodding at the tobacco in the bowl of his pipe with the tip of a used match. 'I thought the father was a Yank. They left a lot of babies behind after the war. And all it cost them was a pack of nylons, maybe a couple of Woodbines or even no more than a stick of Wrigley's.'

'Eddie, behave yourself!' yelled Rosie. 'Catherine's not like that.'

'I did better than that;' said Catherine resorting to sarcasm, 'I got a T-bone steak and a couple of fish suppers.'

'There must have been love in it somewhere,' Eddie continued. 'I wouldn't give tuppence for that chipper along the road. I hardly slept a wink last night for heartburn from that macaroni cheese pie I got there yesterday.'

Eddie always managed to make Catherine laugh. 'I have to admit that Earl meant more to me than a few greasy chips and I shall always care for him, but we weren't in love; simple as that. I'm glad I'm having his child; I always wanted another one. And I've no regrets either. It's not as if I'm some poor Madam Butterfly; I can afford to bring up the child by myself.'

Eddie cleared his throat uncomfortably, put his pipe back in his mouth and fished a box of matches from his pocket before returning to the back door for a proper smoke.

Rosie waited until Eddie was out of hearing. 'A child has a right to know who their father is,' she said. 'It's not up to you to make that decision for them.' Catherine groaned inwardly, fully aware of what Rosie was hinting at. Not that old chestnut, she thought and began to fluff up the cushions on Eddie's chair. Rosie wasn't going to catch her out.

'I'll call a taxi,' she said, 'Jimmy and Patricia will be wondering where you are.'

Chapter 22

It was Stephen's turn next to be told once Rosie and Eddie were clear away over the Border and back in Essex. 'Have you lost your mind?' he shouted. 'Haven't you heard of contraception?' He was pacing the floor like a man possessed. 'You'll be nearly sixty when the baby's my age. What if it turns out to be one of those tearaways? You'll never cope. And don't expect me to play the heavy handed brother when it's running wild in the streets, staying out all hours. I'll have enough with my own by then.' Stephen was already imagining the future. 'Oh my God, if I start my own family in a couple of years' time it won't be much older than its nieces and nephews!'

'Aren't you jumping the gun somewhat? You've got yourself set up with a make believe brood of teenagers and you're still one yourself.' Catherine was following him round the room like a little puppy trying to convince him that she was doing the right thing. She threw out her arms in exasperation. 'I make a good living, I'm perfectly strong and I'm used to taking care of myself. I can't see the problem.'

'But it won't have a father, at least a father that it knows. How are you going to explain that away? - "Oh, I've forgotten who your father is. He was a passer-by who knocked at my door one dark night and knocked me up while he was at it." - How's that going to feel? My father's dead but at least I know who he was, and I have the certainty that he loved me.' Stephen had his hands up over the sides of his head as if his brain was ready to explode.

Catherine's whole body gave an involuntary jerk as the baby gave its first kick and she had to sit down, steadying herself first by leaning on the arm of the chair. Stephen's vehement protestations on fatherhood had also knocked her sideways, especially when he was himself under the wrong impression regarding his paternity. 'I'll tell Earl one day and I'll tell the child all about its father and make it proud of him.' She had to put her head between her knees as a sudden rush of vertigo whooshed over her.

Stephen knelt beside her. 'I'm sorry, Mum. It's just that I care for you so much. I don't want any more upheaval in your life.'

'I'm all right. It would be strange if you thought differently, but you have to understand that this is what I want.' She patted Stephen's hand. 'You're a good boy and I love you for it.'

'I'll make you some hot sweet tea and we'll leave it for now. I'll get my head round it somehow; don't worry.' From the noise Stephen was making as he rattled among the crockery and cutlery in the kitchen it was going to take some time.

Catherine had allowed him to think it was only another bout of morning sickness but his words had struck a chord and given her a nervous reaction. How would she explain to a little girl that she didn't have a daddy? And worst of all, what if Stephen found out the truth about his? She thought of her own childhood and the surge of excitement whenever her father came home after being at sea. The sure, unshakeable knowledge that she had a strong and constant figure in a big uncertain world each time she put her tiny hand in his huge calloused one was something her dear little baby would never experience.

Catherine could see her daddy yet standing in the kitchen doorway beaming his smile across at her before she ran wildly into his arms and climbed up him like a squirrel up a tree. Tears ran down her cheeks at the realisation that her daughter would never know such joy, and although the love Stephen felt for Gregor wasn't for his real father, at least he'd known the love that special bond brings. Perhaps Stephen was right. Maybe she had taken leave of her senses. Her daughter would never have what she had considered being one of the most wonderful joys of her life - the adoration and protection of a real dad.

No one else seemed to share her impatience to see the baby born. They all threw obstacles in her path: doubt, criticism, unsolicited advice. Even Eddie said she should be out meeting people her own age instead of tying herself down, and went as far as to suggest she should have joined the Labour Party and gone out canvassing instead of landing herself in the pudding club. Rosie's suggestion was that she should have taken up singing in the local church choir. 'You've always had such a sweet voice, Catherine. And think of all the nice people you'd meet there.'

Frank gave her the most support if it could have been interpreted as such. 'There's always been a part of you I could never quite understand, Catherine, but if that's what you want and it makes you happy then I'm right behind you and I wish you well.'

She never heard what Jimmy had to say but she could imagine that the words 'weirdo' and 'Bohemian' would have returned to his vocabulary. He called past occasionally on various pretexts of bearing news about Rosie and Eddie at arranged times when he knew Stephen would be there, but he would only stay long enough for a quick cup of tea and be off. Stephen enjoyed these fleeting visits and they would become quite animated as they discussed sport and the latest developments in the oil fields.

Jimmy leaned forward to offer assistance to Catherine on one occasion when she was nearly full-term and was struggling to prise herself up from the chair. She expected him to pass comment then but it seemed he had enough problems of his own. He hesitated at the door and spoke to her almost as if she were his confidante. 'My job's on the line for real this time. No more reprieves. The company's on the verge of collapse. By next year I'll be at the dole office signing on with nothing else on the horizon.' Catherine looked closely at him and realised he was beginning to look his age. Lines were etched round his mouth no doubt from too much smoking, and worry lines were furrowed in various parts of his face that looked grey and no longer fresh and plump. On hearing these worrying comments, Stephen put down the book titled 'How to Strip Engines' that he'd been about to study and joined them as they loitered on the doorstep chatting. He was only two years away from becoming a fully qualified engineer and was interested to find out the lie of the land for future employment.

'I have to think of moving elsewhere before too long,' Jimmy told them. 'I doubt if I'll find anything for a welder here now or anywhere in the whole country for that matter. It's down south as usual for us Scots now that the rest of the world has come and drained our oil dry. However, it's unlikely I'll find anything at my own trade. I'll have to take whatever's around; driving a bus if need be. That's a good, steady job and would bring in regular money.'

'I was thinking there might be engineering work for me at Folkestone in Kent, building the Channel Tunnel but it's all in the lap of the gods,' replied Stephen in an effort to sound cheerful. He didn't like to see Jimmy so cynical.

'I'm sure you'll do well, son. Does it matter where you go now that your mother is preparing to replace you?' This was the first time Jimmy had made a direct comment about the imminent birth. How was it he could always find some barbed remark that would strike home so accurately?

'You know perfectly well that Stephen will still mean as much to me when the baby comes. He's always wanted to be a big brother.'

'When I was ten maybe, but not when I'm nearly nineteen!' protested Stephen widening his eyes in horror at the thought.

Catherine smiled. 'I don't care what anybody has to say. This baby and I are going to be extremely happy together.' She patted her tummy and smiled the secret smile of pregnant mothers.

Jimmy shook his head and Catherine noticed how he and Stephen exchanged glances and rolled their eyes as if she really were crazy. And as if that weren't enough, he turned just as he was about to open the gate and added, 'My mother and Eddie think you've bitten off more than you can chew, but it's up to you what you do with your life.' Catherine stood with her arms folded contentedly over her bump and smiled. She wasn't going to rise to the bait.

It seemed to Catherine that Jimmy waited momentarily for the standard retaliation of their younger days, but instead she lifted her hand and gave him a pleasant wave. 'Well, I'll be off then,' he said and gave Stephen the standard instruction: 'Work hard and make sure you look after Madonna - and child, when it comes.'

As Catherine watched him disappear into his car that was parked at the end of the street her heart beat in time to a song of jubilation that was ringing joyfully inside her head. 'Bye, bye,

Jimmy!' she said quietly.

Stephen hurried back inside to resume his studies. 'We'll miss Jimmy if he moves away,' he said.

'I think we'll manage just fine,' replied Catherine.

Chapter 23

(Christmas 1988)

Catherine was over the moon with excitement. She had indeed had a daughter, a beautiful girl with blonde, wispy curls that haloed her angel face. She had called the child Arlene which was almost a mixture of her own name and Earl's. It was Arlene's first Christmas and the house was coming down with decorations and musical Santas to create a wonderland for the baby girl. Catherine sat with a glass of ginger cordial while she opened the latest batch of greetings cards. One by one she read the messages of goodwill and set them up in front of her on the mantelpiece. The last one was heavier than the rest and had an airmail sticker on the front. She expected it to be from one of her friends in Canada. However, when she looked more closely, she saw that this one had US Mail on the postmark. It must be from Earl. It was no great surprise. He had sent one the previous year although she couldn't return the compliment. He hadn't included his address, no doubt afraid a card from a woman in Aberdeen would jeopardise his marriage.

She took a sip of the throat burning festive drink and carefully slit open the envelope. As well as a beautiful card showing a crisp winter's scene and wishing her and Stephen the merriest of Christmases, there dropped out a family photograph of himself with his wife Theresa and three children - a teenage boy, a girl of about eleven and baby Hannah who was now nearly two. She was a beautiful curly headed blonde, not unlike Arlene. The girl, Rachel, was an older version of her baby sister, while Luke, the grown up lad, was dark haired and wore a serious frown. Theresa, Earl's fair haired wife had a pretty, elfin look and was one of those women whose age would be difficult to determine. Earl stood side-by-side with her, holding the baby in his arms while the other two youngsters stood in front. His face shone with pride. He had left the snapshot to do the talking for him. It was dated October, 1988, one year exactly after she had last seen him.

Arlene, who had been asleep in her cot upstairs, was

whimpering over the babycom. Catherine carefully propped the picture of her daughter's father against the glass and hurried to her. At five months Arlene was a bonny baby, plump and rosy cheeked and always ready to give a sweet smile that showed off her bumpy gums that already needed soothing jelly on them at night. But she slept well and gave her doting mother every reason to believe she was the most perfect little angel in the whole world. Catherine carried her down to the living room and positioned herself on the white painted nursing chair with the Little Miss Muffet cushion and began to breast feed. What better start in life could a mother give her child? She stared at the happy family on the card and wondered how she, a single parent, could provide all the homeliness and company that Earl's little Hannah was going to enjoy.

But, she argued, there would be neighbours' children, friends from nursery and school, and Stephen was proving himself to be an adoring brother. Maybe in a few years' time there would be little nieces and nephews for Arlene to play with, that is, if Stephen didn't move away as he often threatened to do. Catherine sometimes worried that he never brought home any girl friends, or friends at all for that matter. What if Arlene had a lonely life? No daddy and no brothers or sisters. The misgivings that occasionally played on her mind now grew to gigantic proportions as the faces of Earl's family looked out at her with bright eyes and happy smiles. She gazed at the picture so long that it seemed that Earl turned his head towards his wife and rocked the baby in his arms. Staring fixedly at them had created movement in the same way as she supposed religious statues appeared to come to life when meditated upon. She blinked and the characters steadied.

She looked down at Arlene suckling happily. A surge of injustice washed over her. Arlene was Earl's child too and Catherine couldn't get the family photo out of her mind. It was so unfair. 'I wonder if I should,' she said dreamily to herself, and pulled her sweater down now that Arlene was satisfied. She kissed the feather soft curls and whispered as if it were to be a secret between the two of them, 'I think I'll tell your daddy one day soon about his other little girl. There's bound to be a way of finding his address.' During a particularly low ebb soon after Gregor's death and before Earl had turned up on her doorstep she had tried the friend whose number he had given her many years before but that had been disconnected. She wasn't going to give up now that the idea had come to her. After the New Year she would make it her business to find a way of getting in touch.

Catherine stared into the gas flames of the fire. Eddie and Rosie had just bid a poignant goodbye after their annual visit. It was usual for her to shed a tear or two but on this occasion her sorrow ran deeper than that of the usual farewell which usually carried with it the happy anticipation of the next time. On this particular occasion there had been none of the merry debauchery as Eddie had liked to call their endless visits round old friends and acquaintances, drinking and kissing and dancing. It hadn't mattered whether or not they knew the people well; it was an annual event of unbridled hedonistic joy.

This year, however, had seen a dramatic change in him. All he wanted to do was to stay put either in Jimmy's house or Catherine's. 'I was so hoping to see his old self return,' Rosie had said mournfully, looking into the glass of port that she showed no inclination of wanting to drink. Eddie had been at the back door smoking. Catherine had gone over to where Rosie was sitting uncharacteristically hunched and depressed. 'We're all getting older, Rosie. Perhaps Eddie is feeling his age,' she'd said, digging desperately for a reason that would convince both of them that there was nothing much to worry about. Just at that moment Arlene had wakened and screamed for a feed. Catherine rushed to fetch her and thrust into Rosie's arms the baby and a bottle which she sometimes took as well as the breast. Rosie had gladly snuggled the plump bundle cosily into her bosom, the head leaning into her heart, and smiles of contentment had spread over both their faces.

Catherine had taken the opportunity to join Eddie at the back door. It had been dark since four o'clock that afternoon and a thick haar from the sea had closed in like a shroud. The windows at the backs of the houses opposite struggled to shine even a dusty yellow through the impenetrable fog. Eddie stood alone in this grey mist and inhaled the sweet smelling tobacco of his pipe. Catherine shivered and drew the neck of her jumper up around her throat. At last the silence between them was broken as Eddie took the pipe from his lips and gave a dry cough. 'I'm not myself,' he said, his voice struggling to break free from a hoarse whisper. 'I wish I could explain it but I can't. I hope I haven't spoiled the New Year for you. See, now, at this second, I know why we're up here, but there have been times when I haven't understood a thing that's been going on.' He put the pipe back in his mouth but it had gone out and he shoved it into his jacket pocket. Catherine took his arm. 'Let's go inside. Rosie will be wondering what on earth has happened to us.'

Rosie was wiping Arlene's chin with her bib and the empty bottle rested on the coffee table. She stood up and walked over to her husband and held out the baby to him. Eddie took the child and gently nursed her, pacing round the room until she fell asleep in his arms. He kissed her moist pink forehead and a tear trickled down his cheek. 'I can't for the life of me remember her name,' he said.

Catherine watched the flames dancing as she pondered on the troubles that faced Rosie and Eddie. I must make a point of going to see them this year, she thought. She was hoping that all that was wrong was that Eddie was finding it hard to be retired and needed taken out of himself. But before going to Essex there was another matter of vital importance that had to be settled.

Spring was in the air as Catherine drove to the industrial estate on the outskirts of the town. She parked her car just inside the entrance and hurried to the building that had American Oil emblazoned on the frontage. Like the rest of the company offices it was a characterless modern building of concrete and glass. The scattering of wooden tubs that sprouted daffodils and other spring flowers showed at least an effort to make the drab surroundings more pleasing. Taking a deep breath, Catherine skipped up the steps of American Oil, pushed open the swing door and stepped into the carpeted foyer.

A young girl, not long out of school, sat idly at the reception desk gaping into space as if bewildered at having been left in charge. A blue rectangular plastic badge on her chest gave her name as Emma. Catherine approached, her head held high giving the appearance of having every right to be there. She knew exactly why she had come. It was in order to find Earl's home address. Although new drilling had been suspended, business had carried on with the bare bones of a skeleton staff. Catherine gave the youngster a friendly smile and said a formal good morning. When Emma returned the greeting and offered her assistance, Catherine nodded and smiled.

'You seem just the very person who can help me,' she said and stood hard against the counter leaning on it with one elbow and playing on her chin thoughtfully with her well manicured fingertips. She had to convince the girl that she viewed her as the most important worker in the whole firm. This tactic was duly rewarded by an urgent desire to please on the part of Emma who was actually the most junior member of staff and only been there a week. 'I want to locate someone urgently who used to work for you,' Catherine said quietly with authority, moving her face closer towards the girl as if she were the only person worthy of being taken into her confidence and that it went without question that she was entitled to have anything she asked for.

'When did he work here?' enquired the girl. Her eyes had brightened at the thought of having a task of some importance placed upon her. 'Most of our records have been transferred to our main office in Texas. That's in the United States, you know.'

'Umm, I see,' nodded Catherine as if being told something she didn't already know and she cast her eyes over the computer on the desk. 'Well, we can only hope he's still listed. I'm sure you know how to use a database.'

'Oh yes. We got all that at college.' This girl was unbelievable. Emma was so desperate to sound efficient and knowledgeable that she had already switched the computer screen to a page headed Personnel Records.

'I thought you looked as if you knew what you were doing,' Catherine said approvingly. 'So many people have never used a computer and wouldn't know what I was talking about.'

'Look,' Emma said excitedly, 'I've found the list of transferred employees already. What's the name?' The novice clicked her way down the columns while Catherine watched. She had to clench her fists and bite her tongue to keep herself from snatching the machine in order to speed up the laborious procedure. 'It's Schaefer, Earl Schaefer,' Catherine said, careful to keep the excitement out of her voice. She contented herself by simply craning her neck to watch the names revolving through the Ss. 'It's E-a-r-l not E-r-r-o-l,' she said in a precise tone, realising that any simple mistake could cause him to be overlooked. She felt the perspiration forming under her arms and she was sure the girl could hear her heart thumping. It took a few more revolutions of the screen before they struck gold. There it was as plain as day: Earl Schaefer, with all his particulars set out neatly below.

'That didn't take me long,' said the receptionist with delight at her own success. His address is a street in Houston, Texas, does that seem right?'

'You're so clever,' said Catherine. She couldn't believe her luck. The whole procedure had been literally taking candy from a baby. 'Would you mind awfully writing it down for me?' She had come well prepared and produced pen and paper out of her handbag so there would be no time wasted while the girl went scurrying around searching in cupboards and drawers. Emma wrote the address in her best handwriting and handed it to Catherine. She thanked the youngster who was beaming with pride and swept quickly out through the swing doors and hurried head down back to her car, high heels striking the tarmac like pistol shots as she made her getaway with the precious piece of confidential information.

As she drove off her heart thundered in her chest. She had expected at any moment to feel a heavy hand on her shoulder ready to throw her out of the company building. Arlene was with her neighbour Gloria who had planned taking her and her daughter Becky to the Duthie Park. Catherine's mission had taken less time than planned so she decided to join them. As she drove along the riverside that was lined on one side by clumps of daffodils growing on the banks of the River Dee and the park on the other, she breathed in the beauty of the spring day. The swans and ducks that paddled the surface of the sparkling water had families to look after and did so with a conscientiousness that would have put any human to shame. They would never abandon their young. Arlene had a father. Earl had a right to know he had a daughter. As Catherine turned in to the park she spotted Arlene with Gloria and Becky at the swings and she knew she had done the right thing.

Catherine chewed the end of the pen nervously. This wasn't one of her pieces of fiction concocted to entertain housewives while they drank their morning coffee or sat bored of an evening. When she wrote this letter she had to get every single word and nuance exactly right. She had to make sure Earl knew she didn't want to break up his family and she was certainly not expecting a generous financial payoff. It had to be made plain that her only reason for contacting him was because Arlene might one day need him and he had the right to know he had another daughter. She explained that she hadn't told him sooner because initially she had wanted to save him from scandal. But just as Gregor had never known how she had deliberately seduced him in order to lose her virginity, so Earl must never know that she had intentionally used him to father her child. Whether or not he wanted to accept the fact of having another daughter was entirely up to him. She would understand if he never replied.

Catherine didn't allow herself to build up her hopes and daily fought the urge to open the front door and scan the street for a glimpse of the postman on his way. The postman never did deliver a reply. The result was much more dramatic than she had ever anticipated and almost immediate. Earl didn't arrive on the next flight exactly but pretty soon after. The call that he was on his way nearly took the feet from under her. She'd rushed to answer the phone one Tuesday afternoon expecting it to be a builder who was late coming round to finish off work in the bathroom. It took her a good minute to grasp the full implication of what Earl's urgent American voice was saying. He had made a booking at his usual hotel for the following Monday and would be calling round to see her, and of course his child. Catherine was all of a dither. There was more than tiling a shower room to think about now.

For the rest of that week she hardly slept as she imagined all they would have to say to each other. Would he be pleased? Would he be angry? She had to make sure Arlene was in her prettiest dress and she would have to get her own hair styled at the salon and maybe even a facial at the same time. It was important for her to be seen to be dealing with motherhood efficiently and happily. Earl mustn't go away thinking his daughter was unsuitably cared for.

However, when the time came, their reunion went much more smoothly than she could ever have hoped. There wasn't any of the awkwardness that she had dreaded. Earl rang the doorbell and stepped back into their lives as if he had been there only the day before. As they sat talking, Earl had taken Arlene into his arms and cuddled and kissed her so much that Catherine thought she was never going to be able to settle the baby for the night. They sat that evening in front of a roaring fire talking, and naturally enough the conversation turned to why they had moved from friendship to sleeping together, an act that had made Earl into an adulterer.

Catherine tried to reduce his obvious guilt in that regard. She pushed the point that the seduction had been at her instigation but excused herself by giving loneliness and grief as the reason. 'You were a stranger in a strange land and I was a broken hearted widow,' she said, taking a sip of coffee as if to finalise she'd given explanation enough to satisfy anyone, including his wife. 'I was in pieces at the thought of your leaving, but it was the anticipation of all those empty days stretching ahead of me that caused the greatest suffering. I knew deep down we hadn't fallen in love. Your wife has to know that I have no intention of coming between you, but I do think our darling little daughter has the right to know who her daddy is.'

Earl didn't have much to say on the subject. Catherine had expected a blazing outburst from him but he was not the type of person to apportion blame. Catherine told him that contraceptive devices weren't always reliable and he believed her. In his own eyes he had cheated on his wife and there was no valid reason for having done so. He'd just have to face the consequences, like it or not. 'In years to come,' he said, 'I hope Arlene will come and visit me and meet her other family. In the meantime, I'll make damned sure I see her at least once every year.' He talked long into the night about his family and there was no doubt of his devotion to each and every one of them. As it transpired, this was Earl's wife's second marriage and the two eldest kept in touch with their father. There was no hostility from any quarter and Earl was sure that he would be able to carry on an equally happy relationship with his daughter as that which Theresa allowed her ex-husband with his two children. His wife was open-minded but there were limits. She wanted to meet Catherine for herself, or at least speak to her on the phone.

Catherine agreed. That would be the best way of ironing out any misunderstandings and it was arranged for the following evening. Earl left for his hotel. There was no parting kiss or even a hug. 'I'll phone Theresa and ask her to ring you about eight,' he said firmly. 'She's a reasonable woman and I don't foresee any problems.'

It was obvious from the beginning of the telephone conversation with Theresa that Catherine had met her match. This woman was no walkover. 'After all, I am Arlene's stepmother,' she said, 'just as Earl is Rachel's and Luke's stepfather. I want the little girl to know she has a family over here.' Theresa was establishing her own status right from the outset and Catherine realised only too well that she was determined to manage the complicated situation her husband's infidelity had brought into her life. She was no fool. In her mind she had been extraordinarily lenient by not throwing Earl out on his ear, but the fact that nearly a year and a half had passed with no contact from Catherine was vaguely reassuring that any communication would be purely about Arlene. Theresa's voice took on a harder, even threatening tone. 'I have to tell you that the slightest suspicion of Earl messing around behind my back and we're through and he knows that. He comes home to me every night and he has no need of any other woman. But he is so tolerant of the set up with Rachel and Luke and my ex-husband that I'm willing to do the same for him.'

Catherine was beginning to feel her autonomous hold on Arlene loosening and it even seemed possible that her daughter might slip through her fingers all together and into the hands of this formidable woman. Had she made a mistake? Theresa was every bit as involved as Earl and she finished off the call by saying, 'Any time Arlene needs us we'll be there for her.'

Catherine felt the role of sole parent she had cherished being swept away by this tough cookie but she knew in her heart that this arrangement was in Arlene's favour. She wouldn't be living surrounded by a large family but they would be there for her all the same, albeit across the wide Atlantic Ocean. Catherine was glad she'd written the letter. Her little girl would always have loved ones to turn to.

Until now Stephen had been the most important person in Arlene's life after her mother. With his constantly talked about plans for marriage and a large family, Arlene would probably never have any need of her American relatives. But so far there was no steady girlfriend. Stephen hated it when his mother brought this up. 'I like things done properly,' he said. 'Study is what matters to me for now. I don't want to waste precious time gadding about on meaningless dates. When I'm qualified I'll meet a decent woman who will want a settled family life as much as I do. I already have a picture of her in my mind and so far none of those frivolous girls I see in the RGIT have matched up.' Catherine tried not to worry about the evenings he spent alone in his bedroom with nothing but books, music and dreams. Hadn't she been much the same? When the time was right he would find a quiet, home loving girl and set out on the life he wanted as head of a happy household. In that respect he was like his father, Jimmy.

Chapter 24

(Early 1990)

Another year passed in utter contentment for Catherine. Arlene provided her with the joy she had thought was beyond her reach. Stephen was a doting brother and helpful son. His studies were going well and his results so far showed an aptitude for engineering that would guarantee excellent prospects for gaining employment all his life wherever he might choose to want to live. He would have the world in the palm of his hand. Even Jimmy's visits no longer bothered her. As long as she made him a cup of tea and asked how his family were doing there was no problem. If Stephen was at home they would chat about work or sport. Life was treating her well at last.

One worry was blighting the horizon, however, and try as she might to put it to the back of her mind there came a time when she could no longer ignore it. Things were going awry in Basildon. Rosie's phone calls were becoming more frequent and they weren't the chatty, newsy ones that Catherine had once looked forward to. They were longwinded diatribes about Eddie and his various tantrums and arguments. Rosie would be on the verge of tears. Always she ended by telling Catherine that you had to live with somebody to know what they were really like. The hilarious double act that used to keep Catherine in stitches carried a tinge of tragedy now that suggested a not so happy ending. Eddie was forgetting things all the time. He'd been on the phone the other day to Catherine but always managed to turn his stories around to blame other people, especially his wife. 'Twice we've had to fork out the cost of a locksmith because of her carelessness, and something should be done about how much they charge. Thirty-four pounds for fifteen minutes' work, I ask you, and I've told Rosie that she was supposed to be carrying a spare set, but you know what she's like - could give lessons to mules on stubbornness.'

Rosie's version was of course different. 'Eddie loses everything.

His bunch of keys was lost somewhere in the house, God knows where; could have been in the oven for all I know. They were in the fridge last time and in his sock drawer the time before that. We'll have to fit another lock tomorrow and of course Eddie won't stump up the cost of a professional doing it. He's buying the replacement from the hardware stall at the market and putting it on himself. That'll be more fun and games. Even when the keys turn up he has to have a new lock fitted in case anyone else has found them and made copies.'

Catherine listened patiently as each took it in turn to slate off the other. She said yes and no at all the right places to keep both of them happy. She found it easier just to humour them along. At least Rosie's attention was being taken away from the Stephen and Jimmy saga while dealing with Eddie's latest antics.

Catherine eventually made it to Essex. In all conscience she couldn't leave Rosie any longer to deal with Eddie alone; after all he was her uncle. The situation had worsened and Rosie had begged her to come and see for herself. From the moment she arrived Catherine was in no doubt that Rosie hadn't been exaggerating. However much Catherine and Rosie chatted, deliberately bringing up tales from the past that would raise a laugh, Eddie rarely joined in, and when he did there was no spark. His only topic was to complain that Rosie had started hiding his things. 'She stole my spectacles and put them under the sofa so I couldn't read the paper or watch television. I think she's jealous of the attention I pay to newsreaders, especially that dark haired one with the fringe. She wants to keep me all to herself, but I'm too young yet to want to sit drinking tea and holding out my arms to help her wind her blessed skeins of wool.'

Normally Eddie had doted on Rosie and nothing had been too much bother for him. He had loved listening to his wife telling him their plans for the day. After years of living on his own, she had been a godsend and he had loved having her companionship to fill his retirement. Now all he did was moan. 'What do you think is wrong with her?' he'd whine. 'Couldn't you have a word?'

Catherine made a point of sympathising with each one in turn. What else could she do?

Jimmy had been no help when Catherine had brought up the subject during one of his visits to see Stephen. He said they were just getting on each other's nerves from spending too much time together. Apparently Patricia had also suggested he should see them on their 'home territory' but he had reneged, saying he valued his two weeks ashore with her too much and with unemployment growing daily there was no way he could take time off. His imminent redundancy had been on the cards for years so it seemed like just another lame excuse. 'Why don't you go?' he had said to Catherine with a frown. 'It's not as if you're doing much else.'

'So that's how highly you regard my writing and running a home single handed for Stephen and Arlene?' she'd snapped back. Jimmy had opened his mouth to make some kind of apology. He knew that flush of anger rising up over her neck and cheeks spelt danger. He was right. Catherine turned bright red and snarled fiercely, 'So if there's no husband with a pile of dirty shirts and underpants, a woman's life is wasted.'

'I didn't mean it like that. It's just that I'm no good at these things. I bring home the money and that's my contribution to running a home. Anyway, you know what my mother will start on about if she has me to herself out of earshot of Patricia – the question of Stephen being mine. She stopped challenging you because you already had enough on your plate with Gregor and then a new baby.' As he stood up to leave, he spoke more gently. He had to persuade her to be the one to go to Basildon. 'Sorry to have missed the lad this visit, but if you do find the time to investigate what's going on in Essex, I will appreciate it; honest.' Catherine rolled her lips inwards and held them tightly between her teeth. She was determined not to start shouting and let him see he still had it in him to raise her temper.

She held her voice steady as she replied, 'Whatever I do for Eddie and your mother is for them alone. Don't ever imagine I'll do anything for you. Tolerating your coming here once in a while is as far as it goes.' Instead of holding the heavy front door open as they said their goodbyes she let it slam at his back. She leaned against it. Sometimes she accepted his coming round with barely a second thought but at others she just wished he would frizzle up somewhere and disappear off the face of the earth. There really was no one but herself to try and find the best solution for Rosie and Eddie. She would take Arlene to Essex right away. Stephen would have to fend for himself.

Rosie ran to embrace the pair of them at Stansted Airport and fidgeted uneasily until their luggage was reclaimed and she could usher them into a taxi and hasten to Basildon. Catherine was shocked to see how thin Eddie had become and noticed with concern the black circles round Rosie's usually bright eyes. Eddie was overly excited whenever she stepped through the door. 'Oh, Maggie, I thought you'd never come.' Catherine opened her mouth to correct him but Rosie put a finger to her lips. 'It's Catherine, dear, Maggie's daughter,' she said gently, 'and just look at this adorable little girl. Her name's Arlene.' Needless to say she had gathered the child into her arms as soon as her coat was off and was showering her with kisses. When she did at last release her from her suffocating embrace, the toddler ran behind her mother and peeped out shyly. 'Look, darling, it's your Uncle Eddie,' Catherine said picking up her daughter and holding her out for Eddie to kiss. Her own tear filled eyes were hidden behind Arlene's blonde curls.

Rosie was right. Eddie was failing dramatically and confusion was setting in. He was nearly seventy-three after all and had to grow old sometime; but to lose his mind - that would be too much to bear. The doctor suspected a series of mini strokes to be the reason behind his confusion and irritability. Because of the damage caused to the brain he could forget whether or not he had eaten as well as having spells of lucidity when he was able to pass an opinion on any political change he considered to be unjust. It was his memory that was increasingly impaired rather than his intelligence and the implementing of the Poll Tax was his latest hobby horse. There was a well-advertised demonstration due to take place in Trafalgar Square on 31st March and Rosie begged Catherine to take him. At first Catherine refused. She'd lost interest in the latest political protests. She was more interested in searching kiddies' fashion shops for outfits that would suit Arlene.

'So what's happened then to all your principles?' scoffed Rosie. 'After all it was standing up for them that got you where you are in the first place.' Catherine had to admit she had turned from campaigning for the greater good into making sure she personally always got what she wanted. Surely this was a chance for her to fight some cause, climb her way back into investigative journalism and re-energise her way out of the cosy tales of domestic bliss that were now her bread and butter.

'Go on;' said Rosie, 'it's only for one day, and think of the good it'll do Eddie. He's desperate for something exciting to happen in his life. I'm sure it's boredom that's turning his brain to water.' Catherine knew Rosie was right. And it would do herself good to taste again the sense of being involved with a worthwhile cause. The local Anti-Poll Tax group had organised a bus leaving from the community centre. Eddie was beside himself with excitement when Catherine announced they were going. He was like a child. Every day for a week he asked if they were going up to London. When the 'demo day' finally did dawn he was frantic and tore along the street to where the bus would be collecting them a good half hour before it was due.

Once on the coach, he calmed down and they reminisced about their first chance meeting more than twenty years before at an Easter peace march. 'You changed my life,' said Eddie wistfully. 'I was well on the way to becoming a lonely old man.'

'And we wouldn't have had the pleasure of knowing you,' Catherine replied and turned to give him a quick peck on the cheek. As they sped through East London and headed west up towards the Embankment, a fleet of buses full of protesters with banners were heading in the same direction all set to make this one of the most powerful of all demonstrations. 'We'll soon get these Yanks out of Vietnam,' said Eddie loudly, holding up his clenched fist as he spoke. 'It's about time they put an end to that napalm bombing. It's inhuman.' Catherine opened her mouth and closed it again. Was she hearing right?

By now they had reached the streets near Trafalgar Square and the driver ushered them off so he could clear the way for others to stop. He shouted instructions for the return journey but the protesters were rushing off without taking time to listen to details. 'Be back here, same place, at five o'clock and wait. I'll be here as soon after then as possible. It all depends on the traffic.' Concentrating on the busy road ahead, he revved the engine and disappeared along a side street.

Catherine kept quiet about Eddie's earlier comment. He was animated and ushered her along with their group that was speeding on ahead anxious to position themselves near the front to hear the speakers. Eddie hoisted the placard he'd been impatiently carrying by his side ever since they'd been dropped off. 'What do we want ...? Peace! When do we want it...? Now!' he shouted and looked round for people to join him in the chant. But they were gawping at him in amazement. A few had even started to laugh and point, probably thinking he was some sort of comedian. Catherine had to stop him before he made a complete fool of himself. 'Uncle Eddie,' she said quietly, tugging at his sleeve, 'the Vietnam War ended on May Day, 1974.' He turned and stared at her with bewilderment in his eyes and for a moment she thought he was going to argue. But he fell silent as he took in what was written on the banners around them. 'Stop The Poll Tax' was the prevailing message. 'I was having a joke,' he said but a nervous tremble shook his voice.

'It's all right, Eddie,' said Catherine linking her arm through his. 'I understand. We'd been talking about a Vietnam march only minutes before, but these other people weren't to know that.' She was as desperate as he was to find any excuse for this aberration rather than face the real nightmare that was haunting them with such increased frequency that they'd soon be forced to wake up to the grim reality that the strokes were taking their toll. She understood now why Rosie was so frazzled.

It turned out to be quite a day. As soon as Catherine sensed that trouble was breaking out between the police and a swathe of the protesters, she managed to steer Eddie on to the sidelines and past the line of stewards who were struggling to maintain calm and order. It was only by positioning herself between Eddie and a couple of dishevelled policemen did she prevent him from giving them a mouthful. Thankfully, most of their contingent managed to make a clean getaway, albeit an hour later than planned, but three of their young lads had allowed their tempers to flare and joined in the melee, throwing stones and empty drinks tins at the constabulary. Word had it that a bobby's helmet had been knocked off which was proved to be true as another youngster at the back of the bus who had managed to escape arrest was proudly wearing it as a trophy. By now his mates would surely be in the cells somewhere waiting to be tried and fined.

As the coach drew in to the community centre it was met by a crowd of near hysterical neighbours who had been following the News. Rosie was at the head of them trying to pull the door of the bus open. Apparently news reports on all channels had been equally stirring. Three hundred and forty people had apparently been arrested, tube stations had been closed, smoke and flames were rising from Trafalgar Square and placards and cans were being hurled at arresting police officers, not to mention that a group of protesters had attacked the police with bricks. Much of central London had had to be cordoned off due to the riots and wasn't safe for theatre goers or ordinary sight seers.

Instead of a troublesome, possibly bloodied coach load of rioters, a peaceful and justifiably triumphant crew of protesters filed off. Rosie made a grab for Eddie who she was sure would have been in the thick of the trouble. 'News reports are always more dramatic for the viewers than for those actually there,' said Catherine. They were both flushed with exhilaration. 'Just get me home in front of that telly,' said Eddie. 'I want to see what propaganda they're sending out this time.' Catherine ushered Rosie away before word reached her of how three of their neighbours had been hauled into police vans and how near Eddie had come to joining them. She would hear about it soon enough through the local community grapevine.

'There's always a trouble making minority and I'm afraid it's them that'll make the headlines,' murmured Catherine. The majority intention was simply to make a point. She was remembering the demonstrations of her young days when Anarchists had frequently been in the middle of scuffles that had won all the media attention. 'It's the stupid way they shout out "Anarchista" in Spanish as if they were still in Spain in the 1930s,' she said tutting and shaking her head.

'And didn't they just make a right balls up of that too!' replied Eddie heatedly who had fought in the International Brigade against Franco as well as in Italy against Mussolini where he had been taken prisoner at Anzio before escaping and making it home. Now he was older he was referring to his life of active service more and more often.

'Mind your language,' said Rosie to Eddie before throwing Catherine a warning look and mouthing that Spain was a topic to be avoided. 'To hear you,' she said squeezing his arm to make sure she got him safely and quickly home, 'that Brigade of yours seemed to spend more time arguing and fighting amongst yourselves than you ever did against the Generalissimo. Not much wonder he sent you all packing.' Her simplistic analysis never failed to rile Eddie no end, and on such a day as he'd had, her comments made the veins stand out on his forehead and throb like the pipes to a steam boiler that had become overheated and were ready to burst. Worry had made Rosie irritable. 'There's been far too much excitement for one day. I left little Arlene screaming in Mrs O'Riley's across the road over an hour ago. I only hope she hasn't worked herself into a fit.'

'That's not true!' Eddie shouted at the newscaster who had announced that seventy thousand protesters had taken to the streets against the new government levy. 'There were at least a hundred thousand. I can estimate a crowd no bother the amount of football matches I've been to.' Catherine and Rosie let him have his say. After all, didn't they agree with him about the injustice of this new tax? Later on that evening when Eddie was asleep in front of the News after shouting at the television that the reporting was all one-sided, Catherine offloaded her fears to Rosie. 'There may be more to his problem than just age. He's not quite seventy-three. Think about it, you're sixty-nine and have more than all your wits about you.' Sadly she told Rosie about Eddie's various mix-ups that day. She had to lay it on the line or Rosie would do nothing about it. Rosie nodded. 'You're right. I sometimes forget names but not to the same extent. I sometimes wonder if he knows who he is himself. I thought mini strokes just happened and then got better, but the hospital was right, he has to get his blood pressure down and he won't co-operate. They've left his brain damaged and who knows if there can be improvement at his age?'

Catherine spoke to her uncle next morning at the breakfast table. He was calm and deep in thought. She needn't have worried about how she was going to broach the subject because he did it for her. 'I'm worried, Catherine,' he said hoarsely. 'There's something far wrong with me. It's not only Rosie that's noticed.' He stopped and his eyes widened with anxiety. He didn't want to say any more, but he was a sensible man and recognised that something was wrong. 'I may be losing my memory, but I'm not stupid. I'm wise enough to know that there is something crazy going on here and I can't control it.'

'I'll come with you to the doctor if you like. I know that Rosie is desperate for you to get help,' Catherine replied, pouring out their second cup of tea that morning. Rosie came in from the back garden where she'd been hanging out washing. 'Sit down, girl,' said Eddie, 'we've something to tell you, and I think you know what it is already.'

'It's all right, dear,' said Rosie putting out a hand to squeeze his. 'I know all about the strokes. Maybe if you get stronger medicine to keep your blood pressure down it won't get any worse.'

'It'll take more than some pharmaceutical concoction to lower my blood pressure when we have a government like this one in power,' he raged and banged his fist on the table making all the cutlery and plates on it rattle.

It was a wrench for Catherine when the time came for her to return home. Arlene too threw a tantrum for good measure in the airport lounge when she realised that Rosie who had come to see them off wasn't travelling with them. Catherine struggled to carry her screaming daughter bodily on to the small aircraft.

'We'll be back soon,' she managed to shout over her shoulder to Rosie who was beyond speech and had her face buried in a fistful of Kleenex. Eddie had decided he would rather help with the painting of the walls of the canteen at the community centre. Being in the company of snivelling women wasn't really his cup of tea. If truth be told he was bluffing. He had forgotten Catherine was leaving that day and was headed along the road with a collection of brushes and rollers when Rosie chased after him. What choice had he but to make an excuse? Admitting that he had forgotten such an important event would have been the same as telling the world he was losing his mind.

Strangely enough it had been that very morning that a letter arrived from the hospital. The test results were back. Rosie had showed them to Catherine. The likely cause was indeed a series of small strokes that had left patches of the brain starved of oxygen. Eddie was to be given medication and a salt-free diet to follow in order to keep his blood pressure down.

'And you've to stop all that shouting at these newsreaders on the television,' said Rosie, wagging her finger at him as if he were a naughty child. 'They can't hear you so you may as well keep your opinions to yourself.'

Eddie screwed up his face. 'The day I stop putting in my tuppenceworth is the day they nail me in a coffin and drop me in my grave.' He lifted a spoon of muesli to his mouth and gagged. 'And that day can't come soon enough; life isn't worth living without my bacon roll in the mornings.'

Jimmy had finally decided to throw in the towel as far as finding work in the floundering oil industry in Aberdeen went and was heading for East London to find a job. There were a few possibilities there and also he would be nearer his mother. Perhaps he had a conscience after all thought Catherine. Some assistance from Jimmy would certainly not go amiss and who better than him to bring some cheer into his poor mother's life and a male companion for Eddie to compare notes with while watching Saturday afternoon sport.

Chapter 25

At home in Aberdeen, not a day went past when Catherine didn't wait with baited breath for yet another sorry tale from Rosie. She found the rapid deterioration of such a learned man as Eddie beyond her comprehension. It made the rest of her complicated life seem quite acceptable in comparison. Everything was running like clockwork between herself and Earl. He phoned monthly and had sent updated and larger photographs of himself and his family so that Arlene would always know who they were. Stephen was doing well at college although he had been on his own far too much for Catherine's liking. He didn't have friends popping round and even when she was there it was as if he had lost the power of speech and kept disappearing to his room to listen to music and that's where he was now, lying on his bed with earphones on. Punk rock was his 'thing' and any time Catherine complained, he insisted that his music and especially the words made more sense than her wishy washy out of date flower power sentiments. 'It's the music I used to listen to on the radio in my room when we first came to Aberdeen. It matched my feelings of anger at not being accepted. It's remained at the top of my list ever since. I'll never tire of it. This music stands for justice,' he said, 'but you won't take time to listen to the words. You don't like to admit that wearing a bunch of bells round your neck never changed the world and has had its day.'

'Your music's too loud,' she said. 'And it's aggressive,' she argued.

'See, you always know best, Mother, and you can't pass judgement because you've never listened to the words. They're anti Nazi, anti racism and above all it's all about personal responsibility and making your own way in life. And don't start on about drink and drugs. Your sixties songs were full of it. To hear you, you'd think I covered my hair in margarine and sugar and stood it on end, coloured it orange and purple and spent my days hanging around statues in Union Street drinking cider.'

Catherine didn't know what to say. She knew how lucky she

was to have a son who stuck into his studies and he was correct in saying she'd never given his choice in music a chance. She thought back to the glue sniffers in the flat they'd occupied and wondered what had become of them. Perhaps a new type of protest music had been needed because the television and newspapers were always full of the seeming hopelessness among present day youth. Maybe her ways were out of touch now and namby pamby. It wasn't so much the sentiments of the music that got her down but the lack of romance in them. She started on at him again, 'But you won't get girls to dance to that noise.' She was desperate to see him laughing and enjoying himself with a girlfriend.

'Just leave me alone,' came his standard reply followed with, 'I have the girl I want in mind. When the time's right I'll have her, okay?'

'But who is this girl? You haven't even met her,' said Catherine, frightened that her son might be slipping into a world of fantasy, 'and there's not a person living who's perfect.' She paused and gave a half laugh before adding, 'Certainly not me. Why don't you go out and have fun?'

'Jimmy has done all right for himself with Patricia,' retorted Stephen and Catherine couldn't help but detect a scornful note creeping into his voice as he continued. 'Dad was perfect too, if only he'd been appreciated sooner.' Catherine allowed the pain of this comment to pass over her head. Stephen's next few words made her catch her breath and her insides squirmed as if something evil had crept into her intestines. 'Jimmy's forever bragging about Sophie and Sylvie. So, you see, there are good young women around.'

Catherine remembered the warnings from Jimmy that Stephen and the girls must be kept apart. Until now she had thought them the ravings of a dirty mind. But now she wasn't so sure. With a struggle she kept her voice from shaking. 'Jimmy seems to have found a job driving tube trains in East London. The whole family is on the verge of moving down there. Apart from the work, he wants to be near to Rosie.'

Stephen gave his mother a sideways glance and turning up the sound began nodding his head in time to the music. 'As if I'd bother with anyone that had anything to do with this family,' he sneered. By 'this family' she knew he meant her. How she longed to pull him into her arms and comfort him, tell him how much Gregor had meant to her, and in spite of Earl and little Arlene, there was many a night she spent crying into her pillow for him. As she stood at the door of his room she turned and said, 'I know I wasn't always the perfect mother but I did my best. What more can you ask?' Whether he had heard her or not she couldn't tell but he rose from his bed and slammed the door after her shouting, 'Why don't you just leave me alone?' Then he proceeded to bang open and shut cupboards and drawers all the while muttering loudly enough for her to hear, 'The sooner I finish this course and get a place of my own the better. I don't think I can survive another year of this.'

Catherine's heart jumped into her throat and almost choked her when she received the phone call from Jimmy announcing that Eddie had taken another stroke. Rosie couldn't possibly look after him and there was no way Jimmy could give up his new job. Patricia had to stay in Aberdeen for the next few months to see Sylvie through school. Sophie could live in at the nurses' home until she finished her training and then the plan was that Patricia would travel between London and Aberdeen sharing her time between each until their house was sold.

One way or another they had no choice but to put Eddie into a nursing home. Rosie came on to the phone; she was crying. 'Jimmy's quite right. He's done enough for us and I can't lift Eddie on my own. They're sending him home from hospital next week and he can't even walk. I don't know what's going to become of us.' Catherine tried to put Rosie's mind at rest while running all the possibilities for coping through her mind like a computer. 'You've done everything you can for him. Without your care he would have been dead months ago. Give me a couple of days to sort myself out here and I'll come down. Don't worry, we'll view a few of the local nursing homes until we find the place that's right for Eddie, poor soul, but these places are a lot better nowadays or so I hear. The nurses are kindness itself.'

Stephen was given a list of instructions, the freezer was stocked with enough food to see him through an invasion and yellow Post-its were stuck to every available surface: window cleaner, grass cutter, emergency plumber and electrician, dry cleaner, refuse collector – not one service went unmentioned. Stephen heaved a sigh of relief when his mother left and made his way round to the local fish and chip shop for a greasy pie and chips and a bottle of Vimto before attaching himself to his headset and blasting out The Stranglers at such a volume it made his ears ring when the tape finished.

The atmosphere in Basildon was one of despair. Rosie was never without a hanky scrunched up in her hand. Jimmy hung around grim faced not knowing what to do. Eddie's sunken eyes followed everyone's every move like a lost puppy and the look of desperation in them as he tried to form words made Catherine's heart ache. She would sit beside him and relate to him as far as she could all that was happening in the community centre and on the News. An occasional visitor would drop by and give him a smile but most thought that because he couldn't speak that they shouldn't speak either. Catherine would encourage them to keep him informed of any little piece of gossip while Jimmy could always be relied on to make a cup of tea. Eddie's eyes certainly lit up when he heard that the local vicar had been seen out with one of the ladies of the WRI holding hands on a park bench. Catherine made Eddie's mouth twist upwards into a smile when she said, 'I'm afraid that now Rosie has wind of it, they may as well put it straight on to News at Ten.'

Catherine had organised visits to a couple of nursing homes in the area, one of which was only a few streets away in a converted Victorian mansion that must have belonged at one time to a wealthy merchant. Rosie and Catherine sat in the reception area of Sycamore Lodge. The cloying smell of industrial strength disinfectant hit them full on the face as soon as they entered through the front door. There was no disguising their agitation. Rosie clasped her hands to her face, the fingertips digging into her eyes, not to stop tears but to prevent herself from seeing where this latest stage in age's cruel advance had brought her. Catherine gazed downwards and seemed intent on twisting her fingers out of their sockets. Neither spoke. The only movement of Rosie's mouth was to chew her lips and scrape her teeth across the soft skin until it looked as if she had some form of eczema. Catherine's face on the other hand was set without expression as if every last shred of emotion had left her and she had turned to stone. Her fingers were knotted on her lap and she leaned forward with eyes closed as if in a trance or possibly prayer. They had seen such horrific establishments in their tour around these homes that it was for the time being beyond their belief that this one might be better. 'After all,' said Catherine with a note of cynicism, 'weren't these nursing homes simply money making industries where compassion was thin on the ground and the elderly were easy prey.' However, they were in for a pleasant surprise.

At last the heavy oak door of the office squeaked open and Constance Massie, the matron, emerged with a welcoming smile on her ruddy cheeks. Her baleful eyes shone with spiritual goodness. Rosie said later that she reminded her of an ox coming into their lives to shoulder for them the yoke that had grown too burdensome for them to carry on their own.

Rosie began speaking so fast and asking so many questions that she was almost incoherent. Fortunately the matron understood and let her pour the last dregs of nervousness out of her system. Catherine on the other hand had slipped further into a morose silence and hardly acknowledged the woman's introduction to herself and the building. She stuffed the fistful of leaflets handed to her by Constance into her handbag for later when she might have the stomach to open them. Rosie on the other hand was impatient for information and flicked through the pages of her bundle asking questions on every possible aspect of her husband's future care.

Constance showed Rosie and Catherine round the high

ceilinged premises and well maintained grounds sheltered by a wall of sycamore trees and filled with beds of tea roses. All the while she was telling them the history of the building and sharing with them the various positions of responsibility she had held over the years. In the common room, Rosie talked patiently to one or two of the residents and waved to others for whom this was their only means of communication. Some lifted their arms and smiled in return.

There were the unfortunate few who slumped to the side or curled forwards in their chairs oblivious to reality and lost in a world of their own confused memories or horrific dreams. Occasional cries of fear from their dry cavernous mouths brought it home that some inhabited dark, scary places beyond normal human imagination. Others, however, had managed to retain their personalities despite advancing years. Rosie had noticeably calmed down and chatted sensibly to Constance showing her genuine concern and asking questions relevant to the needs of Eddie should he come to live there. She had come to terms with the fact that Eddie would benefit from their round the clock care.

Catherine took time to offer up a prayer of thanks to God for taking Gregor before he had to end his life in a place like this. Constance noticed her discomfort and gently asked her opinion. Catherine commented that most of the patients seemed unable to hold a conversation and that her uncle was an intelligent, well-read man, the insinuation being that he wouldn't belong in such a place.

The matron nodded and the flicker of a smile played across her lips. She'd been in the business for too long not to recognise the signs. There was little she hadn't experienced in the course of her nursing career. 'I see,' she said with not even a hint of having taken offence. She was more than ready to deal with Catherine and her attitude to the elderly. 'If you would like to follow me I think you may learn some points of interest about the people I have in my care,' she said, 'but let's take one immediate example before we set off.' She nodded in the direction of a frail old lady who might have been made of paper she was so thin and fragile. The woman was tapping on the side of her armchair and singing tunelessly.

Constance put an arm round her shoulder. 'You're playing well today, Esther,' she said kindly and Esther responded with a ready smile before resuming her song. 'Come and see her room,' Constance said, and led Catherine and Rosie along the corridor that was lined with lovely prints of well known paintings on the walls and plants on the windowsills.

Rosie and Catherine followed obediently. Constance had an air of authority you wouldn't argue with in spite of her kindness. 'I want you to have an idea of the size of our rooms and how residents can bring in their own furniture and possessions to make themselves feel more at home.' They stopped at a door that had Esther Goldmeyer etched on a brass nameplate. Constance turned the handle and opened the door wide. Rosie and even Catherine gasped in amazement. The walls of the room were covered in amazing photographs of a beautiful young woman in a variety of exquisitely coloured and sequined dance dresses spinning round the floor in the arms of a dashing young gentleman in a dark suit. A glass cabinet was crammed full of cups and shields. On the chest of drawers there was a further array of photographs displayed in silver frames. 'Esther was a competition ballroom dancer in her time,' explained Constance. 'That gentleman was her husband. He was a policeman with the Met before retiring to his hometown in Essex.'

Without waiting for comment, she reminded them of the man who had just thrown a spoon across the dining room scattering custard all over the floor. Her expression had grown smug now that the visitors were beginning to realise the full value of her charges. With pride she directed them to the inside of his room. Stanley's golfing trophies were out on show alongside the pictures of his family and hordes of grandchildren. 'Stanley was a bank manager before a brain tumour struck him down. The operation saved his life but not his mind.' Catherine took a sweep of sadness and felt the tears welling up in her eyes. The golfing trophies had brought back fond memories of Gregor and she felt profoundly ashamed of herself for ever passing judgement on these people whose contribution to society had been equal to if not more than her own.

'Everyone who makes their home here was young once and as full of hope as anyone else on the threshold of life,' said Constance gently. 'I expect that none of them planned on being ill or ever dreamt they would end up helpless and in need of care. They've all served humanity and now they deserve our kindness.' Catherine was suitably chastened. Rosie took the matron's hand in hers. 'I think we've found the right place for my Eddie. I know he'll be well looked after here.' The sociable Rosie was obviously itching to get back to the common room for a chat with some of the residents.

There was no holding her. 'I could do some voluntary work here,' she said excitedly to Catherine. She was remembering her days from before she met Eddie when she had been employed at a home for unmarried mothers. 'I could take craft classes, maybe making simple collages with scraps of cloth. I have some beautiful remnants at home.' She was already in the future helping out and she'd be near to Eddie at the same time. In a twinkling she and Constance were head-to-head thrashing out the details. Rosie had carved out a worthwhile future involving Eddie.

Catherine meanwhile was far away in her own thoughts. For six years she had devoted her time and energies to Gregor and she had been glad to do so. There were no regrets and she had never stopped loving him with all her heart. But what if his time had not been measured so accurately right from the outset? What if his had been a slow deterioration and his mind had failed him as well as his body? Could she have endured watching him fall apart day by day? Would she have been so willing to sacrifice twenty years or even more tending to his most intimate needs? His decline had been quick and his mind had remained sound. She knew deep inside she hadn't been capable of more and doubted if she deserved the volumes of praise that his colleagues had bestowed upon her. He had continued to advise and assist in important research work almost to the end and had died at the very pinnacle of his life, respected and valued as a person with intelligence and integrity. She was glad, not only for him but for herself too if she were honest. Had Gregor ended up as one of those human shells containing little else but a heart that refused to stop beating, bowed, broken and staring as if their souls had already departed, it would have broken her. She offered a prayer of thanks to God there and then that her husband had been taken so mercifully.

Rosie noticed her distractedness and as if reading her mind said in a tone that was a strange mixture of comfort and defiance: 'Eddie will be fine here. I've spoken to several of these people and they're quite able to be good company for him. You're seeing them from a point of view that's been tarnished from having nursed a sick man for so long. I want to keep my Eddie alive for as long as I can whatever it takes.' With that she sniffed, gave a toss of her head and made for the door.

Eddie had his moments of lucidity that would break through the fog of his confused mind. Sometimes he called Rosie 'Daisy' and he always called Catherine 'Maggie'. Every day he would listen to the News and was perfectly aware of who the Prime Minister was. He could also talk about political situations from the past and out of the blue began speaking about the Italian Canale family who had cared for him after he had escaped from a prisoner of war camp in Anzio. It was the day-to-day that gave him problems. Sometimes he asked for his lunch when he had already eaten and of course he kept on wanting to go home.

Sadly another stroke was on its way and one morning he let out a fearsome yell as it hit him. Rosie heard the scream from the adjoining activities room and came running in expecting to have to help with a resident who had fallen or was having a tantrum. She stopped in her tracks momentarily when she saw Eddie lurch forward out of his chair and fall foaming at the mouth on to the floor. In a split second the carers were at his side with Rosie kneeling beside him. But Eddie wasn't to be beaten yet. After a few days of bed rest after this latest small stroke, he was back in front of the television telling the new Prime Minister, John Major, how to run the country.

Rosie managed to hide her feelings while she was in the nursing home but when she got home she would cry. Her evenings were spent flicking through the pages of photograph albums reminding her of happier times. Jimmy's planned move to East London to be near his mother now the depression in Aberdeen had cost him his job was well under way and Patricia had joined him now that Sylvie had left school and was training as a beauty therapist nearby.

Patricia used to take Rosie out round the markets looking at material and into the sari shops. Rosie was so overcome by the colours and patterns of the cloth that she would be lifted out of her melancholy and would be cheerful again. She loved the friendliness of the Asian women and would gladly return the hugs and handshakes when they called her 'Bhanji' the Hindi/Urdu word for sister.

Now that Patricia was a regular visitor Catherine was free to set off for home to check on Stephen who saw her return as an intrusion into his private, solitary life.

Chapter 26

Jimmy had finally lost his job as a welder on the rigs as the slump in the oil industry cut ever deeper and he'd been forced to head for East London as a tube train driver. 'I'll soon work my way up to station manager,' he said to everyone, cocky as ever. He was determined to make something of himself. The big times were over, but he wasn't going to hang around signing on at the Jobcentre for a measly giro cheque and meagre handouts. He had too much pride. He preferred to seek his fortune at the other end of the country.

Although he'd been to Basildon on numerous occasions, it wasn't what you might call his 'cup of tea'. He fancied the buzz of East London rather than the outlying towns of Essex that were expanding due to increasing numbers of indigenous Londoners fleeing the massive influx of immigration that had flooded the East End in waves since the sixties. Incomers were drawn from overseas to work in hospitals and factories or to open shops and restaurants that brought exotic tastes and fashions to grey, rain soaked Britain.

For him it was the multicultural element that especially fascinated him. He'd never been abroad in his life and the racial mix attracted him. 'I feel as though the world has come to me,' he said to Patricia who had joined him since she was to be the one to choose somewhere suitable to buy. Sophie was studying hard in Aberdeen and Sylvie was living with her grandmother in Basildon to keep her company. She had taken to the place like a duck to water and was thriving. Training to be a beautician filled her time and she was delighted with her choice of career.

So far Jimmy and Patricia hadn't got the price they wanted for their lavish home in Aberdeen. For Sale signs lined the streets of both Aberdeen and London. The recession was biting hard the length and breadth of the UK. It pleased Patricia that she was made so welcome in London and was soon well known in the community who called her 'the Scottish lady'. She loved the warmth and friendliness of the people and found it quite overwhelming that on every different feast time she would be given food by those who were celebrating, whether it be Eid, Divali or Guru Nanak's birthday. Kindly Asian neighbours were always knocking at their door with cartons of biryani, dhal or sweet rice. 'Life here seems to be working well so far,' Jimmy said optimistically. 'As soon as the Aberdeen house sells, you can decide what to buy. The houses are cheaper here anyway.'

It was handy too being so near his mother. Jimmy couldn't be faulted as far as supporting her went and he visited Eddie as often as he could. Eddie usually mistook him for a range of people, often one of his comrades from the war. One time it was Joe, his older brother who had died in the fire and another time it was his nephew Kenny who had also burned to death. Jimmy took it all in his stride. 'It doesn't matter if the old fella recognises me or not;' he said philosophically, 'as long as he thinks his family are coming to see him he's happy, and that's the main thing.'

When he and Catherine had come into contact with each other, Patricia was often there too so Rosie hadn't bothered interrogating them about Stephen. Rosie was a clever woman and she didn't need them to confirm what she already knew deep in her heart to be the truth that Stephen was undoubtedly a Simpson.

All wasn't perfection in East London, however; far from it. Jimmy had viewed the situation through rose tinted spectacles and had been sheltered in Aberdeen's nouveau riche suburbia from the horrors of racism that prowled the tree lined streets of the capital, especially at night. It never occurred to him that others might not feel as welcoming as he did to incomers. Why, he was one himself. More than once he had to repeat some words when his accent made it hard to make himself understood, even when he considered himself to be talking in his best 'proper English'.

During the day the friendly shopkeepers were selling fruit, vegetables and stacks of garlic. The sari shops thronged with women trying on the latest designs from Lahore in Pakistan or Bombay in India. He never ceased to be amazed at the stateliness of the African women who carried themselves majestically with folds of colourful fabrics thrown elegantly over one shoulder. Even the immaculately dressed Patricia would watch in wonder. 'If I were wearing that,' she said in admiration, 'the material would have fallen to the ground after only a few steps.'

However, once the daytime people had returned home to cook and tend to their families, another breed of human came out after dark and the windows of the pubs were noticeably crisscrossed with tape to protect against glass shattering during riots. Jimmy had heard of the National Front but never encountered them face to face. He was naïvely unaware of the havoc they could cause. Taking pleasure in cruelty and torture was their motivation and their already warped minds were frequently polluted with various concoctions of street drugs mingled with cheap booze and even lighter fuel or glue. This was an underclass that had risen in response to unmanageable levels of unemployment, and the rabble rousing speeches against immigration from more than one parliamentarian had helped to turn their discontent into hatred.

One of Patricia's friends in Aberdeen had been furious when her fifteen year old son had got his head shaved. The school hadn't been too happy either. But hair grows in again. The boy had simply fancied showing off a bit and wanted to be different from the rest. However, the bovver boys that paraded these East End streets had their heads shaved as a symbol of belonging to the extreme right, a violent army of thugs who based their philosophy on the teachings of Adolf Hitler. The fashion they followed symbolised a philosophy that was not unlike that of the brown shirts of the Hitler Youth. Indeed, the membership of these organisations that admired the man who had masterminded the Holocaust was growing and their violence was on the increase.

Patricia had no need to go out at nights and she too was oblivious of the dangers that overshadowed her neighbourhood after the decent people of the daytime had withdrawn safely behind locked doors. Jimmy, after his shifts, walked quickly home through the streets that were eerily quiet due to people wanting to avoid the racist beatings that had become commonplace and it took some time before he discovered the real reason for the lull that fell after dark.

Jimmy had made friends with an Irish chap, Deaglan, who also worked on the tube trains. He'd been a maintenance man at a factory that had recently made hundreds redundant and like Jimmy had moved to find work. It was on the cards that by sharing Celtic origins in an area where people tended to stick together according to ethnicity they would soon strike up a friendship. Unfortunately, he had horrible digs that were overrun with mice and cockroaches. Deaglan's complaints about the appalling conditions in his lodgings gave Jimmy an idea. 'Why don't you come and live with Patricia and me. We've plenty room and Patricia is occasionally in Aberdeen keeping an eye on our daughter, Sophie, who's still to finish her nurse's training. My other daughter, Sylvie, has gone to live at my mother's to be near the beauty college. I'll be real glad of your company.' Jimmy was also reckoning on the fifty quid a week that a sub-let would bring in. Running two homes was no mean feat. Because Jimmy had set up a monthly standing order the landlord never came near; there wouldn't be a problem.

There couldn't have been a better arrangement. Deaglan was the perfect housemate. He was scrupulously tidy and as many Irishmen were wont to do, ate out at the cafes that sold the homemade stews and puddings that reminded him of home. He'd go to the pub in the evenings with his fellow countrymen - or so Jimmy thought - and would come quietly in at closing time and straight to bed.

One afternoon, Jimmy came home unexpectedly early. He'd made up some hours the previous week covering another lad's shift. Patricia was with Rosie for a day's shopping at Lakeside, the massive indoor mall in Essex. He whistled his way through the front door with nothing on his mind except the possibility of a long soak in a Radox bath followed by a snooze on the sofa in front of a spaghetti western he knew was on television that afternoon.

He'd no sooner set foot across the threshold than he heard a commotion coming from Deaglan's room. The voice that he heard, loud and laughing, was Asian. Somebody must have broken in through a rear window. The best laid plans... he thought to himself as the vision of the steaming bath faded and he cursed loudly as he backtracked and picked up a claw hammer from his toolbox lying in the hallway. Wielding it high above his head like Thor ready for action he crept through to the back room and flung open the door to tackle the intruder full on.

Never in a million years would he have guessed what was happening in there. Deaglan and a young Asian both of them bollock naked were hopping around desperately trying to haul on underpants and socks. The rest of their clothes were strewn everywhere, some tossed on the floor and others draped on the furniture. The bed was in turmoil. They'd been having quite a session. Jimmy stood for several moments his mouth hanging open and his eyes bulging from their sockets in absolute shock. Deaglan and Vikram, as Deaglan's friend was called, took advantage of Jimmy's temporary paralysis to gather the remaining garments and dress themselves.

Jimmy went ballistic. He dropped the hammer, probably scared that if he kept hold of it he might use it. 'What do you think you're using my house for?' he screamed. 'Clear off you couple of queers!' Deaglan started to protest about privacy. Vikram placed the palms of his hands together and held them to his face, bowing and apologising. When Jimmy had lunged into the room like a maniac they'd stumbled over one another backing out of his way, but he wasn't making for them. Shoving past he caused them to tumble together in a heap on the bed. They yelled in fright and covered their heads with their arms when they saw him grabbing the chair from beside the dressing table. But instead of using it as a weapon to crack open their skulls as they had feared, he climbed on it to reach for the suitcase on top of the wardrobe. Laying it on the floor he hauled open drawers willy nilly and began stuffing Deaglan's clothes into it. His silence was more frightening than if he had continued to shout.

Deaglan stood up and dared to speak. 'I told you I had a friend called Vikram. I thought you understood these things.' Jimmy rammed the bulging case against Deaglan's chest. Vikram was already scuttling to the front door, desperate to escape. Jimmy pushed past him and held it open, shouting at them both to get the hell out. Deaglan caught sight of the toolbox beside Jimmy. Aware that they had got off lightly and not wanting to stir up his wrath, he apologised too, but all Jimmy wanted was to be shot of them. As they scurried out like scared rabbits Jimmy gave each one a hefty boot in the backside that made them arch their backs in pain. He slammed the door and wiped his brow. 'Thank goodness Patricia wasn't here to witness that,' he muttered to himself as he gathered up the bedclothes and threw them into the washing machine setting it for the hottest wash.

Jimmy heaved a sigh of relief as he left the tube station after a wearisome day hunched in the driver's cab of the District Line train, but if this was all the recession had to offer then he'd no choice but to stick it out. It was coming down dark and an icy fog caused him to shiver and hurry his steps. Never mind, in less than twenty minutes he'd be in a hot tub followed by a cracking good meal, one of Patricia's specials, lamb roghan josh. She had become quite a curry expert and in the halal butcher's on the corner she had befriended old Imran who was taking great delight in passing on a lifetime's knowledge of Kashmiri cuisine to his new Scottish customer. Jimmy licked his lips in anticipation and the tightness in his low back eased with the thought of his happy homecoming.

The streets here at night were eerily quiet so unlike the daytime when the place buzzed with folks of every nationality and the pavements were chock-a-block with rails of bright saris and rows of tables straining under the weight of crates piled high with every exotic fruit and vegetable. As the day wore on the street would take on the atmosphere of a fairground. Thick branches of sugar cane were fed into the steel teeth of the machine that resembled an old washhouse mangle, and crushed while you wait into syrupy juice; huge green coconuts brimming with milk were prepared with straws and set out in rows ready for thirsty customers; cobs of corn were roasted in the open air and lashed with butter; squealing children queued at the kulfi ice cream cart and voices in every language known to man rose from the crowds in a Babel of excitement.

Now there was only grim silence. Jimmy looked at the deserted stance of the wizened old mango seller whose boxes were daily flown in from Pakistan to Heathrow. He would be safely tucked away with the other traders in one of the flats above the shops and the colourful carnival of the daytime gathered in behind grey steel shutters. Most of the windows of the flats were in darkness. A few showed the flickering lights of television screens and Jimmy imagined families gathered cosily round some Bollywood extravaganza, and sure enough the strains of sitar music filtered through the night air to mingle with the spicy smell of curry. So far he had seen only one person - a slightly built Asian, in white shalwar kameez, looking neither to left nor right as he flitted along in the shadows like a ghost before disappearing up the narrow alleyway that led to the back steps of the flats. Jimmy felt the man's fear and shuddered as if some evil entity had been carried in on the chill damp air from the river.

He quickened his step and turned into the next street. Nearly home. Oh God, trouble ahead. About twenty yards in front of him alongside the pub was a crowd of thugs. They'd cornered a couple of blokes and were laying into them. He was about to cross the road and hurry by unnoticed when he heard an Irish voice shrill and filled with terror. A shiver ran up his spine. He knew that voice. 'Feck off you Nazi bastards. Leave him alone!' it shrieked. Jimmy carried on walking but kept his head down, allowing only his eyes to glance upwards in order to have a closer look. You've too vivid an imagination he thought to himself. This area is crawling with Irish. It won't be Deaglan.

Knowing he was taking a risk, he decided to move slowly closer and screwed up his eyes to get a better look. But he wasn't mistaken. It was Deaglan. He was shouting and screaming and kicking while two skinheads restrained him. The other three bovver boys were laying into his lover, Vikram, who was curled on the ground covering his head with his hands while they kicked into his face, his head and his sides with their lethal metal toe-capped doc martins. Vikram was screaming and praying to God. Deaglan was frantic as he struggled to break free and help his boyfriend. The mob threw taunts at him. 'Ha, ye Fienian c***, enjoying the show? We've only just started on your Paki lover boy. You won't think much of him once we're finished.' They began to laugh, the crazy laughter of madmen. 'Think he's suffered enough?' yelled one particularly ugly beast whose nose was squashed flat to his face and his red-rimmed piggy eyes flashed wild with bloodlust and no doubt some vile infusion of street drugs. 'It's your fault we have to do this to him,' yelled the other Neanderthals. 'You need the likes of us to come and patrol an area like this and keep the streets clean.'

Deaglan began to sob. 'I'm sorry Vikram. We shouldn't have come this way together. We should've stayed separate. I love you Vikram. I'm sorry.' One of the thugs let out a wild cry before shouting, 'See how this turns you on!' And as he swung his boot against Vikram's skull there was the unmistakeable sound of bone breaking and Deaglan threw his head back and screamed into the air, tears flooding his broad Celtic face.

Without a word Jimmy strode up to the door of the pub and started banging on it. In a flash one of the ruffians left off kicking Vikram and rushed at him. Jimmy struggled to shake him off so he could carry on kicking at the door. He was shouting at the top of his voice for whoever was in there to come out. He could hear somebody moving behind the door, but when he felt a wallop behind his ear he turned and punched, kicked, bit and tore at his assailant throwing him to the ground. A voice from inside the pub shouted at him to clear off, but he persisted in battering at the door. In other towns, lights from the surrounding flats and houses might have been switched on. People might have gathered. But where you had the National Front with their big boots and baseball bats no one made a sound or interfered. They couldn't risk their family's lives by being seen to disapprove. Also, it was in the nature of Asians in particular not to react. They were a mild mannered race of people and the older generations especially behaved submissively rather than retaliating with violence. However, the up and coming impressionable youngsters who were witnessing this unfettered cruelty night after night might not be so meek and mild when they reached an age to fight back.

At last the door was opened and the anxious white face of the publican peered out. 'You've got to help,' insisted Jimmy. The man closed the door and Jimmy hammered on it again. The Nazi he'd thrown to the ground had recovered himself and charged at him lifting high his jackboot which caught him a heavy blow on the side of the thigh. Jimmy felt as if some force rose up through him from the very core of the earth itself to give him the energy he needed to annihilate the bastards. There was no holding him. The adrenalin that coursed Jimmy's body had speeded up his responses and when the second kick came his way he grabbed hold of the iron segged heel and threw the leg up in the air, much as a strongman might toss a caber at the Highland Games, and the piece of human debris was flung a fair distance before crashing flat out in the gutter where it belonged.

His mates threw Vikram and Deaglan aside to concentrate on this mad Scotsman. Jimmy was set to fight them all but it was fear now that fired him up. He landed another one a punch that sent him stumbling backwards to fall on top of his mate. He felt hands tightening round his throat from behind while the other enraged beast rained blows on his chest. Just as his head began to spin from lack of breath the pub landlord pulled open the door. He brandished a shotgun menacingly at the louts. 'Clear off you scum!' he shouted and without further warning fired it into the air. He meant business.

The cowards took to their heels apart from the one Jimmy had knocked out earlier. He rose sobbing from among the burst open rubbish bags and hobbled away like a rat from the sewers after the rest of the vermin. Jimmy staggered against the wall but soon gathered himself.

Deaglan was crouched over Vikram whose crying had faded to a whimper. He managed to force out a hoarse whisper to his boyfriend, 'Khuda Hafiz, meri jaan.' (God protect you, my life, and my love.) His breath rattled in his throat and the blood that seeped out of his mouth was starting to form a crust on his chin. Deaglan looked up at the two men with pleading eyes. 'Get him inside,' he begged between sobs.

'I'll get rid of this first,' said the landlord once he had made sure the way was clear, and he hurried inside with the gun. 'Nobody will ever find it,' he said, reappearing and out of breath. 'It's for emergencies only. Never had to use it before, but nice to know it's there.'

Jimmy and Deaglan took Vikram's top half and the landlord took his feet. Jimmy started to shake as they went through the door and a common opener to a joke sprang weirdly into his mind and he blurted it out with a crazy sounding laugh: 'A Scotsman, an Englishman and an Irishman went into a bar ...' His voice was shrill and he was giggling. Deaglan told him to shut his feckin' gob.

They struggled over to the clear space in front of the counter and laid Vikram carefully down. Jimmy knew there was no hope for the boy that hung limp and silent in their arms and he finally gave way to hysteria. Deaglan landed him a punch smack in the middle of the mouth. Jimmy tasted the salt blood that trickled between his lips and he wiped it quickly off with the back of his sleeve as his laughter turned to sobs. 'I deserved that,' he wept. 'It was nerves made me say something so stupid.' He looked at his friend's distraught face and it dawned on him that he and Vikram had been in love, every bit as much as if they'd been a man and a woman like himself and Patricia. He thought of how he'd treated them only a few days before and he retched with disgust at himself. Deaglan was bent over his lover howling, his ear flat to his chest and feeling the side of his neck desperate to find a pulse. 'I'll swing for these Nazi bastards,' he yelled. The words echoed round the silent, smoky bar. Jimmy and the barman whose name was Sid looked on helplessly as the broken hearted Deaglan gazed with longing at his beloved's face that had been pulped to a jelly.

Satisfied that Deaglan had had sufficient time to say his last goodbyes to Vikram, Sid walked over to the phone but some neighbour must have already dialled for help because just at that moment the Old Bill came bursting through the door, batons at the ready. 'Somebody said there was a shooting,' said the first one in, a ruddy faced lad not much more than twenty. His three colleagues looked at Vikram. 'He been gunned down?' they asked almost in unison.

Deaglan immediately jumped back from the body. 'Just checking to see if the guy was still alive.' He didn't want the police knowing his relationship to Vikram and blabbing it to his family. Neither could he trust them with the knowledge he was gay and making a marked man of himself.

The landlord was quick, thinking on his feet. 'There's been a lot of shouting maybe but no shooting.' He turned to Jimmy and Deaglan. 'Any of you two hear anything?'

They replied without hesitation, 'No, we've been too busy getting away from those thugs.' Jimmy's mind was working fast too. The unmistakeable smell of burning that follows gunshot wafted in from outside. 'Maybe one of that crew did fire a gun after they took off,' he said. 'They looked the type and one of them was definitely carrying something.'

'Do you think it was a racially motivated attack?' asked the young bobby. The landlord wiped his mouth with the back of his hand. 'What d'you think? He's Asian ain't he, and the crowd that attacked him were skinheads.'

'You know their names?'

'These Nazis all look the same to me,' muttered the landlord. He face was pale. He was tired. What with one thing or another it had been a long day. He looked at the criss-crossing of masking tape on his window put there to prevent shattering during riots. He'd had it smashed in before at the last killing - a West Indian who'd dared to marry a local English girl. They'd stubbed out cigarettes on his face as he lay dying. He sighed as the memory he would have liked to forget flashed into his mind as clearly as if he were watching a film. What was wrong with people these days? 'Sorry lad,' he said abstractedly to the youngster with the notebook who was desperately licking at the blunt point of his pencil, 'I didn't recognise any of them.' Who in their right mind would own up even if they did?

'How come you two got involved?' asked the constable in an effort to make himself seem important and capable of a bit of detective work. After all he had been left in charge of the investigation while his mates were giving chase to the killers.

'These hooligans were laying into the lad there when me and my pal came by,' added Jimmy. 'We've just come from the Underground off a late shift. We work together and he's also my lodger.' There was nothing strange about a Scotsman and an Irishman teaming up. The policeman nodded. Deaglan wouldn't be implicated. They'd both be in the clear; just a pair of interfering passersby. 'A bit foolhardy getting involved; you could have ended up like that poor bugger. Next time, walk on by and dial 999. That's what we're here for.' Three red in the face and out of breath coppers gasped their way in through the door. 'Got clean away. They must have had a car waiting.' Catching his breath, the chubby one went on to his walkie-talkie. 'Another racialist killing,' he announced and gave the location. 'Nothing stolen as far as I can see ... I found the deceased's wallet on him ... Yes ... Skinheads ... Saw their scalps shining in the street lamps as they took off.'

Jimmy felt like taking a swing at the copper for trying to be funny, but after all the man probably had a family at home the same as himself and who could blame him for trying to make light of yet another gruesome find among the backstreets where he faced being murdered himself any night of the week? The landlord had meantime brought Jimmy and Deaglan a large brandy after first taking a steadier for himself. They took their medicine gratefully while filling in the blanks for the copper who was still scribbling like fury. He wasn't interested in drink being dispensed after hours. No money had changed hands and he'd more important business in hand.

A siren sounded outside and the ambulance men rushed in. They checked Vikram, shook their heads and his dead body was stretchered out. Deaglan let out a whimper but didn't follow. One of the policemen had already found Vikram's personal details in his jacket pocket. The formal identification would be left to his family. They wouldn't ever know the truth about their son. He would be buried with his honour intact. Deaglan wouldn't be a part of it. It was better that way.

'Let's get you home,' Jimmy said. He took his friend by the arm and led him away. 'Sorry lads,' said Sid. 'I can't go out every time there's trouble. I don't want to get myself killed. Get yourselves as far away from here as you can get and if I were you I'd clear out of the area all together. These streets are going to see a right blood bath one of these days; that MP was right.' Jimmy stiffened but forced himself to stay calm; he was in no mood for further argument. All he said in a quiet, controlled voice was: 'Now there's a man that would've done better to keep his mouth shut.'

Holding each other up, Jimmy and Deaglan headed off down the poorly lit and empty streets. 'I know who Vikram's parents are,' Deaglan told Jimmy as the hurried home. 'They have the sari shop next to the library. They'll be better pleased to accept a racist murder than a gay bashing any day. The father's on the local borough council and head of the Muslim charity for the homeless. I don't mind leaving it at that. Their grief will be painful enough without adding public humiliation to the agony they already have to bear.'

'Surely they would want to talk to you. After all you were both so close,' replied Jimmy. He was desperate to make up for the tirade he'd had against them.

'Wise up, Jimmy,' said Deaglan impatiently. 'I've already had a beating from his father and a few of the uncles. But not on any grand scale, just a roughing up as a warning to keep away. Don't you know homosexuality used to be illegal in England until 1967 and still is where I come from? (Note 1.) And not only that, it's a social stigma wherever you go. My own father in County Wicklow would rather skin me alive himself than have the neighbours find out my sexual preferences as he calls it. Why do you think I'm over here? My father more or less threw me out and warned me never to let word of it slip out in his local drinking den.' Deaglan was still wiping tears from his eyes as he told Jimmy about the prejudice he'd had to live with. 'And especially round here ..., it's best keep your nose clean and not give the local constabulary anything to pin on you that will keep them banging on your door at every squeak of trouble. Being Irish is bad enough. They'll haul you in for questioning every time a bomb goes off up west.'

On the way back to the house they watched a gang of National Front supporters rolling through the streets swilling from cider bottles and throwing them across the road to smash in smithereens so cars would get their tyres torn to shreds. One hit his against a wall and carried the weapon threateningly in front of him. Another had a pit bull terrier straining at the leash ready to obediently tear out the throat of anyone who might cross its crazy owner.

'Just keep your great gob shut so they don't hear the accents,' warned Deaglan. 'I'd rather face their bovver boots than have my face torn off by the slavering jaws of one of their dogs. See the scars on that animal's body? It's probably been in so many fights it can't wait to taste any kind of blood. It would go for the jugular on one simple command from its idiot owner. The money that's at stake between dog fighting and drug dealing, I wouldn't be surprised though they're not armed with guns. A machete too is another weapon of choice. I don't fancy my head rolling down one alley and the rest of my body down another.'

The yobs were shouting incoherently, just noises to scare anyone who passed their way. They spotted Jimmy and Deaglan who'd crossed to the other side of the road and were walking close into the shadows of the buildings. 'Hoi, you two! Wot yer finkin', eh?'

'Aw riyt miyt!' Jimmy called and kept walking, imitating as best he could the local accent and greeting. He put his arm round Deaglan as if to support a drunk, and Deaglan played along, head down to hide his bruises when he passed under the glow of the street light. Pretending to be drunk was no problem. He was staggering with pain any way. The bully boys passed on by. They weren't on the lookout for white faces.

Outside the carpet shop, two street girls, fifteen if that, were standing at the edge of the pavement enticing passing men in cars. One stopped. It had four passengers. The two in the back slid along to make room for one of the girls. Then it sped off, tyres screeching. The young girl left behind gave them the V-sign as they drove away, but she hadn't long to wait. Hard on its tail came another bunch of kerb crawlers and picked her up all set to have their night's fun with her.

'What a bloody country,' said Deaglan. 'Makes me sick. Probably married too. Get these poor kids to entertain them in a way they wouldn't ask from their wives.' Deaglan was getting quite het up. 'If that's heterosexuality you can keep it.'

'Don't go preaching, Pal,' said Jimmy. 'What about the rent boys? I'd like to string up all of them bastards who'd lay a hand on youngsters. I'd kill anyone who touched either of my daughters or my ...' He nearly said son, but stopped himself. He didn't want any slip of the tongue to get back to Patricia. 'I'm sorry about the other day,' he said quietly. 'It was such a shock. I never realised that you lot, you know what I mean, felt the same way about each other as any other couple.' He scuffed his feet along the street in embarrassment, both at his behaviour and because he wasn't used to talking about personal things. He kicked an empty can across the pavement, rattling it into the gutter. 'Maybe if I hadn't thrown you out, none of this would have happened.'

'It's all right,' said Deaglan. 'I understand. After all, "the love that dare not speak its name" as they call it, is still against the law where I come from and carries a two year jail sentence. Can you believe that? Ending up behind bars for falling in love with someone? And each year up to 200 people are dismissed from the armed services for being gay. And even after it is legalised like it was here a few years ago, the attitudes will take generations to die out. Why should I have expected you to be any different?'

The two friends walked on in silence for a while. A flashy car with smoked glass windows thundered past. The heavy beat of rap music vibrated through the cobbles of the street and a bright blue light flared out from underneath it giving it a space age look. Seconds later, a police car sped past, siren screaming as it gave chase. It was on a loser. An old banger turned out of a side street and lurched, engine stalling, straight across its path. Jimmy and Deaglan both laughed as the cops jumped out and started haranguing an old bloke who obviously couldn't speak a word of English and was under the bonnet muttering in what sounded like swear words in any language.

'Maybe it won't be long before gays are no longer hounded out,' Deaglan started up again, now that a touch of humour had relaxed the atmosphere between them. 'It's surely better we're allowed to live the lives we've been born into rather than marrying some hetero and ruining everybody's lives.'

'When you put it like that, it certainly does make sense,' replied Jimmy thoughtfully. He was trying to imagine what life would be like if he had inadvertently married a lesbian who had done so just to conform to what was expected. 'What are you going to do now?' Jimmy asked. He found he was actually concerned about Deaglan's future.

'I'll move to Seven Kings where there's an Irish community. I've mates there. It'll be a long time before I get involved with anyone after Vikram. I'll be living the straight life to all intents and purposes. But at least I'll be among my own people.' He heaved a sigh. 'You see, however much you try to be friendly and mix with people around here, it's tribalism that wins through in the end; safer and more companionable for everyone. Take a long time for that to change, but I could never go back to County Wicklow. As I said before, my old father would be the first to have me strung up.'

Patricia peeped out from behind the curtains before opening the front door when she heard the squeaking of the gate. She'd been sitting up waiting for Jimmy whose supper was beginning to stick to the pan on top of the cooker. Half asleep from drifting off in front of a late television quiz show, she stared at them with a look of horror on her face. It wasn't the fact that she recognised Deaglan who'd been asked to leave, but the state of them that shocked her. 'What's happened to you two?' she cried clutching at her throat as every last drop of colour drained from her face.

'We'd a bit of a set to with some idiots on the way home, that's all,' said Jimmy. Patricia went to the kitchen. In her distress she continued robotically to do the normal things like put his tea on the table. Jimmy followed after her. 'I thought you'd thrown Deaglan out for not paying his way,' she said. 'Will he need feeding as well?'

'That was a misunderstanding,' Jimmy explained. 'It's all been sorted out.' Patricia didn't look too pleased and who could blame her? It was nearly two o'clock in the morning. Jimmy looked longingly at the freshly made curry and couldn't help inhaling deeply the heart warming spicy smell. Without hesitation he said, 'Give Deaglan mine and I'll have a few fried eggs on toast.' He took Patricia by the waist and kissed her cheek. 'Do you think you could make up his bed again, nice and warm with a hot water bottle?' Jimmy had noticed his friend trembling with shock and wanted only the best for him now.

Patricia tutted. 'As long as I live I'll never understand you men.' She was a patient woman and she would do her best to look after any poor soul that came into her house, but at this time of night her good nature was being stretched a bit too far.

'I'll explain it all tomorrow,' Jimmy called after her. He knew perfectly well he wouldn't. As was his wont, he would keep Patricia in the dark about all matters unpleasant.

'I'll tell you this much, Patricia,' Deaglan called after her, 'if it weren't for your man here, I would be lying stone dead in a gutter. He saved my life.'

'I didn't do anything anyone else wouldn't have done,' snapped Jimmy, giving Deaglan a silencing look. He didn't want Patricia to get hold of the story. As far as she was concerned he'd only thrown a few punches at a couple of youngsters before the police came on the scene. She must never know there had been a murder.

The next morning he told her to start packing. Her instructions were to go back to Aberdeen for a while and get the house sold at any price. They would be looking for a home out in Essex beside his mother as soon as possible. He was going to clear things with the landlord, give up the house and find somewhere to rent in Basildon near to Rosie and Eddie for the time being. 'Once Aberdeen is sold,' he said, 'you'll come to Basildon and choose the house you want, any house, because we're moving. I've had enough of the excitement of London. It's no place for my family. It's all very well you liking the area because the quiet living Asians are kind and give you food, mango juice and pretty bangles, but out there at night is a different world of drug dealers, pimps, thugs and thieves.'

(Note 1.) Homosexuality between consenting adults of 21 years was made legal in England and Wales in 1967, in Scotland in 1980, Northern Ireland in 1982, Guernsey in 1983, Jersey in 1990 and the Isle of Man and Southern Ireland in 1992. Since 2003 it is unlawful to discriminate in the workplace against someone on the grounds of his/her sexuality or perceived sexuality. Gay men (and women) have been allowed to serve in the military since February 2000.)

Chapter 27

(1991)

Another new year came and went and Catherine visited Basildon frequently now she was satisfied Stephen could manage without her, and during her visits would accompany Rosie nearly every day to Sycamore Lodge. Rosie loved the voluntary work. She would never have guessed there were so many reasons why people required such care. Catherine couldn't help but admire the patience of the staff and especially was full of wonder at Rosie's ability to be such an excellent companion to the residents. She would sit herself in the middle of a group and sing favourite songs with them. Often she would talk to them about the past. Old radio characters were brought back to life as they remembered catch phrases and popular melodies. She would participate in their ramblings as if they were making sense, just to give them a sense of companionship.

'What you must remember,' Rosie would say, 'is that each and every one of these dear souls was young once. You should see how the ladies look forward to the hairdresser on a Friday morning. Nobody ever forgets being young. There's many a Saturday night when they would have put on their dance dresses, done up their hair and gone out to looking for romance. Inside all of them is a young girl or boy who was once in love. Age is a fact of life, and as long as you don't die young, it comes to us all.'

Catherine screwed up her face. Even when she was young she hadn't gone to the dancing, preferring the debating society instead. She remembered Jimmy asking her to go with him and her scornful refusal. Maybe she was the strange one. He'd only been asking her to do what all the other young people were doing. Why had she always been so stuck up? Why had she never fitted in? Why had she never been normal? Even Gregor had been a bit of a lad in his day. She certainly hadn't been his first. And here was she, the great journalist, unable to understand the basics of human kindness. As always, it was Rosie who was the true people person, the philanthropist, the carer.

She'd no choice but to agree all the residents had mattered to somebody at some stage and done all sorts of interesting jobs, not to mention being pretty young girls or swaggering young lads sprucing themselves up in the hope of finding a sweetheart and falling in love. Eddie sat amongst them, nodding and mumbling, allowing his eyes to close and occasionally opening them for a lazy look around before drifting back to sleep again.

Catherine would frequently take Rosie and Arlene up into London for a change of scene. Arlene loved the boat trips on the Thames and would jump up and down on Catherine's knee like a jack-in-the-box. They'd had a particularly perfect day that Friday in May when Catherine and Rosie swung Arlene between them in through the front door of the nursing home. How they'd laughed as she squealed with delight at being lifted so high. Her screams must have been heard all through the building. Suddenly two carers ran past them along the corridor and into the common room. That's where the merry trio were heading doubled up and giggling in order to visit Eddie, but as soon as they walked through the door their expressions changed immediately to shock and dismay. Arlene immediately sensed their anxiety and began howling. The scene that met their eyes was what they'd been dreading for months. A nurse, with the two assistants, was kneeling over Eddie who was lying face down on the floor. Catherine turned Arlene quickly away and took her through to his room to wait. Rosie was down on the floor beside him in seconds, stroking the sparse white hairs of his head.

It didn't look good. This was no ordinary fall. His mouth was twisted down on one side and his eyes were rolling in his head. A white froth bubbled between his bluish lips and he was mumbling incoherently. His left arm hung limply by his side. This time the stroke had hit hard. Rosie took him and held him tight. His eyes fixed on her momentarily and his mouth moved as much as he was able to as he tried to rasp her name. 'Oh, Eddie, Eddie, don't go. I love you so much,' wailed Rosie.

Eddie had suffered a massive stroke and they knew there was no more hope. Rosie clutched tightly to his hand and prayed for him as he slipped gently away. 'If ever a man should go to Heaven it's Eddie,' she said and declared to all and sundry that there was a smile on his face after he died which was evidence enough to her of his arrival there. It was probably a blessed relief. He was at peace and happy to be on a journey to meet the loved ones who had gone before. Catherine thought of Gregor and her mum and dad and little Lucy. Would her darling baby sister have grown up in Heaven or would they all be the same ages as they had been when they were alive? Her sense of loss and the shock of Eddie's great influence in her life coming to an abrupt end gave her the sinking feeling that perhaps there was nothing more beyond this life. In desperation she conjured up in her imagination the huge welcome the family would be giving Eddie and managed to draw some comfort from this vision of a happy reunion.

Chapter 28

(Aberdeen, June 1991)

Stephen straightened his tie in the mirror and rubbed his palm along one side of his unshaven face and then the other. The beard was coming along nicely. It made him look and feel grown up. With his mother back in Basildon to look after Rosie while she came to terms with Eddie's death, Stephen had a free hand to do as he pleased. She would have nagged him he was sure to shave it off, regardless of how much hair Earl had had when she went around with him in her younger days. Those two had lived the high life and no mistake. Now he wanted to see for himself what was out there and he wondered what sort of night lay ahead, not that he expected to enjoy himself. Socialising wasn't his strong point and he felt more at home studying logarithms or acquainting himself with engineering terminology but he had agreed to join some student friends for an evening in the pub and possibly a nightclub later to celebrate the end of their exams.

This would almost be their farewell get together before they went their separate ways. Nights out with the lads weren't his idea of fun but perhaps a bit of company would ease the tension he'd been feeling lately. It wouldn't be any skin off his nose to make the effort just this once. After being uprooted from his childhood pals in Canada he hadn't found it easy to make friends. Even at almost twenty-two he still had a trace of the accent and was bored with the interminable explanations that he wasn't American. How could he ever become a local when every new person he spoke to said, 'You don't belong here; which part of America do you come from?' For him there were none of the long term school friends - the ones that last a lifetime. It may have been a mistake, his mother sometimes said, to have put him to a fee paying school instead of the local comprehensive where fellow pupils would have lived nearby. Many of his classmates had moved on, their having come from other parts of the country or overseas, the sons of oilmen, or, like himself, with fathers working in the hospital or university.

Apart from the swimming club he had no other social outlet, and even that was simply a part time hobby and not the all consuming passion it had been in his younger days. Caring for his father had taken up much of his time although it was Stephen himself who had insisted on it. Because of taking his father swimming he hadn't developed his own ability. Why would he when he could be enjoying his father's limited few years of life? Gregor had tried to encourage him to achieve championship standard but Stephen's heart wasn't in it. And so, spending time with his father had taken care of early teenage years when bonds with school mates might have been strengthened.

After Gregor's death he'd taken on the responsibility of making sure his mother didn't slide into depression. She hadn't asked him of course, but caring for her wellbeing had become an integral part of his nature. Although they didn't always see eye-to-eye and frequently fell out, an overwhelming sense of duty drove Stephen to protect his mother and she in turn continued with her instinctive impulses to smother him. The result of this intensive one-on-one relationship was that each felt stifled and would react against the other's seemingly overwhelming need for control. But how could he forget the drinking bouts of his childhood? And he dreaded their return. A little sister had been next on the cards for him to deal with and it was only now with his mother spending so much time in Basildon that he felt the urge to become his own person at last and spread his wings.

As he scrutinised his image in the full length mirror of the wardrobe, especially when he caressed his manly stubble, a sense of freedom swept over him. Although she was no worse than the average well-meaning mother, he had recently been on the verge of finding his own flat to escape her interference, but that move could be put on hold for the time being. For the first time in his life he was at liberty to come and go with no questions asked. Perhaps this outing was his opportunity to branch out and start living. As he closed the front door behind him and stepped out into the balmy evening air that smelt of honeysuckle and new mown grass he knew that tonight would be a night to remember.

With a few drinks inside him and having enjoyed a few laughs, Stephen had gladly queued with his pals at the entrance of a popular nightclub. After all, he thought, the world was his oyster and he might strike lucky. Wasn't this the ideal place for a casual pickup and get some practice in before he met the woman he would want to marry? He stood at the bar watching the girls. He'd never had a serious relationship, only meaningless fumbles in the back of his car or a furtive grope on a settee while parents slept upstairs. Tonight would be different. He had the whole house to himself. No holds barred.

A blonde, that seemed somehow familiar, sat quietly alone at a nearby table. Her pals were on the dance floor flailing their arms and wiggling their hips to make sure the men who'd asked them to dance would be enticed to stay and buy drinks all night. This girl wasn't like that. You could tell from the shy way she kept her eyes cast downwards instead of glancing around to get a 'trap' as these female hunting packs called their pickups. If a bloke was looking for a 'dead cert' for the night, she wasn't the type to approach. It was obvious from the way she was clutching at the hem of her skirt every few minutes and pulling it discreetly down over her slender thighs that she wasn't trying to flaunt herself, quite the opposite. Stephen watched how she twisted her fingers anxiously; she was out of her element in a place like this.

Stephen let his eye rove freely round the other wallflowers for a suitable candidate for the christening of his bedroom but he kept returning to the blonde. Something about her was familiar but he couldn't quite place where they could have met before. His mind flicked through possible locations for having encountered this lonely young female.

Slowly, filtering its way from the distant past, came the memory of talking to her at his father's funeral five years ago and more recently they'd exchanged fleeting glances at Eddie's. He recalled too their meeting as children. This was just a vague dream and he remembered his disappointment at Rosie's grandchildren being girls. The conversation between them after his father's funeral was becoming clearer and he remembered her mother whisking her away as if he were a bad influence. There had been no conversation between them after Eddie's because he and his mother had to collect Arlene from a childminder. It had been his place to accompany her due to her state of near collapse. She had worshipped her uncle all her life and needed Stephen by her side. Rosie had Patricia and Jimmy to see her through that heartbreaking occasion and his mother seemed disinclined to talk to them. As a result he'd hardly noticed the other mourners and barely spoken to anyone but his mother before hurrying back to Aberdeen to complete his studies.

Although he hadn't been in her company properly for such a long time, he was certain that this was Sophie Simpson. What was someone as goodie-goodie as she was supposed to be, according to all that her father said, doing here? Curiosity won the day and thoughts of finding a one-night stand temporarily flew from his mind as he went over to introduce himself. 'Hi, didn't expect to see you here. Remember me?'

Sophie eyed him suspiciously for a moment before answering, 'I can't say that I do.' There wasn't even a glimmer of a smile. She sat up straight and pulled her black tailored skirt even further down over her knees before turning away.

'I'm Stephen, Stephen Bruce.' He paused to allow this information to sink in and continued, 'You're Sophie, right? Sophie Simpson. I was at Eddie Clark's funeral only a couple of weeks ago.' He wished now he'd never spoken to her and that the floor might miraculously swallow him up. Sophie screwed up her face trying to place him. When he'd met her as a child he'd dismissed her as a girl wanting to do nothing else but play with dolls. Even as a young teenager he thought she was rather quiet and never given her a second thought and was beginning to wish he'd left it at that.

Just then, a tall redhead in a low cut top and tight leather trousers went slinking slowly past and gave him the eye. What stupid impulse had made him bother with Jimmy's sullen daughter? He had missed the perfect opportunity he'd come here for in the first place. Perhaps he could follow that sexy female and explain he was only talking to an old friend. He turned to walk away when Sophie gave him a closer look and nodded. 'Of course, you must be Catherine's son.' Her eyes took on a gentle softness. 'I remember you now from your father's funeral. It's the beard that threw me.'

'That was years ago. We were just silly teenagers then,' said Stephen fingering his chin proudly. 'I'll get rid of this when I start work,' he laughed, but his chest puffed out noticeably as his attempts at facial hair were at last being properly acknowledged. His friends had been mocking him and nicknamed him 'Bum Fluff'. Sophie laughed when he told her this. Stephen's confidence grew. She actually enjoyed his jokes. Maybe she was worth talking too after all. He had lost his appetite for a pick-up now that he'd missed his chance with the redhead who had her arms wrapped tightly round some other bloke's neck. 'Do you mind if I join you?' he asked and pulled up one of the black PVC stools that were lying around and sat down beside her.

Sophie was on a girls' night out to mark the end of their final nursing exams. Stephen nodded and gave a heartfelt sigh. 'Sat the last of mine on Tuesday. Such a relief to get them over with,' he said with an understanding grin.

'I feel lighter, like a great load's been taken from my shoulders,' answered Sophie. They were having to shout to make themselves heard above the music. The disc jockey was taking great delight in spinning and holding the records with his fingers to make a freakish sound that squealed discordantly around them making conversation almost impossible.

Stephen had moved in closer towards her at the low table in order to hear better, when a swarm of giggling girls desperate to get up to dance pushed past and made him spill some of his drink. 'So here we are with nothing better to do than come out to this awful place for a good time,' he said picking up a beer mat and scooping a pool of lager from the Formica surface beside him into an empty glass from the table so that none of it would run on to her clothes. They began to laugh as each simultaneously cast an eye round the packed night club.

'I've never been here before,' said Sophie raising her eyebrows, 'and I'm not sure I'll be back.'

'I'm glad I came though, otherwise I wouldn't be speaking to you now,' Stephen said, draining what remained of the lager from his glass. Sophie's face flushed a bright shade of pink which Stephen thought made her look even more attractive. 'What would you like to drink?' he asked noticing that her glass was empty too.

'A St Clements,' she said with a smile. 'That's what the barmaid called a mixture of orange and lemon.'

'Whatever you want you shall have,' said Stephen and soon returned with her order and a pint for himself.

In no time at all they were chatting like long lost friends. Stephen brought up the subject of her father's redundancy and subsequent move. Sophie knew that he'd sometimes visited Catherine under Granny Rosie's strict instructions to make sure she was all right. 'I always get on well with your dad,' enthused Stephen, determined to ingratiate himself as a close friend of the family and to convince her he was a person she could trust. His voice carried a note of understanding for her family problems as he continued, 'Jimmy was devastated when he lost his job and moved away. I'll miss our little chats.' Sophie seemed to be impressed by this show of sympathy and thanked him for his concern. There was something that puzzled him and he wondered if perhaps Sophie could provide the answer. 'My mother seems glad for some reason that he's stopped coming round,' he said and waited for her response.

'I suspect she likes to be independent and not have my gran finding out everything about her from my father,' Sophie replied. 'I know for a fact that my own mother has to be ever so tactful dealing with Gran. She would like to run our house as well as her own. She still sees Dad as her little boy.'

Stephen was pleased that Sophie shared his opinions on the family dynamics and added, just to put another theory to the test, 'I'm not sure my mother and your father get along all that well anyway.'

Sophie agreed wholeheartedly. 'Gran has mentioned they used to fight like cat and dog when they were children.' They looked at each other and burst out laughing at the same time. 'Families!'

'Let's forget them and not spoil our evening,' said Stephen now that the ice was well and truly broken. 'Would you like to dance?' He placed his hand gently on Sophie's waist and led her up the carpeted steps on to the highly polished wooden floor. As her hair brushed softly against his face he was aware of the fragrance of fresh blossom instead of the tobacco smell that often surrounded other girls and his heart unexpectedly skipped a beat. His eyes never left her as they danced. She was a natural beauty. Not for her the thick plaster of heavy makeup. Her eyes shone with sincerity as she returned his smiles. He was enjoying himself more than he could ever remember. Although neither was an expert dancer, they managed to shake themselves around the cramped floor without standing on too many feet. With Stephen, Sophie seemed to overcome her shyness and was at ease, comfortably talking and laughing without awkwardness. Stephen couldn't remember any girl he had relaxed with so much. After two more dances they returned to their seats. 'This is more fun than I expected,' said Sophie. She even giggled as she tried to catch her breath. Their eyes met and instead of looking away in mild embarrassment they held the gaze and broad smiles of genuine affection spread across their contented faces.

Sophie's friends flocked round intrigued that the quietest amongst them had been the one to strike lucky. From the way they were giving Stephen the once over it was obvious they wouldn't have said no to a night out with him. But he had eyes only for Sophie. In any case it wasn't long before each girl had been snapped up and Stephen's pals had long since faded into the crowd, no doubt each one having pulled for the night. Sophie and Stephen were alone. 'I wish we'd got together sooner,' said Stephen, daring to reach over and take her hand. 'You're so easy to talk to. I feel we've been friends all our lives.'

Sophie didn't pull away as he half expected her to. 'You're a lot nicer than I remembered,' she said, 'so I'm surprised Dad didn't invite you and your mum round for tea occasionally seeing as he went round to yours quite often. I think it's maybe because Mum let him know I'd been cheeky to her at your dad's funeral. He's like that; never wants to upset Mum.'

'Thought I'd be a bad influence no doubt,' Stephen said with a mischievous twinkle in his eye.

'Well, he couldn't have been more wrong. You've been a perfect gentleman all evening,' replied Sophie. For several moments they looked deep into each other's eyes, liking what they saw and a strong link of friendship was forged between them with the promise of more to come. As Stephen waited while Sophie fetched her jacket from the cloakroom he couldn't stop a broad smile from spreading across his face. As they left the nightclub it seemed only natural that Sophie should link her arm into his and Stephen felt a surge of pride at having her by his side.

'I'll see you into a taxi,' Stephen said gallantly as they strolled through the night streets. He hurried Sophie past the rank where a fight had broken out. 'I can't possibly leave you out here on your own,' he said and put his arm protectively round her to steer her clear of the rowdy revellers. After making arrangements where and when to see each other again, he flagged down a passing cab and saw her safely into the back seat. She lived in a different direction from him in the nurses' home and Stephen gave the driver more than enough to cover the expense. The evening had ended differently but much better than he'd planned. Sophie was already special. She made him feel manly and he wanted to look after her.

Exhilarated from his surprise encounter and also the brisk walk home, Stephen wanted to think of nothing or nobody but Sophie. There was a message on the answering machine from his mother. Rosie was getting on her nerves by trying to organise multiple reunions between her and Jimmy whenever he and Patricia visited. So far she'd managed to avoid them on most occasions and had escaped into the city to spend time with Arlene. She was going to have to tell Rosie straight that she and Jimmy just didn't get along.

Stephen's jaw tightened. He'd grown weary of it all. Hadn't there always been strained relations between his mother and Jimmy? Some nonsense from the past as far as he could gather and it seemed as though Auntie Rosie was the one who stirred them up. Stephen leaned over and pressed the delete button firmly. He couldn't be bothered with all their shenanigans and went to bed whistling happily.

Sophie and Stephen really hit it off. Every moment they spent in each other's company drew them closer together. The next few weeks were bliss with both Catherine and Patricia away from home. The Aberdeen house was under offer at last and Patricia and Jimmy were in the throes of finding somewhere suitable to buy. Sylvie was too caught up in her beautician's course to ever want to visit or even phone her sister.

Chapter 29

Over the next few weeks Stephen continued to treat Sophie with the greatest respect, dropping her at the door of the nurses' home with a gentle kiss, nothing else just yet. She was what he'd dreamed of all his teenage years and would be well worth the wait. They enjoyed the cinema, long drives in the countryside and walks along the beach. 'It's such a pity our parents don't always see eye-to-eye,' said Sophie one Sunday when they stopped off for lunch at a country hotel. 'We've missed years of friendship and happiness because of their differences.'

'I know; such a waste. But maybe not. We might not have got along so well if we'd played together as children. We could have been at each other's throats by now,' mused Stephen.

'Reading between the lines,' replied Sophie thoughtfully as she scanned the menu, 'that's the reason my dad and your mum fell out. They were too much like brother and sister being brought up in the same tenement since birth. Gran tried to force them together and they were having none of it.'

'I agree,' replied Stephen signalling to the waitress that they were ready to order. 'Rosie's so busy trying to make them friends that it's driven them further apart. She's been annoying Mum something awful recently. When your dad visited us I always had the feeling it was to please Rosie and Eddie. They wanted to know Mum and I were surviving, what with Dad's illness and all that.' As always when he mentioned his father, his eyes misted over and his face grew sad. He was aware of this and pulled himself together, forcing a smile. 'We got along well your dad and I, so there should be no problem for us in the future. I'm sure he'll be happy for us and Mum will just have to get used to it.'

'My mother was making the same complaint about Gran when I phoned her this morning,' said Sophie. 'Apparently Dad was shouting at Gran to keep her nose out and if he chooses not to visit any time Catherine's there then that's his business. Mum says she understands her wanting to get on with her own life looking after Arlene without being under constant scrutiny.'

Stephen screwed up his face. 'They're so childish!' He added with a mischievous glint in his eye, 'We're like Romeo and Juliet caught in the middle of a family feud.'

Sophie pressed her lips together and began straightening the cutlery before responding with a note of impatience in her usually soft voice, 'It's all so stupid; and probably over nothing, knowing Dad.' Then she looked up and said optimistically, 'Maybe when they find out about us they'll bury the hatchet and forget the past. Anyway, as soon as Mum's found a house not far from Gran, she'll be back in Aberdeen until the house sales are completed. You can meet her properly then.'

'My theory is,' said Stephen seriously, 'that it's when Rosie's around that they stay apart because she stirs up the trouble. Anyway, I don't think my mother has properly grown up.' He fiddled with the edge of the tablecloth and seemed embarrassed. 'Imagine having a baby at her age. She always did make a big thing about wanting a family and a happy home life but what I remember most from my childhood is her packing a case and chasing after some story for the newspaper as if we meant nothing to her. Sometimes we didn't see her for days at a time when she went off with her reporter friends setting the world to rights over a few drinks or many drinks come to that.'

'I thought your mum didn't drink,' said Sophie, screwing up her nose from the tickly bubbles of her cola.

'Not now she doesn't, but she used to. Dad was very patient. There was a time I'd hear them arguing constantly. If it wasn't about having more children it was about her drinking. So, for whatever the reason, the little girl Mum wanted wasn't to be at that time. Neither of them knew I was lying awake listening to their angry voices.

'When we came on our own to Aberdeen I was sure that we would never see Dad again and Mum began drinking really heavily. I remember times when she wasn't able to get out of bed in the morning. It got really bad and she was hardly ever sober. That's when I think she saw sense and gave it up. There were lots of on goings I knew about but never mentioned. She must have thought

I was blind or stupid. But once Dad did arrive home, and it turned out he was sick, they grew ever so close, like Darby and Joan. They were so engrossed with one another that sometimes I felt left out and just went to my room with my music and videos for company.

'But Dad and I did go swimming and he did help me a lot with my homework. That's when the penny dropped and I began to understand and enjoy maths. Who would ever have believed it, and now I'm a fully qualified engineer.' Stephen cleared his throat with embarrassment and rubbed his forehead as if these childhood memories were causing him pain. 'Sorry, Sophie, I must be boring you. I've never told anyone all that stuff before.' His heart began to sink. Maybe he had frightened her away opening up like that. He reached over the table for her hand. 'I don't really care what my mother does, honestly.'

Sophie gave his hand a reassuring squeeze. 'Why shouldn't you tell me how you feel? I want to know what makes you tick. I am your friend after all.'

Stephen looked deep into her eyes. 'Please tell me we're more than just friends. You mean a lot to me, Sophie. I can't imagine what life was like before I met you properly.'

Sophie gave a broad smile. 'Of course we are. I enjoy being with you so much.'

'Even if you leave and go to London or thereabouts to work, I won't be far away,' said Stephen initiating the idea of a future together. 'I'm thinking of applying for work in Kent. We'll still be able to see lots of each other, well at least at weekends.'

'Remember, if I'm a nurse, I'll have shifts to consider,' Sophie replied. She held his eyes with hers as if testing his true determination to pursue this relationship to a happy conclusion.

Her heart leapt with joy when Stephen didn't flinch, and with unblinking sincerity replied, 'We'll sort something out. Don't worry; love will find a way.' In spite of his beard it was noticeable that he'd flushed deep red. He'd meant to tread carefully with Sophie and take it easy to be sure of winning her over, but from the brightness of Sophie's eyes and the glow of happiness that shone from her pink cheeks Stephen had said exactly what she wanted to hear. It was settled. They would have a future together. Nothing would tear them apart. Stephen lifted his half drunk pint of lager high in the air. 'To us!' he said with a loud note of cheer in his voice.

Sophie laughed and clinked her glass of cola against his. 'To us; we're going to be so happy.' For the rest of the meal they whispered and giggled with excitement as they made plans and dreamed dreams. 'I would like a large family when I get married,' said Sophie. 'And although she is older, I can understand your mum having another child. That's what life is all about.'

Arms around each other they walked down the hotel path that was overhung by deep red rhododendron blooms. A soft summer perfume rose from the fallen crimson petals strewn underfoot as if laid out especially for them. Stephen turned to Sophie just before they reached the car and took her hand in his. It was so small and fragile. He bent to kiss her fingers and when she drew closer he shivered as her hair fell like an angel's caress across the back of his neck. He looked up and saw the longing in her eyes. As he put his arms around her he felt his lips tingle as her mouth met his. Her body softened as she leaned into him and he held her tight, their bodies moulding like molten liquid into every secret part of each other. They teased each other with moist, tickling tongues until, with shared breath they were caught in their first long, lingering kiss. As Sophie sank deeper into Stephen's enveloping embrace she knew that this was where she wanted to spend the rest of her life.

'I think we'd better go,' said Stephen after what seemed an eternity in Heaven. He was suddenly nervous. He'd become fully aroused and wanted more. But this was Sophie. She was special and he didn't want to rush her. He looked down at her upturned face. Her cheeks were flushed and damp. There was unmistakeable longing in her eyes. She kissed him again and her firm youthful figure quivered like a live wire touching and electrifying him. There was no doubt in his mind now. She wanted him as much as he wanted her. 'Let's go to mine,' he said in a hoarse whisper. 'Mum's still away. We'll have the place to ourselves.'

Sophie nodded. She seemed too breathless for speech. Her eyes were heavy with desire. 'I'm not on the pill,' she said quietly.

'Don't worry,' said Stephen, 'I'll see to that side of things.' He was in a daze. Today was the day he had been waiting for the whole of his life. 'I'm going to take care of you from now on,' he said, and holding her hand gently but firmly he led her to the car. Sophie smiled. Falling in love had been so easy.

Although they were impatient to be together they were nonetheless shy. On the doorstep as Stephen put the key in the lock and let them in, their laughter changed to an awkward silence. They went upstairs on tiptoe even though there was no one else around. Stephen asked Sophie one more time if she was happy and she assured him that this was what she wanted. 'Why are we whispering?' he laughed as they entered his room. It was still tidy in preparation for the conquest he had planned all those weeks ago never suspecting it would be Sophie, who was now his fiancée in all but a ring.

Gently he took her hand in his and led her over to the bed where she sat on the edge. She looked around her nervously saying nothing. Stephen noticed her breath was coming in quick short bursts; she was ready for him and waiting. He drew the thin summer curtains that allowed the afternoon sun to shine through and provide the subdued lighting that kindles romance. Pulling Sophie up into his arms he whispered sweet promises in her ear and kissed her soft, silky white neck. A shudder ran through her and she gave a little cry. Slowly he removed her clothing and dropped it piece by piece on to the carpet at her feet. She was beautiful, like a goddess. Her body was still that of a young girl, pure, untouched and virginal. He buried his face in the arch of her neck and inhaled the perfume of her skin. The heady fragrance that emanated from her nakedness filled the room with that most powerful of aphrodisiacs and transformed the musty bachelor pad into a paradise garden.

He ran his fingertips down from the gentle curve of her waist and over her hips that were as slender as any boy's until he was stroking her thighs that were as smooth as silk and the inner part of them as soft and sweet as honey. Her long golden hair draped her perfect porcelain shoulders and fell in soft ringlets to where her breasts began to rise. They were small and pert with nipples erect like tiny pink rosebuds begging to be plucked. He stooped down and kissed them, taking each one in his mouth in turn.

He stopped and looked into her eyes for confirmation that he should continue and although her overall appearance was one of maidenly innocence, her eyes burned with womanly desire. The build up to this moment had taken every ounce of his patience and now he could no longer wait. He tore off his own clothes in record time. His athletic broad shoulders and well defined torso led Sophie to gasp with admiration and longing. Taking hold of his muscular arms she bent forward and allowed her warm, parted lips to brush his chest and let them follow the contours of his body until he tingled from head to toe as she used her teeth and tongue to tantalise him with little bites and tickles until he could stand it no more.

He pulled her with him on to the bed where he began kissing every inch of her until she could no longer hold back and was as desperate for him as he was for her. His secret stash of condoms, hidden under a corner of the fitted foam backed carpet that could be lifted and flattened out again, would come in handy after all. Stephen was sure that if electricity were visible to the naked eye, the powerful surges of energy between Sophie and him would have appeared like explosions in a rainbow.

To describe the rest of the evening in his room as bliss would be an understatement of the pleasure each one experienced at being with the other. They were perfect together. A match predestined by Heaven itself. He had been right to wait until the right girl came along. Once she realised how delightful Sophie was, his mother would love her too, regardless of who her father was. Sophie was his princess. As she cuddled down beside her beloved Stephen for the night she whispered in his ear, 'I can't believe this is how our future's going to be. It seems that living happily ever after doesn't only happen in fairy tales.'

'Nothing and no one can ever separate us,' Stephen murmured and kissed her once more on her soft, moist lips.

Chapter 30

Sophie had been crying when Stephen collected her at the gates of the hospital. 'I'm late,' she blurted out without waiting to be asked the reason for her upset.

'What do you mean late? We said eight o'clock and it's only five to,' said Stephen naïvely. He put his arms round her to give her a welcoming kiss but she pushed him away.

'Not late to meet you, Stephen but something much worse.' Sophie looked down at the ground and scraped the toe of her shoe over the loose pieces of gravel on the asphalt. 'I think I might be pregnant.' She burst into tears and became almost hysterical in her distress. 'What will Mum and Dad say? They'll be furious. I've let them down.'

Stephen took hold of her firmly by the shoulders that heaved up and down uncontrollably and spoke in a voice that was suddenly filled with agitation. 'You can't be pregnant. I thought you said you'd started taking the pill.'

'I have, but that can take a while to start working. And I've been feeling dizzy; and there are other signs.' Sophie looked up at Stephen. He was supposed to have 'taken care' of everything.

'Damn these bloody condom machines in the Gents,' he said. He was chewing at his lips and the inside of his mouth. Beads of sweat broke out across his furrowing forehead. 'I should have bought them from the chemist, but I was too embarrassed.' A stab of remorse hit him hard in the stomach when he saw the suffering in her pale little face and the dark circles ringing her careworn eyes. 'I'm so sorry,' he said. The heavy ache of unexpected responsibility settled across his back and black clouds seemed to gather round his fogged up head. He took her tiny hand in his and kissed it as they walked forlornly to the car. It wasn't supposed to be like this. Sophie was sniffing into a handkerchief and Stephen didn't know how to get her to stop. As he reached down to open the car door for her a thought came to him and the sun rose brightly in their horizon again. Once seated inside he shared his latest idea with her and said quite matter of factly, 'We were going to be married anyway. This just brings it forward.'

Sophie stopped crying and turned quickly towards him. 'Do you mean it? You're not going to abandon me?'

Stephen shrugged and gave a laugh. 'Don't be ridiculous; why would I leave you when you mean everything to me? You're my whole life and the baby will only make it more special.'

Sophie sighed. She was full of apprehension about what her parents might say. There had never in the whole of her life up until now been what might be called 'words' between them. Her life had been mapped out for her and this wasn't part of their plan. Stephen put his arm tightly round her shoulders. It was as if he had read her mind. 'We're a couple now. We've grown up and we're soon to be parents ourselves. I'm the one who will be looking after you from now on.' Sophie blew her nose and tucked her hanky into her pocket.

Stephen was right. No more crying. They would face this situation together. Surely her parents would want her to be happy. Stephen put the key in the ignition and started the engine. Sophie put her hand on his arm to stop him moving off. 'I have something else to tell you. Mum came home yesterday. They've found a house that suits them at last and they're going to accept the offer made on our one. I went to see her for half an hour after my shift last night and she's been packing boxes like fury.' Stephen let the engine stall. He felt suddenly sick to his stomach. The courage he'd felt while they had their lives to themselves ebbed quickly away. Jimmy's face loomed large in front of his mind's eye. He would have some explaining to do.

Sophie sensed his discomfort. 'Why don't you come round and meet Mum properly. She'll take to you, I know it. I told her I had a boyfriend but I kept its being you as a surprise. I knew that you wanted to tell your mother first before my dad.'

Stephen looked sheepish. 'I've a confession to make too. My mother's been home over a week now but it's never been the right time to let her know about us. The truth is that I've been putting it off until she stops moaning about Rosie and Jimmy. I didn't want our relationship blighted by their never ending squabbles.'

Sophie pursed her lips and then a smile spread across her face. 'Start the engine. I have an idea. It's too late to turn the clock back but we could visit Mum now instead of going to the pictures. Once she's used to the idea we'll tell her about the baby.'

Stephen had no choice but to agree. He rubbed his sweaty palms down the rough denim of his jeans, gripped the wheel and pressed hard on the accelerator. 'Brace yourself, Sophie; we're in for a rough ride.'

They stopped outside Patricia's beautiful home. This was Stephen's second visit and the night they would drop the bombshell. The previous evening had been a great success. There was no reason to postpone telling Patricia who would make a strong ally in the face of opposition from the other parents. The SOLD sign was plain for all to see and there was already a pile of cardboard boxes blocking one of the bedroom windows. Patricia had been busy. The four bedroom detached house in Basildon had obviously monopolised her mind and she couldn't wait for their new life to begin. It was roomy enough too for Rosie should the day ever come when she would need their care. Stephen and Patricia got on like a house on fire, especially when he offered to stack the boxes neatly that were lying everywhere and too heavy for a woman to lift on her own. Sophie had told her mother she'd strained her back lifting a heavy patient and couldn't help when in truth she hadn't wanted to risk any harm coming to the baby that had recently attached itself to her womb.

Stephen gave Sophie a quick peck on the cheek. 'Yesterday went better than I ever expected. Your mum definitely likes me and was quite impressed by my being a fully qualified engineer and willing to move to Kent to be beside you.'

'I would imagine she's heard nothing but good about you from every quarter: my dad, Eddie of course and especially Rosie who always said Mum overreacted that time we were a bit cheeky.' Sophie spoke excitedly and clutched her hands in front of her as if offering up a final prayer that news of her pregnancy would be received with equal acceptance. 'Now she thinks you're the ideal man for me. The only thing she objected to was the beard.' After a quick little laugh she added, 'And I notice that won't be a problem anymore; and just look at you all dressed up in your Sunday best. Mum must have made quite an impression on you too.' She gave him a thorough once over before raising her lips to kiss him on the cheek. 'You're wearing the same clothes you were wearing on the night we met. You're a sentimental fool after all and I love you so much.'

Stephen smiled and stroked his baby soft chin. 'I shaved it off this morning and of course I want to look smart. I'm ready to take on my role as family man and I have to look the part so your mother will trust me.'

'I'm sure it'll make all the difference. And when it comes to Mum telling Dad she'll be singing your praises so much he'll have no option but to be as happy as we are. But what about your mother? When are you going to tell her?' Sophie leaned towards him and began stroking his smooth face. 'You're even better looking now than you were before and my parents will be delighted that I've chosen you.' She didn't look so confident when she said quietly, 'I only hope I can win the same approval from yours.'

Stephen took her hand that rested now on his thigh and patted it gently as if he were reassuring a child. 'She'll be fine. I told her I had a great surprise in store for her but I'm sure she thinks it's a job. Don't worry, I'll definitely tell her tomorrow.' Stephen felt the butterflies in his tummy giving a quick flutter. Sophie didn't realise that the gulf between his mother and her dad had widened. Rosie had been giving Catherine an immense amount of grief while living under her roof. The short but welcome respite from non-stop interrogation had ceased. Rosie was back in full fury now she had recovered from Eddie's illness and death. In fact, without him to bark at all day she had all the more time and energy to concentrate on getting to the bottom of Stephen's parentage. Although he had no inkling of this being the cause of the rift, he knew his mother was going to go through the roof when she discovered they were all about to become in-laws.

But she would have no choice. Whatever issues his mother and Jimmy had from the past they would have to let bygones be bygones if they wanted to be included in their grandchild's life. Sophie was a woman he would be proud to show off as his wife anywhere and anything his mother said wouldn't make one whit of difference. He was going to marry the girl of his dreams and that was an end of it. But he wished he could feel this brave when in her actual presence and she was tearing Rosie to shreds for having tried so hard to inveigle her into Jimmy's company.

Patricia had set the table especially for the happy couple coming to dinner. A centrepiece of dried flowers she'd made herself and the highly polished silver cutlery set out complete with linen napkins spoke volumes. She was delighted with her daughter's choice. When the bell rang and they walked in, there was no containing her excitement as she rushed from the kitchen to welcome them in the hallway with warm hugs and kisses. Her heart gave a skip and a jump when she saw the joy in her daughter's eyes and she nodded with pleasure to see that Stephen had lost the dark stubble that she normally connected with vagrants and ne'er do wells. He certainly was a handsome lad. She liked a man with a generous mouth, not one of those thin-lipped, mean, mousy characters. She gave him a second kiss on the cheek and gratefully accepted the box of chocolates he handed her.

During the meal she confessed to having told Jimmy. 'We were on the phone last night,' she said, her voice brimming with happiness before biting into her bottom lip like a little girl who couldn't keep a secret, 'and I was so excited I could hardly get the story straight. He did go strangely quiet but that's to be expected from him. I've always known that any boyfriend of Sophie or Sylvie would have difficulty matching up to his expectations.' She smiled across at Stephen and Sophie who were tucking into their rack of lamb as she spoke endlessly about their high hopes for the girls. 'I don't think he'll be disappointed, and even if it takes a while we'll talk him round. He trusts my judgement.'

'That was a delicious meal, Mrs Simpson,' Stephen said politely, rising from the table and insisting on going through to the kitchen to help Sophie with the dishes while Patricia prepared a tea tray for later, all the while singing happily to herself. 'You know, Stephen,' she said between verses of a little love ditty, 'don't you think it's about time you started calling me Patricia. Mrs Simpson is so formal and we are going to be family after all.' She winked over at Sophie who was up to her elbows in soap suds and grinning like a Cheshire cat. 'It may not be long before you're calling me "Mum"', she said to Stephen, handing him a fresh tea towel.

Stephen smiled and wiped at the plates with renewed gusto. 'It'll be a pleasure, Patricia.' Perhaps the news of the baby might not go down so badly after all.

Seated in quiet harmony, sipping tea and nibbling little biscuits, Sophie felt the time was right to introduce this next snippet of information. 'Mum,' Sophie said, 'we have something to tell you. You know we said we were planning on getting engaged? Well there's more ...' Sophie wanted to get this over with quickly. She knew her mother had been pregnant when she married her father, so hopefully what she had to say wouldn't cause too much trouble.

Suddenly there was the slam of a taxi door outside, and heavy footsteps running up the gravel. The cosy tea party stopped in mid-conversation. 'Who could that be?' said Patricia. She was annoyed that the evening of celebration she'd been looking forward to all her married life was being so rudely interrupted. She let out a sharp cry of surprise when the front door crashed open followed by Jimmy bursting into the living room like someone possessed. Without stopping to explain, he lunged past his wife, who sat mouth wide open, to reach for Stephen who was sitting beside her with a bone china cup in one hand and a pink wafer biscuit in the other. Jimmy grabbed him by the collar and threw him to the floor, scattering the hot tea and dishes in every direction bringing to life the old saying 'like a bull in a china shop'. But this bull was crazy and stamped and bellowed fit to explode. His nostrils flared and he was roaring beastlike.

Patricia and Sophie both screamed and rose to their feet and clung to each other in shock. Jimmy managed to force a struggling Stephen back on to the floor and was astride him, taking him by the shoulders and hammering him against the carpet so hard that Stephen seemed to have stopped breathing and had turned as purple as his attacker. Then Jimmy set up a wail like the wild cry of a banshee in the night. 'Don't you dare lay a finger on my Sophie. Stay away or I'll kill you with my bare hands.' He repeated 'stay away; stay away' until tears spurted from his eyes and ran down his face.

Patricia knew Jimmy might not be too welcoming to either of her daughters' suitors but she had never expected anything like this. After she'd told him on the phone about Sophie and Stephen last night, he must have taken the first available flight home. 'Leave him alone Jimmy!' Patricia's voice rose above his in protest. She clutched her howling daughter trying to shield her from the brawl in the middle of her so tastefully decorated lounge. 'Sophie's in love with Stephen. He's the one she's chosen. Leave him alone; they're happy.'

Jimmy ignored her. Sweat was pouring down his face and he was shaking Stephen by the throat now like a terrier shakes the life out of a rat. Sophie sat down and burst into tears and began nursing her tummy where the new baby was already starting to grow. 'Stop, Daddy, please;' she cried, 'we're going to be married. I think I might be pregnant ...'

There was no stopping Jimmy now. He was beyond speech and grumblings in his throat rumbled like a volcano ready to erupt. Sophie screamed and tried to pull him off Stephen who was trying to protest that he loved Sophie and wanted her to be his wife. Jimmy held his grip round his throat all the tighter and Stephen's face turned a deeper blue as Jimmy applied more pressure to his windpipe. Stephen tried to shove Jimmy back by the face and even pushed his finger tips into his eyes but he was fighting with the super strength of a madman and couldn't be stopped. Frothing at the mouth, he prepared to spit out the words that were going to change happiness to horror in one fell swoop. 'You can't marry her!' he wept. 'You're my son.' Having finally spoken, he fell against Stephen's chest exhausted. His next utterance was said almost in a whisper. 'Sophie's your sister.'

Stephen had been trying to heave Jimmy off him but fell back on to the floor for a few seconds, too stunned by what he'd just heard to make any effort to get up. There was a deathly hush as the women took a moment or two to absorb the awful truth. Stephen, lying flat out staring at the ceiling, was first to break the silence. 'But how? I can't think straight. Nobody's ever said anything before.'

Jimmy had resumed his position on top of Stephen determined to keep him from going anywhere near Sophie. He snarled for all to hear, 'Don't be such a bloody fool. Do you really think I would readily own up to you being mine and Catherine's son and ruin my whole life? Gregor wasn't your father. I am.' He was staring straight down at him but there was no love in his eyes this time, only revulsion and deep hatred. Stephen snapped when he realised that Jimmy was speaking the truth and he tore the skin of Jimmy's face with his nails as if wanting to destroy any similarity between them.

As the two of men struggled on the carpet the striking resemblance that had been masked by Stephen's recent beard became apparent. No one but Rosie had thought to look for it before and it was usually only Catherine who saw them together. Although Jimmy's hair was receding and grey at the sides, what he had stood up in spikes around his head the same as Stephen's. The confirmation of a definite blood relationship couldn't be missed. The shape of their heads was identical, Stephen's lips were slightly fuller than Jimmy's whose had thinned with age. But the most pronounced similarity was the look; the way they glared at each other, shock in Stephen's eyes and defeat in Jimmy's as he realised that even murder couldn't solve the problem. Stephen got up and his whole face contorted with loathing as he turned his back on the man he had only known as a visitor to his house. It was beyond belief that this brute was his real father.

He could not bear to look at Sophie who was nursing the new life within her, the life that he was responsible for putting there, the child that was part of them both. The possible outcome of their incestuous union struck home. 'No child of mine is going to be born a freak,' he cried over to her. 'If you're my sister, you'd better get rid of that foetus pretty damned quick.' He brushed down his clothes that were covered in tea dregs and crumbs and took a couple of steps to go and collect his jacket from over the back of a dining chair. Jimmy grabbed him back and threw a swing at him but missed. Stephen caught him by the clenched fist, twisted him round and pushed his arm up his back in a half nelson. Jimmy's muscles tightened and he mustered all his strength to wrench himself free. He squared up to Stephen. He had seen the look of horror that had passed across his daughter's face – the daughter he had worked for and sheltered from all the world's evils. Although Stephen had put into words exactly what he himself had been thinking about his grandchild, he would not stand by and watch Sophie being bludgeoned into madness with the god awful suggestion that the child she carried might be a monster.

'Watch what you're saying, lad, in front of my daughter,' he growled and landed Stephen a punch that sent him sprawling across the floor. Jimmy was immediately on his knees beside him and hauled him to a sitting position by the front of his shirt, ripping the buttons from it as he did so. His vision blurred as he pressed his nose against that of his son. He longed to smash that face - the face that reminded him of his own cruelty when he'd behaved like an animal in rut when he'd forced himself on Catherine against her will. Who would have believed the events of that night could come back to haunt him with such torturing consequences? He'd been a totally different person then. He'd changed and had dedicated his life to living decently as if in recompense. He doted on his wife and daughters and there was nothing he wouldn't have done for them. This was worse than if the devil himself had spawned his seed in an angel of goodness.

Worn out, he released his son and lay with his face on his shoulder and cried with despair. Stephen lay under him eyes closed as if knocked unconscious. Sophie couldn't help herself as she moved forward to help him, but he opened his eyes, and, as he shoved the sobbing Jimmy off, Stephen drove her back with a murderous look, 'Don't ever come near me again.' His lip curled as if she were disgusting and evil and she stumbled back on to the sofa as if she had been physically struck. She laid her hand protectively on her tummy. 'It can't be true. It can't. I'm going to have your baby.' She began to weep and rocked backwards and forwards as if already nursing the little one in her womb.

Patricia sat beside her, cradling her in her arms. She had watched and listened in silence. Surely she was hearing things. Surely she must waken soon. All she wanted now was for these two men to get out of her house and leave her with her daughter who would need her as she'd never needed her before. Jimmy was on his hands and knees trying to stand up but Stephen kicked him on his underbelly and sent him sprawling to lie sobbing on the carpet. Jimmy crawled to his wife's lap and tried to squeeze in beside where Sophie was snuggled, but when he laid his head on the soft, warm cushion of Patricia's thighs and cried, she felt such revulsion for him that she pushed him roughly from her so that he cowered at her feet like a beaten dog.

'When did it happen?' She spoke slowly and deliberately between her teeth. 'Sophie's older than Stephen. It must have been after I was expecting her ...'

Jimmy made no effort to rise. 'We weren't married at the time. I didn't know what I was doing,' he sobbed.

Stephen stood over the man whose blood he shared and the reason for his mother's hatred of him took seed in his mind. Swaying from mental and physical exhaustion he closed his eyes and took deep breaths. Somewhat recovered he rubbed his fingers round his neck and throat that already showed signs of bruising. 'You fooled us all, you bastard,' he said. 'You're no better than an animal; you're scum.' He kicked his father hard on the backside sending him rolling over into the foetal position. Jimmy drew his knees hard up to his chest and whimpered like a whipped animal. Stephen gathered up his jacket and headed for the door without a backward glance.

Sophie let out a cry of anguish and called after him to come back but Patricia restrained her. 'You have to let him go,' she said gently before striking her husband hard smack in the middle of his snivelling face with the underside of her shoe as he grovelled at her feet. Stephen crashed blindly out the door into the dark night, the questions he'd always asked himself about the relationship between his mother and Jimmy well and truly answered.

He bolted like a runaway horse into the street and away from the hell where less than an hour before he had been talking and laughing about a heavenly future. He threw himself into the car and revved the engine, crashing through the gears as it took off like a rocket along the street. He had no thought for safety. All he wanted was a quick burst of acceleration that would enable his escape from the horrific reality that had changed in minutes from the pleasure of looking forward to a wonderful life with Sophie and the new baby to a black pit of destitution and nothingness. They had set out that night to break their joyous news to Patricia, who was now a broken woman holding her destroyed daughter in her arms. He blasted his way through the roads taking corners like a maniac, screeching past every other vehicle in his path until he had left the city and was driving along pitch dark country lanes.

Stephen sped on through the night. Sometimes, when he came to the narrow zigzag bends he would close his eyes as he turned the wheel taking the chance that he might go hurtling down some wooded embankment into the oblivion that would have brought him blessed relief. His youthful craving for life was too strong to make him do anything deliberately, but he was desperate enough to play Russian roulette with fate and dice with death. He was well clear now of any buildings or houses. He veered without even changing gear up a side path near a gravel pit and into a dark lay-by. He pressed his feet on the clutch and brakes with such force that he almost catapulted himself through the windscreen.

Chapter 31

Catherine had settled Arlene for the night and was hoping for a quiet evening with a book when loud banging at the door along with a simultaneous ringing at the doorbell had her running to answer it. She knew immediately there must be something wrong and her hand flew automatically to her throat. Whoever it was had their finger pressed hard on the bell and wouldn't release it. She hoped it wasn't the police. She knew Stephen loved driving fast and her heart fluttered to think something might have happened to him. Preparing herself for the worst she turned the handle but she had barely opened the door a crack before Jimmy, without so much as a by your leave, pushed his way past her and stormed into the living room knocking over the standard lamp in his haste. Catherine thought he must be blazing drunk and ordered him out. She stood with her hands on her hips at the door of the lounge fuming with rage at the cheek of him frightening her like that. Who did he think he was? 'Get out of here with your drunken carry on,' she screamed in fury as she picked up the lamp and straightened the shade. 'Stephen will be in shortly, and I won't be responsible for anything he does to you when he arrives.'

Jimmy ignored her rantings and threw himself into a chair. Catherine stared in a mixture of rage and amazement as he rocked backwards and forwards with his head in his hands. When he heard Stephen's name mentioned he let out a roar that frightened Catherine into silence. 'I'm not drunk,' he said. He could barely speak; his voice was shaky and hoarse. She stepped towards him and noticed that his body was trembling and sweat was dripping off his forehead. Something terrible must have happened.

'Is it Rosie?' she asked, thinking that maybe his mother had taken ill or even worse. There was no answer. Catherine clutched the back of the sofa as if she were about to faint. His agitation had passed to her and she had to sit down as her knees grew wobbly beneath her. 'Is it Patricia ...? The girls ...?' she asked. Surely there must be some serious reason for him being in this deranged state. Jimmy let out a cry like the squeal of an animal caught in a gin trap and she actually rose to her feet and walked over to him and laid a comforting hand on his shoulder. At her touch he lifted his head and looked up at her. His eyes were sunken in a way she had never seen them before and had the hollow look of someone who found being alive too painful to bear. His face was a dingy yellow as if he were jaundiced and blinding tears were streaming down his cheeks that were smeared like a mucky child's from where he had been wiping them away. His nose had been bleeding and his knuckles were skinned and bloodied. He'd been in a fight but with whom? What if he became violent again? Catherine grew frightened and backed away. Nothing he said or did was making any sense.

'I went into a church years ago like you and your mother used to do. I was the only one there. I went down on my knees right at the very front and prayed. I spoke my repentance out loud and all the time I looked at Jesus hanging on the cross and swore to live a good life to make up for the evil I had done.' He stared at her and she grew nervous. Crazy people often took to religion in this melodramatic way. She didn't know why but it was a fact. Nothing she said would stop him shouting at her.

'Nobody ever knew how sorry I was. I've lived my whole life to the point of perfection trying to compensate. I've had to live with the regret of what I did but you never believed me. I thought God would listen. I prayed so hard, I really did. I said I was sorry, but where was the forgiveness? All I've got in return is this cruel retribution. It's God's vengeance and a punishment worse than any I could have ever imagined. I'd rather be dead.' Catherine was worried. He was like a maniac. And where was all this biblical stuff coming from? She was sure he must have taken a brain storm. She didn't know if she should call the police or an ambulance. Jimmy fell to his knees on the floor with his forehead pressed to the carpet.

'Please tell me what's wrong?' Catherine persisted. 'Maybe I can help. Are you sure you're sober?'

'Of course I am. You know I hardly touch the stuff. Who would have thought it would come to this?'

Catherine put her hand under his arm to help him up. 'Come

on, Jimmy, come and sit down. I'll make you a cup of tea.' She was scared for his sanity and repeated her questions. 'Where is Patricia? Is Sophie all right? Is it your mother?'

Jimmy paid no heed. He was incoherent and his lips were sprayed with saliva like somebody who had really lost their mind. 'Sophie, my little darling ...' He was weeping now and threw his head back and roared up to the ceiling, 'Have you no mercy?' It was obviously God he was calling upon.

Catherine didn't know what to think. She poured him a large glass of whisky left over from New Year and offered it to him straight.

He pushed it away and then, changing his mind, reached out for it and took a slug. 'Why did you let it happen?' he said, looking her straight in the eye. His voice had become a harsh whisper.

Catherine was at a loss and feeling frightened backed off and sat on the sofa waiting. She knew he had to calm down eventually. She couldn't think of anything she'd done that would cause such a reaction. And from the sound of it, something awful had happened to Sophie. Jimmy drained the last of the whisky and put down the glass. He spoke slowly, robotically, as if he couldn't believe what he was saying. 'Stephen and Sophie have been seeing each other,' he said and started to sob. Catherine was speechless for a moment until the full meaning of his words hit home.

'What ...?' she cried and fell back against a cushion in shock. She thought for a moment. The solution was simple. It would upset a few people, but they would get over it. If Jimmy was worried about Patricia's reaction then that was his problem. She would have enough on her plate dealing with Stephen. She tried to speak soothingly, to make him see sense and be rational. Even if the youngsters had become friends, the truth could be explained calmly to them and that would be an end of it. 'But if you've told them the truth they'll just have to stop seeing each other. It will be hard, but they must,' she said gently, but she had become worried about Stephen. Where was he?

'If only it were that easy,' he shouted, 'but it's not. Sophie's pregnant! She's ruined.' He started to wail again like a child who is beyond consolation. 'If you want to destroy a man,' he cried, 'destroy the thing he loves most. That's what they say isn't it? This is pay-off time for what I did to you.' Catherine stared at him speechlessly. She should have felt pleased to see him broken but she wasn't. There was nothing sweet about this horrifying revenge. If Jimmy was like this, how had Stephen reacted? For one awful second she thought that maybe Jimmy had killed him. Her heart leapt in her throat. She thought it was either going to choke her or thunder to a complete halt.

'I think you'd better go now,' she said without leaving her seat. She knew her legs would never hold her if she tried to stand. 'See yourself out. I have Stephen to think of. You'll have to sort things out with your own family.'

Jimmy looked across at her and eased himself out of his chair. He was blubbering, a lost little boy who had been caught out and couldn't face the consequences. 'Who would have thought it ...?' He carried on his lament as he made his way reluctantly to the door and out into the darkness of the night.

Chapter 32

Stephen screeched to a halt at the side of the gravel pit deep in the wilds of the countryside where he and Sophie had often stopped to discuss their future and spend an amorous hour or two together. 'Those damned cheap condoms from the machine!' he cursed. 'I should have known better.' He flung open the car door still bursting with rage, climbed out and slammed it behind him. All around was pitch black. A massive blanket of stars twinkled in the sky above but they seemed to be mocking him. The tiny sliver of an old moon curled away with its back to him. He didn't deserve its light anyway, a pervert like him.

He groped his way to the boot and jerked it open. The light came on just enough to enable him to locate the hammer. His mind raced with memories of Sophie and him cuddling on the back seat and making love. He could see the shadowy ghosts of the two of them now as if they were solid living beings in each other's arms and not just the figments of a mind that was tinged with madness. He swung the hammer like a club high above his head and brought it down to smash every window one by one into smithereens. He beat hard against the bodywork thrashing it as if it were a heinous monster that he wanted to kill. He pummelled at every inch of it until there was not a fragment left and the tough metal bodywork was beaten beyond recognition. The ground round about looked as if it had been snowed on with crumbling pebbles of broken glass that crunched underfoot. He smashed the light too and he was glad that he could no longer see the remains.

He felt his way round the misshapen wreck to the boot again and lifted out the can of spare petrol he always carried since once being stranded miles from a filling station. He unscrewed the metal cap and the petrol trickled cold on to his hands and mingled with the blood where his hands had been torn during the onslaught on the vehicle that held such guilty secrets; where he'd had sex with his sister, not just once but nearly every night since his mother had come home and many times before that. Waves of nausea poured over him and he began to throw up.

The truth was beginning to penetrate and change from an ordinary nightmare from which it was possible to waken to a reality he would have to face for the rest of his life. Panic struck and his stomach churned. This would be on his conscience forever and meant his future held nothing now but misery dogging him every step of the way? He dowsed the upholstery, the floor and the boot itself. The fumes struck at the back of his throat making him gasp for air. Feeling for the evening paper that he knew lay on the back seat he rolled it up tightly. He stepped well back and drew a box of matches from his pocket. He struck one and a small yellow flicker lit up the darkness. He shielded the flame with his hand from the night air until it became a flare. He lit the cylinder of paper and screamed like a madman as he threw the fiery torch into the wreck. The flames licked up the petrol which exploded into a violent raging fire, which spread quickly and turned the car into an inferno. There was an almighty blast as the tank of fuel blew up. In seconds the heat from the conflagration was unbearable and lit up the countryside for miles around. When he felt sure that the car was destroyed beyond all retrieval he turned and walked away, his life burnt out and wasted. The agony in his heart exceeded by far the pain in his scorched hands.

He hadn't gone far when he heard the sirens of police cars and fire engines. He sidestepped into the bushes at the edge of the road and strode further into the woods, crashing through the undergrowth like a hunted animal. He lay down among the sharp bracken and soon the blackness of unconsciousness brought about by exhaustion closed over him. The human mind can only take so much and his had reached saturation point.

He may have lain like that for minutes or even hours until a creature, small like a vole or a mouse, scampered over his face and he woke up wondering at first how on earth he had come to be in the middle of a dark wood almost buried in a pile of rotting leaves. From the branch of a tree nearby an owl hooted and he heard the slow, steady flap of its wings as it hunted its food. The agonising scream of captured prey made his heart race and he broke out in a cold sweat as he simultaneously remembered the events of the previous evening.

When he was sure the fire brigade and police must have done the necessary and were gone, he turned up the collar of his jacket and walked out into the rain. He could barely lift one foot after another from fatigue. His face was soaked with tears and rain mingling together. The cuts and bruises from earlier began to sting and his bruised body ached from the fight with Jimmy. He stopped and held his burnt hands under the cold rainwater that ran deep in a ditch at the side of the road until the pain in them slowly eased. As his feet squelched in his shoes, every step he took seemed to be saying 'Sophie, Sophie'. Was there to be no release?

He couldn't face going home. His mother must have known the truth. If Jimmy knew then so must she. How could they have kept such a secret? His whole life was a lie. And Dad wasn't his father! He howled at the stars that sparkled in the dark sky as if they had gathered to cry shame on him. It would have been better to have had no past at all. His life held no meaning now. Better if he'd never existed in the first place if this was how it was to end.

He had no concept of the passing of time, or memory of having walked miles as he approached the outskirts of the town. A few vehicles rumbled past. Lorries were taking off in the early hours to beat the morning rush and vans were bringing workers to the first shift of the day. Already there was a hint of pink and yellow in the east where the sun was preparing to rise. Seagulls screamed a territorial warning from the rooftops before setting off in search of food among the bags of rubbish left out for collection. The insistent peeping from the nests among the chimneys alerted the adult birds that there were hungry mouths to be fed and one or two large speckled fledglings staggered to the edge of the high buildings to supervise their parents' scavenging techniques and to learn how to do it when they would be expected to fend for themselves in only a few weeks' time.

Other sweeter birdsong filled the air as the dawn chorus struck up its early morning wake up call. Stephen wished the night had never ended. While it was dark he could remain hidden and keep walking until he dropped. Why did life have to begin again?

Mornings would always bring dread to him from now on. But regardless of how dead he was inside, the grey morning mist penetrated to the marrow of his bones and he felt cold; he would have to rest but he had nowhere to call home.

Everywhere he passed was shut. He went into the doorway of a corner shop to light a cigarette, sheltering it from the wind as he struck a match from the damp box against the corner of the wall. He sat on the step to think. He edged his way further in until his back was leaning against the door itself. He closed his eyes to enjoy the satisfying sensation of the nicotine hitting the back of his throat. When the cigarette was finished he pulled his knees up to his body and drew comfort from clutching them like a child that's been punished and thinking over its misdemeanours. Sleep overcame him but not for long. Something struck him hard on the chest and jolted him from his welcome oblivion. It was the early morning delivery of newspapers. The driver hadn't seen him hunched in the shadows as he chucked the bundle carelessly out through the front window of the van on his routine morning round of newsagents.

Feeling like a vagrant and chilled through in his damp, clinging clothes Stephen pounded the streets that were deserted except for an occasional bus heading from the garage to start on its route or an occasional weary person yawning their way to or from work. Daylight had broken through the last shadowy remnants of night and the streets were filling with people again. What was there to do? He was up against a brick wall. He imagined himself wandering homeless, aimless and unnoticed through crowded streets for ever. It wasn't the most appealing of futures. If only he could get some respite, but life wasn't like that, was it? It carried on relentlessly.

Just ahead, he spotted a B & B sign. At least there would be food and shelter and no questions asked. Straightening his jacket and tucking in his shirt back into his trousers he paused outside. Rain had washed away most of the earth and smoke from his body and clothing. He had to hope they would take him in and walked resolutely up the path. He knocked and waited desperately, still trying to pull himself together knowing he must look like a derelict. The landlady opened the door, suspiciously at first, but when he pulled some notes from his pocket and assured her he would pay, she gladly let him in. After all she had to make a living. Most people who came to her door were strangers and it wasn't unheard of for someone to turn up in the early hours after having been thrown out by an angry spouse.

As if by telepathy Stephen made the excuse he'd had a fall-out with his girlfriend and had nowhere else to go for the time being. The landlady shoved the required amount of notes into her apron pocket and showed him to his room which was basic but clean and there was an ensuite shower. He turned it on full blast and scrubbed himself down with scalding hot water. He covered himself with so much lather the drain clogged and the water rose in the shower unit almost to overflowing. Would he ever be properly clean again he wondered as he scoured his body with the nail brush? He towel dried his back so harshly it was covered with abrasions and looked like the marks of self flagellation that mediaeval monks inflicted on themselves as punishment with a cattail whip of knotted cords.

He hated having to wear the same clothes that he would have gladly burned there and then, but at least he managed to get most of the wetness out of them with the hairdryer. By then the smell of sizzling bacon was rising from the dining room to fill his nostrils. This was going to be the perfect hideaway. He didn't want to face anyone he knew as long as he lived. What was the point of going to university again when he wouldn't be working for a family? And anyway he'd finished his exams. They were only filling in time.

Much as he would have preferred to hide under the blankets, the landlady liked her lodgers out in the mornings. Having devoured a huge breakfast which would set him up for the day he stood on the doorstep and realised there was nothing he wanted to do and nowhere he wanted to go. The heavy fog in his mind refused to clear so he began walking round and round the block countless times. Thinking that he must be drawing attention to himself and possibly arousing suspicion he walked in a straight line into town. He took money out of his account from the hole in the wall and bought a complete new rigout from a cheap chain store and wore them straight away leaving in a bin at the corner of the changing rooms his expensive designer clothes that carried not only the memory of meeting Sophie but also the revelation she was his sister.

Back out in the street he was gripped by a sudden urge to revisit the scene of the 'crime'. Wasn't that what murderers and the like felt compelled to do and he considered himself no better than one of them. So, like a ghost retracing the haunts of a past life, he took a turn past Sophie's house. There was no one to be seen. The SOLD sign was still on show. Hopefully they would all move away soon. Head well down, he walked past his own or rather his mother's house like a prowler ready to run if he was spotted. He couldn't consider that house a home any more. His bedroom was a place of depravity.

Was this what it meant to be an outcast? Better if he'd been a leper with a warning bell to ring. At least he would have had a recognisable place within society. This was surely the end of him belonging to a family. They would despise him, even Frank. Rosie would want nothing more to do with him and as for his mother ... how could either of them look each other in the face?

Cups of tea and coffee in out of the way cafes kept him occupied for the rest of the day, and with a newspaper to hide behind no one bothered him. Come late afternoon he returned to his digs with some sandwiches from a shop. Why did they always have to smother them in sickening mayonnaise?

There was nothing on the local news about him being missing or about the burnt out car. His life had been worthless ... no more than a dream. Time hung heavy on his hands. There was nothing to do or that he wanted to do. A succession of meaningless rubbish on the television acted as a sedative until he fell asleep. And so he followed this routine for a couple of days until curiosity about the events leading up to his birth got the better of him. He had to talk to his mother.

Chapter 33

Two police officers were hammering at the door when Stephen crept like a fugitive along the street towards his path. It was now or never. Peering sideways over the high hedge of the neighbour's front garden he saw his mother was already on the doorstep talking to a couple of policemen. On sight of the uniforms she had obviously feared the worst and her hands instinctively clutched her heart. Stephen was horrified at the state she was in. Every emotion from guilt, love and scorn swept over him. Her hair was an uncombed bush sticking out in a matted tangle on either side of her gaunt face and her clothes were crumpled as if she'd been sleeping in them.

She looked up and spotted Stephen hovering at the gate. She gasped and stretched her arms out past the policemen to her son who was filled with amazement that his being missing could cause his mother to let herself go so badly. Part of him wanted to hold her close and tell her that everything would be all right, but it never could be again and would be a lie equally as bad as the make believe life she foisted on him. The thought of her betrayal took precedence over every other emotion and he stormed past the huddle on the doorstep. He shot daggers at her with a deranged look in his eyes that was enough to curdle the blood in his poor mother's veins.

The policemen accompanied her into the hallway. One of them had to take her by the arm as she collapsed against the wall of the hallway in a torrent of tears. He was furious at how this young hooligan was treating her.

'Here, lad, your mother says you were driving that vehicle we found burned out near the gravel pit.'

Stephen turned and glared at them. 'Nothing to do with me; I left it outside the pub and it was gone when I came back.' Without another word he carried on up the stairs taking them two at a time.

Catherine had reported both him and the car missing. 'I don't think he's in the mood to talk,' she stuttered. 'He's going through a difficult time, exams and all that ...' She slumped into the easy chair and the two men hovered over her; one had his notebook at the ready. They were itching to get their hands on Stephen and have him charged. 'I'll sign the statement to the effect that my son is safely returned and the car was stolen,' Catherine said meekly. 'I was the one that bought it anyway, but it was for him to use. He was driving it with my permission and was fully insured.' She wiped her eyes and put her handkerchief back in her pocket before saying quite firmly, 'I hope you manage to catch the thieves,' knowing full well that it must have been Stephen who had set fire to his pride and joy and it didn't take much imagination to guess why. Whatever their suspicions, the policemen had no choice but to leave.

Back behind the wheel of the squad car they had plenty to say on the matter. 'These bloody sons that run rings round their mothers! I'd like to see him banged up for a month or two.'

'And throw away the key,' replied the other.

Catherine breathed a sigh of relief when she heard them drive away. She was on the point of following Stephen upstairs when his bedroom door crashed shut making the whole house shake. Catherine took herself into the living room where she sat with her head in her hands well beyond tears. Filling her lungs and screaming would have brought some relief but no point in providing a reason for the policemen's return. She listened as Stephen banged about in his room. Things were being thrown from one side to the other and then the Clash being turned up to full volume perpetuated the vibration. At least the house was detached but Catherine wasn't bothered about neighbours; all that mattered was that her son was alive.

She knew she should give him his space but for her own peace of mind she had to check if he was all right. After creeping upstairs, arguing with herself on every step whether she shouldn't just leave him alone and preparing herself for total rejection, she banged at the door of his room. 'Stephen we have to talk. Either let me in or you come out. But please speak to me.' Stephen turned up the volume even louder. He needed the grating repetition of steel guitars and drums to drown his spasmodic cries as he lay across the bed mourning the death of his dreams. It was only in the words of the music that he gained any sense of being understood. The world was a cruel and vicious place and his favourite band with their lyrics that cried so vehemently against injustice and suffering offered him commiseration in a way his mother never could. Catherine pressed her ear hard against the door and listened to his agony, but it broke her heart to witness such pain and she tiptoed quickly downstairs.

At least he was safe. Various platitudes came to mind but none fully convinced her. They all seemed meaningless and twee. Was it possible that time could heal such a deep and poisoned wound? Would he ever meet another girl and find happiness? And what of Sophie? Jimmy would have to come clean with Patricia. As for Rosie, that was Jimmy's domain as well. The responsibility for the whole sorry mess lay firmly at his door, not hers and at long last he was going to suffer. She didn't mind at all what happened to him but the thought of all those other lives in ruins made her feel sick to the stomach.

Taking a comb through her hair and securing it with a rubber band, Catherine went into the kitchen to make a cup of milky coffee. Perhaps after a night's sleep she might come to believe that this whole affair would eventually blow over, but even as she stood pouring milk into a pan she couldn't help wondering what would happen to Sophie and her innocent baby. She rushed through to the living room and picked up the phone to call the neighbour who had been looking after Arlene. Thinking of what Sophie must be going through made her desperate to hold her own child in her arms. She shuddered as another thought struck home. That poor baby was her first grandchild.

The following morning Stephen dragged himself down to breakfast. His mother was drinking coffee and Arlene was supping cornflakes. Following years of habit, Catherine poured him a coffee and spread him a few slices of toast and marmalade.

'What can I say, Stephen, except that I am so sorry. Our intentions were for the best. Who would have guessed this would happen?'

'Well now you know different. My life is finished and so is Sophie's.' He looked at his little sister who was over the moon to see him home again. She was clapping her hands and saying his name over and over. He reached out to her and gently stroked her satin soft hair. He would have to speak quietly and not terrify her although he was desperate to let rip with vile accusations against his mother and the rest of his family. 'Why couldn't you have come clean? Neither you nor Jimmy gave a thought for me. It was all for yourselves.'

'I'll never forgive myself for that, Stephen. But why didn't you tell us you were attracted to Sophie? All this could have been averted.'

'Why are you always so quick to pass the blame? You're not exactly the sort of person someone comes to when they need to talk. If you're not working, you're out enjoying yourself. How many more kids are you going to have with men you're not married to?'

Catherine winced as if she had been struck. 'There's no reasoning with you. You don't understand how hard it's been for me.'

'You always lay first claim to any suffering that's going around,' Stephen scoffed. 'What's so special about you anyway? I think it's best if I leave. I don't want to contaminate you any further. I just feel sorry for Dad. He can't be held responsible for having married trash. For all we know you and Jimmy were carrying on behind his back all the time he was ill.' Catherine's face crumpled but she managed to control herself for Arlene's sake. Such insults would have made her show him the door at normal times, but what he'd been through was far from normal and she absorbed his stinging words as part of her punishment. She gathered up the child who still had a half eaten slice of toast in her hand and carried her through to the living room where she planked her down on a cushion on the floor much to her amazement and joy in front of a children's cartoon programme on television.

Catherine hurried back through to Stephen. She had to make

the peace. 'I'm your mother,' she cried. 'Have you no respect? It all happened before any of us were married.'

He had fallen into silence, and looked at her blankly which she found worse than anger. A blazing row she could have handled; some more harsh words and then moved on. 'I have to get out of here and far away,' he said quietly. 'I'm going to Perth, down to Frank's for a while. He's always glad to see me. Well, he used to be ...'

Catherine's face was grey. 'I thought I was protecting everyone. There are some things you will never understand. Your dad, Gregor I mean, loved you as his own even before you were born. We all thought it would be easier on everybody to say nothing.'

'Easier on yourselves you mean. If you'd been honest when I was a young child I would have grown up knowing the truth and got used to it. Now it's abhorrent and makes me sick.' Catherine was too worn out to say any more and watched with a sickening ache as Stephen turned away and went up to his room. Half an hour later he marched out the door with a bulging rucksack but not one word of goodbye.

Chapter 34

Patricia took Sophie to the doctor. There was no question about it. An abortion was the only answer. 'It's early days yet – about five or six weeks,' the doctor said, averting his eyes and scrutinising Sophie's notes. 'I'll do my best for you and phone round to get a bed a.s.a.p.' He moved his pursed lips from side to side as if he would rather keep his mouth closed. It was at times like these he found his job especially hard and longed to be at home with a stiff brandy. He rubbed his mouth with the flat of his hand and leaned forward, his elbows on the desk looking Sophie straight in the eye. However painful, she had to face the truth. 'You see,' he explained, 'even though you are only the half-sister of the baby's father,' - he seemed to gag on his words - 'the chances of its being born with a defect, even multiple defects, are high. It would be quite cruel to knowingly inflict such health problems, not only physical but possibly mental too, on a little baby.'

His eyes bored into Sophie's as he passed judgement. He drummed his fingertips on the table, and the tap, tap, tap of his well manicured nails against the polished wood echoed round the small surgery. 'The other important aspect of this whole sorry mess is that a sexual relationship between a brother and sister, albeit unknowingly, is against the law and could carry a jail sentence for you both if you were to continue. However, I'm satisfied it's over and because it was unintentional and because you are willing to put an end to this unfortunate pregnancy then the matter need go no further. I'll just write in your notes that you have separated from your boyfriend and your parents are unwilling to support you.'

'That's a lie!' shouted Patricia.

'Do you want "incest" on your daughter's notes for the rest of her life? Do you want this to fall into the wrong hands or possibly be available to any future husband? A crime has been committed. Don't you understand?' He tightened his mouth and clenched his fists and waited in silence for the truth of his words to register. When he saw there were to be no further protestations he continued. 'There is scarcely a worse crime imaginable. Incest is an abomination in any decent society.' Although the man was wishing this distasteful consultation would end, Patricia felt her skin crawl. She interpreted his determination to emphasise clearly the facts as they stood as a dirty old man seemingly taking a perverse delight in repeating the word, almost as if he were titillated by it.

Sophie shuddered. All she could think about was how much she loved the baby. Her hands never left her tummy as if sheltering the unborn mite inside her. 'We were in love. Why did this have to happen to me?'

The doctor frowned at this unexpected outburst. He'd quietened the mother and now the girl was starting up. 'Surely you can't want it now? It could be deformed.'

Patricia began crying too. 'She's a good girl. She always has been the most caring darling angel that any parent would be proud to have. She doesn't deserve this.'

Sophie nursed her already rounding belly. 'I can't help it. It's a new little person and I love it.'

The doctor looked at his watch. He had a queue of patients in the waiting room and they would all be bad tempered now from having had to wait so long. 'That's life, I'm afraid,' he said. 'These things happen. The natural chemistry between a brother and sister who unwittingly meet in later life can be misconstrued as attraction. You're not the first to be caught out this way. But we have to think of the laws of nature as well as the laws of the land. We can't deliberately stand by and allow a handicapped child into the world.'

Sophie curled further forward in her chair as if to cover the baby's ears. She was moaning, her arms clasped round herself as if rocking the dear soul that was condemned to death before it had even drawn breath. 'Keep a close eye on her, Mrs Simpson,' the doctor said. 'We don't want any more mishaps.' She knew what he meant, but Sophie didn't realise the implication. She was too wrapped up in the child that she was sure was kicking against her hands in its bitter struggle for survival. In her mind she was carrying a fully formed baby that was as much a human being as anyone else. To the doctor and her mother it was only a cluster of cells that could easily be washed away.

    Satisfied that Mrs Simpson had agreed to go along with his reasoning, the doctor wrote hurriedly on Sophie's notes, the tip of his tongue peeping through his lips as he scribbled the inoffensive white lies. With a great sigh that made his shoulders heave, the air puffing in and out of him like a giant bellows, he laid his pen down on the polished walnut desk in front of him. That was that. He picked up the phone to make the necessary arrangements. 'I'll be in touch,' he said. 'Would you mind letting the receptionist know I'm ready for the next patient?'

Chapter 35

In the waiting room of the maternity hospital Sophie sat staring blankly ahead. Her hand was on her swollen tummy as if she were stroking the never to be born child inside her, comforting it. She had all the appearance of a disembodied wraith with tears rolling down her thin, almost transparent cheeks that were framed by lank colourless hair. 'We didn't know. We should have been told.' She said this to her mother who sat grim faced beside her. These had been practically the only words she had uttered over the past two weeks as they waited for the hospital bed in the day ward. Every moment of that time Sophie had to endure the pain of watching her body change as the child grew and developed to no purpose in her womb. Bouts of morning sickness had caused her already thin frame to waste away and depression too meant she ate virtually nothing. Anything she did eat was taken by the demanding embryo so that although the rest of her was emaciated and her arms and legs turning to skin and bone, the bulge became daily more pronounced.

Even at the eleventh hour Sophie wasn't convinced she should have it taken away. 'This baby inside me is innocent and now it must die and it hasn't done anyone any harm. I'll never have another child. I'll never love another man. My life is over ...' She continued to weep in protest but her mother had long since stopped listening. It was too much for her to bear. It wasn't only the trauma of seeing her daughter suffering but the sheer disbelief that her husband had carried the awful secret all these years. Jimmy, who had always been her total support, was more distasteful to her now than the dirt on the sole of her shoe.

Patricia had been pregnant with Sophie before she married Jimmy and remembered how her parents had wanted her to have a termination. However, in those days it had been harder to obtain. When her father heard that a psychiatrist would have to be involved he had vetoed the whole idea. This had delighted Patricia. She recalled how she had hurried round to Jimmy's house to give him the good news that her parents not only wanted the child but were anxious for her to get married. When she had given birth to Sophie she had been ecstatic and had devoted her life to making a home for her and the little sister who had followed soon after.

Now, as she looked at Sophie's young body swollen with her half-brother's child, she wondered for the first time ever if having her had been such a good idea. She might have married somebody other than Jimmy; anyone would have been preferable to him now she knew the truth. A sudden hot flush bathed her in perspiration and she had to make a dash for the Ladies. She leaned against the cool porcelain sink as she rushed cold water on her wrists and splashed her face. How could she think such a thing, that her life might have ended on a better note if her mother had had her way and they'd destroyed the unborn Sophie? That was a cruel and horrible thought but nonetheless it had crossed her mind more than once in the past couple of weeks. The normally sweet Patricia burned with the fierceness of a she-wolf as she considered how that stuck up Catherine must have led Jimmy astray when she knew he already had a girlfriend!

Patricia squashed down the memory of how drunk Jimmy used to get in the early days and how he had turned moody and sullen when she became pregnant. Maybe it was Catherine he'd wanted all along. Once Sophie was born he had improved but it had been hard work to finally make a man of him, as even his own mother had had to admit. She pulled at the roller towel until it rotated clean and white. You never knew in a place like this what kind of person had been using it before you. They could even have one of those diseases people got from sleeping around. She dried her face and opened her well organised handbag for her powder compact and lipstick. Having reapplied a presentable face she returned head held high to look after her daughter in the waiting room.

Sophie was gone. She'd been called. Inwardly Patricia heaved a sigh of relief and rejoiced. At last they would be clearing out the remains of the blight from her daughter's insides and she'd be able to live a proper life again. Stephen's existence would eventually be forgotten, perhaps in a few months' time. Sophie was young and girls were notoriously fickle, well that's what they were always saying in the problem pages of the women's magazines she read. Girls went quickly from one infatuation to the next with hardly a second thought.

Later that day, Sophie walked out through the gates of the bleak grey hospital and into the car, all dreams of motherhood gone, ripped out of her and thrown into the incinerator with other patients' bits of appendix, cysts, amputated limbs and old wombs. The little soul would be reduced to ashes before it had even had a chance to be born; gone up in smoke as if it had never existed.

At exactly the same time, Stephen was stepping through the door of the Army Recruitment Office. He had to make a new life for himself away from old memories. He was British by birth so it wasn't a problem that he'd been raised in Canada. He completed the form impatiently and resisted any question from the officer in charge that might have been asked in order to put him off. He was desperate to get away. A life that he would previously never have considered in a million years was the perfect kick start he needed. In days gone by he would have joined the French Foreign Legion, he thought to himself. He was informed of all the procedures he would have to go through in order to complete his training. Northern Ireland was the most likely destination for him after that. He couldn't have cared less. As long as it was somewhere far away, it didn't matter where, and as for being dangerous, wasn't that even more of an attraction?

Chapter 36

Stephen went to live with Frank in Perthshire until the time came to join up. Frank was retired. At seventy-one he lived in a little cottage beside his brother who had enjoyed vast success with his jam making business and sold his own brand to one of the major supermarkets. The factory was run by a manager these days but Frank and his brother would go for an occasional scout around the works just to keep their hand in.

Stephen spent a lot of time on the hills round about, setting out at daybreak with a knapsack of sandwiches and a flask. There was no one he wanted to be with. Frank was the only human being whose company he could bear, but it was more often than not simply a matter of sitting watching television in silence together in the evenings. Occasionally, they would stroll down for a couple of jars to the local pub where Frank had a few cronies that kept him from the loneliness of old age.

While they played dominoes and chatted over old times, Stephen would sit brooding in a corner seat in a world of his own. He had always known Frank couldn't stand Jimmy but never been sure why, and had noticed his lips tighten at every mention of his name. One evening he decided to ask him once and for all why his mother and Jimmy had always seemed at loggerheads and yet they'd managed to have a child together. Yes, he was going to have this out before he began his army career. He waited until the present game of dominoes was over. Frank as usual looked across to try and entice him to play in the next one. However, this time Stephen signalled to Frank to come and join him at his table.

Frank carried his drink over but was reluctant to speak on the subject and began to fidget impatiently. At least when he was occupied in a game his mind was taken off matters he would rather not think about. But when Stephen announced with tears in his eyes that he was finding it impossible to come to terms with the deception and couldn't get his head round his mother being unfaithful to Gregor, Frank decided that perhaps the time was right to say something.

'Don't be hard on your mother,' he said, looking longingly over at his friends as they shared out the dominoes. 'It's wrong of you to judge her.'

'How can I not?' Stephen persisted. 'Perhaps with a bit of honesty my life wouldn't be in shreds.' He looked suspiciously at Frank. 'I wouldn't be surprised if you didn't know already that Mum and Jimmy had a thing going.'

To Stephen's surprise, Frank grew angry. 'There was no "thing going",' he said. 'It seems the time has come for the truth, however brutal. I can't allow you to go on thinking so badly of your mother. She's a decent woman and has always done what she thought was best for you, albeit in what has turned out to be a cack-handed way.' He looked into his pint as if he were a fortune teller seeing past events in the glass.

'What do you mean?' asked Stephen. 'There must have been something between them if Jimmy's my biological father.' He scraped his chair across the stone floor right under the table and leaned towards Frank, as if by staring into his eyes hard enough he would be able to read the true facts written on them. 'I don't care what it is. You have to tell me.'

'Your mother hated Jimmy; despised him. She couldn't bear to have him near her.' Frank spoke through his teeth. His cheeks had taken on a purple tinge and he had to take a puff of his Ventolin inhaler before he could continue without losing his breath.

Stephen waited until Frank's breathing had settled. Use of his inhaler had become commonplace and an added worry, but Stephen was so desperate for information that he asked the ageing man who had played the part of grandfather all his life to continue. 'Then how come she became pregnant if that's how she felt? Was she drunk? Did they quarrel afterwards?'

'Your mother didn't want it – if you get my meaning.' Frank bit into his bottom lip. 'This is a very painful subject for me to talk about. I've spent years, more than your lifetime, son, trying to erase it from my mind.'

Stephen sat back in his chair. He was hoping against hope that he wouldn't hear put into words what Frank had so far only been insinuating.

Frank clasped his hands together under his chin and closed his eyes for a few moments. 'Right, lad, you asked for it and you're not going to like it.'

Stephen called to the barman for two double brandies and told Frank he was ready for anything he had to say as long as it wasn't more lies.

Frank who was not a drinking man raised the brandy glass to his mouth and knocked back a large mouthful of the much needed alcohol. He coughed as it caught his breath and then continued. His face was by now a network of purple veins. 'You see,' he began, 'Jimmy always fancied Catherine, but she would have nothing to do with him.' He paused to make sure that point had sunk in. Stephen's face was flushed red from a mixture of alcohol and rage as a vague suspicion intensified in his mind. 'I regret it now but I used to pull her leg about him and she would go crazy; it was all in fun. But there was one time when she went over the top. She was so riled up I knew that something bad must have happened. It was a struggle but I got the truth out of her. She told me how he had attacked her. It was during one of the weekends I was away from home down here. It was when Maggie was still alive. You know when someone's telling the truth. He even hit his own mother when Catherine was fighting him off. I'll bet nobody's told you that. Now I'm wondering if he did it again, but went further the second time ...' His fists clenched and his knuckles shone white. 'I know for a fact that he and Gregor hated each other. They never went to Jimmy's wedding. Neither did I. You would have thought Rosie would have been furious but she accepted it. She knew the score. She'd not only witnessed the first vicious attack but been on the receiving end of it herself.'

Stephen's eyes nearly started out of his head. 'What on earth do you mean?'

'You know fine what I'm getting at. Your mother would never have slept with Jimmy willingly. I saw the state she was in at the very mention of his name. I'll bet she's been putting up with him all these years for your sake, maybe as part of some agreement so that he could watch you growing up, but no more. He probably took some perverted delight in sitting there, the three of you, his secret second family.'

'You don't know for sure that he attacked her a second time.'

'I saw the loathing in her eyes for him. She wouldn't have him near her. And what struck me as strange was her accepting his little visits when you all returned from Canada, even Gregor who hated the very sight of him. Perhaps they agreed to his coming round rather than have Jimmy take you from them. They loved you that much, Stephen. Think about it. There was no easy way out of their predicament.'

Stephen ordered a second round of spirits. He had nothing to say. There was too much going on in his mind.

'I think they all must have twigged that you were Jimmy's instead of Gregor's.' You yourself may not realise it but there is an unmistakeable resemblance between you and Sophie, especially when you were kids, despite the difference in the colour of your hair. I've never seen you together even at your father's funeral where I was more concerned with setting the world to rights with Eddie. Recently, however, I've been taking a closer look at all the photos of the two of you I've been sent by your mother and Rosie over the years and there's no mistaking it. And although I hate to say it, and I'd never given it a second thought before the truth came out, you do resemble Jimmy. But there is no way Catherine gave her consent to him. It must have happened by force.'

Stephen curled forward and held his stomach as if it were giving him great pain. 'Have you any idea what all this is doing to me?'

Frank, who wouldn't have hurt a living soul, bowed his head as if ashamed of what he'd just done. 'You forced it out of me. You just wouldn't let it go.'

Stephen jumped up and ran off into the darkness of the night and ran blindly up lanes and across fields, scrambling over dykes and tearing himself on brambles. Why was he being tormented like this? What harm had he ever done anyone? He hated them all. Even Auntie Rosie was a hypocrite. The only one he still loved with all his heart was his dead father, Gregor. He couldn't wait to get away, anywhere. They all made him sick.

Chapter 37

When word came to Catherine via Rosie that Sophie had had an abortion she decided to keep it to herself that Jimmy had forced himself on her. How could she have this broken young woman find out that the father she loved had attacked a woman? Nor could she allow her own son to know that he was the result of a rape. She told Stephen that she and Jimmy had had a drink one evening together and got 'carried away' as the popular phrase described it. Sophie was told the same story and although it showed neither in a very good light, each having had another partner at the time, they were protected from a hideous truth that, added to their being brother and sister, would have been an intolerable burden for Sophie and Stephen to bear and blighted their futures for ever more. Little did she know that Frank had guessed the truth and already passed his theory on to Stephen. But her son was naturally too distressed and embarrassed to tell her and he would soon be too far away from it all to care.

When Jimmy had turned up at her door uninvited while Stephen was at Frank's wanting to 'discuss things' Catherine grimly told him that she would keep silent about the rape for the sake of two innocent young people who would already have to carry enough emotional scars for the rest of their lives. 'I would rather die than have them know what you did,' she hissed. They stood at the gate. Catherine wouldn't allow him to set foot in her house again. Those days of pretence were over.

'Don't you think I haven't struggled against ending it all myself?' Jimmy said and Catherine couldn't be sure if this wasn't another bluff to win her sympathy or if he really had changed his spots. He carried on speaking, but almost to himself, rather than to a listener. 'But that would be the easy way out for me. As it is I'll go to my grave a coward for what I've done in the past. I've had to live with my conscience for the past twenty-odd years, and now my life has become one long suffering act of penance. Patricia can't stand me near her and Sylvie won't talk to me. Even my mother has hardly spoken two words to me.' Catherine let him ramble on but barely heard him. If only he would just go and never come back. She told him bluntly she had important things to see to indoors and turned her back on him.

Frank, however, had guessed the truth and would have nothing to do with Jimmy under any circumstances. Catherine was furious when she eventually found out that he'd let the cat out of the bag, but then Frank was an honest soul, much like her Uncle Eddie. How could he have been expected to keep such suspicions to himself? At least when Stephen left for Northern Ireland, he knew his mother hadn't willingly slept with Jimmy and was able to fathom out for himself that she and his dad had probably done what they did only because they thought it was for the best.

Rosie preferred to continue with her belief that Catherine and Jimmy had had an affair and it had been selfish of both of them to keep her grandson from her. 'I didn't know what you two got up to half the time,' she said as if exonerating herself of any blame. Catherine decided to leave her to her own ideas. She was too old now to be told outright what a nasty piece of work she had spawned. Her overdeveloped maternal instincts had always clouded her senses. She had turned on Catherine angrily, blaming her for the secrecy as if Jimmy had been all innocence. 'You see the cost of telling lies. If I had been allowed to claim Stephen as my grandson when he was a child, none of this sorry mess would have happened. Sure, he would have been upset and Patricia and Gregor would have had to deal with it, but they would have come round to the idea of you and Jimmy having a fling. After all, none of you were married at the time. At least these two beautiful young people would have been spared this terrible tragedy.'

Catherine bit her tongue and merely replied, 'That's exactly why we covered it up, to save our marriages. With the wisdom of hindsight I realise that your way of handling the whole sordid mess might have been the correct one; however, none of us had a crystal ball, and without this happening, the way we chose might have been proved right.' A surge of injustice that she was being blamed and Jimmy being let off scot-free caused her to add with a vinegary sourness, 'And where would your precious son be now if Patricia had taken the girls and left him? They only stay together now for Sophie's sake, but I doubt if all is hunky dory in that household. Jimmy will be paying over the odds for his part in the deception, and it's not a moment before time.'

This unexpected spurt of venom took Rosie so much by surprise that she made no answer. Her eyes flickered as she weighed up the evidence not only from more recent times but from the past as well. She ran her tongue along the inside of her lower lip and frowned as the vision of Jimmy hurling himself at Catherine in an outburst of violence played in front of her and she relived the pain of him striking her too, his own mother, and she flinched involuntarily. Common logic led her along a road she didn't want to travel. Hadn't she witnessed with her own eyes a drunken Jimmy taking Catherine by the throat and pushing her roughly against the kitchen sink? And even worse, she could feel the wrenching of her own shoulder as he'd turned to attack her too.

Catherine was watching her closely, as if trying to read her mind. She knew that Rosie's intuition rarely missed the mark and it was clear she had reached the obvious conclusion much as a clever detective would when trying to solve a murder mystery. Eventually, Rosie cast her eyes heavenwards and heaved a great sigh. Then, with tongue in cheek, she turned to Catherine, 'I expect it was six of one and half-a-dozen of the other, but what's done is done. Let's leave it at that and deal with the here and now.' She had backed down and in doing so had given Catherine her answer. Rosie did know the truth, but would never admit to something that would mean her having to cast Jimmy out once and for all as she had done so readily to his father. That had been easy to do, her first husband being merely another woman's son. Now at last Catherine had the compensation of knowing that Rosie would no longer judge her as having been unfaithful to Gregor, and she promised herself she would put Jimmy wise to his mother's suspicions.

Jimmy wrestled with his conscience but it was no surprise that in the end he fabricated an excuse to Patricia. He explained that although 'it' had happened after she fell pregnant it was during the time she and her parents were planning an abortion. He'd felt confused and unwanted and turned to Catherine for advice at the same time as she was mourning her mother. They'd been drinking and given each other a shoulder to cry on. It was a simple mistake, but from his side it had happened through the worry of losing her, Patricia, if she carried out her parents' wishes. Life would have been worthless if she'd left him. He wept. He pleaded. Patricia decided it was in everyone's best interests if they stayed together and more importantly, the share out from a divorce would only provide her with a little flat. Her house meant everything to her. She was shrewd enough to decide on maintaining her lifestyle while treating Jimmy as if he didn't exist. In her heart she would never believe him. She had heard too many stories over the years from Rosie reminiscing on how close Jimmy and Catherine had been as teenagers and how she had expected them to marry one day.

Jimmy had taken Patricia in his arms and said he'd try even harder to be a good husband. He was the luckiest man alive to have her as a wife. They would work together to salvage their marriage and dedicate their lives to caring for Sophie and making sure Sylvie's life took a more straightforward direction. Patricia had no choice but to stand by her man. Sophie was in need of constant care and Sylvie too had become withdrawn due to the shock of her prim and proper sister's sudden involvement in one of the most unsavoury aspects of human life. The solution seemed to be for them all to move in together in the new house in Basildon. A fresh start for everyone and no one left on their own. In fact, Patricia would be glad of Rosie's help and she'd divert Jimmy's attention away from herself. He made her flesh creep if truth be told.

Now that the baby had been disposed of and Stephen would

never darken their door again, Jimmy felt great relief. He imagined he was off the hook and had successfully soft soaped Patricia. He thought his mother too would be a walk over. He hadn't realised they were simply keeping the peace for the sake of the girls and primarily themselves. In reality neither woman had the smallest shred of respect for him. His life was a sham. But at least he was safe from the law and his family hadn't thrown him out. The real punishment was in having to witness the destruction of Sophie which was a greater torture than any prison sentence might have been. It was a valid saying that if you want to destroy someone, you destroy what they love most. His greatest love had been and always would be his girls. He had been proud of having bred a son and enjoyed acquainting himself with him but he didn't have the same sense of ownership over him as he had with his daughters. Pure vanity at having fathered a boy especially to Catherine had been the true foundation on which his relationship with Stephen had been built. He could happily live without him.

Chapter 38

Stephen knew the only way he could ever erase the pain of losing Sophie was to continue with his plans to join up. He would have willingly joined the French Foreign Legion or become a mercenary in some remote African conflict rather than hang around surrounded by memories. Frank was dead against what he called a foolhardy piece of nonsense and wouldn't cease from reminding Stephen of the cruelty and futility of war. In desperation he wrote to Catherine hoping she would be able to influence her son. How could she allow him to be trained to kill people he had never even met?

'There are still numerous limbless and headless corpses flying around me in my nightmares as a result of the Second World War, even after nearly fifty years,' he said to both Stephen and her. 'Some of the men I watched dying were friends I knew well. I wouldn't want my worst enemy to go through that hell. Unless you've experienced war first hand you can't imagine the full horror of it.' Catherine remembered how, when he was first introduced to her by her mother, he had a nervous stammer resulting from his being on active service, and which he had struggled for years to overcome. However, it wasn't until now that he had revealed exactly how devastating his experiences had been.

There was no reasoning with Stephen. Living on the precarious edge between life and death was the only way he could reasonably keep sane and he placed no more value on his own existence than a couple of quid placed on a game of black jack in a casino. She didn't want Stephen in the Forces any more than Frank did, but she knew that if she were to harp on about it then Stephen would stop phoning her all together. Their relationship hung by a wispy thread and she knew she couldn't cope if her son cut off all ties with her and never spoke to her again. She had no choice but to wish him well in whatever he wanted to do. But she felt pain as nerves flooded her stomach with acid at the thought of her only son being involved in any kind of warfare and swallowing food became almost impossible.

During a lengthy phone call to Frank she explained that unfortunately this was maybe the best step for Stephen and that because the trauma he had suffered must be unimaginable then maybe the solution might be unthinkable too. Perhaps in years to come Stephen would be able to live without self-condemnation and lead an ordinary life with a family to love. She explained as gently as she could to Frank that Stephen felt he belonged nowhere and felt there was no one in the whole world he could turn to or trust.

Frank wasn't convinced but he'd had his say. 'We'll have to leave it in the lap of the gods then,' he said quietly. 'I just hope and pray that Stephen will be all right.' He had hung up without his usual goodbyes and telling her how much he loved her. Catherine knew from this and the return of his stammer that his nerves were in bad shape. He saw himself as Stephen's grandfather, just as he had been like a father to her after he married and took care of her widowed mother.

Catherine took solace in the fact that she and Stephen were now on speaking terms. She would have preferred Stephen to think he was a love child rather than the result of an attack, but at least he could no longer taunt her with accusations of unfaithfulness to Gregor. She didn't care that Jimmy's family saw her as a scarlet woman who had seduced him deliberately in order to lure him away from his fiancée.

However, because Stephen knew the truth, he couldn't relax in his mother's company; the very sight of her reminded him of the circumstances of his conception. It would take years packed with intense experiences before he could come to terms with that. The only benefit to come out of it all was that Jimmy would never show face near him or her again.

Jimmy's family made their permanent home in Essex. They had found an even more spectacular house, sold Rosie's and taken her to live with them. Sophie took to her room and spoke to nobody. She read the Bible and said prayers. 'She'll soon be her old self again,' said Jimmy. Like a true stoic Patricia patiently endured the pretence of standing by her man. There was no danger of him ever coming into contact with Stephen or Catherine again. Young Sylvie quickly recovered her enthusiasm for life and worked tirelessly on her beautician's course. She planned going into business on her own and driving a van round her customers. Her choice of career was a growing industry and she was sure she would achieve her ambition of becoming the proud owner of a beauty salon in a few years' time. Although she had been shaken to the core by Sophie's misfortune, she nonetheless welcomed her own rise in status within the family since Sophie's decline.

Sophie's response to the tragic end of her baby was to set off on a constant quest for answers through endless prayer. Despite all her family's efforts to entice her out of her room Sophie was slipping in front of their eyes into a pit of despair. 'We'll have to take her to see somebody,' Jimmy urged but Rosie objected. She didn't want any psychiatrist tampering with her granddaughter. However, after the weeks stretched into months of watching her daughter sink further into a world of her own, Patricia resisted Rosie's objections and took her to the local GP. He diagnosed reactive depression and a course of pills was recommended. No one listened to Rosie's protestations. Patricia asserted herself as being in charge. This was her house and she was determined that her word would be law and Rosie, like it or not, had no say in the matter.

    Sophie slowly began to respond to the medication combined with her family's unconditional support. Rosie especially took her under her wing. She was obstinately determined to prove that patience and love were more effective than drugs. They would go for long walks in the countryside or round the shops. Gardening also provided the wretched girl with a reason to get up in the morning and she soon had the flower beds planted with an abundance of hardy annuals of every colour and a core of perennial shrubs. She particularly loved the faces on the pretty pansies that seemed to smile up at her when she went to weed or water the flowers that responded to her loving care with such vibrancy that passersby would stop in their tracks to admire the rainbow of pansies, petunias, antirrhinums, stocks and asters. In the evening especially, their fragrance would waft around her as she strolled amongst them deadheading in order to keep them blooming throughout all the summer months.

In an effort to rehabilitate her and entice her away from solitary introspection, Rosie would insist she join her for walks. A favourite outing was showing her round the shops filled with the lovely bales of cloth that had been driven in vans all the way from Kashmir, Pakistan and India. Sophie was overwhelmed by the vividness of the dyes. They reflected brightly in the translucent pallor of her skin as she held the wonderfully patterned materials against herself in the mirror and eventually she began to take pride in how they set off her own natural beauty and took great delight in wearing the blouses and skirts that Rosie would skilfully make for her. Although it would take some time, there was a growing optimism within the family that she was on the road to recovery and they had to admit that Rosie's techniques were paying off.

After a long wait she saw a psychologist who seemed pleased with her progress. She recommended meditation in addition to her other activities and Sophie decided to give this a try. She went with a friend she had met at the day care centre to a course being run by Buddhist monks at the local temple or Vihara. The head monk was adamant that in her condition she should only do short spells of meditation under close supervision. She found the talks and the basic practice of concentrating on her breath as it entered and left the tip of her nose of great benefit and she learned to relax and calm her mind with the simplicity of this exercise. But she found meditating on loving kindness impossible. How could she when so many horrible thoughts were in there chasing out the good; when the only chance she'd ever had of having a family of her own had been taken from her?

When she told the monk that she preferred to concentrate on trying to kill her love for Stephen, the forbidden love, he shook his head and explained that this was not a good idea and would be damaging to her mind. He advised that although it might take time and hard work she must try to transform the romantic love into normal sisterly love for a brother. This would be healthier, as nothing destroys the mind more than hate, which has a detrimental effect on physical health too.

Feeling love for Stephen as a brother would be wholly acceptable and only then could the healing process begin. She wouldn't have to meet him of course. It was the black thoughts about him and the consequences of their relationship that were harmful. Importantly too, she had to learn to love herself and then self-forgiveness would follow. If she could eradicate all sexual feelings for Stephen the guilt would disappear. After all hadn't they both been innocent participants?

She must stop training herself to despise him at once which was distorting her mind to the point of mental illness. She tried to imagine herself wishing Stephen well and for him to have a happy future. Over time, with practice and help, her feelings for him did change and there was hope at last that the turmoil in her mind was calming down, and acceptance, especially of herself, was bringing relief. However, she knew she must never see him again as the pain would be unbearable and possibly throw her into another bout of depression.

Chapter 39

Once Stephen had finished his preliminary training he was posted to Northern Ireland. He and his comrades had looked death squarely in the face in Belfast, hiding in doorways, never knowing when the next shot or bomb blast would be the one that would finish them off. An incendiary device had torn through a public house and Stephen was one of the soldiers called on to clear the damage.

There was mayhem as ground troops, ambulances, army trucks and police vehicles rushed to the scene. The wailing of sirens mingled with the screams of terrified human beings fleeing for their lives carried for miles. The door of the pub had been blasted off its hinges. Only half the front wall was still standing. Shards of glass crunched underfoot as Stephen and his companions crept stealthily inside, fearful that a second explosion would send them to kingdom come.

The stench from the burst open bodies of the dead and dying made him throw a pile of vomit into a corner where a limbless youngster was whimpering for help. He had never seen such carnage. Few of the bodies of the dead were in one piece. The agonising cries from the dying would ring in his ears for the rest of his life. He knew that. He knelt beside the young lad whose legs had been thrown God knows where into the array of what looked like fresh butcher meat scattered over the floor.

Mindless of the blood that seeped from this poor mother's son into his combat trousers and flak jacket, Stephen held him until the last breath left his body. Should he say a prayer over him he wondered, looking at the crucifix that hung round his neck. In these gruesome sectarian killings innocent victims from both communities fell in the crossfire. Silently he hoped that each and every one of the dead, from whichever side, would make it to Heaven, if there was such a place, to compensate for this Hell on earth.

It wasn't only in the city that Stephen saw action. Sometimes they were sent to places in the countryside where munitions were suspected of being stored in some farmhouse or outbuilding. The danger on these occasions was from snipers' bullets. He'd lost a couple of mates that way. Life and death was no more predictable here in Northern Ireland than throwing two sixes with a pair of dice.

This latest assignment was to check out a tipoff that there were suspicious activities taking place in a house outside a village along the coast. The object of this exercise was to fly his group of soldiers by night in a helicopter, drop them off nearby and surprise the enemy. Stephen had been on one such excursion before, flying up over the sea, and when they were over the land again and near, but not too near the target, the men would slide down a rope that was suspended to about a yard from the ground and then jump and roll, fanning out so they could all land safely. They had to be quick about it as the boots of the man behind could come hammering down against their helmet and shoulders if they didn't move fast enough. They all knew that the sound of a helicopter would be quickly picked up by a lookout and the snipers would take up position and fire at anything that moved. So far, Stephen had escaped with his life but he'd lost two of his pals on the last such raid.

Trained to act in spite of fear the soldiers ran to board the helicopter. The roar of the propellers was deafening and the rush of air as the men ran under them would have floored a lightweight. The adrenalin was already coursing Stephen's veins as they clambered aboard. His body was on full alert, stomach fluttering and hands slightly tingling. It wasn't unlike the exhilaration of thrilling fairground rides had it not been so fraught with real danger. The engine vibrated his whole body. He stiffened with the excitement of take off. The blades thundered as they tore through the air. Stephen felt his pulse quicken and his body quiver with the rush that was like having had a shot of amphetamine. He enjoyed the sensation as the helicopter toppled sideways and then rose, higher and higher in the sky before hurtling forward at great speed as it veered off towards the coast and the sea.

Stephen was proud to be a man amongst men. Recently, on the occasions he found himself possibly facing death, he had acquired the habit of mulling over the past. Earl who had stirred in him an early love of helicopters suddenly entered his mind and a sweep of shame caught him unawares when he thought of how he had compared his father unfavourably with him. He remembered the shock of seeing his dad hobbling from the plane at the airport and his mother's sharp intake of breath at the sight of her invalid husband. He knew even as a child what his mother had been up to with her cowboy friend, betraying that decent man whose main purpose in life was to struggle despite ill health to be a good husband and father.

Perhaps it was guilt at his own temporary rejection of his father, but suddenly he heaved and he felt a surge of stomach acid burning its way up through his gullet and into his mouth. He gulped it back down. Forget the past. That's why he was here wasn't it? Around him most of the chaps were quiet. If thinking had made a sound the cabin would have been full of it as loved ones that might never be seen again filled everyone's minds. The engine gave a roar and the helicopter faltered. Turbulence he thought. They often hit pockets of air that could toss even a jumbo jet around the sky like a toy.

Stephen looked round the faces of his companions. Who knew what thoughts went through the minds of men who worried that every mission might be their last? Gary, who was sitting next to him was first to start a conversation. He was new, one of the replacements for the men who'd been lost the previous week. 'What are you doing here then, Steve? What drove you to joining up?' Gary spoke quickly, his voice shaky with nerves.

'The usual story, wanted to get away, clear my mind, that sort of thing,' Stephen replied. 'It wasn't for the skiing holidays and foreign trips, I'll tell you that. The only way I'm going to forget my problems is to risk getting my bloody brains blown out.' He surprised even himself with the bitterness of his tone. He'd been caught off guard and hadn't had time to put on the front of joviality that usually carried him through these dangerous manoeuvres.

'Got some slapper in the family way?' asked Gary in an offhand way that suggested he wouldn't have been surprised to hear it. Was that derogatory word a cover up; had he cared deeply for someone who had let him down? Stephen chose not to answer but Gary persisted. 'That's not so bad these days. Throw her a couple of quid and leave the State to bring up the sprog.'

'Wish it was that easy,' he muttered and as soon as he said it, he regretted it. He'd spoken his thoughts aloud and now everyone would know.

'Ah, see what you mean; you were in love with her.'

'Something like that. I just want to forget.'

Gary was silent for a moment or two and then he cleared his throat ready to speak, but before he could get any words out, the helicopter's engine made a sound like two pieces of dry metal scraping against each other and gave such a lurch that all the soldiers would have been thrown off their seats had it not been for their safety belts.

'Turbulence,' said Dave, Stephen's companion on his other side. His ears had noticeably pricked up on listening in to Stephen's personal life story and, like Gary, he wanted to hear more.

'Quite a jolt that,' replied Stephen, rubbing the back of his neck. 'Nearly dislocated my spine.'

'At least if I die it will be in a worthwhile cause,' said Gary who, being new, still spoke with the ingenuousness of the idealist.

'You really think,' said Stephen, 'that it's all right coming over here and shooting at people in their own streets?' Some of Frank's arguments had taken root.

The helicopter lurched again.

'Hey, take it easy, you're not driving a corporation bus,' shouted one of the men near the front. Two benches of six men faced each other. They could see plainly the fear in the eyes of the men opposite.

'I wondered what the L plates were for when we got on,' quipped another.

'You ever see her?' Gary asked. Stephen thought Gary would have dropped the conversation by now and felt his hackles rise when he wouldn't let up, but Gary was scared and glad of any diversion.

Although Stephen was annoyed that his life was under scrutiny, at least they never suspected that the girl in question was his sister.

'Never,' he said sharply. 'It's all in the past. I was hoping the streets of Belfast would blast the whole sorry business from my mind.' And they had almost succeeded. After seeing dead bodies in pieces around him Stephen's personal problems had seemed to fade like so much mist rolling back up a hill, but he knew that, like Frank, there would be horror movie pictures in front of his eyes many a night, possibly forever. Most of the troops had fallen silent, each one deep in thoughts of their own. Stephen hoped Gary had finally shut up, but he continued on the same tack burrowing into Stephen's brain like a weevil. It was his way of fighting off fear.

'There'll be other girls for you,' he sneered lecherously. 'I'll bet there are hundreds of them around ready to let any soldier in uniform into their knickers.'

Stephen chewed his lips wishing he'd kept his mouth shut. He didn't want his comrades thinking he was some kind of weirdo hankering after a lost love. 'I know that,' he said as if he was interested in finding a replacement. 'I've seen a few crackers already. Won't be long I suppose until I find one for myself.' He couldn't let these men know how crushed he was; that he had no desire for another woman ever again.

'It's a dangerous game going with local girls,' said Dave who was older and more experienced. 'We're viewed by most as the enemy. There can be reprisals. You couldn't go down on one knee if your kneecaps had been smashed in.'

'Well, I'm game to have a good try. These Irish girls take some beating. I've seen some right beauties amongst them,' said Gary.

Dave laughed. 'You've a lot to learn, my young son.'

As they sat occasionally exchanging a wandering thought, Stephen's mind turned to his mother. He was glad he'd called round to see her before he left. He had especially missed that little bundle of mischief, Arlene. It had been Frank who had insisted he pay that visit after telling him the truth about how Jimmy came to be his father. He wished he'd known sooner. What his mother must have suffered all those months while he refused to speak to her. He'd make it up to her when he went home on leave.

Even the fact of having taken up with his sister seemed to carry less weight these days. His attitudes were losing their rigidity, and a little voice in his ear grew louder with each atrocity he saw, making his experience with Sophie seem almost miniscule in importance compared to what went on in the greater scheme of life where basic survival was the order of the day. 'So what! You're not the first and won't be the last,' this inner voice kept shouting at him. And it had somehow gathered momentum all the time he was telling Gary the sorry tale. Men and women were splitting up constantly the world over. He would get over it. He felt lighter, almost happy. Life was on the up and up. There might be a future after all.

He looked at his watch. Another half hour should do it. Suddenly, the helicopter gave a fierce jolt and began jumping about in the sky. 'What a driver!' came the shouts from the men. The tension in the air was mounting as they approached their destination and humour was one way of deflecting it. The joke of pretending to be on a bus had taken off. They were all at it.

'Hope he's passed his test. Let me off at the next stop.'

The comments came thick and fast as they lurched their way through the darkness.

A raised voice came from the cockpit, louder than all the rest: 'Surely you can do something!' It was the support pilot.

'I am doing my best.' The pilot sounded desperate. 'The fuel seems to be sticking. It's not flowing right.'

The soldier in command down at the front who had been trained to face danger calmly at all times disappeared in beside them. He emerged. His face was drawn. 'Prepare for the worst; we're in for a rocky ride until this little blip gets sorted out,' he cried and cleared his throat as if struggling to force the words out.

'Too many cigarettes when I was on leave,' he laughed huskily and drew out his handkerchief to mop away the beads of perspiration that had formed on his forehead like droplets of rain running down a window on a dark stormy day. 'Must be coming down with flu,' he said, wiping his sweaty hands on the damp square of cotton before tucking it back into his pocket. He had to think of something to say that would reassure the men but the engine spoke for him as it faltered and spluttered and faltered again before giving a whine and finally dying.

'We'll have to get out of here, men!' roared the co-pilot, his voice rising to a scream of panic not at all like the controlled command he'd used during training. 'The pilot's put out the Mayday so all sea going vessels will have been alerted and every coastguard station. You know the drill.' He took a deep breath. 'Right lads,' he shouted, 'prepare for sea landing.' In rapid response, they made for the exit struggling to throw off their heavy flak jackets. No point in being weighed down and dragged to the bottom of the sea. The ballistic protection had to come off; being hit by shrapnel was the least of their worries now. They knew that life in the ocean would be quickly snuffed out at this time of year if they weren't picked up immediately.

'Jump for the love of God, get yourselves clear of her!' It was the pilot himself who was giving the order, the officer in charge having lost his voice from sheer terror. The engine made a grating sound as it ran dry of fuel and then became silent. The massive beast took a dive and hurtled into the freezing cold jaws of the Irish Sea. The speed at which she plummeted like Icarus was too fast to give anyone a chance. Men pushed each other clear to take a jump, hoping to land as far from the wreckage as possible, not wanting to be dragged down with it to Davy Jones's locker. Better to stay afloat and be spotted by a passing ship or plane. The helicopter had landed in the water tail up in the air, propellers still spinning, where it remained like a seabird diving for fish before slowly disappearing beneath the waves leaving nothing but an effervescing circle of bubbles in its wake.

As he hit the surface and went under, Stephen offered up a

prayer for his mother, little Arlene, Auntie Rosie and Frank. He asked God to look after them all and to take special care of Sophie whose life he had ruined. 'Daddy! Mummy! I love you.' Down through the salt waves he sank, his lungs bursting with the pressure of holding his breath. Then the turning point and holding his arms above him like a sharply pointed arrow and kicking his feet back and forth like flippers he cut his way to the surface where around him the sea was closing for the last time over young heads and others were already bobbing lifeless after drowning in the freezing water. Some wreckage floated nearby with the remaining handful of soldiers clinging to it for dear life. Darkness was falling fast and their chances of being spotted were slim.

Stephen struck out in the direction of the distant shore. 'Daddy!' he shouted and continued swimming full force from the carnage. 'Daddy, please help me.' Rushing through his mind like a fast running video came the reasons for his death wish that had made him join up in the first place. He'd needed to place his life in danger as if punishment for what he'd done. Now he was about to pay the ultimate penalty and he relaxed as the anointing touch of heavenly forgiveness stroked him lightly across his tired shoulders. As he struggled to keep afloat in the icy water a blinding light burst across his vision. Was it a searchlight or was it the gates of paradise opening ready to receive him. He felt his father's hand reach out for his as it had done when he was a little boy and had taken him for walks along the shores of Lake Ontario at Rouge Hill. He saw the sunlight strike the surface of the lake and reflect the shimmering colour of the red autumn leaves on the trees along the shore.

Automatically he continued to swim and he heard his father say through the screaming of gulls and the rushing of waves that filled his ears, 'You know you shouldn't swim in this dirty water. Come with me to where it's crystal clear and fresh.' Stephen allowed his father to lead him by the arm on to the sand dunes, over lush green grass and through the trees until they came to a forest pool surrounded by flowers of the brightest colours. He slipped into its welcoming warmth and gladly allowed his weary body to surrender itself to the overpowering blackness of oblivion.

Chapter 40

(March, 1992)

Catherine was bouncing Arlene on her knee and they chortled with laughter at the latest antics of the little green frog on the children's television show. They both jumped at the sound of a heavy knock at the front door. They hurried to answer thinking it was Gloria from along the road bringing Arlene's friend, Becky for tea. Catherine's smile froze when she saw the serious face of the uniformed man on the doorstep and the unmistakable dog collar of the padre by his side. Catherine knew at once why they were there. They were responsible for notifying the next of kin that a soldier was injured, missing or worse. Arlene held out her arms to her mother to be picked up. She sensed something was badly wrong and began to cry.

After the preliminary check that she was in fact Mrs Catherine Bruce, the padre had to take her arm and help her into the living room to sit down. Arlene clung round her mummy's neck. He gave a cough. He didn't know whether to sit down or stay standing. In the end he took a seat on the edge of the chair opposite where Catherine had collapsed on to the sofa, Arlene curled up on her knee, cuddling in for protection.

'I'm afraid it's your son, Stephen ...' he began trying to break the news gently but in a nonetheless firm and authoritative voice. He wasn't supposed to get emotionally involved. Catherine sat open mouthed but silent. She crushed Arlene closer to her. 'He has been officially named as lost in action. The helicopter in which he was flying took a dive into the sea a good half mile from shore.' The man spoke robotically as if he had been rehearsing the awful words on the way to her house.

Catherine found her voice, but it was not to make normal speech. She let out a heartrending cry followed by sounds which could only be described as whines and whimpers. Arlene began to scream, 'Mummy, you're hurting me. Stop squeezing so hard.' Catherine loosened her grip on the child and buried her face in her golden hair sobbing uncontrollably. The army officer squeezed the top part of her arm as if imparting strength through it. Heartfelt compassion for this anxious mother gave him the strength to take up the telling of the latest run of events. 'The search is on and a few men have been rescued by a trawler that was in the vicinity. We don't know any more than that.' Catherine knew from what her father had told her that the cold of the sea alone could kill as well as drowning. A person would have to be picked up almost immediately in order to survive. The worst scenario was that his body would never be recovered.

Bravely Catherine pulled herself together. She couldn't allow herself to give way completely. She kissed the tears from Arlene's cheeks while all the time tears of fear were running down her own. She would allow herself to break down later when she was alone. Catherine glanced past the grim faced padre at the television screen. The News was on and the helicopter crash was the main item. She grabbed the controls to turn up the volume. From what they were saying the bodies of all but three of the fourteen men had been found, but only two were lucky enough to be alive. No further identifications had been made as yet. The search would continue into the night. The reason for the helicopter coming down was thought to be some kind of engine failure but that was only conjecture and had yet to be verified.

Catherine pressed the off button. All she could do now was wait. A ring at the doorbell meant Arlene's chum and her mother had arrived. Catherine would have someone to talk to for the evening so the two men let themselves out telling her they would let her know as soon as they had further news. Reluctantly, Catherine gave them Jimmy's phone number and address. She was in no fit state to phone but it was only right and fair that he and Rosie should know.

At quarter past ten, during the News, the phone rang. It was Jimmy. He had been informed and from watching the film footage of dark stormy seas he feared that Stephen would never be found. He was crying. 'We don't know for sure,' Catherine snapped. The last thing she needed was to listen to Jimmy blubbering on the line and told him she didn't want to talk. 'I'll ring back when we hear something definite,' he said, arrogant enough to think he was giving her reassurance. 'I haven't told my mother yet. She's had enough upset lately.'

'Losing Eddie has been hard for everyone. We'll have to be brave whatever happens,' Catherine said and hung up, unable to take their strain as well as her own. Jimmy was already floundering and would turn to Patricia to pick up the pieces as usual. That snivelling bastard had his family but she would have to face the outcome on her own. So far, she was determined not to lose hope. Stephen might be lucky and have been one of those picked up alive by the fishing vessel. Becky's mum, Gloria, had been a tower of strength. She was an intelligent woman and had fetched a light hearted video for them to watch together. She had the sense to know that endlessly going over the possibilities would only wear Catherine out.

It was two days later at half-past six in the morning when there was a second lot of banging at the door. Why did these people never use the bell? On sight of the padre she let out a scream. A stab of pain tore through her innards. She didn't need to be told the rest and suddenly she was falling, falling into a thick black fog so dense she felt its solidity beneath her. I must go to him was her only thought. There was no way that anyone but herself would lay claim to her son's body, certainly not that evil skunk Jimmy. She had to be the one who would look on Stephen's dead face and name him.

Her body felt as if it were made of India rubber as she struggled up from her knees to fight her way out from the darkness that seemed to be holding her tightly in its grip. There seemed to be so many hands holding her and so much noise and so many voices. Gritting her teeth she imagined her mother's sharp voice telling her to get a move on or she'd be late, much as she'd done when she'd been a little girl going to school. 'Stay with me, Mum. I need you more than ever today,' she whispered. Was it herself or someone else who was washing her face and pinning her long curls into a tidy knot at the back of her head? Did it really matter as long as she was made presentable?

It was as if she were astral travelling in an out of body experience with no sense of concrete reality. Merely going through the motions, she sat or stood or walked as required. She stared through the people she had to communicate with as if they were transparent spectres, and her voice echoed eerily from somewhere beyond. She stepped out into the cold drizzle of Northern Ireland. The army representatives rushed forward to greet her and ushered her to the mortuary. Such was her state of mind that they seemed to be able to get her there without the use of a vehicle.

She felt the presence of both her parents as well as that of her husband. They had drawn near to help her. Once there, an attendant as well as an army officer accompanied her and their footsteps echoed ominously as she was led down stone stairs and along bleak corridors to where her dead son would be lying in a metal drawer with a tag round his big toe like a carcass of meat lying in the back of a butcher's shop. There was no sensation of walking only travelling and she seemed to float for part of the way. The news had knocked her senses for six. She braced herself for what she knew would be waiting for her behind those swing doors that someone in a dark green apron, rubber boots and mask was holding open.

She had seen it all before in films. She knew the score, but never thought that she would one day be playing the main part. Although it was the attendant's hand that she held on to for support, it was her parents, Maggie and Sam, who had given her the strength to survive that stretch of hard concrete corridor with cold, bare, tiled walls. As they entered the morgue itself the icy air struck her face like a blade. The smell of formaldehyde clawed the back of her throat and she was glad she hadn't eaten as she began to dry heave.

Silently, a man she took to be a forensic doctor came forward. He too was wearing a bottle green overall. She was glad of the hard backed chair they brought over for her to sit on while various formalities with bits of paper were gone through. Why was everyone whispering? The officer put a supportive hand on her back as she rose trembling to take the necessary steps over to the stainless steel table where the corpse lay.

She almost choked and had to grasp tightly to the rail that ran along the edge of what was little more than a shelf as she watched the doctor's hand in slow motion move towards the top of the linen sheet and draw it back. A high pitched cry escaped her as she looked down on her beloved Stephen. She remembered how she had checked him over as a newborn baby, carefully counting every finger and toe, and how proudly Gregor had held him that very first time. It might have been the chilling air of the cold basement but she could have sworn she felt her husband's lips brush across her cheek exactly as they had done on the first day of Stephen's life. She'd never expected to be there on the last.

If she'd had even one ounce of energy left in her, she would have shouted her rage to God who could take for himself a good young man and let live the evil bastards that scurried in every corner of the world like vermin. All she had left in her was pain and she kept choking as if something was catching the back of her throat. The pangs of giving birth were as nothing compared to the agony of seeing her child on a slab. Stephen's dear little face was bluish grey but not as bloated with drowning as she had dreaded it might be. She hoped for his sake that death had come quickly and painlessly.

'Yes, that's Stephen Bruce, my son,' she said quietly. The words tore harshly from her dry throat. She steadied herself against the table and bent over him to plant one last kiss on the ice cold, purple mouth. Only by leaning backwards against her parents was she able to remain upright before being led back upstairs by faceless people holding tightly to her wrists. She heard them arranging for her to be given a cup of hot sweet tea for shock but she knew she would never drink it. She was sick to her stomach.

There was a vague awareness of travelling to what she took to be a hotel. It wasn't until she was alone in her room that she finally gave way to grief. She was on her knees on the floor banging against it with her bare fists until the skin along the sides of her hands was grazed and bleeding. She tore at the pillows so much that the seams ripped open and she hauled out the foam and shredded it into tiny pieces that she threw about her like falling snow. She dragged at the very flesh of her face as she howled and pulled out her hair in handfuls. At last, exhausted to the point of collapse, she lay on top of the bed and closed her eyes, falling into unconscious rather than sleep.

Chapter 41

Patricia looked with scorn at her husband, his face buried in the pillow too distraught to come out from under the duvet. 'It's your lovely daughter you should be thinking about, not some bastard son,' she sneered. With Jimmy's slump into depression with the worry over Stephen her suspicions that he would have preferred to marry Catherine instead of herself returned. How had she been weak enough to believe his excuses? He would never get round her again and she would never forgive his unfaithfulness to her while she was in the early stages of carrying Sophie. On top of this, watching her daughter slide from one depressive episode to another had brought her to the edge of despair. Now she had her husband whimpering over the loss at sea of his illegitimate son born to that Catherine whose house he'd been forever running off to for 'cups of tea'.

But Patricia wasn't one to fall by the wayside. She would organise her life to her own best advantage. It was Jimmy who brought in the money. He would have to be allowed to stay. She looked round her beautiful home. She wasn't prepared to give it up, but Jimmy's life would become a misery; she'd make damned sure of that. She forced down a plate of cereal followed by a strong cup of coffee and braced herself. Sophie would have to be told. Rosie hadn't given her a moment's peace looking for a shoulder to cry on since Stephen went missing but that was for Jimmy to take care of too. In future, all that mattered would be her two daughters. She would have to keep a close eye on Sophie and not allow her too much time with her granny. If the worst came to the worst, Rosie would be so full of her own distress she would be capable of pushing Sophie over the edge. Sophie would need handling with the greatest of care and, as her mother, she was the only one capable of doing so.

She tapped at Sophie's bedroom door and a little voice invited her in. There were days when Sophie was up and dressed and would take a walk round the garden and do some light work on it; other days she stayed in her room with the Bible open in front of her, desperately trawling through the chapters and verses in her search for answers and for God's forgiveness. The Buddhist Vihara which had been a large terraced house taken over for the purpose of meditation and meetings had been closed down because of complaints from neighbours about the noise from chanting and the amount of cars needing to park in their street. Sophie had taken to reading the Bible instead, but without guidance or the necessary fellowship of a church group. Patricia didn't like to be cynical but she had always gone through life with a steely determination to survive and didn't go looking for props to lean on. She had worked hard, been honest and hopefully kind to other people. She didn't deserve this tragedy, but by hook or by crook she wasn't going to allow it to spoil her own or her daughters' lives.

She was perplexed that Sophie didn't share her fortitude. How could a girl that she had brought up so carefully have allowed notions of the perfect romance to reduce her to this state? Probably spoiled by her father who had fussed at her too much and cushioned her from reality and trained her into thinking that everyone in the world would love her and take care of her like some helpless little princess. Take Sylvie now; she was different. Quiet but no nonsense; just got on with it. If it had been her that this had happened to ... Patricia stopped herself. It was unfair to compare them. Sophie was her own person, an individual, and it was her genuine trust and compassion for others that had caused her to take the abortion so badly. After all, wasn't it a desire to care for the sick and infirm that had led her to nursing as a career?

Patricia went over to where Sophie sat with the Bible open at the Psalms. She turned and smiled at her mother. 'You should read these sometime, Mum; the words are beautiful and so comforting.'

Patricia stroked her daughter's face. 'Darling, I have something to tell you. You are going to have to be brave.' Sophie's eyes widened. She didn't know if she could endure any more bad news.

'Come and sit by me on the bed,' said Patricia. She held Sophie to her breast and stroked the flaxen hair that had lost its golden lustre. 'I don't know how to tell you this but Stephen has been in an accident.' Without giving Sophie time to react she quickly followed on with the final blow: 'He's missing. He was on a helicopter that crashed into the Irish Sea.'

Sophie stopped breathing for so long Patricia thought she would never start again. She clawed her mother's arms but didn't say a word. Patricia peeled her hands off - she was tearing into her flesh with her nails - and held her away from her so she could look her straight in the eye. 'Some bodies have already been recovered. We are waiting to hear definite news on Stephen. Your father is naturally upset.' She felt her lips tighten as she said this. Patricia waited for Sophie's reaction but there was none. She felt like shaking her to provoke a response. This wasn't what she'd been expecting. It wasn't normal. Why didn't she cry? Sophie looked blankly up at her mother and from the dull emptiness in Sophie's eyes Patricia knew they were back at square one and maybe worse.

Sophie rolled back on the bed and lay on her side clutching her knees up to her chest. Her eyes were closed and God alone knew what was going on in her sad and muddled little head. Patricia grew anxious. Could Sophie survive another breakdown? She put a hand on her shoulder and heaved a great sigh of relief when her daughter began to cry. The tears poured from her eyes and her cries were like those of a fox in heat screaming in the night. Hopefully she was going to be all right.

Sylvie put her face round the door. 'What's going on now?' she asked impatiently. She had heard her father sobbing in her parents' room. 'When are the people in this family going to stop crying?' She disappeared down the stairs calling out behind her, 'I know the ropes, Mum; I'm putting on the kettle.'

That night Sophie's high pitched wailing wound its way into every crevice of the house and this was accompanied by the regular creaking of the floorboards as her father paced backwards and forwards into the early hours of the morning. Sylvie blasted garage music through headphones into her ears and sighed. Rosie cried silent, burning tears that seemed to bring little relief, and she prayed to God that he would take her soon away from all this pain.

Patricia lay quiet and still. She knew that this too would pass.

Chapter 42

Catherine was aware of someone shaking her by the shoulder. Surely it couldn't be a member of the hotel staff. She must be imagining it. Her eyelids were gummed together and swollen. She tried to lick her sore, cracked lips with a dry tongue but there was no moisture in her mouth to give relief. She shivered as an uneasy tingle ran up and down her spine. The nightmarish reality engulfed her and she longed to just roll over and lie face down and cover her head with her arms but she was restricted in her movements. One hand especially was so heavy it seemed as if it had been tied to the bed. She didn't care what anyone did to her now. She couldn't bear to stay alive anymore? It was only thoughts of Arlene forcing their way in that stopped her planning anything stupid. Her life wasn't her own to destroy. She would have loved to lie there forever and be allowed to fade away, but that was a luxury forbidden to woman with a young child. She tried to prise herself off the bed. She must get some water to ease her raging thirst.

However much she struggled she just couldn't get up. Had someone really come in the night and tied her down? She cried out in fear and soft cool fingers took hold of her hand and squeezed it. Someone really had come into her room. 'Catherine, are you awake?' said a gentle voice with a highland lilt, a voice she didn't recognise. Other voices in hushed whispers floated around her. She tried to move her arm but once again felt it drag on something. She blinked hard in an effort to open her eyes. 'What's happening?' she tried to say but her throat was too dry and her tongue stuck to the roof of her mouth.

The voice with the breathy highland accent said, 'I think she's coming round. Come on, Catherine, waken up.' She did at last manage to force open her eyes but the glare from a light shining down from behind her made her close them again. Again she was urged to waken and the unknown but kindly woman was tapping the back of her hand so there was no chance of slipping back into the sleep she felt she so desperately needed. Through the narrow slits between her eyelids, fringed by her eyelashes she could see only blurred and meaningless shapes. There was the heavy scraping of a chair across vinyl and she knew a figure, large like a man's, was leaning over her and he took her free hand in his, the one that the woman had been holding. She tried to move her other hand again but it was still secured to something and she began to struggle. Had she been taken prisoner in the night?

'Please don't fight me off, Mrs Bruce,' said the man firmly but gently, 'you really must listen to me.' Catherine wanted to push him away; she had to escape but her strength gave out and she lay still and closed her eyes again. What was the point of anything, even life itself now that Stephen was dead? She wasn't afraid of anything or anyone anymore. Let them do to her what they would.

Accustomed now to the light, she looked at the white coated figure at her side. He held her gaze. 'You must listen to me carefully now. And try not to interrupt. It's about your son.' At his words, Catherine let out a cry and pulled her hand from his and up to her face to hide herself from the awful truth which she just couldn't bring herself to confront. But why was there a tube coming out from her nose? And why was her other arm restricted? She looked around properly this time. This was no hotel room. There was nothing but white drapes hanging round her and a bright beam of light at her back.

'What am I doing in here?' she asked in alarm and began tugging at the tube which caused her captor to lay his hand firmly on her arm to restrain her. 'Please, Mrs Bruce,' he repeated. 'You really must listen.' Catherine detected the impatience in his voice as he repeated himself. Suddenly, another voice joined in, one she recognised this time. It came clearly from the foot of her bed. 'Mother, please. I'm all right. I'm alive.' Catherine gasped and if she had had the strength would have become hysterical.

'Stephen,' she mouthed. 'Stephen. What are you doing here?' Momentarily she thought that she had arrived in Heaven to join him but the gentle young girl had drawn back the curtains and as she became accustomed to the light her gaze took in the hospital side ward where she lay with a drip in her arm. As Stephen walked slowly round the bed to take her in his arms her hand went up to her throat as it tended to do when she was anxious and she felt an oxygen mask lying loosely under her chin ready in case she might need it. Seeing her distress, the doctor placed it over her mouth and told her to take deep breaths. 'We've been trying to tell you, Mrs Bruce, but you wouldn't listen. You collapsed before the padre got a chance to tell you that your son was safe.' He stood up to let Stephen take his place beside her.

Stephen kissed her on the cheek while she struggled with the mask desperate to be allowed to speak. He shook his head and smiled at her and then at the doctor and the nurse. 'Getting a word in edgeways has never been easy where my mother is concerned.'

Catherine took deep breaths of the oxygen as she tried to take in the miracle return of her son. She looked from one to the other of the people gathered round her bedside. There was the padre who had come to inform her about Stephen and was obviously there now to support him. She knew now that the white coated man must be a doctor and at his side was a pretty nurse. The doctor frowned anxiously and said some words she couldn't quite overhear to the nurse who went away and returned in minutes with a dish of ice cubes.

Now that Catherine seemed sufficiently calm with Stephen seated beside her and stroking her hand reassuringly, the girl stepped forward and removed the oxygen mask. 'Suck on this, Catherine,' she said, popping one of the ice cubes into her parched mouth. 'It'll help your thirst.' Catherine sucked vigorously on it like a baby at the breast to encourage it to melt, and the cold liquid slowly seeped into her mouth and throat and the relief she felt from its refreshment was almost magical.

Catherine began to cry. She couldn't believe that Stephen was alive. The nurse stepped forward and Catherine was terrified she would send them all away again. She sniffed back the tears. She had to appear to be coping. 'I'm all right, really. I thought I was in Belfast, in a hotel,' she said, 'but it's all beginning to make sense now.' She realised that she must have been having those vivid dreams about mortuary corridors in Ireland while she herself was being rushed into hospital. Stephen who still held tightly to her hand laughed. 'I hear you've been giving the staff in here a run for their money.'

'And a few of our pillows paid the price when you first arrived,' said the nurse with a wry smile.

The doctor added sternly with a warning note in his voice. 'You just wouldn't listen,' he said. 'You were an emergency admission. You collapsed with a violent bleed from the stomach. It's lucky for you the padre and his companion were there when it happened. You wouldn't be here now if it had happened while you were alone.'

He looked over at a machine only a few feet from the bed. 'We had to use suction to clear the residue from your stomach and thankfully the bleeding was superficial. Heavy sedation prevented any relapse and you were put on a slow milk drip by naso-gastric tube to heal the stomach. We also gave you a bottle of blood intravenously before starting the glucose and saline.' Catherine was incredulous. But I don't understand. The doctor's eyes pierced hers and his voice was reprimanding. 'You went for days without eating and stupidly took pain killers on an empty stomach which burnt off the lining. The empty packets were found on your kitchen worktop by the paramedics.'

Catherine knew now the full meaning of her hallucinatory trip to Belfast: those long corridors, the green overalls, the pain and most of all the sense of floating above it all.

'I've had such a sore head, for months now, and I've been taking pills for it and not eating as properly as I should.' Catherine spoke with a meekness that was unusual for her, like a child, and she felt like a child, a naughty child. She had behaved irresponsibly. 'I haven't been able to swallow food this last while, and with the extra worry while Stephen was missing I couldn't even manage biscuits or milky coffee without heaving. 'I'm sorry,' she said and closed her lips tightly together as if showing remorse.

She allowed the doctor's explanation of months of worry at having a son caught up in the middle of a war zone to be the cause of her headaches. She remained silent. She wasn't going to reveal anything about the love between her son and his sister having shattered her nerves and his subsequent rejection having brought her to the edge of a breakdown.

The doctor sighed. 'Well, I hope you've learned your lesson. You're a very lucky woman in every respect. You could have given yourself an ulcer and bled to death.' He finally smiled and looked across at Stephen who sat head bowed as if he too were in receipt of a telling off. 'Look after your mother. She's been through a lot.' He picked up Catherine's chart that hung over the foot of her bed and, adjusting his spectacles that had slid half way down his nose, scrutinised it with a tightening of his lips that indicated he was deep in thought. 'Ten minutes maximum with your visitors, Mrs Bruce, and then nurse will remove all these accoutrements from your person and bring you some porridge and toast and a cup of tea.' He said all this before adding as an afterthought, 'By the way I want you back sometime soon for a barium meal to rule out a stomach ulcer, but that only takes an hour or two as an outpatient.' He screwed up his face. 'I believe the barium tastes ghastly so hopefully another badly needed lesson for you to start taking care of your health will do the trick.'

His face took on a thoughtful look and Catherine thought she was in for another lecture but he turned and gazed longingly towards the door of the ward. 'I'd better get a move on and see if there's enough porridge left in the urn on the breakfast trolley for me. If I don't have my daily fix I'm hell to work with.' He turned on his heel and hurried from the ward. The nurse too excused herself and followed after him in the hope there might just be a plateful for her as well.

She was about to comment on the sling on Stephen's arm when the padre took up the story. 'Your son is a remarkable swimmer, Mrs Bruce. He must have covered more than half a mile fully clothed.' It transpired that Stephen had dislocated his shoulder by holding firmly to a piece of floating wreckage and had been able to swim ashore on the incoming tide. Catherine laughed. Her eyes shone with pride as she looked up at him. 'Stephen has been a champion swimmer since his earliest school days and I've never known him come anything but first at the life saving events which are carried out fully clothed.' She looked up at him and tears of joy flooded her pale face.

'We were flying over water,' Stephen added, 'and I knew I would have to swim if I wanted to make it alive. Those few seconds it took for me to haul off my boots made all the difference,' he said. 'In fact I'd started undoing the laces at the first sign of trouble. I knew they would have weighed me down. Lifesaving practice all those years paid off in the end.' Catherine sighed and turned to Stephen with the broadest smile that lit up her face that had already lost its sickly pallor. But their smiles faded as they thought of his comrades who had not shared his forethought or good fortune.

The padre took up the story again. 'And then, whether with the luck of the devil, or the fact that the sun shines on the righteous, he was washed up on a beach where he must have dragged himself clear of the turning tide and into a small clearing of trees where he must have lain floating in and out of consciousness for at least another twenty-four hours. A man walking his dog found him and called for help. A day in a warm hospital bed soon sorted him out. A touch of hypothermia and a dislocated shoulder is nothing that a red blooded man like Stephen can't overcome.'

The padre gave the young hero a hearty pat on the back before leaving them in private. As soon as his back was turned, Stephen said quietly, 'It was Dad who took me by the arm and pulled me ashore. I would have never managed by myself. I know for a fact that my body was useless with exhaustion when he half carried me clear of the waves.'

'I quite believe it,' Catherine said quietly. 'If at all possible I know he would have come to your assistance. My parents have helped me on numerous occasions when I would have fallen apart on my own. But how did you get here?'

'As Padre said, they found me washed up along the shore. A touch of hypothermia that's all and an overnight stay in hospital saw me as right as rain.' He gave a rueful smile. 'I was kept under armed guard for my own protection. I don't like this war game at all. It's not me.' He stopped as if too many thoughts had rushed into his head all at once. 'And then they flew me back home. I'd been told you were being treated for a haemorrhage. You'd hardly eaten and you hadn't slept. You've been out of it for nearly three days. They decided to sedate you and put you on drip feeds.' He looked past her at the drip stand that still held a half full bag of liquid nutrients. 'I'm sorry I've given you all this worry Mum. I've done a lot of thinking both before and after the accident.'

'You're sorry. Whatever for?' she asked and held out her hand to point at the jug of water the nurse had kindly left. Even propped up against a pile of pillows she was feeling faint again. Stephen poured some into a glass and added a good splash of blackcurrant from a bottle that he'd brought in and had placed on the cabinet by her bed. He added a handful of the rapidly melting ice-cubes from a dish beside it. Thoughtfully he put a straw in the glass and held it to her lips that were raw and peeling from using the oxygen mask. Catherine guzzled the sweet juice until with a gasp her thirst was fully quenched. 'It's I who should be sorry,' she said in a firm voice. 'And where's Arlene? Is she still with Gloria? That poor little child will be terrified with both of us away.'

Stephen smiled broadly. 'That poor little child, as you call her, was playing as happy as a sand boy with Becky when I went to see her yesterday evening. You have nothing to worry about. She's not the only one who thinks you went to Ireland to fetch me.' Catherine only smiled. She wasn't going to tell him the gruesome content of her dreams. They'd arisen because of a mixture of fear and heavy medication, but he was all right now and the quicker that awful nightmare faded from her mind the better.

He grew serious again. 'After the sights I've seen in Northern Ireland I've come to realise I was making too much of my own problems. Worse things are happening to people all the time. I told Padre everything and he had a long talk with me. Sophie and I were unfortunately caught up in a sequence of events that were beyond our control. I refuse to use the word 'victim' because I'm determined to rise above a disastrous event that was not of my making or Sophie's. That single act of violence had far reaching consequences. And that's the lesson we have to take from all this. Every word, every action and every misdeed carries repercussions exactly as a thrown pebble causes the ripples on a pond to spread to shore disturbing the settled life that lies below the surface. The main thing is that I'm alive. I have my whole life in front of me. Dad will always be my real father as far as I'm concerned and Jimmy is little more to me than a ...' - here he hesitated - '... well, sperm donor, to put it crudely.'

Whether it was from the shock of Stephen using such language or because it was a phrase that had already crossed her own mind, Catherine laughed, openly and heartily. 'That's so true, Stephen. He counts for nothing.'

Stephen joined in the laughter. 'Sorry to make so light of it, Mum, but humour is the best way forward for me.' However, he still had a long way to go yet in order to recover from his heartbreak. He wrung his hands as he spoke and a film of perspiration moistened his brow. 'What happened between Sophie and me was a mistake and a tragic episode in our lives, for her especially. I don't know if that poor girl has the wherewithall to recover as easily as I. She's too nice a person to handle the harshness of real life. But at the end of the day neither of us was to blame. And I really don't want to see her or Jimmy again. I have plans and the sooner I get on with the rest of my life the happier I shall be.'

Catherine clutched Stephen's hand tightly in hers as if the word 'plans' meant he was ready to go right at that very moment. She forced a smile. 'What are these plans then?'

'First on the agenda is finishing my three years with the army, but I've been advised I can transfer to engineering, maintenance of army vehicles, aircraft and all the equipment. I'm fully qualified and that's the job they wanted me for before I insisted on active soldiering.'

'Another couple of years won't take long to pass,' Catherine reassured him, 'and I'm delighted you're going to further your career properly.' Catherine was relieved that active service was no longer on the cards. 'And where will you go after that? What will you do?' she asked. There was optimism in her voice as she imagined that he might just come back to her, if he were still single that is.

Stephen sucked at his lower lip before answering. 'I'll be going back to Canada.' His voice was quiet but slow and deliberate. He meant every word. 'I want a proper fresh start, and after all, I was brought up over there. I consider it my real home. I'll miss you and Arlene of course but I have to make my own way.' He gnawed anxiously on the skin along the side of his fingers that he had pushed between his teeth as he waited for her response.

'I understand,' she said quietly. 'You'll have a good life. I'm happy for you.'

The pretty nurse came towards them pushing a trolley of silver dishes and various mysterious instruments. 'I'll remove all these tubes and then you can enjoy a proper breakfast,' she said in her chirpy voice. 'And the good news is that the doctor says you're fine for going home tomorrow – but on condition you eat properly mind.' She turned to Stephen. 'I'm sorry but your mum needs her rest now.' Stephen kissed Catherine on the forehead and went to join the padre who was waiting patiently for him just outside the door of the ward. 'I'll be here tomorrow about eleven to take you home.'

Catherine felt she was going to burst with happiness.

Chapter 43

Catherine snoozed comfortably. Gloria had phoned the ward to say that Arlene was well and they all sent their love. Expecting nobody, she had asked for the screens to be drawn round during evening visiting. A steady hum of voices lulled her into a trancelike state and she was sure she must be dreaming when she heard her name called by another familiar voice and a well known face peeped round the edge of the curtain. It was none other than dear old Frank and she struggled to sit up properly and held out her arms in welcome. He was leaning heavily on a stick as he staggered in on his wobbly old legs towards the chair beside her. He was looking particularly old and frail after the shock of Stephen's accident and from the effort of the train journey through hail and snow.

After chastising him angrily for having travelled all that distance in such wintry weather, they settled to a lovely chat that brought the colour to both their cheeks. Together they had shared the loss of Maggie, Gregor and Eddie and now they were giving each other some honest support through the agony of nearly losing Stephen. With Frank she was able to say how she had felt in those harrowing hours after he had gone missing instead of glossing over them as she had with Stephen himself. However, their cosy tête-à-tête was rudely interrupted when another head poked its way into their little sanctum.

Catherine let out a cry of horror when she saw who it belonged to. It was none other than Jimmy. 'What the hell are you doing here?' she shouted and turned wide eyed to Frank as if he had the power to make him disappear. Jimmy who had entered with a smile now shrank back from her withering look like a weed that had been sprayed with herbicide. He was on his own. His wife hadn't accompanied him. She wanted no reminder of his involvement with Catherine. For Rosie, flying to Aberdeen would have proved too much. He flushed bright red and hesitated as if sensing he was so unwelcome he would have to leave. However, he gathered his composure and stood his ground. 'Stephen phoned my mother and told us what had happened to you. I took the first flight I could get. We've all been so worried.' Catherine knew Stephen had had no choice but to tell Rosie. If only Jimmy would stay away. 'I'll go and find a chair from somewhere,' he said and disappeared back out through the curtain.

'I wish he'd stay away for good,' muttered Catherine. 'He's like the veritable bad penny.'

Frank spoke quietly. 'You need never see that man again after today, but you must break that thread of hatred or you'll never have the freedom to follow your own happiness. Look at him. He's a broken man. Give him his due, he cares for Stephen.'

Catherine was always willing to give consideration to anything Frank said. After all, it was dear, quiet, reliable Frank who'd seen her through so many of her troubles. He had come into their lives and held her mother steady, like an anchor, through her illness and ultimately her death. She knew his words came from a wise and honest heart. 'And would you ever have wanted to be without Stephen completely?' he continued. 'Jimmy provided the gift of a child for you and Gregor to share.' Catherine gazed at the crack in the screens through which Jimmy had crept in and out again like a snake slithering in the grass. She knew Frank was right but the sight of Jimmy made her feel nothing but disgust.

He returned pushing his way in with the legs of a chair he'd managed to find from somewhere. He perched on the edge of it with his hands clasped nervously and neatly in front of him. An awkward silence hung thick in the air. Jimmy began to rock backwards and forwards like an insecure toddler abandoned by its mother. Desperate for acknowledgement he began to speak. 'At least we can be thankful he didn't get his brains blown out in some Belfast back street.' Immediately he knew he should have stopped himself from saying aloud the thoughts that had been running wildly in his mind over recent days. Catherine stared at him in disbelief. Were these the only words of comfort he had to offer?

Frank was on his feet. 'Good God, man,' he snarled, 'have you no sense at all? Haven't you damaged her enough as it is?'

Jimmy was immediately on the defensive. How dare they think

he wasn't every bit as upset as they were! Why couldn't they see his pain was as intense as theirs? He'd almost lost his only son after all. 'Don't come the high and mighty with me,' he retaliated. 'I know full well that I did wrong. I've had to live with the guilt most of my life and don't be fooled that the social retribution of a prison sentence is the worst punishment a man can bear. At least if jailed, society recognises the price has been paid, but this way I'm never going to be free.' He turned to Catherine who, although in bed, seemed to be on the point of collapse. She grabbed Frank's arm and made him sit down again because she knew from the glint in Jimmy's eyes that worse was to come and she was right.

Bitterness at their obvious wish to exclude him overflowed like a river of muddy water after heavy rain and, like so much debris carried along in the deluge, so all the resentment from the past poured out of him. 'Have you forgotten that you were as much a party to it as I, flaunting yourself? You choose the bits you want to remember as if I were the evil one. But you're no angel, Catherine. You enjoyed taunting me. And even though you've been ill, you still manage to wallow in self-pity.'

Catherine gasped as if she had suffered a wound to her physical body. Jimmy's face contorted, his lips and eyes tight shut as if trying to recapture the hurtful words that already he regretted saying. Tears forced their way out from the corners of the squeezed eyelids but there was no sympathy coming his way.

'Get away from here,' growled Frank, his nostrils flaring. 'Can't you see you're not wanted and never have been?' His face had gone from pale to bright red and his breathing had become laboured.

'All right, I'm leaving,' said Jimmy, 'but how many times do I have to grovel and say sorry? How many times before you stop looking at me as if I were something that had crept out of the slime? I've tried to make good but it gets wasted on you.' He stood up, flung the chair aside and stormed out through the curtain as if leaving the stage at the end of a cheap melodrama.

Catherine started to cry. 'You know, Frank, I've been thinking over what you said earlier and you're right. I must try and forgive him. He was only speaking out of desperation. He's lost a lot of weight and his face seems to be shrinking away.' She was the one on the side of forgiveness now while Frank had completely changed his tune.

'When a man is violent towards a woman it is equally as bad as when an adult is cruel to a child, a bully using brute force to get his own ends.' Frank glared at the overturned chair.

'Rosie said he'd saved a man's life in London,' Catherine said. 'Maybe he's not all bad.'

'Rosie phoned me with that story as well,' said Frank, rolling his eyes upwards as if Rosie's stories about Jimmy had to be taken with a huge pinch of salt. 'Sounded more like a common brawl in some bar if you ask me,' he concluded with a sneer.

'I expect we'll never know the rights of it,' said Catherine, 'but he did contribute a lot towards Eddie's nursing home fees and he did visit him a lot.'

Frank nodded. 'Of course, you're right, Catherine; nobody is all bad but he's no good as far as you and Stephen are concerned. Don't encourage him or he'll step back into your life and cause a whole heap of trouble.'

Catherine told him what Stephen had said about him being no more than a sperm donor and Frank thought it was hilarious. 'That lad Stephen is a character and no mistake,' he said, visibly cheered after the distressing row with Jimmy. She wished she hadn't repeated that story. It sounded so coarse coming from her own lips, and deep down, she felt decidedly uncomfortable. Jimmy had flown all the way from Stansted and had been genuinely out of his mind with worry. She struggled to remember the past more clearly. She had played the incident so often in her mind that she was losing track of what had really happened and she was no longer sure of the exact truth. Maybe she had led him on ... Maybe she had made fun of him ... There was one certainty, however, in all of this, and it was that before she could make any move into the future she had to make her peace with Jimmy, if not here, then at some future date. She would never condone what he had done but she had to accept that he was sorry and had spent his life trying to make amends for a juvenile act of brutality that was alien to his nature since growing up.

Chapter 44

Stephen was given a few days' compassionate leave. Catherine loved having him at home again. She'd given up hope of that ever happening again. Just to hear him pottering about in his room was comfort enough and the everyday events such as sharing breakfast or watching television together in the evenings were experiences that could only be described as heavenly.

On his second afternoon at home they sat in the living room in a silence of anticipation. Both knew the time had come to talk about his plans for the future. They needed to be alone to do this and waited awkwardly for Gloria to come for Arlene who had clambered up beside her brother on the sofa and now lay across his lap screaming with delight as he tickled her and rubbed his face into hers. He stood up with her held tightly in his arms and he swung her around as he counted to three and threatened to throw her away. The child screamed with pretend fear and instead of being tossed in the air she was clasped safely against his chest. 'More, more,' she cried and so the game continued until Stephen crashed backwards with her on to the sofa. The two of them gasped with laughter as they struggled to sit up straight again. Catherine had watched them with a glow of satisfaction.

'I think that's enough now,' she said as there was a ring at the doorbell. 'That'll be Gloria and Becky who've come to take you to the park.' Arlene squealed and ran to fetch her jacket before chasing her mother to the front door to have it fastened before disappearing down the path all set for an afternoon at the swings and maybe an ice cream if she was extra lucky.

Catherine brought through a tray of tea and biscuits and placed it on the coffee table between her and Stephen. There was a strained atmosphere between them for a good few minutes and both stared downwards, he examining his shoes and she twisting her fingers into a variety of knots. Catherine didn't want to hear what she knew he was about to say and Stephen didn't want to burst her bubble of happiness any sooner than he could help. At last he cleared his throat and Catherine jumped as if startled. They glanced across at each other and their eyes met. They didn't have to speak. The look said it all. Stephen went first. 'I did think of buying my way out of the army but that would cost thousands. I only signed up for three years so another two will soon pass and will accustom me to being out there in the wide world on my own.'

'Have you any idea yet where you'll be posted? Surely they won't send you back ...'

'It's all right, Mum. They're not shipping me off to Northern Ireland. As I said before, I'm transferring to engineering work so to begin with I'll be training for membership of the Royal Electrical and Mechanical Engineers which will add to my university degree. That will take place in England. After that I'll be sent somewhere to repair and maintain all the army equipment. All good experience.' He sucked in his bottom lip as he waited for her response.

Thankfully she seemed happy. 'Well that's a relief and a wise choice to continue with your real career.' She drew a deep breath. 'And any ideas for what you'll do after that?'

'I'm thinking of emigrating back to Canada as I told you before. It shouldn't be too much of a problem as I have dual citizenship and should have no difficulty finding a job. Whatever happens, I'm willing to turn my hand to anything and work my way up. I've been doing my homework and I should have no problem gaining the "Professional Engineer" licence in Ontario. I want to go back there so I have a sense of familiarity with no bad memories. I'll be attending courses throughout my army career for further qualifications such as City and Guilds and BTECs. These are all transferable to Civvy Street and will make me highly sought after by employers. It's the road to success for me from now on.'

'Well, I must say, Stephen, it seems you have it all sewn up. I shall miss you terribly but I know you'll do well. You're grown up now and you must lead your own life and not be tied to your mother all your days.' She laughed in order to mask her sadness at finally losing her little boy to manhood. But she was glad. He would be successful wherever he went. His lessons in life had been hard won but they had made him a son to be proud of.

Stephen watched her pulling at her intertwined fingers on her lap. He walked round and sat beside her. He took the moist, trembling hands in his before planting a huge kiss on her cheek and drawing her into his arms for a hug. 'Thanks Mum. You're a swell.'

'I've a confession to make,' she said, trying to keep a straight face. 'When you were missing and I feared the worst I went into your room.'

'I suppose I can understand that,' he said, 'but surely that's not something you should be apologising for.'

'I looked through your collection of records and CDs,' she said and a giant smirk spread across her face. 'I played some of your favourites and listened carefully to the words. I also read the lyrics printed on the insets in the cases.'

'And?' he asked intrigued to find out what she thought of his taste in music.

'I have to say I was greatly impressed and agreed with every sentiment. Society has changed so much and when governments become increasingly draconian then the style of protest and demands for justice are bound to adopt a tougher and more explicit approach. The words were so true and I especially liked how they hit out at the hypocrisy and tyranny of the people who run the country. I saw the changes for myself when I took Eddie to that Anti-Poll Tax demo in 1990. The carnival atmosphere of the peace marches of the 1960s had changed and the tension between the protesters and the police was new to me. I couldn't wait to get Eddie and myself away from it. The anger among the crowd was particularly noticeable and was no doubt due to the cuts and restraints imposed by a government lacking in compassion. In fact, I wouldn't mind buying a few of these CDs for myself, not only to remind me of you when you're away, but to enjoy them for their own sake. Times have changed and it's about time I stopped living in the past.'

All he could do was laugh and kiss her again. 'I hope you don't want me to start playing your stuff,' he said with mock horror, 'and I emphatically refuse to wear flowers in my hair!'

Chapter 45

It was almost time for Earl's annual visit but he had decided to come earlier to make sure that Catherine was fully recovered. Both he and Catherine agreed that he should book into his usual hotel. She needed space as well as his comforting presence. Also, they knew they had to treat his marriage with proper respect even though there was nothing between them but friendship. It seemed only right and proper that the platonic nature of their relationship be made obvious, especially to Theresa who was already showing more than reasonable consideration by allowing this extra visit.

They saw each other for a couple of hours each day. Catherine benefited from the company but also felt the need to spend most of her time alone without the strain of anyone else being there. Earl enjoyed days out on his own with Arlene who shrieked with joy every time he appeared at the door and ran into her daddy's arms. When they had left for whichever treat he had planned for that day Catherine could hear her shrill, piping voice chattering excitedly as she skipped along with her hand in her daddy's firm grasp. She loved her father and he loved her. What a pity she was going to lose him again so soon.

'Leave quickly,' Catherine begged him on the day before his flight. 'I don't want to say goodbye.' And so, in order not to cause her any more heartache, Earl gave Arlene and Catherine quick kisses as if only returning to his hotel for the night. He paused at the front gate and turned back to look at them one last time. The engine of the waiting taxi was revving impatiently, so loudly that he had to shout. His eyes were wide and pleading. 'Promise me you'll phone if you want me to call in past tomorrow.' She saw his face was drawn and the healthy glow of his tan had faded to the dingy buff colour of a used envelope. He was as worn out from the agony of leaving as much as she was from seeing him go. How would she handle Arlene's distress? She bit her lip to keep it from trembling, all the while longing to call him back, to drown out the insistence of the cab. But she knew that was impossible and waved him goodbye. She turned quickly and after slamming the door behind her, picked up Arlene and rushed through to the back of the house so she wouldn't hear the taxi pulling away.

She spent the next day watching the clock, counting the minutes and mopping her eyes with a handkerchief. 'Is Daddy coming to see us today?' asked Arlene with childish innocence. 'He can bring medicine for your cold.'

'We'll see Daddy again another time,' Catherine replied, forcing a smile. 'He has to go back to work.'

Frank, like all old soldiers, never died. He faded away several months after Stephen's ordeal. He slipped peacefully away in his sleep and never suffered. His family held a small private funeral in the small local church. Stephen had been posted to Germany by this time and Catherine had to attend without him. She was plunged into a sense of loneliness she hadn't felt since her first days back in Aberdeen. She sat head bowed beside Frank's brother and sister-in-law thinking over all the wonderful times they'd had when he was first married to her mother.

A few evenings later she was on the phone to Earl telling him about it and in her grief couldn't help revealing how her sense of isolation had intensified. All she had been expecting was a phrase or two of condolences to make her feel better but she was taken completely by surprise when Earl said, 'Since there's nothing to keep you in Scotland, why don't you come to Houston? There are plenty Scots here because of the oil. You will have me and my family as friends, and Arlene need never be alone for the rest of her life. Think about it, Catherine, it makes sense. What better place for you to start a new life? We have newspapers and magazines here too, you know. Before you can turn round Stephen will be in Canada and what will you do then? Much better for you to be settled over here before that day comes.' She realised he was serious, but this outrageous idea had never crossed her mind before. Surely she was too old to set down roots in a brand new country.

Catherine pulled at the belt of her trousers. She'd to take it in yet another hole. She had lost so much weight since Stephen had left and then Frank's death so soon after, but at least she was making an effort to get dressed and not shambling around in a dressing gown waiting for time to pass. She had been doing just that for days, so many she'd lost count, and then wandering the house during the long dark hours of night longing for morning to break. She would gaze out at the quiet, still street longing for the reassurance of even one sign of life. Occasionally, she would be rewarded when another human being would hurry by, unaware that they were being observed by the glow of a street light.

She was gradually getting back on an even keel and had managed to take Arlene for walks in the park much to the child's delight. The never ending chatter about Stephen and her Daddy was like a constant drip of torture to Catherine. Sometimes she would be playing with her dolls and Stephen would be mentioned. 'Stevie in a country faraway. Uncle Frank gone to stay with the angels. Daddy gone fly 'way, bye-bye. Back soon.' Catherine didn't know what to do with her. She tried more walks and more nursery rhymes but there was no end to Arlene's questions about these absent loved ones. Catherine could have coped with her own pain but the knowledge that her daughter was grieving too cut a deep wound in her heart. At least the stomach x-ray had shown no sign of an ulcer and she did make efforts to eat regularly. The weight would start to go on soon, she thought. What she really needed was a holiday. Yes, that was definitely the answer. She would go to London and stay at a hotel, booking Rosie into the same one so they could spend time together.

Catherine remembered the happy times in Weymouth with Gregor's parents. His dad had since died of a coronary. Thelma had jokingly warned him about his craving for cream teas. Maybe she had been right. Left alone, Thelma's own health had gone rapidly downhill and she was now in a nursing home. Due to the increasing confusion of her mind, Catherine had spared telling her too much about Stephen. She didn't have the capacity to understand so had been told during one of their confusing phone calls that he had been posted to Germany but the details of what had happened in Northern Ireland were carefully left out. It would kill her to know what had really happened. In fact it was the death of Gregor that had been the start of her mental decline.

Catherine remembered the sunny seaside days she'd spent with Stephen and Gregor on visits to his parents. Arlene would love the donkeys. There was so much there for a child to enjoy. Thelma knew about Arlene and had been quietly understanding. Their visit would bring a touch of happiness to her as well and it would be so simple, a train to London followed by a further jaunt to the south coast. Catherine felt a surge of excitement. After breakfast she would make a few phone calls and get things underway. She was even humming a little holiday tune to herself when she heard the letter box rattle. Arlene waddled after her. She was squealing with delight in accompaniment to her mummy's singing and the singing became happier and louder when Catherine saw the instantly recognisable blue airmail letter postmarked Houston lying in the centre of the mat behind the door. She couldn't wait to read Earl's news. There was always something special about a handwritten letter. She wanted to savour it to the maximum. She made a cup of coffee and gave Arlene some juice and a biscuit. With great precision, she slit open the envelope with the silver paper knife, a long ago present from Gregor's colleagues. She eased out the paper, not wanting to tear off any of his precious words.

But the writing was unfamiliar. She hadn't noticed it on the envelope, simply taking it for granted it was from Earl. Instead of his flamboyant loops, the words in this epistle were penned by a steady and deliberate hand. Catherine flicked the pages over to see the signature at the end. It was from Theresa. Catherine's heart gave a lurch. Surely nothing was wrong. Her hand was trembling as she took a gulp of coffee before bracing herself for bad news. A sweat had risen uncomfortably up over her body and soaked the small of her back and chest. The perspiration on her hands was marking the flimsy notepaper with wet smudges.

The Letter

My Dear Catherine,

I hope this letter finds you and Arlene both well. Please take time to read it before assigning it to the waste bin. I shall be grateful if you try to bear with me as I am trying so hard not to sound patronising or judgemental. Earl has of course told me all about the tragic death of your stepfather, Frank, so soon after you thought you had lost your son, Stephen. You must miss him dreadfully now he has gone to Germany. However, I believe he plans to emigrate back to Canada and that decision of his may help you to take what I am going to suggest more seriously.

I know we have spoken on the phone, but in view of what I have to tell you, I must have my say regarding your relationship with my husband first. Unless the air is cleared on that matter, I cannot move on to the next part of my letter. When you first met him and had an affair, it was none of my business because we hadn't made any definite commitment at the time. However, when you resumed the relationship, we had been married for four years and I had not long given birth to Hannah. None of us are perfect and I have to admit that Earl and I were undergoing a particularly difficult time in our marriage, mainly due to my frequent meetings with my ex-husband, the father of my other two children. Earl understands this situation all the better now that he has a daughter by you, and he accepts the need for discussion over the upbringing and welfare of a child although living apart from the other parent.

I am utterly convinced that you are no longer a threat to my marriage. I myself have several male friends that are valuable but will never become sexual partners. I like to consider myself a fair-minded and compassionate woman. Earl noticeably misses Arlene and, I have to be honest, he worries deeply about you as well. If he didn't I wouldn't consider him worthy to be my husband.

The crux of the matter is, and please don't think me condescending because I know you are a strong, capable, professional woman, but would you find it in your heart to consider moving to Houston? You would have our companionship, friendship and support. Arlene would have her father and the children as well as myself. I don't want to presume to judge how you must be feeling over there in Scotland, and you no doubt have your own circle of friends, but please don't dismiss this idea out of hand.

This is the last page of my notepad and the floor around me is littered with about a dozen discarded attempts at persuading you to join us, so this must be my final request to invite you over, even for a holiday just to find out that none of us bite. I can guarantee that you and little Arlene will be perfectly safe around us. The schools are just great and I'm sure you will have no problem finding work. Please give this suggestion your most serious thought. We have discussed it thoroughly and we both agree it is a wonderful solution for all of us.

Kindest regards,
Theresa

Catherine was stunned. Her stomach fluttered with at least a thousand crazy butterflies and she knew her mouth was hanging wide open just waiting to catch any stray fly that might want to dart in. She looked down at Arlene who was chortling with glee. She had seen her mother's distractedness as an opportunity to empty the plate of custard creams and cram every one into her mouth which was smeared with the crumbs of half a dozen biscuits. Catherine was rendered helpless with shock and simply looked on as Arlene toddled through to the kitchen by herself to return with a tea towel trailing on the floor behind her saying, 'Wipe mouth.'

Catherine swept her mucky daughter into her arms and carried her upstairs to the bathroom where the warm, soapy sponge was duly administered despite howls of protest. Her head was reeling and once Arlene was cleaned up she sat holding her daughter firmly on her lap in order to re-read what Theresa had written. Earl must have told his wife that she was struggling with loneliness and grief.

Earl had already described his wife as an open minded, friendly woman who saw the good in everyone despite having endured a faithless first husband. Perhaps an over developed sense of trust had led her into the wrong relationship when she was younger. Catherine asked herself if she would have shown the same compassion if the roles had been reversed. She knew immediately the answer was no. Any woman who had borne her husband's child would have been given pretty short shrift. Theresa must indeed be someone special and she was glad to have her there in the background for Arlene's sake. To clear her mind she decided to take a long walk round the park. Theresa's missive was placed carefully in the bureau where she kept vital documents, and not amongst the detritus from the letter box that overflowed from the junk drawer in the kitchen unit.

Although this latest development had jolted her into a state of agitation, and although the warm summer days were past and autumn chilled the shortening days, Weymouth remained uppermost in her mind. Whatever happened in the future, she knew that she needed a holiday in order to make some happy memories with her daughter. She fastened Arlene into the pushchair and took off into the fresh air. The child screamed with delight as they sped along the pathways. There was no stopping to look at little birds or fallen leaves this morning.

Catherine's mind raced as they hurried along. In no time at all they had covered both parks and were soon hurtling through the streets of the town until they arrived breathlessly at the railway station where Catherine queued impatiently to make enquiries about train times to the south west of England. Whatever happened, that much needed break was top of the list. A stopover in London on the way back would enable Rosie to share a day or two with them in the capital, another highlight to look forward to. Life was taking off at last.

The second post had arrived while they were out and two more letters had arrived, one official with her name and address shining through a cellophane window and the other obviously a bill from the Hydro Board. These could wait until later when she was in the right frame of mind. She had to have time to mull over Theresa's invitation. Of course, there was no way she would take her up on the offer. She was capable of resurrecting herself out of her depression and making a life for herself in Aberdeen. There was no real reason to move.

It wasn't until evening and Arlene tucked up in bed that Catherine casually cut open and scanned the bill from the Hydro Board. The money she would have to fork out for electricity was more or less what she had expected and she set it aside. It was when she opened and read the other that her jaw dropped for the second time that day.

It was from the magazine she wrote for. There had been no prior warning, no hint of trouble ahead, but here in black and white, glaring at her underlined and in bold type were the words that would strike terror into any working person's heart - bankruptcy for the firm and redundancy for the employees, with only enough pay-off to last a few months. She dropped the letter into her lap and dug the nails of both hands into the soft upholstery of the arm chair as if expecting to fall off it at any second. The room and its contents began to spin and rise and fall around her as if she were out at sea in a storm and the sharp taste of bile rose in her throat as a bout of nausea overwhelmed her. She swallowed quickly and clenched her teeth until the sickness passed.

Unemployed - she had been given notice - another casualty of this blasted recession. Companies were falling by the wayside every day. Why had she thought she would be any different? She had Gregor's pension, some savings and she had made good inroads into the mortgage. Due to the nature of Gregor's illness when they had taken it on there had been no insurance cover to pay it off completely on his death. Her mind ticked off the possibilities. She had previously thought about going to the College of Education for a year to become a teacher of English Language but she knew from acquaintances in the local writing group that there was little guarantee of work at the end of it unless she was willing to live somewhere like London's East End, and going by Jimmy's experiences there, she wasn't prepared to bring up Arlene in that environment. Furthermore, it was too close to the Simpsons for comfort.

A quiet life on the West Coast of Scotland had appealed to her often over the years, but once Arlene was old enough to make her own way in life she would have to leave Catherine to make a life for herself in a city or town. The threat of the appalling loneliness that would accompany that future event would hang over her like the sword of Damocles during every moment of the sublime pleasure of raising her child.

As she poured the frothing milk into a mug and stirred in the chocolate powder until the soothing drink resembled soft brown silk, she made her plans. There was no time for hesitation. These troubled times called for a stout heart and a strong will. But she would carry out her own investigations first.

Chapter 46

There was no faulting the short break they had in central London itself. Arlene was old enough to be thrilled by the dinosaur skeleton in the National History Museum and Catherine was overwhelmed by the art work in the Victoria and Albert Museum especially the wrought iron exhibition and the pieces of marquetry crafted with mother-of-pearl, pewter and ivory made her wonder in disbelief at the skills of these artistes. Boat trips along the Thames, a visit to the Zoo and the Doll's Museum drove them on with fierce energy to feast on every bit of excitement the fascinating city had to offer. While they watched the street theatre in Covent Garden a magician asked Catherine if he could include Arlene in the show. The little girl's face was a picture of delight as he pulled what seemed to be miles of streamers out of her hat and she stood bravely albeit with a look of perplexity on her face when a dove flew out of the hat and landed on her head.

Essex was a different story. She had to make arrangements to meet Rosie in a tearoom, not being welcome of course in the Simpson house. Rosie, who had turned down Catherine's offer of staying at the same hotel, nervously approached her table and crushed her in a breathtaking hug before sitting down. Jimmy had dropped her off at the corner and would collect her in a couple of hours. 'I can't walk so far these days,' she explained with a frustrated smile. 'The doctor says I have to lose weight.' Catherine said how sorry she was to hear that but Rosie's many failed attempts at losing weight were legend. Catherine placed the order for two coffees, a fruit squash and an assortment of fancies. She gave Rosie a kindly smile. 'Surely the diet can wait for one more day.' Rosie's eyes filled with delight when a giant chocolate éclair with fresh cream was placed in front of her.

'It's so hard trying to do without cakes and biscuits, they're the only pleasure I have left in life,' Rosie said with a whimper before shoving the éclair into her mouth as if she'd never seen food for a month. She waited until the giant mouthful was safely devoured before adding in a plaintive note that would have made the hardest heart melt if Catherine hadn't known her better, 'You've no idea what it's like for me here. Patricia rules the roost and Jimmy always has a face like a flitting. The only cheerful one is Sylvie but she's out all the time. I must say though that her travelling beautician's business has taken off and she's raking in the money. She's thinking of opening a shop soon and taking on a couple of newly qualified girls to help out.'

'How's Sophie?' Catherine dared to ask, selecting a custard slice from the plate of goodies which would surely help her through any bad news. She hoped that Sophie was beginning to recover but within herself she knew the girl was probably suffering unbearably, not only from losing Stephen but also a first child.

'Well,' began Rosie, licking chocolate and cream from her lips, 'we thought she was coming out of her depression and then ...' Both women lowered their eyes for a minute in case if they looked at each other they would burst into tears at the memory of Stephen being lost in the sea. Rosie cleared her throat and carried on. 'The whole episode has torn her apart. And Jimmy went to pieces too as you know. After all Stephen is his son ...' Catherine said nothing and deliberately cut through her cake concentrating on not making too much mess with the custard and pastry.

After a short pause Rosie continued. 'Sophie had been going to meditation classes to help her to relax. The psychologist suggested it. We'll never know if it was that or the antidepressants or all that ferreting through the Bible with prophets seeing wild apparitions on every page, but Sophie started seeing things too, like angels hovering over her bed in the night and ...,' She took the paper napkin from her plate and wiped her eyes with it.

Catherine put down the cup she'd been about to drink from and put her hand to her mouth in surprise. She had no idea that Sophie had come so close to losing her reason. 'The poor girl,' she said quietly and Rosie continued, speaking quickly now to get the sorry tale over and done with. She obviously wanted to get it off her chest but it made her choke with emotion as she did so. 'Poor little Sophie said she saw Stephen's face too, floating amongst them, as if he was trying to talk to her from Heaven. That was during the time she was convinced he was dead. We all thought she had lost her mind completely. Well, Jimmy and I did. Patricia said it was all in her imagination.' Rosie took a deep breath. She was noticeably upset and her hand shook a little as she took a sip of her tea. 'It wasn't taken too seriously until the hallucinations became worse. Demons this time threatening her with Hell.'

'You've never told me any of this on the phone,' said Catherine wiping crumbs from Arlene's mouth and handing her a second chocolate marshmallow. She didn't feel the conversation was suitable for a child and had to distract her.

'How could I?' Rosie said trying to justify not having told Catherine before. 'There's not often I have the living room to myself in that house and someone could have come in at any time and heard me. Patricia would go mad if she knew I'd let on to you.'

'So what's happening to Sophie now?'

'The psychiatrist says she'll recover. He suggested that maybe she gives the Bible a rest. It's not as if she'd been going to a church and helping with coffee mornings and jumble sales and listening to stories about Jesus. She'd immersed herself in all that stuff about seven headed monsters and lakes of blood and burning in Hell. He says the Bible should only be studied with the help of a vicar. Anyway, they're giving her stronger medication. She still goes to the day centre and that gives her a bit of company. She likes it there, so she says. The doctors are quite hopeful that she'll recover as her condition has been more of a reaction to a particular trauma and not as a result of a chemical imbalance or mental illness inside her. She was coming on so well too before the Northern Ireland carry on. We would work together on the garden and go round the shopping malls. Then when that happened ... Well, all of us have suffered ...'

'I'm not surprised the poor girl is ill,' said Catherine thoughtfully. 'If Stephen hadn't been found I know I wouldn't have survived.'

'I don't think any of us will get over what's happened,' replied

Rosie and she pressed her lips tightly together. 'Too late now to point an accusing finger but I'm hopeful Sophie will be fine given time. She mentioned to me that she's been thinking of becoming a classroom assistant or a nursery nurse. She can imagine herself working with children but never with a husband. She looks frail but her eyes have a glimmer of life in them at last and she is able to have short conversations. The new young vicar is a tremendous help. He's managed to get Sophie involved in some of the youth activities of the church, rambles in the countryside and discussion evenings. According to him, these vivid dreams aren't unknown when someone distressed buries themselves in the Bible without proper guidance as they can lose track of what is real and what is metaphor.'

Catherine listened intently, her heart aching more and more with each of Rosie's words. How that poor girl must have suffered. Although she said nothing to Rosie, she recalled the visions she had seen when coming off alcohol and how frightening they had been. 'Please don't think my conscience is clear,' she said, 'but how could we have foreseen the future?'

Rosie bit her lip. She had to resist accusing Catherine of hiding the truth if she didn't want them to fall out. 'It's all our faults. I should have shared my suspicions with Eddie. But it's happened and thankfully Stephen at least will have a decent future and who knows, Sophie might too in time.'

Catherine turned away to hide her tear filled eyes. She knew she would always have a pain in her heart for not having guarded against Stephen and Sophie becoming involved. Rosie understood and patted her on the hand. 'I'm sure she'll be all right in time,' she said gently. Catherine whispered a thank you and wiped her eyes. It had taken her by surprise just how much she really did care about that lost young girl. There was a bond that couldn't be denied. Hadn't Sophie been carrying her grandchild, and Rosie's great grandchild?

Catherine looked at her watch. The time had passed so quickly. She quaked at the thought of telling Rosie her plans and decided to get it over with quickly. Surprisingly, Rosie took the news in her stride. 'I'm not surprised, Catherine, with all that you've been through. You deserve to have people around you.' Her voice was steady but her eyes clouded over as she looked longingly at Arlene who had been given a colouring book by her mother so the adults could speak freely.

'How's Jimmy?' Catherine asked. That was always a sure and certain way of taking Rosie's attention off the subject in hand.

'He's not so good. He works every hour God sends and he and Patricia have separate beds.' Suddenly she stopped speaking and took a large bite of a chocolate truffle before nodding towards the door. Catherine nearly jumped out of her skin when she saw who was coming towards them – Jimmy. He looked old and even his lips were thin and surrounded by deep lines, no doubt from smoking too many cigarettes.

'I hope you don't mind,' he said hesitantly but I got through the traffic sooner than I expected. Catherine coped with the situation by calling on the waitress to bring more tea. That always went down well with him.

'Rosie and I have had a nice chat,' she said, these being the most innocuous words she could think of. Arlene smiled at him and asked his name. She was intrigued to hear that he was Rosie's son. 'You look too old to need a mum,' she said with childish innocence.

It was while they were still laughing at her comments that Catherine shocked them all, including herself. The words just came blurting out. 'We have to forgive and forget ...' she said seriously. There was a stunned silence for a few moments. 'I've been doing a lot of thinking recently ....' She held out her hand to Jimmy who stood looking down at her his eyes full of wonder. 'I think it's time to put the past to rest. It's caused so much unnecessary anguish and we have the rest of our lives to consider. We mustn't carry these horrible feelings anymore.' She had to release herself from the gnawing hatred that had been eating at her all these years, but she would never completely forget and certainly not condone what he had done to her.

Jimmy was visibly taken aback but took the hand of forgiveness without hesitation. What surprised them even more was when he reached into his jacket pocket for a neatly folded white handkerchief. He was crying. Catherine had finally offered him the understanding that he had craved for more than two decades and it had proved too much. Tears rolled down his cheeks and he sobbed without restraint. 'Sit down with us, Jimmy,' both women said in unison and Catherine added, 'you must have been suffering terribly too.' She knew that Jimmy was truly sorry. Why not live the rest of their lives freed from years of disharmony? Bemused by Catherine's unexpected show of charitable hospitality and kindness towards her son, Rosie looked from one to the other and smiled to see them finally talking together in a civilised manner. She'd had such dreams for the two of them. But when Rosie took the hanky from him and handed him a fresh napkin on which to blow his nose, Catherine, who had experienced an intoxicating rush of relief and even warmth in her heart, couldn't help but pity this man who seemed unable to cut the apron strings however much else he achieved in his lifetime.

As Catherine packed the suitcases later in her hotel room she was glad the day was over and that an unhappy chapter of her life had been dealt with and was now closed and put away forever.

Chapter 47

Catherine took Arlene's hand up the steps of the nursing home in Weymouth where Thelma, Gregor's mum, had spent the last two years of her life. As they made their way to her room, Arlene clung on to Catherine and asked to be carried. 'Don't like it here. It's a sad place like where Uncle Eddie got sick.' What an amazing memory this child has thought Catherine and picked her up and cuddled her close. 'Thelma is Stephen's granny,' she explained, 'and I'm sure she would love to be your granny too.'

Arlene thought for a second or two. 'I would like to see my new granny,' she said and wriggled back down on to the carpeted floor and dragged Catherine along the corridor. Thelma's room was bright and airy and she was sitting in her comfortable armchair watching an afternoon chat show. Fortunately, she was having a good day and the sight of Catherine and her honorary granddaughter lifted her spirits no end. One of the carers brought them tea and biscuits and juice for Arlene. The visit was going great guns and there were plenty of smiles and laughter, mostly at the recounting of the various antics of Arlene who loved to be the centre of attention. However, it wasn't long before Thelma grew tired and Catherine stood up and said they would have to be going but would return as often as they could during their holiday.

'Before you leave, go into that top drawer,' said Thelma. 'There's a red plastic folder with all my documents.' Catherine handed it to her. Thelma dug into a corner of it and drew out a business card. She handed it to Catherine. 'While you're here, would you mind going to see Mr Sharp? He's the solicitor handling my will. I have you down as executor.' Catherine's eyes opened wide. She had never considered herself in line for such a task. Thelma, although confused on many day-to-day issues, spoke confidently and with surprising lucidity on the matter of her estate. 'Much of the money from the sale of the house has already been drained away on fees for my care, but I will be allowed a certain amount left in my bank account.'

She broke down in tears and Catherine held her in her arms

until she was calm and ready to continue. 'Whatever is left, I want it to go towards research into that disease that killed Gregor.' Catherine was lost for words. Thelma's voice quavered as she continued bravely. 'We couldn't do anything for poor Gregor, but after I'm dead and gone I want to make a contribution to research that might help some other poor souls. I know that you and Stephen won't mind. After all, you're both earning and Gregor was my only child.'

'These are the dearest and kindest word I've ever heard,' said Catherine kissing her mother-in-law repeatedly on the cheek. 'I'm sure that money will make a difference in researching the cause and improving the treatment of Lou Gehrig's disease.' The bravery of this twice bereaved woman was admirable.

As Catherine and Arlene walked along the road towards the seafront for a feast of fish and chips and an evening stroll along the beach, Arlene announced in a loud, carrying voice, 'Granny Thelma is a nice lady. I want to go back and see her lots of times.'

Chapter 48

(Early summer, 1993)

Catherine took Arlene by the hand as they walked through the streets of Toronto. They were having a wonderful time. They'd visited the Royal Ontario Museum and wondered at the stuffed animals, pandas, lions, tigers and wolves to mention but a few. Arlene never stopped talking and asking questions. When they went to the zoo her face was a picture of delight and when she saw a real tiger creeping through some bushes behind the wire she wanted to run over and put her hand through to pat it. She was in her element in High Park. With her paper bag of monkey nuts, she could safely entice the squirrels that ran around. They would come scampering almost right up to her hand to snatch away the titbits she'd scattered and she squealed with excitement.

They walked up and down Yonge Street, the longest street in the world, and marvelled at the variety of shops although she had been there countless times before. She took Arlene to the cinema and fed her popcorn just as she had done with Stephen when he was a child. The city was buzzing. They took a boat trip round the harbour and out to a Thousand Islands. When they went out to Rouge Hill and Scarborough on the Go-Train, Arlene insisted on sitting upstairs. But the highlight of the trip was a visit to Niagara Falls where moving underneath the gigantic flow of water on the pleasure boat was like something out of a dream.

It was early summer before the sun became burning hot and the countryside was lush green with a promise of tree blossom to brighten further the landscape and soon the parks and gardens would be a riot of colour with a variety of flowers. Catherine found the whole visit exceedingly moving and her eyes often smarted with tears. In their hotel room at nights she had to smother with her pillow the sound of her crying. So many memories. It was as if Gregor and Stephen as a child walked with them every step of the way.

Of course, she had to see old friends and find out what

changes had taken place and spent much of the two months' visit renewing acquaintances. Mrs Thomas cried when she opened her door to welcome them into her arms. She was still at nearly eighty a strong, capable woman and Catherine leaned into her warm embrace as if she had seen her only the day before. Mrs Thomas had kept in fairly regular touch with her and Stephen and their meeting was dominated by her reminiscing over his childhood.

The meeting with Marion had been particularly difficult but Catherine knew it was essential to make her peace with the woman she had wrongly suspected of trying to steal her husband. Marion was kindness itself and explained how tortured Gregor had been in coming to terms with a death sentence, not so much for himself but for her and Stephen. Who could have blamed him for behaving so out of character? 'It is so easy to expect perfection from a person as steadfast as your husband,' said Marion over coffee. 'He was a brilliant doctor but a terrified patient, probably because he had seen too much. Your husband was a wonderful human being and I was proud to give any help I could.'

Catherine nodded her agreement. 'I want to explain how sorry I am for misjudging you and to thank you for being such a strong support to him. I realise that it can take a good friend from outside the family to give the correct advice, and you knew more about his illness than he did himself.'

Marion smiled. 'Don't worry. I'm not surprised you got hold of the wrong end of the stick. I'm sure I would have done the same.' When they stood up to leave, Catherine gave a smile full of warmth and genuine appreciation. 'Let me shake you by the hand for being such a wonderful friend. You were willing to let me think the worst of you rather than break Gregor's confidence. I'll never forget you.'

As well as old friends, she revisited old haunts. Walking along the shores of Lake Ontario with Arlene, she told her all about Gregor and that this was where Stephen had spent his time when he was a little boy. Although Arlene wasn't aware of it, Catherine was holding Gregor's arm everywhere they went and imagined Stephen running ahead playing dragons and calling out for them to join in. When it was time to say goodbye to Toronto, Catherine knew that part of her would stay there forever as if she too were a ghost. These had been such happy times. But happy times would come again. With one last look across the waters of the lake and up at the crimson tinted sky, she walked with Arlene back along the street and on to a main road.

She hailed a taxi back to her hotel. Stephen was there waiting. Over the past few weeks he had had his own round of friends and places to visit as well as the vital job interview that would see him securely settled again in Ontario. 'I'm glad I saved the money to buy myself out of the army. I'll more than make it up in only a few months with the wages I'll be earning here.'

Catherine let out a cry of joy. 'Congratulations, Stephen,' she said. 'I was sure you were perfect for it.'

'And can you believe my good fortune? Granny Thomas is putting me up until I find my own place. She was almost rendered speechless when I phoned and said I would be calling in past. She didn't know I was coming over so soon after you. I was barely in through her front door than she had me seated in front of a plate piled high with homemade pancakes doused in maple syrup.'

He turned to his mother with eyes as bright as polished diamonds and a smile that stretched from ear to ear. 'You've no idea how happy I am. I've contacted so many of my old school friends in Pickering and Guildwood and I feel properly at home again. This is where I belong. This is where I spent my childhood and I can feel the real me resurfacing as if I've been buried alive all these years in between.'

Catherine looked at the glow on her son's face that had been missing all those tortured years when he'd been uprooted from his friends and had sacrificed his youth caring for both parents as well as undergoing one traumatic event after another. 'You don't know how happy I am to see you like this. I'll miss you dreadfully, of course,' she said biting her trembling lips, 'but all I want is for you to enjoy your life. We'll visit each other as often as we can and I expect to hear all about your latest adventures on the phone.'

Stephen helped his mother into the taxi with her luggage and went with her to Toronto's Pearson International Airport where she and Arlene were due to catch the plane to Houston.

The sorrow of parting changed to the thrill of anticipation as the jumbo jet sped along the runway and soared up among the clouds. She felt elated. At forty-six she was still young enough to embark on a new life and one she felt sure was going to be well worth living.

The End/The New Beginning

(Houston, 2011)

Catherine

Catherine never looked back after her arrival in Houston. She became firm friends with Theresa and the rest of the family. For a number of years she earned her living by teaching at an adult education institute and writing freelance for a Texan newspaper. At a creative arts convention in 1995 she met a musician, Ralph Newberry, who played jazz saxophone. Together they established a centre for new writers, artists and musicians, which was an astounding success and brought people from far and wide to share their talents and gain a foothold on the ladder to greater achievements. Catherine and Ralph are officially retired now and spend their lives deservedly in travel and holidays although Ralph still plays the occasional gig with his band, the Jaxaphones, and Catherine reads stories to children in local schools and libraries, encouraging their writing by organising and judging competitions. She and Ralph are also frequent visitors at the Schaefer home where Earl delights in Ralph's company. Catherine enjoys occasional sojourns back to Toronto whenever she and Ralph can spare the time. Of course, the highlight of her life was when Stephen and his family came to live nearby. Christmases are extra special when the whole family gang gathers together and they have a whale of a time, especially having musical talent in its ranks. There is no shortage of laughter and fun, and happiness is the order of the day.

Stephen

Stephen, once more back in his element, worked his socks off to become as successful at engineering as his father had been at medicine, becoming a technical engineering manager earning well over the equivalent of £50,000 a year. Only a few blocks away from Granny Thomson lived Ruth, a girl he'd been friendly with at primary school. Ruth's father had taken off with another woman when her mother was killed in a road accident when she was a child, leaving her to be brought up by her grandparents. Once Stephen had established himself in a good job with career prospects and driven with the urge to be the head of a family, asked Ruth to be his wife. He had decided it was best to let Ruth know his 'unfortunate' history. She said yes without any hesitation. Her philosophy based on being determined to challenge the biblical saying that 'the sins of the fathers are met in their children'. She is adamant that no matter what hers or Stephen's real father (Jimmy in this case) had done, they were going to rise above it all and have the happiest family life.

In only a few years they had a lively brood of three children, two boys and a girl. Christmas was always spent in Houston with Catherine's extended family but the wrench of leaving his loved ones behind grew harder each year and when Ruth was travelling with three children plus being pregnant with her fourth, she suggested that it might be a good idea for them all to live closely together. By this time her own grandmother and Granny Thomas had departed this earth so there was no reason to deprive themselves of a wider family life in Texas. Stephen whole heartedly agreed and they moved to the oil city of Houston where he found himself in even more demand than he had been in Toronto. These four teenagers keep Stephen and Ruth on their toes these day but they are youngsters to be proud of. George and Frederick both show great promise as future baseball champions. Katie is already a keen participant in swimming competitions, whereas Thelma prefers a quiet life with her books and music.

Arlene

Arlene, now a fashionable young woman of twenty-three is a qualified accountant and works in an oil company. She lives with her partner, Dwayne, who runs his own home security business. So far, they have shown no interest in having children. She keeps in close contact with her mother and her father and step-mother. They are a large extended family and she has a growing number of nieces and nephews from Rachel's, Luke's and Hannah's marriages, and delights in taking them for sleepovers and weekends. For the time being that provides her with enough of the enjoyment of having children in the house, but she is young yet and who knows how she may feel in a couple of years? Theresa has been like a second mother to Arlene and this has delighted Catherine who dreaded her daughter ever experiencing the loneliness she had known.

Earl

Earl is happily retired too and spends his time gardening, listening to music and playing with his grandchildren by Theresa's daughter Rachel and son Luke. Even Hannah, at only twenty-four is married with one girl and a baby on the way. His grandchildren, one by one, have had a turn of falling about with laughter when he shows them old photographs of himself with long hair and cowboy boots. He has no urge to travel and simply loves family life, although his recent efforts at playing the guitar have caused some 'discord' (his joke) when he gets carried away and starts singing. He loves when Catherine's Ralph calls round so he can get tips on playing. His ambition is for the two of them to have a jam session and perhaps be allowed to play a couple of numbers with the Jaxaphones. Theresa, who has always been the mainstay of the family, thrives on having grandchildren although arthritis has slowed her down in recent years. 'Once I get those new hips,' she laughs, 'I'll soon show you. I'm going to take up salsa dancing.'

(Essex, 2011)

Rosie

Rosie lived with Patricia and Jimmy until the ripe old age of 86. She never stopped doing as much as she could to help, especially in the garden and was a familiar sight to neighbours and passersby in her sunbonnet and floral dress with a basket over her arm busily picking up papers or deadheading the flowers.

In the summer of 2003 she was found seemingly asleep in her chair outside in the sunshine with a freshly picked bunch of flowers and a cup of tea and a cake on the patio table in front of her. Although saddened by the loss, everyone said she couldn't have finished her long life in any happier way.

Sophie

Sophie did gradually recover her confidence and composure. After all, her emotional problems were the result of unimaginable distress and bereavement. However, she was an intelligent woman and a fully qualified nurse, and over the years, with patient support from Granny Rosie and the more practical advice from her mother, she was eventually able to take part-time work at a nearby hospital in the orthopaedics ward. By 2000 she was working full-time and had met Harry, a radiographer in the same hospital. Two years later they moved into a rented flat together and hope to be able to buy soon. When they are not working they go to the theatres and cinemas up west and Sophie has never been so happy. Although Patricia doubts if there will ever be a grandchild, she lives in hope of Sophie having a lovely wedding one of these days.

Sylvie

Sylvie has ambition and in only a few years of running her own beauty business visiting clients in their own homes in a small van with her name painted in rainbow colours on the side, she put down a deposit on premises only a stone's throw from the town centre. Rosie was delighted to have a beauty parlour in the family. It was like a dream come true. It wasn't long before Sylvie had met Bernard, a computer programmer, and flown the family nest. Neither of them wanted children and they have had instead a succession of cats, two at the moment, one called Scissors because of his sharp claws and the other Silk because of her soft fur. Sylvie was lucky to take out mortgages on both a flat and her own shop before property prices shot sky high and now a second shop is on the cards. She and Bernard who is also self-employed put in long hours and are lucky that despite the current recession they are both still in business. They work hard but take a couple of exotic holidays every year to compensate.

Jimmy

With the money from the sale of her house, Rosie bought a hardware shop for Jimmy only a ten minute drive from the house. She thought it was better for him to be available for the family due to Sophie's ill health and it would be too much for Patricia to manage everything on her own. Jimmy enjoyed being nearer to his family and worked like a Trojan to build the business. With the help of a manager he extended the business to include DIY and his shop developed into an Aladdin's cave. In its convenient position near the town centre it became a hive of activity from morning to night. All his life Jimmy's main focus has been his work and being a good provider. As the years went by Patricia softened towards him especially after his mother died and he slumped into a state of melancholy helplessness. After a few months, however, and with Patricia's patient but strict direction he resumed the running of the business and regained his status as head of the family. When he finally retired early in 2011 he sold the business and shared the proceeds equally between Sophie and Sylvie. Sophie was able to put this towards a home for her and Harry while Sylvie used the money to open a second beautician's with all the latest electronic equipment. Jimmy followed Patricia's advice and they have downsized to a bungalow with enough money left over to enjoy a comfortable retirement. When he is not following his favourite pastime of reading a newspaper with a cup of tea and a cigarette, Jimmy spends his time helping Sophie and Sylvie with any minor building work they might need.

Patricia

In spite of everything Patricia continued to put all her energies into her family. She spent endless hours with Sophie, taking her places, encouraging her to join social groups and helping her with her studies to pass a refresher course in nursing. Sylvie too benefited from her mother's positive attitude and it was partly due to her push that she bought her first shop. Although Patricia had to occasionally keep Rosie in her place, she was like a daughter to her. Content that her daughters have settled lives this capable woman has decided that the time has come for some well deserved relaxation for Jimmy and herself and has booked a world cruise.